Praise for *Death of a Dyer*

"Kuhns creates a marvelously chilly atmosphere throughout this suspense tale about seemingly upright people guarding evil secrets. Rees, the weaver, is a wonderful creation."
—*Booklist* (starred review)

"Absorbing . . . [Kuhns's] finely done historical makes frontier Maine come alive." —*Library Journal*

"Kuhns's follow-up to Will's debut offers a sensitive look into matters of the heart woven into a nifty puzzle."
—*Kirkus Reviews*

"Well-constructed . . . Kuhns does a good job integrating the political developments of the time into the story line, especially the Fugitive Slave Act of 1793, and delivers a logical and surprising solution to this traditional whodunit."
—*Publishers Weekly*

"Kuhns's characters are engaging, and she expertly re-creates the world of the Shakers." —*The Bay Area Reporter*

Praise for *A Simple Murder*

"A gripping historical mystery . . . With an ingenious story line (including a truly surprising conclusion), fascinating characters, and a profound sense of time, place, and culture, *A Simple Murder* marks a debut brimming with promise."
—*Richmond Times-Dispatch*

ALSO BY ELEANOR KUHNS

A Simple Murder

Death of a Dyer

ELEANOR KUHNS

MINOTAUR BOOKS
NEW YORK

DEATH OF A DYER. Copyright © 2013 by Eleanor Kuhns. All rights reserved. Printed in the United States of America. For information address St. Martin's Press, 175 Fifth Avenue, New York, N.Y. 10010.

www.minotaurbooks.com

Designed by Steven Seighman

The Library of Congress has cataloged the hardcover edition as follows:

Kuhns, Eleanor.
    Death of a Dyer / Eleanor Kuhns. — 1st ed.
        p. cm.
    ISBN 978-1-250-03396-3 (hardcover)
    ISBN 978-1-250-03397-0 (e-book)
    1. Male weavers—Fiction.   2. Murder—Investigation—Fiction.
I. Title.
    PS3611.U396 D43 2013
    813'.6—dc23

                                                        2013006982

ISBN 978-1-250-04225-5 (trade paperback)

Minotaur books may be purchased for educational, business, or promotional use. For information on bulk purchases, please contact Macmillan Corporate and Premium Sales Department at 1-800-221-7945, extension 5442, or write specialmarkets@macmillan.com.

First Minotaur Books Paperback Edition: March 2014

10 9 8 7 6 5 4 3 2 1

To my husband

Chapter One

D ead?" Rees repeated, staring at George Potter in shock.
"Dead?" A spasm of unexpected grief shot through him.
Although he hadn't seen Nate Bowditch for eighteen years, not
since Rees had marched away with the Continental Army in
1777, as boys they'd been closer than brothers. "Are you sure?"

Potter put down his cup with a clink. "Of course I'm sure.
His wife herself told me of his death."

"I've never met her," Rees said.

"After almost twenty years? He lives—lived on the other side
of Dugard, not the Atlantic Ocean. What happened? You were
such good friends."

Rees shrugged; that story was too long to tell. "We . . . went
in different directions."

"Nate has children, too, did you know? Two sons and a daughter," Potter continued, his expression stern. "I'm sure they'd like
to know what happened to their father."

Rees expelled his breath as Lydia Jane entered with more coffee and cake. Potter cast her a glance, his eyes lighting curiously
upon the square linen cap covering her dark red hair. Rees did
not introduce her, although his eyes involuntarily lingered upon
her face. He didn't know what to say. He'd met Lydia, a former
Shaker, when he'd pursued his runaway son to the Shaker village

of Zion this past summer. Although Rees had fallen in love with her, he was reluctant to marry again, but he hadn't wanted to give her up either. When she had nowhere else to go, he'd invited her to stay with him—as his housekeeper—just until they sorted out their feelings.

Potter turned his attention back to Rees. "It looks like he was beaten to death with a scutching knife, Will. It's murder. And the constable believes Nate's eldest son is the murderer."

"His son," Rees repeated. He was still struggling to digest the news of Nate's death. Nate remained in Rees's memory as the laughing dark-haired boy of his youth, not a middle-aged man with a wife and family. "Why does he suspect Nate's son?"

"They were always at loggerheads, those two," Potter said. "Nothing serious, I'm sure. But everyone knew. And Caldwell, with Richard in his sights, won't look at anyone else. The constable is a drunken lout and the crew he hires to help him is worse, tavern rats from the Bull." He paused and when Rees said nothing, went on in a rush. "You know Caldwell will take the easy way, Will. Is that what you want for Nate's son?"

Rees sighed. "And what if he's guilty? Have you thought of that? It won't be the first time a son murdered his father."

Now Potter lapsed into a thoughtful silence, staring off into the distance for several moments. "Yes, I know," he said at last. "But if he is, I would prefer knowing you were the one to come to that conclusion."

"If I look into this, secrets—secrets kept by anyone with the slightest connection to Nate—will come into the light," Rees warned. "You live here, George. Do you want to know everyone's dirty laundry? Know all the little ugly things about the people you love? Including Nate?"

"Nate was my friend. I want his son cleared if he's innocent and the guilty man punished. Besides," Potter added "we have no secrets in Dugard. We're too boring and know each other too well to have secrets."

Rees shot his friend a scornful look. "Everyone has secrets, George, large and small. Illuminating them will bring out anger and fear."

Potter shook his head. "I'll risk it." After a short silence, he said, "Please, Will. You'll work impartially. I know that. Please. I'd look upon it as a favor."

Now, although Rees thought to refuse, he couldn't. Without Potter, Rees wouldn't have been able to recover his farm from his sister Caroline and her husband, Sam. And he'd loved Nate once.

"Very well," he said. "But not tomorrow nor the next day. We're still bringing in the hay, or what there is of it after Caroline's and Sam's poor stewardship." Potter nodded, and the two friends sat again in silence. Rees recalled the expulsion of his sister and her family from the farm a month back. An ugly experience. He hadn't seen Caro since then, but he thought of her every day with regret.

"You had to recover your property," Potter said, reading his old friend's expression without difficulty. "You had no choice. You had to do it for your future and for David's." Rees said nothing. After a pause Potter said, "So, you never visited Nate?"

Rees shook his head. "I wish I had," he said. But the break between them had been so abrupt, he could never figure out how to bridge the chasm. "Didn't he inherit the Bowditch family farm?"

"Yes, but he didn't live there. Thomas farms that one. You remember Nate's brother?"

"Yes," Rees said. Thomas, a paler and younger version of his brother, had tagged after them like a shadow.

"Nate may still own it. . . ." Potter stopped and thought.

"Well, no matter. Besides working the farm, Nate served as our local weaver and kept ten to fifteen of the local housewives spinning for him. He required a larger place with a separate cottage."

Rees heard Potter's reproof, but knew that settled life would not suit him. As soon as good weather arrived with the spring, the road would sing its siren song and he would pack his wagon and head out again. Born under the traveling foot, that's what his mother always said.

"Good for Nate," he said.

"Do you know where it is?" Potter asked, extracting a piece of paper from his waistcoat pocket and handing it over. "I've written out the directions. I suggest you drive out first thing tomorrow; Molly is waiting on you and will not bury Nate's body until you've taken a look at it."

"Your confidence in my acquiescence astounds me," Rees said, not entirely joking.

"Your passion for justice, if for no other reason, assures your compliance," Potter said, clapping his friend upon the shoulder. "Besides, you loved Nate once. You'll want to do right by him."

Rees inclined his head in acquiescence. Guilt and regret could be powerful spurs. "Yes, all right."

"Good." Rising to his feet, Potter added, "David can manage the harvest. Hire help if you must. Molly will pay a goodly sum to save her son from hanging."

"Wait," Rees cried, gesturing at Potter to resume his seat. "I need more information."

"I don't want to influence you with my opinions," Potter said, remaining upright.

"How old is the boy? Tell me about Nate's wife. I don't remember anyone named Molly."

Potter sighed. "I have an appointment, so I must leave you.

Quickly, then. Molly is Margaret Brown. You must remember her older brother, Billy? She was the little tagalong, always at his heels, copying everything he did."

Rees cast his mind back into the past, recalling Billy and the sister who rode and fought as skillfully as any boy. "The bootmaker's children. Nate married her, that little rooster in a hen's body?"

"Yes. You'll scarcely recognize her now. She grew into a lovely and very feminine woman. And Richard, who is just seventeen, was born a few months early, if you catch my meaning, when his mother was but sixteen." Potter grinned at Rees, who nodded. Many girls stepped up to the altar, pregnant, at fifteen or sixteen. Potter clapped his tall hat upon his head. Despite the day's heat, he wore a cutaway swallow-tailed jacket over his pantaloons and glossy riding boots.

Rees, also standing, suddenly felt self-conscious in his rough tow shirt and loose breeches. At least he'd dropped his old shoes with the stink of the barnyard clinging to them on the porch. Called in from the fields and fearing an emergency, he'd raced in without stopping even to wash his face and hands. He followed Potter out to the porch and watched him mount his fine bay gelding. The law had proved a successful career for Rees's old friend.

"You'll do this for Nate," Potter said from his elevated seat on horseback. "And you need this puzzle. Admit it, you crave a challenge. The four walls of this farmhouse must already be pressing in upon you." Without waiting for Rees's response, he wheeled his mount in a circle and galloped down the drive. Dust rose behind him in a cloud.

Rees remained upon the porch, staring into the distance until his friend was long out of sight and the dust had fallen back to earth. He still could hardly believe that Nate was dead.

"Will you do it?" Lydia asked, coming up behind him.

Rees turned and looked at her. She'd left her home with the Shakers to follow him here and seemed to be struggling with the adjustment. She'd been unusually subdued of late. "Of course," he said. "It's the final favor I can offer an old friend."

"You loved him, and when you love you're loyal," she said. "Once you knew about your friend's death, Mr. Potter did not need to ask. And I think he's right about you. You've been a bear with a sore head lately." Rees frowned in disagreement. "Yes, you have. Don't worry. You won't be abandoning us. You'll still be able to help David with chores in the mornings and evenings."

"Potter said Mrs. Bowditch promises to pay me enough to hire help."

Her smile illuminated her face. "Both David and I can use some extra hands," she said.

Rees looked at her. "I haven't been that terrible, have I?" He was embarrassed.

"You don't enjoy farming and make your feelings very clear."

Rees longed to reach out and touch her, but he didn't know if she would welcome it. He wanted her and prayed she wouldn't return to the Shakers, but he wasn't ready to propose marriage and anyway he didn't think she was ready to accept. He suspected she thought of her deceased Shaker lover every day. Well, he often thought of his former wife, Dolly.

"And I'll help you," she said now, gazing up at him with expectant eyes.

"Not this time," he said. No, he wouldn't allow that to happen here. Unlike in Zion, where she'd served as his assistant, in Dugard she knew no one. The excitement in her face drained away. Turning abruptly from her disappointment, he slipped his feet into his old shoes and clumped down the stairs, heading back to his interrupted chores.

No opportunity to speak to David presented itself until suppertime. Then, as Rees sat down to a meal of leftover chicken and a ragout of cucumbers, he took his chance. "I'll be . . . in town . . . for a time," he said. "You've heard me speak of Nate Bowditch. Well, he passed away and his wife asked me to look into the death."

"We're approaching a busy time," David said with an angry frown. "We've got the rest of the hay to bring in and both wheat and the corn. And then there'll be the oats and pumpkins. . . ."

Rees took a moment to respond, holding his temper in check. He knew he would spend a long time making amends after abandoning his son to the rough care of his sister Caroline and her husband, Sam. "Mrs. Bowditch will pay me," he said. "We can hire some help. You've wanted to take a few hands on anyway."

"But that included you," David said, only slightly mollified.

"Of course he must go," Lydia said from her position by the hearth. "God gave him a gift for untangling such snarls. He must use that gift. And the victim was his friend."

David scowled at her.

"If there is even an unnatural death in this case," Rees said.

"Mr. Potter must be fairly certain, else he would not have driven all the way out here to ask such a favor of you," Lydia said, turning around to look at him. "And, if there isn't one, why, you'll be back in the fields all the sooner."

Rees tried to pretend that the thought of returning to farmwork did not depress him.

"David and I will gladly relinquish your company for a little while. Won't we, David?" Now she stared pointedly at Rees's unhappy son.

"I suppose," he said. He did not sound enthusiastic and he never looked at Lydia.

"It's just for a little while and then I'll be back," Rees said.

"Yes, and for how long, then? I know you'll pack up your wagon and leave as soon as spring arrives," David said.

Rees expelled a short impatient breath. "Weaving is how I make my living," he said. "Weaving brings cash to the farm." He never knew when David would explode. Not that Rees entirely blamed him, but sometimes it seemed the boy would never accept his father's apologies. And David, like Dolly, loved the farm, loved the work. He just couldn't believe his father would never settle to it. "And I've promised." Although he dreaded the prospect of uncovering all the secrets, large and small, of those he'd known since boyhood, he had to admit that the anticipation of escaping the farm's drudgery even for a little while excited him. "I'll ride out tomorrow," he said. "Speak to Mrs. Bowditch and take a look at the body." Nate's body. Rees suppressed a shiver.

David sighed. "Daniel Freeman asked if I had work," he said. "It's a large family; he could use some extra pennies."

"Does he have a sister?" Lydia asked, only half-joking.

David threw his father a quick look and said, "I believe so."

Rees, who didn't want anyone in the house observing his irregular relationship with Lydia, said firmly,. "Outside work first," he said. Her mouth drooped in disappointment. "Chores," Rees said, and fled.

Thunderstorms blew in during the night but did not diminish the unseasonable heat. Although the clouds continued to spit rain the next morning, Rees hitched Bessie to the wagon and set out for Dugard and the Bowditch farm west of town. The shops were opening as he passed through the village. A few men nodded to him. Rees did not recognize them and wondered if he'd known them as boys.

Once out of Dugard, he did not turn left down the dirt lane that led to the Bowditch homestead he recalled from his childhood. Instead he continued straight. According to Potter's notes, all the property visible from here belonged to Nate. Rees stared around in amazement, noting the lush fields of wheat, corn, and rye as well as pastures of cattle, horses, and sheep.

"Nate did very well for himself," Rees muttered. Not envious, exactly, as he did not want such responsibility. And the farm-house! Far larger than the rough clapboard in which Nate had grown up, this structure was built of brick. A long low porch ran the length of the front, littered with discarded boots and a whip and stacks of baskets. The red barn lay across the road with stables and other outbuildings behind it, and Rees realized he'd driven up to the back. Rather than ride out and circle around to the front, he thumped up the steps and tapped upon the wooden door.

A thunderous deep-throated barking greeted his knock. Rees waited a few minutes. Finally, a black man flung open the door. A large brown mastiff leaped at Rees, barking. He held himself still, offering his hand for inspection.

"Leave him, Munch," the servant commanded. Munch sniffed but did not trot away. "Mr. Rees? I'm Marsh."

The black man stood as tall as Rees and they stared at each other eye to eye. Rees was so used to being the tallest man in a crowd that he found their equal height disconcerting. An apron spotted with dirty water and bright dye spots protected Marsh's nankeen breeches and waistcoat. His sleeves were rolled high above his elbows, and a strange bluish cast tinted the coppery brown of his hands and wrists. Since only a few strands of gray glittered in Marsh's curly black hair, Rees thought they were probably near the same age, mid-thirties.

"Mrs. Bowditch is expecting you," Marsh said. His precise phrasing, and the very faint singing cadence underneath, betrayed an accent that was still present despite all attempts to erase it.

Probably Southern, Rees thought, although it was not a drawl he heard underneath the careful enunciation.

"Come in." Stepping aside, he motioned Rees through the door. Munch fell into step behind them, his nails clicking on the wooden floor.

Inside the house and out of the sun, the temperature dropped slightly. Rees looked around. The wooden floors, although frequently swept, were scuffed and worn. A hall ran across the width of the back, offering access to the rooms on left and right and to the narrow servants' stair that rose to the second level.

"You entered through the servants' door," Marsh said, taking off his apron and hanging it over the stair rail. Rees said nothing. Since when did farming folk have a servants' entrance?

They circled around to the east side, passing a small dining room with white walls and a scatter of silverware on a cloth over the table. Some of the cutlery glowed, polished to a shine, evidence of Marsh's recent activity. A door, propped open to catch any breeze, revealed stairs going down to the lower level. When they crossed to the front of the house, they entered elegance and wealth; polished wooden floors covered with Chinese carpets, a formal dining room painted in the fashionable emerald green, and a large front hall with wide curving stairs rising to the second floor.

Marsh crossed the hall and guided Rees to a small plain room with a battered wooden desk and a few chairs. Stacks of bills and a pile of folios told Rees this was Nate's office. "I'll inform Mrs. Bowditch of your arrival," Marsh said with a bow. Rees sat down on a chair to wait. He dared not put the backside that had so recently warmed a wagon seat upon the one upholstered couch.

"Mr. Rees." A woman several years younger than Rees swept

into the room. He rose to his feet as Munch rushed to Molly's side and tried to leap upon her. She swatted the dog away. "How good of you to come. Nate spoke of you often and I always regretted not knowing you."

Rees murmured a polite response, unable to control his staring eyes. Her dark brown hair was cut *à la victime*, a style he'd seen adopted by a few of the more adventurous ladies in Philadelphia and New York. But in Maine? A tall woman and slender, she wore a filmy pale blue gown with long sleeves ending in ruffles. She looked more like a young girl than like a mother of three. Rees thought in surprise that he would never have expected Nate to choose such a fashion plate as a wife. But a closer look revealed the marks of discontent and unhappiness creasing the corners of her eyes and forming a permanent pleat between her brows. "Please, sit down."

"I dare not, not with the dirt of travel upon me," Rees said.

She smiled without warmth. "You are a considerate gentleman, Mr. Rees. My husband would never hesitate." Rees said nothing. "Please, sit where you choose, then," she said. "Marsh will bring refreshments. I understand from George Potter's letter that coffee is the drink you prefer."

"I changed from tea to coffee during the War, in the spirit of patriotism," Rees said, "and now find it a habit I cannot break." He wondered what else Potter had divulged.

"I do hope you can help us," she said, clasping her hands in entreaty. When the ruffles fell back from her wrists, Rees saw long scratches marring the white skin of her right forearm, from dog nails.

"I will attempt my poor best," he said.

Marsh entered the room carrying a silver tray with a coffee pot, delicate porcelain cups, cream in a silver jug, a bowl of sugar chunks and a plate of small cakes. Mrs. Bowditch poured Rees a cup and then took one of her own.

"Where is your son now?" Rees asked as he added cream to his beverage.

Mrs. Bowditch put down her cup without tasting her coffee. "Working somewhere on the farm," she replied. "I've been trying to keep Richard working elsewhere. That drunken constable is on the verge of jailing him."

"I'll need to speak with him," Rees said.

"He would never kill anyone," Mrs. Bowditch said emphatically. "I know my son." When Rees did not respond, she burst into hasty speech. "The constable points to the quarrels between Richard and his father, but, well, it's common for father and son to disagree, isn't it?"

Rees recalled arguments with David. "Sometimes," he said. Some of the tension went out of her. "And what did they argue about?"

"Well, Richard and Nate, they've never gotten along, and now Richard is courting a girl of whom Nate did not approve. . . ." Her words trailed off.

Rees, who remembered Nate's own conflicts with his own father, dipped his head in agreement. But, watching her carefully composed expression, he noted the trembling of her eyelids and wondered, what did she hide from him? "So you're saying Constable Caldwell suspects Richard on the basis of a lifelong rebellion demonstrated toward his father?" Rees asked.

Mrs. Bowditch nodded, leaning forward and stretching out an eager hand. "It's foolish, I know. As though Richard would ever harm his father." She uttered a quick laugh, tinny in its falsity, and those betraying eyelids flickered again. This time Rees clearly identified fear behind her girlish manner.

"Does Caldwell have anything other than that to suggest Richard's involvement?" Rees asked. The constable might have additional evidence. Molly's opinion of her son, Rees discounted completely. A mother always saw her child through a rosy mist of love and hope.

"No," she said so vehemently, he jumped.

"If you know something, tell me now. Others will talk," he warned. "I'll hear everything about Richard's life, every childhood prank, every quarrel." Molly did not choose this opportunity to unburden herself, although her eyelids fluttered again. "Caldwell will hear everything as well, and he will use it."

Mrs. Bowditch hesitated, contemplating her clasped hands. "I don't know," she admitted at last. "Nate spent much of his time in the weaving house. Not weaving," she added, meeting Rees's gaze. He and Nate had apprenticed together many years ago. "He lost his enthusiasm for weaving long ago. He's working with dyes now. Nate is—was obsessed with it." The sudden realization of the past tense brought tears into her eyes. She wiped them away with a dainty handkerchief.

"To what end?" Rees asked. "Did he sell dyed cloth?"

She nodded. "Some. He also dyed yarns for women who wove on their own. But he usually sold his dyes at market. He was looking for dyes he could extract from the plants and flowers that grew around here—that would be less expensive than indigo or Spanish red. And he wanted to know why certain plants yielded a dye and others did not. Why do iron pots fix some dyes and copper pots work with others?" Molly sighed. "Nate didn't care about the money either. He tasked Marsh with the selling of his dyes."

Rees digested this. He had never wanted to do other than weave; he found the repetitive movement of the shuttle relaxing.

"He was working on a substitute for that fashionable green now. . . ." Her hand clutched convulsively at her throat and she closed her eyes.

"I know this is difficult for you," Rees said. He paused for a beat and asked, "What happened?"

"A field hand heard raised voices. Richard admits to visiting his father that night and arguing with him. But that was before supper and he came home. We all saw him. Someone must have visited Nate afterwards. Next day when the girl went down with the breakfast tray, she found Nate's body. He'd been bludgeoned to death." All the blood leached away from her cheeks, leaving them ashen.

"Was there blood upon Richard's person?" Rees asked.

"Of course not," she snapped.

Rees eyed her. One lie after another. "I'll need to speak to the hand."

"His name is Fred Salley," she said. "And George told me you would want to see Nate's body. Dr. Wrothman moved the body into the root cellar for you." She shuddered, a deep bone-shaking palsy that shook her entire body. Rees thought it the first truly genuine reaction he'd seen from her. "Please forgive me," she whispered, pressing a handkerchief to her face. Rees waited while she struggled to regain her composure. He was glad to see this evidence of grief.

"Mama," cried a piping voice.

Mrs. Bowditch quickly scrubbed away her tears and turned, her arms outstretched. "Ben, my little man. Come to Mama."

The little boy—so young, he still wore skirts, and with a mop of blond curls any girl would envy—rushed to her. From the circle of his mother's arms, he regarded Rees with his mother's sky blue eyes.

"A very pretty boy," Rees said. "He resembles you."

The young girl who pursued Ben into the room was the spitting image of Nate, down to the dimple in her chin and the dark curl hanging over her forehead. "I'm sorry, Mama. I know you are entertaining company." Rees swallowed past a sudden lump in his throat. Laughing gleefully, Ben ran behind Rees's chair. "He got away from me," the girl continued. She was on the cusp of her teens, with her hair still in two dark plaits down her back.

"He's not your responsibility, Grace," Mrs. Bowditch scolded. "Where is that lazy Kate? I hope she isn't weeping in her room again." A tide of revealing scarlet swept into the girl's cheeks. "I do wish you wouldn't befriend the help." Grace didn't roll her eyes, but Rees saw the effort it cost her. "Come and meet Mr. Rees. He was an old friend of your father's."

Grace quickly moved forward and curtsied, her lanky body all lean angles, and looked at him curiously from Nate's dark blue eyes. "Mr. Rees," she murmured. He bowed over her hand.

"Cake," Ben said.

Mrs. Bowditch offered him one from the plate. "I shall have to speak to that lazy wench. Again." She pushed the little boy toward her daughter. "Take Ben outside. And remind Kate I employ *her* to watch him." Ben clung to his mother's arm. "Please, Ben, you're tearing my sleeve." As Grace dragged Ben from the room, Mrs. Bowditch said apologetically, "Forgive me, Mr. Rees, for exposing you to this domestic drama."

"Such beautiful children," Rees said. They were beautiful, but he sounded false.

"Thank you." Mrs. Bowditch smiled at him. "My children are my world." Both heard the clatter of buggy wheels and Munch's loud barking. "I daresay Dr. Wrothman has arrived." A faint flush tinted her cheeks; she looked like a young girl caught in the first blush of love. "More coffee?" Lifting the silver coffeepot, she poured, her excited hands spilling the liquid upon the tray.

Rees murmured his thanks, shocked by her attachment to another man so soon after Nate's death.

Munch's barking stuttered into silence, his recognition of the visitor proclaiming him a regular caller. "Down, Munch," commanded a resonant male voice. A gray-haired balding gentleman strode into the room, the dog at his heels. Rees rose to his feet and extended his hand.

"Dr. Wrothman, Mr. Rees," Mrs. Bowditch said, smiling warmly at the doctor. Rees looked hard at the other man. Portly and barely an inch taller than Molly, the doctor was at least fifteen years senior to her. He bent over her hand. Rees noted the furtive caress of her palm and the easy manner between them; their connection was long-standing, then. A spasm of pity and anger in Nate's behalf swept through Rees, leaving him very sad.

Wrothman turned intelligent gray eyes upon Rees. "Ah, the weaver who will prove Richard's innocence." His jovial tone didn't quite mask the mockery in his voice.

"Only if he is innocent," Rees said quietly. "In that case, I will do my very best." He met the doctor's gaze, and after a moment Wrothman's expression relaxed.

"You will find Richard troublesome," he predicted.

"But a good lad nonetheless," Mrs. Bowditch cried with quick intensity.

The doctor glanced at her and said to Rees, "I know Mrs. Bowditch will find your efforts a comfort."

Rees bowed. No love lost between him and Nate's son, then, he thought.

"Will you escort Mr. Rees to the root cellar?" Molly asked, a touch of acid in her voice.

"Of course." Wrothman turned. "Are you ready?" Rees nodded and reluctantly deposited his cup on the table. The doctor threw him a quick mocking glance. "I find such examinations easier on an empty stomach."

"I've seen my share of the dead," Rees replied shortly.

"Oh yes, you were a soldier in the Continental Army, weren't you?" Wrothman motioned Rees to his feet.

"Yes," Rees said. Although the War for Independence was twenty years and more in the past, for the men who'd fought in it, the War might have happened yesterday.

"You must have been just a boy," Wrothman said. "I served with General Washington at Trenton."

Rees looked at him with more interest. "Did you, now? . . ."

"Gentlemen," Molly cried with an impatient clap of her white hands. Wrothman bowed apologetically to her.

"And Mr. Rees." Molly held out a small leather bag that jingled. "Something upon my account."

Rees took it with a bow. David and Lydia would be glad to see it.

Chapter Two

Rees followed Dr. Wrothman through the front hall and to the back of the house where they descended the stairs to the lower level. That proved to be the winter kitchen. Windows ran along the northern wall. A large fireplace, built angled into the room with an attached stove in the German fashion, occupied the southern wall. Although the stone floor was swept and the kettle simmered gently over the coals, no one seemed to be about. Dr. Wrothman walked toward the door at the other end of the kitchen, and the woman sitting on the step snapping beans leaped to her feet. Rees had a confused impression of a light brown face above a blue dress before Wrothman made an abrupt turn to another door, flung it wide open, and started down the four wooden steps to the darkness below. Shelves on either side contained pickled vegetables, relishes, and even from the top step, Rees could see barrels of brined meat and other foodstuffs lined up in orderly rows against granite walls. One tiny window on the northern wall struggled to light the entire interior.

Wrothman lit a lantern and handed it to Rees. "Mrs. Bowditch refused to allow the body in here, with the food. Or in the springhouse, for that matter. It's in the back. . . ." He nodded to a low door set in the middle of the wall ahead.

"Nate is not an 'it,'" Rees said, taking the lantern and going to the door. In the cool damp, the wood had swollen and he had to yank with all his strength to open it. Even bent almost double, he smacked his head upon the lintel. The walls inside were partially of granite bedrock and partially of stone blocks, the floor dirt. It was very cold. Rees stared at the canvas-shrouded form, suddenly unwilling to approach. He wanted to remember Nate as a boy—so handsome and funny, all the girls circled around him like bees around a honey pot, and arrogant with that air of invincibility. Rees shuddered. He dreaded uncovering Nate's secrets, but he could easily imagine a cuckholded husband coming after him.

Swallowing convulsively, Rees forced himself forward and slowly teased the shroud away from the body lying upon a bed of ice. He would not have recognized the lined gray face on the bier as his boyhood friend. He jumped back, fighting an almost inconsolable sorrow. He never got to say good-bye, he thought, wiping away the tears that filled his eyes despite his effort to prevent them.

"I'll find the man who did this to you," he whispered to his old friend. Penance for the long estrangement between them.

"Are you all right in there?" Wrothman called through the door.

"Fine," Rees growled. A moment's deep breathing and a stern lecture on treating this body as he would any other gave him the strength to continue. Carefully he rolled the linen down to the foot of the table. He couldn't—wouldn't look into Nate's gray face again, at least not yet. He looked instead at the shoeless feet. Dirty from long wear, one stocking bore a hole in the toe. Rees could clearly see the nail with its pattern of white lines. And the stockings, like his breeches and linen shirt, were harlequin colored with a rainbow spattering of dyes. Rees's gaze focused upon Nate's collar. Green spray fanned across the linen, touched his lips, and speckled his right arm but did not color the chest. He must have been wearing an apron, Rees thought, glancing from side to side for it. He did not see it. Green dye stained Nate's callused hands as well, occluding the red scaly rash covering his palms. Rees spotted white lines identical to those on the toenails ridging the fingernails.

Rees gulped and determinedly dragged his gaze to Nate's colorless face. The dimple in his chin was the same, but not that curly dark hair, of which Nate had been so proud. His pallid bald pate shone through the few remaining white strands. Deep furrows ran from nose to lips and scored his forehead. Nate, the beautiful boy, now looked twin to his father. Rees wondered if he looked so old. At least he hadn't lost his red hair.

The same angry red rash visible on his palms stippled Nate's cheeks. Some time close to his death he'd been struck in the face; dried blood trickled from one nostril and a fist-sized bruise marked his right cheek. Bruises like fingers upon his nose betrayed a determined effort to cut off his breathing, and something like a scutching knife, the heavy wooden blade used to beat the bark from flax, had been brought down upon Nate's skull. The right side of his head was bruised and bloody, but then head wounds did bleed heavily. The wound did not look serious enough to cause death. Rees muttered, "Oh, Nate, what happened to you?" How he wished he and his old friend had talked, at least once, to make their peace with each other.

"Are you all right?" Wrothman asked again.

"Fine!" Rees shouted.

He examined the body once again, holding the lantern high so as to have the maximum amount of light. When he was sure he'd seen everything, he lowered the lantern to the dirt floor and pulled the canvas shroud over the bloodless face. He stood still, eyes closed and hands folded, saying good-bye. Then he picked up the lantern and joined Wrothman on the other side of the door.

"Who found Nate's body?" Rees asked as they walked up the stairs.

"One of the kitchen maids; Mary Martha something. Young woman with hair as red as your own." His eyes rested with disfavor upon Rees's coppery mane. "She brought his breakfast down to the weaving house and found him."

"Did he commonly spend the night in the cottage?" Rees asked, allowing his surprise to show.

Wrothman nodded. "More often than not. He was passionate about his work." Rees heard Wrothman's censure but didn't comment; he also thought Nate's behavior odd. "Marsh will take you down to the cottage. But, I should warn you, nothing has been cleaned. . . ."

"Good," Rees said. Frequently the killer left something of himself only to have a zealous maid scrub it away.

"Few of us visited him there. We were not invited, and that includes Molly and Richard," the doctor added, almost as an aside, his mouth puckering.

"What happened after the girl found the body?"

"What do you think? The silly wench fell into a fit of hysterics and ran back to the house screaming." Wrothman gestured Rees ahead of him into the kitchen. "Molly sent a boy to fetch me and I drove over immediately." Again Rees noticed the doctor's intimate familiarity with Mrs. Bowditch's given name.

"Marsh?" Rees asked as he followed the doctor outside.

"He was visiting his sister." Wrothman went into the kitchen garden and picked a few mint leaves. "Crush them under your nose. I find it helps with the smell of corruption." Rees did as instructed and inhaled the spicy scent.

"Thank you."

"You'll want to wash your hands before dinner. Rachel will show you." Wrothman nodded at the woman in the kitchen door standing with a large bowl in her arms. Rees recognized the blue dress. "Rachel, this is Mr. Rees. Please show him where he can wash." With a nod, Wrothman turned and walked up the grassy slope to the front of the house.

Rees shot a glare of dislike at the doctor's back. Although accustomed to disdainful treatment at the hands of many a master and mistress, he could not abide such snobbery from another visitor, nay, employee. Then he turned his attention to the cook and, for the first time, her appearance registered. Rees stared. She lowered thick black lashes over unusual amber eyes, her expression resigned. Pale golden skin, a delicate rosebud mouth, a dainty nose, and thick glossy hair pulled back into a bun. The severe hairstyle emphasized her startling beauty rather than detracting from it.

Suddenly realizing he was behaving with unacceptable rudeness, Rees glanced away.

"Come inside, please," Rachel said. She went lightly up the step and into the shadows.

Rees followed her into the kitchen and past the cellar door. Although the fire had been banked, the stifling heat from dinner's preparation lingered. Perspiration popped out all over his body.

With another slight smile, Rachel directed him to the right side and the small alcove next to the cellar door. A small window high up on the wall allowed entry to a narrow band of sunlight that illuminated the sink underneath. Rachel splashed water from a jug into a small basin and handed Rees a bar of coarse soap. He plunged his face and arms into the water, gasping with the shock of the cold.

Rachel handed him a roughly woven towel. "Please follow me, sir," she said. "The mistress is waiting dinner on you." Rees dropped the towel and followed her deeper into the room.

All the natural light came from the windows on the northern wall and the narrow slit over the sink. As they walked past the large oak table, scrubbed white, and past the pantry, the kitchen became progressively darker. Rachel opened the door by the stairs leading to the main floor, and light streamed in. She did not ascend but stood aside with lowered eyes.

Rees went up alone, pausing at the top to get his bearings. Marsh saw him hesitating and took a few dignified steps in Rees's direction. "This way, please," he said, gesturing Rees into the small family dining room at the back. Only Mrs. Bowditch and Dr. Wrothman sat at the table, although a third place awaited Rees. He didn't rate the larger formal dining room, and he was glad of it. Even sitting down at this table felt awkward. He wouldn't have minded so much if Nate sat across from him, instead of Dr. Wrothman. He seemed to be waiting for Rees to use his fingers or tear at the meat with his teeth like a savage.

Rees looked at the vacant chair beside him and asked, "Is Richard not dining with us?" No one replied, but a self-conscious blush flooded into Mrs. Bowditch's cheeks. *He's bolted*, Rees thought.

"The truth is, Mr. Rees, we don't know where he is." Dr. Wrothman said, just a beat later.

Rees regarded Mrs. Bowditch in disbelief. "No one has seen him?" he asked.

Mrs. Bowditch leaned forward. "After the morning when his father's body was discovered and the constable all but accused him of the murder, Richard told me he didn't do it and fled." Her voice throbbed with passion. "We haven't seen him since."

Rees looked into Molly's terrified eyes. *She's afraid,* he thought. *She believes her son did murder his father.* "So, he's gone," he said aloud, "and no one knows where he is?" Molly nodded. Rees wondered if she was lying. He must speak to the constable, and soon.

Marsh brought up the fricasseed chicken steaming in its own gravy. Rachel, carrying a plate of greens and a basket of hot biscuits, hastened after him. Her pretty calico skirts whispered with her movement, and Molly threw her an angry glance. "Where is your apron?"

"Is there anyone who might have wanted Nate dead?" Rees asked abruptly. "Excluding Richard, of course." His bluntness, and obvious rudeness, shocked everyone into silence. But, as he'd hoped, Rachel took the opportunity to flee the room.

"Everyone," Wrothman said.

"No one," Molly said at the exact same moment. She turned a frown of reproof upon the doctor.

"He could be . . . irritating sometimes," Wrothman said.

I'll wager you knew that firsthand, Rees thought, staring at the other man. The relationship between the doctor and Molly Bowditch implied a strong reason to remove Nate. "I'll want to see the cottage as well," Rees said.

Mrs. Bowditch shuddered delicately. "No one has gone in there since . . ." She turned her face away, her dainty handkerchief fluttering.

Dr. Wrothman, gently touching her wrist, leaned across the table. "Please, Mr. Rees. Let's not discuss this horrible event at dinner."

"Very well." Rees nodded at Molly. "Where are Grace and Ben?"

"With Kate, eating dinner in the nursery." She made a face seemingly even less willing to discuss this topic.

"Molly strives to maintain a high level of culture, even on the frontier," Dr. Wrothman said.

"I hardly consider Dugard, Maine, the frontier," Rees said. "And won't your wife be missing you at dinner?"

Mrs. Bowditch glared at him, but the doctor replied easily. "I am a widower, Mr. Rees, and my children are long since married, so my time is my own. I respect Molly's attempt to achieve a more graceful style of living." He bared his teeth at Rees, pretending to smile.

Rees nodded but couldn't resist firing a quick glance at Mrs. Bowditch. She was gazing at Dr. Wrothman and didn't notice.

Rees sat back, allowing the conversation of domestic matters, children and patients, to swirl about him. Despite Nate's death, this was not a house of mourning. *I'm sorry, Nate,* Rees thought.

As soon as dinner concluded and Rachel appeared to clear the table, Rees made his excuses and escaped to the kitchen. Marsh glanced at him and, rolling down his sleeves, gestured to the kitchen door. "Shall we?"

As they trudged down the dusty road, Munch joined them, pushing his head under Marsh's hand for a pat. Although the cottage lay merely a short distance away, the steep downhill grade of the property meant only the roof was visible from the road. As they descended the hill, the wide lane itself changed to two wagon tracks outlined by weeds. It ended abruptly at the cottage. Nate had planted several small fields: one of flax and at least three of madder at different ages. One seemed ready to harvest; several plants had been torn up by the roots and lay waiting for the dyer's attention. Mostly wildflowers dominated this small valley, and Rees wondered if Nate had been trying to extract dyes from them. The flax was already cut and bundled, the seeds removed, and the stalks ready to be retted. Rees saw the glitter of moving water behind the cottage and heard it chattering down the spillway; the cottage fronted a large pond. No doubt Nate had a special stream or trough in which to soak the flax stems until the outer sheath rotted.

The cottage itself was a simple box with a peaked roof. The door sat squarely in the middle. Two windows, one on each side, permitted light into the cottage. Although the right-hand window was the typical small size, the window in the left wall was large, a three-feet square of small panes. Rees wondered how expensive that much glass had been. He knew it must illuminate the weaving room.

He walked up the slate path to the front step, a massive slab of granite. Marsh did not follow him. When Rees looked back over his shoulder, he saw Marsh staring at the cottage with a mixture of grief and horror.

"I can't go inside," he said, moisture glittering in the dark brown eyes. "The master welcomed no one here, not even his wife." He shook his head. "I carried his body out. . . ." He stopped, unable to continue.

Rees turned to look at Marsh in surprise. "You and Nate were friends?"

"We worked together for many years," Marsh said, choosing his words carefully. "He trusted me." He stood in silence, struggling to compose himself. "Mrs. Bowditch asked me to clean this place, but I just can't, not yet."

"Has anyone been inside since Nate's body—?"

"No one has gone in since Mary Martha entered with his breakfast tray." Seeing Rees's question, Marsh added, "Only Mary Martha and the other maids were permitted inside, and only to the front kitchen. If Master Nate was still working inside at dinnertime, one of us would stand out here and call him. Sometimes he would join the family for dinner, but most often not, and then I would send one of the maids down from the kitchen with a tray."

"How long has Nate been so reclusive?" Rees asked. This was not the boy he remembered.

Marsh shrugged. "Since I've known him."

Rees shook his head disbelievingly. Marsh did not break the silence and finally Rees said, "I'd like to talk to Mary Martha."

"She was much distressed, and her parents are keeping her home for now. I'm sure you understand. But she'll return in a day or two." Rees sighed in frustration and turned toward the house. Marsh said to his back, "I'll wait out here."

"Of course." Rees went up the boulder that served as a step and into the house.

The stench of sour milk and old blood assailed him. He pushed the door as far back as he could and fresh air swept in. Gradually, the terrible smell lessened. The midday sun poured across the floor and fetched up in a bright splash against the opposite wall. Two doors led off this tiny hall—one to the left, through which Rees could see two looms and bags of yarn, and one to the right. He stepped through the one on the right. Two windows—one that opened to the front and one on the side, directly across from the large fireplace—allowed light to flood inside. A strange green plant dusted white sat on the windowsill, and scraps of dyed cloth hung from a rope nailed to the ceiling. Upon the long oak table that stood between him and the fireplace sat a tray, still covered by a white linen napkin. But the ceramic pitcher lay smashed upon the floor and a long spray of sour milk fanned across the floor. Large fat black flies buzzed over the remains. Munch shoved past Rees and sniffed it with great interest.

"Go home," Rees commanded. "Go home. I don't need you here." Head hanging low, Munch dragged himself reluctantly outside and settled down to wait next to Marsh.

Holding his breath against the stink, Rees stepped over the

spoiled milk and went around the table. An enormous fireplace dominated the central wall, no doubt sharing the chimney with the fireplace in the weaving room and providing some heat to the loft upstairs. And in front of the fireplace was the blood-stain, a brown pool of it. Rees knelt, tracing the gap made by Nate's head with one finger. Splashes of carmine and indigo as well as green glowed bright as jester diamonds against the exposed flooring. Green dye overlay some of the blood as though the dye pot had tipped over.

"But there's not enough blood," Rees said to himself. "Nate lay here, there is no doubt of that. But he didn't bleed to death. . . ."

A large copper pot hung on a hook over the dead fire. Rees peeked inside; cloth was soaking in the green dye. A piece of rough canvas protruded from the liquid. Was that Nate's apron? And why would Nate dye his apron?

Rees stepped over the bloodstain, pausing in the narrow hall at the back, right in front of the back door. To his left he could see the weaving room and a flight of stairs up to the second level. He flung open the back door. It did not lead to the outside, as he'd expected, but into a small workroom with another door at the back. Indigo-dyed fiber, wool he thought, hung on a cord along the wall, dyed in shades from the palest sky blue to a navy so dark, it was almost black. More dye samples in linen and cotton hung from suspended cords, but this room seemed to be devoted to the dyes themselves. Whole plants hung upside down from the ceiling, and knobby roots lay upon a table to dry. He thought he recognized madder, but there were others he didn't know. Leaves—were those rhubarb leaves wilting in a drifted pile upon a tow linen square? The reddish spears of the staghorn sumac filled a flat basket. Another basket held berries—berries he recognized as the dark reddish purple of pokeberries. Jars of all shapes and sizes contained a variety of powders and liquids and other things—coffee beans in one—and jostled for space upon the shelves. Mingled with the scents of drying vegetation and the stink of mold was a peculiar metallic odor.

Nate must have built this room himself, Rees thought, eyeing the fresh new wood. Water stains already darkened the walls and edged the floor. He leaned over and picked up the scutching knife lying on the floor. Commonly used to beat away the flax husks, the heavy wooden blade was stained a dark brown with blood. Nate's blood. Gasping, Rees flung it from him. He fled through the back door to the little courtyard outside and retched into the grass.

When his stomach was empty, he leaned weakly against the wall and looked around.

A path led off to his left, and when he followed it for a few steps he spotted a rope strung from tree to tree. Hung with wet dyed fibers for many years, the rope and the vegetation beneath it were spattered with every color, from bright imported reds and greens to the muted browns and tans of onionskins and tea leaves. He turned back to the cottage and paused at the top of the slope, staring down toward the pond. Behind the thick, lush brush, he could hear water lapping at the bank. The red barn on the other side of the water was just visible, but not the summer kitchen or the laundry. The location of the weaver's house and the thicket of vegetation enclosing it effectively blocked all views from the barnyard.

Rees returned to the cottage, passing through the dye room and closing the door behind him when he entered the kitchen. He saw Marsh standing in the weaving room and looking blindly around. Rees quietly walked down the hall. "Is something the matter?" he asked.

Marsh jumped and quickly shook his head. "Of course not," he said. "I just haven't been here since . . ." He turned around again, staring.

"Hum. Well, I'm going upstairs," Rees said.

Marsh shook his head firmly. "Don't bother. Nothing happened up there."

"Even the smallest detail will help me," Rees said. Marsh's expression remained obstinately opposed but he did not dare argue with a white man. "I'll just walk through," Rees added. He was very conscious of the other man's eyes following him as he trotted up the stairs.

The staircase gave out in a loft bedroom. Two windows, one in the front wall, one overlooking the field of flax, illuminated a rope bed and a bedside table. The chimney from the double fireplaces below formed the center wall. When Rees walked through the narrow opening by the chimney, he found himself in an empty room over the kitchen. A grate in the floor, intended to allow heat to rise in the winter, now allowed the pungent stink of the dyes to fill the room. Although Rees heard no scrabbling in the walls, he could smell mice.

He returned to the main room. As he looked around, he wondered how often Nate used this bed. Was he so devoted to his craft, he abandoned the comforts of home and family? One long strand of graying hair lay upon the pillow. The sight of it brought moisture to Rees's eyes and he had to turn away. Usually the sight of death did not affect him so deeply, but the stew of grief, regret, and anger left him edgy and vulnerable. Rees wished—oh, how he wished—he had made the effort to drive over and say hello to his boyhood friend. They might never have been friends again but could at least have strived for acquaintances.

"Mr. Rees?" Marsh's voice floated up the stair.

Rees called down, "Coming." He glanced around once more

and started for the stairs. But as he put his foot upon the top step, he saw something protruding from underneath the bed. A chamber pot? He turned back. But when he drew out the object, he realized it was not a chamber pot but a basin filled with vomit. Rees recalled the rash upon Nate's hands and wondered what illness had afflicted his old friend.

"Mr. Rees," Marsh called.

Rees shoved the basin underneath the bed and hurried down the stairs, determined to return and examine the cottage again, without Marsh's looming presence. Anyway, it was getting late. It must already be after three, and it would be suppertime before he reached home.

"Have you finished?" Marsh asked.

"For now, but I'll return. I want to look at the cottage again and talk to you and Rachel and the girl. Mary Martha, is it?"

"I know nothing," Marsh said, his words clipped. "I was away. And Mary Martha won't be back, at least until tomorrow. Maybe after that."

"I understand," Rees said, following Marsh out of the cottage and up the hill. "Until tomorrow, then."

He did not allow his grieving tears to flow until he was driving home.

Chapter Three

B y the time Rees unhitched Bessie, rubbed her down, and released her into the field, Lydia had supper on the table. As he walked to the house, he met David plodding up from the lower meadow with two full buckets of fresh milk in his hands. Rees took a pail.

"Milking is done," David said as they carried the brimming pails into the mudroom.

"The cows are producing well," Rees said in approval.

"Between six and eight gallons a day," David said. "I learned much at Zion." He sounded proud.

While David shucked his boots, Rees lay linen cloths over the pails and left them there for Lydia. He could not help thinking of Dolly; she would have been making cheese by now.

"Mother would want this milk," David said, just as if he'd heard Rees's thoughts.

"I know," Rees said, and clapped his son gently on the shoulder as they passed into the kitchen.

The results of Lydia's industry filled the room: jars of applesauce and pickles. Her face burned with a scarlet flush, and red hair darkened to sable strings by perspiration dropped out from under her cap. She looked both hot and harried. Chicken sliced from the roast served at dinner already sat upon the table, and as Rees entered she put a plate of sliced cucumbers beside them. David looked around and returned outside to wash his hands and face in the trough.

"So," Lydia said to Rees, "what happened? Do you believe Richard killed his father?"

"I don't know," Rees said. "I spoke to Molly, but Richard has disappeared."

"And what did you think of 'Molly'?" Lydia asked. Disconcerted by the sourness in her voice—such attitude was unlike her—Rees turned to look at her.

"All right, I guess," he said. "George Potter and Mrs. Bowditch were in school together. I just met her today."

"Still, you must have some opinion?" she persisted.

Rees paused, thinking. "She is attractive," he said at last, "but unhappy, I suspect."

"She would be," Lydia said. "She lost her husband, possibly at the hands of her son."

"That's not it," Rees said, recalling the discontented creases at the corners of her eyes and the sad droop to her mouth. "Her sadness is long-standing, I believe."

"An unhappy marriage?"

"I don't know," he said, recalling the bed in the weaver's cottage. "But I think so."

Lydia paused, her deep blue eyes examining Rees's face. "And what was your friend Nate like? Mr. Potter said you were such good friends."

"He was fun. The first time I met him, he was spitting through the gap in his front teeth for the amusement of a group of boys. I thought that the most wonderful skill. Nate always had an idea for a new adventure, usually something no parent would countenance. And we both disappointed our fathers, so we shared a bond. Then, when we both apprenticed to Mr. Samson, the local weaver . . ." He shrugged, his throat clogging up. "I wonder if Richard Bowditch is as entertaining as his father."

David entered, his hands and face still damp from recent washing. He looked at his father curiously. "Richard who? Bowditch? I knew a Richard Bowditch in school," he said. "In fact, I knew a Grace Bowditch, too. She is a year or two younger than me. And there were several boys. . . ." Of course David would know them; they all went to school together.

"Those boys probably belong to Thomas," Rees said. "And what did you think of Richard?"

"He was a bully," David replied promptly. "He made Miss Bair cry."

"The teacher?" Rees asked. David nodded.

"Disgusting," Lydia said.

"What happened?" Rees asked.

"I don't know. He said something to her. I heard several of the fathers spoke to Mrs. Bowditch, and Richard stopped coming to the dame school. I believe he was sent away. Anyway, I didn't see him for over a year. But then, I wasn't in school either." Rees nodded grimly. He still had not forgiven his sister and her husband for taking David out of school and working him like a slave on the farm. "Augie would know," David added.

"Augie? Who's Augie?"

"Augustus. He's Richard's half brother. Son of a slave," David explained.

Rees's thoughts instantly flew to Rachel. Was Augustus her son? And why hadn't Molly told Rees about him?

"I'm planning to return to the Bowditch farm tomorrow. I'll ask about Augie." After a beat, he added, "Thank you, David." Rees reminded himself that his son knew more about Dugard and its inhabitants now than he himself did. He found that a disturbing realization. "Look, Mrs. Bowditch paid me." He took the small sack and dumped it out upon the table. Although most were English pence and shillings, there were several French and Spanish coins. Rees, who appreciated coins instead of scrip printed by the states, valued the hoard at more than twenty-five dollars. "We'll use it to hire help. This should pay a few hands more than fifty cents a day." David nodded and, rising to his feet, swept the money into a jar.

Lydia removed the dirty plates and brought a warm Indian pudding and a pitcher of cream to the table. "I feel sorry for Mrs. Bowditch," she said.

"She is certainly concerned about her son," Rees said. "But about Nate . . ." He shook his head in regret.

David, uninterested in the Bowditch crisis, scraped his spoon across his bowl with an air of finality. "I'd like to buy a few more ewes and another heifer, too," he said. "Mr. Mitchell has extras and he's willing to part with one. She could be bred next year. We need to build the herd. . . ."

Rees nodded to show he was listening and allowed David's voice to wash over him. Although the purchase of another cow meant little to him, he wanted to demonstrate interest in the farm. "How much?"

"Seven dollars."

"I daresay, we might be able to afford that," Rees said, thinking of his strongbox in his bedroom. Most of the money he'd earned weaving earlier this summer remained untouched in the box. He didn't want to spend too much of it, though, since they would probably need to live on it this winter.

"Can we afford a heifer and help, too?" Lydia asked.

Rees nodded. "Yes. We'll supplement with my weaving money."

"I have some honey to bring to market," she offered.

"And eggs," David said.

"Perhaps I'll have some cheese as well, the soft cheese," Lydia said. "I thought I might use the extra milk. . . ." Her words trickled to a stop as she realized David was glowering at her. Cheese had been his mother's talent.

"Good idea!" Rees said with such gushing heartiness, he sounded false. "With the approach of winter, I'll pick up a little more weaving."

"I have chores to finish," David said, and headed outside. Lydia stared after him and sighed.

"His mother made cheese," Rees explained. Understanding flashed across Lydia's face. "He'll adjust." He hoped his son and Lydia would become friends. Of course they would, he assured himself. They must. I have weaving to work on," he said and turned his steps toward the stairs.

Although a weaving cottage had been built many years ago upon the farm, Rees's father had converted it to a residence when the conflict between his mother and wife exploded into open war. And now Lydia lived there. Although he wished she would move into the house and share his bed, she'd made it clear without speaking a word that she wouldn't, not without a wedding band. Her experience with Charles in Zion, and the daughter their union produced, had left her wary. Rees thought she blamed herself for the baby's death, just as guilt tortured him for Dolly's. So his loom went upstairs into the bedroom once shared by his parents, the one with the best southerly exposure, and Rees slept alone in his boyhood room.

On the road, he could assemble and disassemble the loom in little more than an hour. Here, with all the demands of a farm, and a family clamoring for his attention, he'd been trying to set it up and warp it for weeks. He picked up the beam, his thoughts turning to the many peculiarities surrounding Nate's death. Running away certainly made Richard appear guilty. And a young man in the full flush of his strength could easily lift the heavy scutching knife and swing it at his father's head. But there was also Mrs. Bowditch's connection to Dr. Wrothman to consider, a connection that seemed not only long-standing but also deeply felt. Rees, recalling the several signs of Nate's illness, reflected that this would not be the first time he'd seen a wife poison her husband. In this case, however, poison hadn't taken Nate's life. Instead someone had administered a beating. Dr. Wrothman could certainly handle the scutching knife—and he had good reason to wish Nate gone.

"Will?" Rees jumped and turned to the door. Lydia stood hesitantly in the opening. "One of the cows is stuck in a mud hole. David needs you to help pull her out." Reluctantly Rees put down the beam and rose stiffly to his feet.

She put out a hand to stay him. "Take me with you tomorrow. I'd like to meet Mrs. Bowditch, make my own interpretation of her behavior."

Rees firmly shook his head. "It's too dangerous." Her mouth set mulishly. But she said nothing as he pushed past her and ran down the stairs.

By the time the cow had been released to join the rest of the herd and Rees and David tramped muddily back home, the light was beginning to fail. Rees, thinking of the still unwarped loom, scowled and kicked at the stones on the path in frustration. But David, pleased with the outcome, and with his father's help saving the cow, began to whistle. And after a few minutes, Rees joined him and they marched home whistling "Yankee Doodle" in harmony.

Dawn next day found Rees already on the road back to the Bowditch farm. This time, although he pulled into the back as he'd done the day before, he drove into the barnyard and allowed

Bessie to be unhitched and sent into the paddock with Nate's horses. He did not stop at the back door but went around to the kitchen.

Rachel, frying bacon in a skillet over the fire, jumped when she saw him. "Why, Mr. Rees," she gasped. "You're here early."

"I wanted to talk to you," he said.

She stiffened. "Forgive me if I continue working," she said, her voice taut with strain.

"Of course," Rees said. "Where's Marsh?"

"Upstairs." Rachel lowered her voice. "The constable is here."

"Another early riser," Rees said.

"Ale, Mr. Rees?" Wiping her hands on her apron, her shoulders rigid, she turned to him. "It's another warm day; the summer doesn't want to let go."

"Thank you."

Rachel brought him a tankard of ale. The spicy pungency of the aroma and tangy taste flooded Rees's senses. "This is excellent ale," he said, following her from the hot kitchen into the cooler air outside. "Do you brew it?" He hoped to ease her tension, but she still looked frightened.

"Marsh does it," she said, twisting her hands in her apron. "I only help him."

"When Master Bowditch died—," Rees began, but she cut him off.

"I still sleep in a room off the summer kitchen," she said. "I heard nothing. I wouldn't be able to hear anything."

Rees found the quickness of her response interesting. "But this was suppertime. You must prepare the master's trays."

"Of course."

"And what did you serve him that night?"

"He always ate everything the family ate." She stared at him, perplexed by the question.

"And Mary Martha always brought down the tray?"

"Usually. But the night before Master Nate—" She stopped suddenly, her lower lip trembling. Rees waited for her to compose herself. Marsh and Rachel both grieved for Nate more deeply than Molly. Interesting. "Marsh brought it down. He was leaving anyway to visit his sister, so he offered."

Rees nodded, recalling the untouched tray. Nate had died before he'd eaten his supper. "Where does Marsh's sister live? In Dugard?"

"No." Rachel turned and walked back into the kitchen. Rees followed. "Marsh had to borrow a horse. In Rumford, maybe? I don't know. He speaks about himself very little." Rachel lifted the bacon from the spider and laid the thick meaty strips upon a plate. She added a wedge of fresh bread toasted in bacon fat and offered the plate to Rees.

He took it absently. "Did you see Richard here, on the farm, that day?" He saw the struggle on her face.

"I don't know," she said at last.

Rees looked at her, sympathetic but stern. "I know you want to protect Richard," he said, "but lying won't help."

She hesitated and then said reluctantly, "He was home that day."

"Did you see him go down to the weaver's cottage?"

"I saw him come back—" Rachel stopped talking, blood surging into her caramel-colored cheeks.

"And?" Rees said. She shook her head and became very busy stirring up the fire. "Rachel?" He stared at her implacably.

"I heard him. It was going on dusk. I heard his running feet, running like the hounds of Hell were chasing him, right up to the back door. He was calling for his mother. . . ."

"And do you know where he is right now?"

"No one knows."

"What about Augustus? Would he know?" The poker fell out of Rachel's nerveless fingers and fell to the stone floor with a clatter. "I only want to speak to him," Rees said.

"I don't know where he is," she whispered.

Marsh came down the kitchen stairs and moved rapidly towards Rees and Rachel.

"I thought you wanted to speak to Mary Martha," Marsh said, his brusqueness almost rude.

"I do."

"She has returned to her duties. The constable wants to speak to her also." He looked at Rees. "You may wish to speak with her first. Where is she, Rachel?"

"In the springhouse. I'll fetch her." Rachel picked up her skirts and fled at a run.

"You've frightened her," Marsh said.

"I didn't intend to," Rees said, staring after Rachel. "Why is she so frightened?" Marsh did not reply, and when Rees looked back at the other man, his face was as blank as carved wood. "And Mary Martha? Is she going to flee from me as well?"

"No. She's more excited than horrified," Marsh said with a lift of his eyebrow. "She is . . . young."

A few moments later, Rachel returned with a young girl, her hair as fiery as Rees's own and her skin even more heavily freckled. The smooth rounded curve of her cheeks gave her the appearance of a child. But Rees revised her age upward when he looked at her womanly form.

"This is Mr. Rees," Marsh said. "He'll ask you a few questions about the master's death. Answer them as fully as you can."

Mary Martha turned her light blue eyes upon Rees. "Will you catch the master's killer?" she squeaked in excitement.

"I hope to help," Rees said gravely, depositing the plate upon the table. "Why don't we step outside to talk?"

But when they went outside, Rees realized there was nowhere to sit. Mrs. Bowditch did not provide chairs for her servants, and dew spangled the grassy slope leading to the front of the house. Moreover, Rees towered over this diminutive child and to look into his face she must bend her head all the way back. Finally Rees gestured her to the granite wall separating the kitchen yard from the lane. They perched upon large stones, Mary Martha spreading her skirts around her. Then she folded her hands primly in her lap and looked at him expectantly. Rees met her eager gaze and agreed with Marsh's assessment; the child was more excited than horrified.

"Did you enjoy working for the master?" Rees asked, hoping to set her at ease.

"I never spoke to Master Bowditch," she said in confusion. "I saw him once in a while, when I brought down his dinner. But he was always too busy to speak to the likes of me."

"Did you enjoy working here?" Rees amended with a sigh.

"Yes," she said. She didn't sound entirely convinced, but Rees moved on.

"What did you see that morning when you found Master Bowditch's body?"

"Everything seemed as usual," Mary Martha said. "Until I went inside. And I saw him." The memory pulled the blood from her cheeks. "He was lying on the floor."

"In what direction did his head point?" Rees asked.

She screwed up her face, remembering. "Toward the table."

That was not right. The blood stained the floor directly in front of the fireplace. "Are you sure?"

She nodded. "I thought he was sleeping. He'd been sick all over the floor."

"I didn't see any vomit in the kitchen," Rees said.

"He'd tried to wipe it up. I finished the job and picked up

the cloth in a towel. . . . Then I realized his eyes were open and all filmy and he was dead and I screamed and dropped the tray and ran out screaming." She inhaled a deep gulping breath.

"And where is the cloth now?" Rees asked. Nate couldn't have wiped up after himself if he had been beaten to death.

"I don't know." Mary Martha's face contorted as she struggled to remember. "I didn't take it." She shuddered.

Someone must have been in the cottage after Richard, Rees thought. But who? Filing that question away for the moment, he asked, "And what happened then?"

"Rachel said we should wait for Marsh to come home, so I did my usual work until my brother came for me."

"You did your usual work? I would have thought . . . Wasn't it very distressing for you?"

"Yes." She nodded her head at him. "I was crying. But I couldn't just sit. . . ."

"So, you worked until your brother arrived?"

"Yes. Rachel told him what happened." She paused, her smooth forehead wrinkling. "I wasn't sure they would let me return, they were that anxious."

Rees eyed the girl with her red curls and round blue eyes and the sheen of innocence upon her like dew upon a rose and nodded. "I would be as concerned," he said.

"But Mr. Bowditch pays—paid well." She looked up at Rees, her freckles standing out against her sudden pallor like scars.

"He paid well," Rees repeated, nodding at her in encouragement.

"He had to. Many families won't allow their daughters to work under the supervision of a colored person, but my parents are Quakers and they say everyone is a person under God. Anyway," she added artlessly, "we need the money."

Rees nodded sadly. Even here in Maine, people he knew,

good Christian people, hesitated to work alongside black people. They certainly refused to accept instruction from persons of color. And Marsh did enjoy an unusual level of authority.

"Do you know Richard?" Rees asked.

Scarlet flooded her cheeks. "He would never hurt his father," she cried, her voice trembling with conviction. A flock of chickadees rose squawking into the sky, and Rachel came to the door. "Well, he wouldn't," Mary Martha said more softly, but no less passionately.

"You must know Richard well to be so sure," Rees said.

She shook her head, the pink in her cheeks spreading to her neck. "We talked sometimes," she admitted, "but that was all."

"How old are you?" Rees asked suddenly.

"Fourteen."

"And Richard is seventeen," Rees said, instantly understanding the relationship. Richard probably did not recognize the girl's existence. "And what did you and Richard speak about?"

"Oh, things," she replied. "He complained about his father." Leaning forward, she confided, "They fought all the time."

"I see. And do you know where Richard might be now?"

"No," she said with a shake of her fiery curls. She straightened her cap. "But I don't blame him for running. Why, the constable accused him of killing his father. It was terrible." Her voice rose. Rees did not speak. "But I must go back to work," she said. "Rachel will be looking for me. She depends upon me."

"I'm sure," Rees agreed in the bright manner adults use with young children. Then, already knowing the answer, he asked his final question. "Do you know the names of the young men Richard might consider friends? From school, perhaps."

"No," she admitted. "I left school a few years ago. I was needed at home. And Richard left before that, for a gentleman's school, I think."

"Do you know the name?" Rees asked without hope. She shook her head.

"Mary Martha!" Marsh came out of the kitchen door. From a distance of several feet, so he would not intrude, he summoned the girl. "Constable Caldwell wishes to speak with you now."

Mary Martha rose reluctantly from her stone seat. "Why don't you ask Augie?" she suggested over her shoulder.

Rees nodded grimly. "I will."

"And Mr. Rees," Marsh said as the girl hurried toward him. "The constable also wants to speak with you. He asks you not to wander away."

"I want to speak to him as well." Rees followed them across the kitchen yard and into the house. But he paused just inside the stifling kitchen, his back to the door, and waited while they went up the stairs. Rachel bent over the dishpan, scrubbing the dishes with ferocious attention. Rees was not fooled.

"Tell me about Augie," he said.

"He doesn't live here anymore," she said, ducking her head.

"Turn around and face me," Rees said. "Please." She turned as bidden but kept her eyes lowered. "Where does he live, Rachel?"

"He lives in Dugard now," she said.

"But he lived here once," Rees said.

She nodded reluctantly. "He grew up here."

"So he knows Richard well?" Rees persisted. She nodded. "Is he free as you and Marsh are?"

"Nate freed Augustus when he was a boy. I'm not free."

Rees stared. As a boy, Nate had hated, in his words, the "pernicious institution" of slavery. Now he owned slaves?

"He didn't free you?"

"He wished to," Rachel admitted. "I refused. Nate was very good to me."

Nate? Not "Master"? Or "Mr. Bowditch"? Rees now understood everything. Rachel was uncommonly beautiful, and Nate only a man.

"But surely you could remain here as a servant," Rees said.

She shook her head, her gaze involuntarily turning upstairs.

"I see," he said. She was afraid of Molly, who might, and probably would, turn her out. But only Nate could sell her. Would that now be Richard, as the eldest son and heir? "So, Richard and Augustus grew up together and thought of one another as brothers?"

She nodded. "Yes."

"Isn't it possible Richard fled to his boyhood friend for protection?" She didn't speak, her reply in the scarlet of her cheeks. "Does Caldwell know?"

"No." The single word exploded from her lips like a shot. She raised her eyes, staring at Rees beseechingly.

He sighed. "Where in Dugard does your son live?"

"I don't know. Nate apprenticed him to the blacksmith behind Wheeler's Livery."

"Amos Isaacs?" Rees asked.

She nodded. "Yes. I believe he works there still."

"But you don't know," Rees murmured, staring at her.

"No. I never visit town and he doesn't come here." A solitary tear made its glistening trail down her cheek.

"Mr. Rees," Marsh said, pausing at the foot of the stairs. "The constable wants to see you now."

Rees glanced quickly at Rachel and followed Marsh from the kitchen.

Chapter Four

The floor above was much cooler. Fresh air blew through the windows, and Rees paused for a moment, enjoying the crisp relief. Marsh looked back over his shoulder, his expression one of impatience, and Rees fell into step behind him, heading, as he expected, for Nate's office. The man waiting there turned from the window, and the two men regarded each other with interest. Much shorter than Rees, Caldwell wore a rusty black coat and breeches, dirty stockings, and a linen shirt stained by food. His thinning salt-and-pepper hair was scraped back into a queue from a pockmarked face shining with sweat. But what Rees noticed first and most powerfully was the odor eddying out from the constable: a stink composed of old sweat and new whiskey. Rees circled around, trying to move upwind of the man. Caldwell matched Rees's movements to keep the distance between them. Removing a toothpick from his pocket, he began worrying at a morsel of food, displaying his stained and rotting teeth.

"Mrs. Bowditch said you was a friend of the family," he said, eyeing Rees from tired black-circled eyes.

"I grew up with Nate Bowditch," Rees said.

"She hired you to look into her husband's death?"

"She did. I have experience investigating murders," Rees

said, "beginning with my first case while a soldier in the Continental Army."

"And you believe that fits you for this now," Caldwell sneered.

Rees shrugged. "I'm here, looking into Nate's murder, whether you like it or not," he said. This was not the first time, nor would it be the last, that the local constable opposed him. At that moment, Marsh entered with a tray: homemade doughnuts and cold tea garnished with fresh mint.

"Don't you have anything stronger?" Caldwell demanded disdainfully.

"Whiskey?" Marsh said, glancing at Rees.

"Not for me." He picked up a glass of tea and drank. "It's good," he said in surprise. "Sweet." Caldwell grunted. Ignoring the tongs, he helped himself to a doughnut with a grimy paw. Rees stared at the filthy hand, the nails rimmed in black, and refused the plate. Caldwell would never make a weaver; any cloth he wove would quickly be too grubby to sell.

"What have you learned so far?" Caldwell demanded.

Rees, temper flaring at the constable's tone, said, "What makes you think I learned anything?"

"You were born and raised here. You know everyone. Don't you?"

"No," said Rees. "I don't know you."

"My family moved here after the War. You know Mr. and Mrs. Bowditch. Yes?"

"I knew Nate," Rees said. "But I hadn't seen him for almost twenty years."

"You must know more than I do. Nobody will tell me anything. Or they lie."

Rees nodded in reluctant sympathy. "I know. They lie to me, too."

"I find that hard to believe. Mrs. Bowditch hired you to clear her son's name, not find the killer."

"Maybe. But I will find the murderer, her son or no."

Caldwell caught the determination in Rees's voice, and after a long steady scrutiny of the weaver's expression, he nodded. "Then I see she has mistaken her man," he said.

Rees sat down, relaxing for the first time since entering this room, and the two men regarded each other more warmly. "Did you learn anything from Richard?" Rees asked at last.

Caldwell dropped into a chair opposite. "He didn't like his father. But I knew that. Their arguments were the stuff of gossip throughout Dugard. And he certainly didn't help his case when he bolted."

"He's frightened," Rees said.

"With good reason," Caldwell said. "One of the hands, a Mr. Fred Salley, saw Richard leaving the weaver's cottage. He was covered with blood."

Rees stared. He remembered Molly alluding to Mr. Salley, but not as though he had anything important to say.

Smirking at Rees's startled expression, Caldwell helped himself to another doughnut. "I daresay Mrs. Caldwell forgot to mention that little fact. I suspected so." Rees did not mistake the gloating expression that flashed across Caldwell's face. "Talk to Mr. Salley; he'll tell you. What's more, I'm sure other people saw Richard but are keeping their mouths shut. The Bowditch family is important hereabouts." He added in a low voice, "And I admit I hope Richard is innocent as well. I'll have the devil of a time making anything stick against him."

Furious, and trying not to reveal it to the constable, Rees said, "I'll speak to Mrs. Bowditch again. As soon as possible."

"You might want to speak to the nursemaid, too," Caldwell added, grinning.

"Kate? Why? Surely you don't believe she's the killer," Rees said.

"You'll understand when you see her." Caldwell grunted in frustration. "I haven't managed to speak to her at all; she runs from me. But maybe you, as a friend of the family, can persuade her to talk. Perhaps she knows where he's hiding."

Rees, resenting Caldwell's sneer, elected not to mention Augustus's connection to the family. It was possible the constable already knew—Dugard was not that large a town, and God knows, people talked. But he gave no sign that he did, and Rees knew Rachel hadn't told him.

"I'll speak to her," Rees said. Caldwell nodded and, snagging another doughnut, went out whistling.

Rees sat for several minutes longer, trying to control his anger. He couldn't wait to speak to Molly Bowditch, and when he deemed himself calm enough he stomped determinedly out of Nate's office. But, although he peered into every room he passed, he saw neither Mrs. Bowditch nor Marsh. Finally he ran down the stairs into the kitchen. The hot air floated up to envelop him with the sweet aroma of roasting beef.

"We need more help," Mary Martha was saying as Rees approached the women. Rachel looked at him almost accusingly, but it was Mary Martha who spoke. "We don't have time to speak to you now, Mr. Rees. Not with dinner barely an hour away."

Gasping in the stifling heat, Rees nodded and fled through the open door into the kitchen yard. Even the warmth of a September day felt cool after the hellish temperature inside. Cows lowed in the distance, and somewhere nearby he heard the shrill treble of a child.

He stood for several minutes in the kitchen yard, growing angrier by the minute. No wonder Caldwell whistled. Whatever threat he imagined Rees represented had now been effectively dismissed. Rees knew he'd come off as a fool, a fool played by Molly Bowditch. He was so angry, he almost considered handing the widow back her money. But he'd already promised, and besides, Nate, his boyhood boon companion, was the victim. Rees would not allow Nate's killer to go free.

"Not even if it was Richard," Rees said aloud.

He pondered the tasks demanding his attention. Although speaking to Mrs. Bowditch might be most important, he was momentarily confounded in that. But he intended to speak to Fred Salley and the nursemaid and examine the cottage once again. He hesitated, irresolute, and then set off up the slope toward the child's voice. He suspected the high treble belonged to Ben, so could Kate be far away? As he climbed the hill, he wondered why a nursemaid was even necessary. Certainly Mrs. Bowditch did not have a large family to care for and she employed help for all other responsibilities. She seemed to aspire to living as a lily of the field, a lazy life at odds with a busy farm.

"Me no want horsie!" The statement ended on a scream that pierced the quiet like a knife. Rees changed course and soon saw Kate and Grace sitting with Ben under a large maple. The more Grace galloped the wooden steed in front of the little boy, the more fiercely he pushed it away.

"Me run," he declared. "Chase me." He set off across the field. Grace jumped to her feet and then, recognizing Rees, stopped short. She looked startled, but Kate stared at Rees in frozen terror. His six-foot-plus frame, broad shoulders, and fiery hair intimidated many. Smiling, Rees slouched and tried to look less frightening.

"He's helping Mother prove Richard's innocence," Grace said quickly. "I'll catch Ben."

"Your mother will be angry with you," Kate said, casting Rees a frightened glance from under her lashes.

"Oh pooh, I don't care."

Rees watched her take off in a sprint after her brother. Even her gait: the outthrust shoulders and rocking motion of the hips were her father's. Then he turned his attention to the nursemaid. She rose slowly to her feet and he instantly understood Caldwell's sneering laughter. Kate was pregnant, at least four months gone, maybe five, if he correctly judged the size of the bulge beneath her apron.

"Please sit down," Rees said, lowering himself to the grass so he did not tower over her. She hesitated and then slowly dropped to the grass beside him. Rees regarded her silently. A pretty girl with soft round cheeks and blue eyes, her face was swollen and flushed with crying.

"What do you want?" she asked, turning frightened eyes upon him.

"Richard is suspected of murdering his father," he said. "I'm sure you know that." He waited courteously for her nod.

She looked at him impatiently. "Of course," she said.

"You're close to Richard?" Rees asked, his eyes dropping involuntarily to her swelling belly.

"No," she choked out. "No, we aren't close." Tears filled her eyes and she quickly wiped them away with a corner of her apron. Rees waited. "I haven't seen him for weeks."

"But you both live here," he said gesturing to the farm around him.

"He stopped speaking to me after I told him about the baby."

"Who else knows about the baby?"

"Only Grace." She raised tear-filled eyes. "Oh, and I am so scared to tell Mrs. Bowditch."

Rees nodded. He suspected Mrs. Bowditch would be neither kind nor understanding. "Is there anyone who will take you in?" he asked.

She shook her head, sniffling. "My father is dead and my mother has enough to do to feed my younger brothers and sisters. What will I do if Mrs. Bowditch turns me out?"

Rees let her sob until she ran out of tears and then returned to his questions. "How long since you spoke to Richard?"

"Three weeks, I think. I had to tell him—" She gestured to her belly. "I'm beginning to show."

"I must believe you've seen him since then," Rees said. "Even if you didn't speak." She hesitated and he knew as clearly as if she'd shouted at him that she knew something important. "You have seen him, haven't you?" he asked. And then, with dawning understanding, he cried, "You saw him the night of the murder, didn't you?" He leaned toward her. "Kate, he's facing the rope. If he's guilty, he should be punished. But if he's innocent, then I need to know everything I can to save him from hanging." Still she did not speak, although she swept her eyes away from him, her cheeks reddening. "One of the hands saw Richard come up from the cottage," Rees said. "I know he was there and argued with his father." He watched the words percolate through her mind, and finally she nodded.

"I saw him that night from the window of Ben's room." She gestured to the house at the foot of the slope. "I was putting Ben to bed."

"And what time was this?"

"Dusk. Just getting dark." Rees nodded. It was probably about seven, then. "Munch had been barking for a long time. Unusually long. Then he stopped. I glanced out the window and saw Richard."

"Was he going down to the cottage or coming back?"

"He walked across the field and went inside. But he came home only a little while later. Ben was saying his prayers. . . ."

A sudden clear picture of Kate, lingering by the window, hoping to see the father of her baby, popped into Rees's mind. Poor child. "How long?"

"Just a few minutes, really." She stopped short and then added in a hushed voice, "I heard him arguing with his father. And then Richard came flying up the road, Munch at his heels, back into the house."

"What did he look like?" Rees asked. "What did you see?"

"He . . . he . . ." She stumbled to a stop.

"Tell me," Rees demanded. She flinched. "Tell me."

"His shirt was dirty, the right arm spattered with—with dark splashes."

Rees sat back, nodding. Blood, of course. "And what time did you leave Ben's room?"

"I sat with him until he fell asleep. It was dark by then and Mrs. Bowditch's grandfather clock was striking the half hour."

"Seven thirty," Rees said.

Kate nodded in confirmation. "You don't really think he killed his father, do you?" She looked down at her clenched hands. "He wouldn't. I know him."

"It's possible he didn't," Rees said, pitying the poor wench in front of him. She did not know Richard as well as she claimed. "But what you told me helps."

"Then someone else killed the master," she said, raising hopeful eyes. "Maybe one of those wandering tinkers? . . ."

"Maybe," Rees agreed, although he discounted that possibility as unlikely. "Please don't worry about this anymore. I'll discover the truth. You concentrate upon your baby."

She smiled sadly. "But they're connected. Don't you see? How will my baby have a name if Richard is hanged?"

Rees said nothing. Likeliest, Richard would not acknowledge

the baby anyway, but it seemed cruel to say so. She must know it, too. As Rees set off down the slope, she threw her apron over her eyes and began sobbing again.

As he passed the house, he looked up, trying to identify Ben's window in the row of three. On the house's top level, the windows were high enough to easily overlook the weaver's cottage. Pausing to study those windows, Rees wondered if Kate might have seen something else and not realized its importance. She lacked the mental quickness possessed by Grace, and he had asked only about Richard. He made a mental note to ask her if she'd seen anyone else.

From the crest of the hill, he could see the cottage and imagine a witness watching Richard hurtle out of the door and sprint up the incline. The boy would be easily identifiable. Deciding he would speak to the stable hand as soon as possible, Rees descended the hill and went through the cottage's open door. The spoiled food on the kitchen floor was gone, but neither the ashes in the hearth nor the pot over them had been cleaned up. Although a pail of soapy water stood by the dried blood, and dark streaks on the floor betrayed recent scrubbing, the room was empty. Rees paused, staring down at the stain. The brownish mark had been scoured so hard, the wooden planks were furred. Soon Molly would inter Nate's body in the family graveyard and only this mark would remain, the last remnant of Nate's presence. Rees sighed.

A sudden sound drew his attention, and he advanced cautiously into the weaving room. Marsh stood at the back, staring around in bewilderment. "It's gone," he said.

"What's gone?"

"Rachel's shawl." Marsh stared around as though the shawl might suddenly appear.

"Maybe she took it up to the main house," Rees suggested.

Marsh shook his head. "She wouldn't. She's still knitting it. Anyway, the mistress . . ." He stopped and started again. "Nate gave her a bag of dyed yarns to use. Rachel knows Mrs. Bowditch will envy her those yarns. . . ."

Now Rees looked around as well. "What did the shawl look like?"

"Nate sampled new dyes by staining yarn, so the shawl is many colors; Rachel's coat of many colors, we called it," he said with a faint smile.

"Upstairs?"

"No. No one ever went up there."

"It'll turn up," Rees said. He understood why Marsh was focused on this small problem; he wanted to avoid thinking of Nate's death. "Maybe I should look around upstairs just in case. . . ."

"No one ever went up there but Nate!" Marsh shouted.

His protectiveness sparked Rees's curiosity; this was the second time Marsh had discouraged Rees from searching the loft. Why? What was he trying to hide? Rees had seen nothing of note upstairs. But now he would search everything.

"All right," he said now. Turning, he went into the dye room. As he looked around at the roots and flowers, he wondered how Nate knew which would produce a color. Rees ran his hand over a scattering of pokeberries drying upon a sheet of rough tow cloth. Burgundy streaks appeared under his fingers. The stains looked uncomfortably like blood. With a shudder, he went out the back door. This time he looked around more carefully. Except for the closely cropped vegetation just outside the door and the path to the left, the trees and underbrush grew wild and jungle thick. He followed the sound of running water, struggling through the intertwined underbrush until he found the pond. A large beaver dam built before the spillway had created another stream that rushed down the new channel and disappeared into the thicket. Nate had adopted it for his own purposes. Bundles of flax stems rotted underneath the water, and when Rees ran his hands over them, pieces of husk broke and floated away with the current. They were ready to be heckled, the fibers removed. He walked alongside the stream away from the pond, tracking the bright flecks of dye until he came again to the rope where Nate had hung his samples.

Rees returned to the edge of the pond. From here the barns, the stable, and the brick summer kitchen were clearly visible and the lowing of a sick cow carried over the water. He looked back at the cottage, almost completely hidden by the trees and lush greenery beneath them. Even the leafless trees of winter would not reveal this cottage; several evergreens tucked in between the maples knitted their branches together into a green wall. A man familiar with this farm could easily escape through the underbrush with no one the wiser.

Rees battled up the hill, through the brush, and around to the front of the cottage. The steep slope provided a barricade. And, to the east, behind the small fields, grew another thick wall of trees. These obstructions could not be coincidental. Rees shook his head; Nate had paid a dear price for his privacy. What had he been so desperate to hide? Somehow Marsh was involved. Rees considered him as a possible murderer. He seemed to love Nate, but perhaps there was a secret Rees hadn't discovered yet.

A sudden clang rang out, its clamor summoning family and help alike to dinner. Rees did not want to eat with either group, too awkward by half, and before Marsh could appear with an invitation, Rees hurried to his wagon. He collected Bessie and soon they were on the road home.

Chapter Five

David, along with the few hands he now employed to help him, was back in the fields by the time Rees arrived home. He unhitched Bessie and released her into the paddock. Then he went around to the back door. Lydia sat on the back step, snapping pole beans. She looked up in surprise. "I didn't expect you so early," she said. "Have you eaten?"

"Not yet," he said. As Lydia jumped to her feet and hurried inside, Rees went to the trough to wash up. The water was cool and refreshing on his skin as he scrubbed away the dust of the road. When he stepped into the kitchen, Lydia put a bowl of thick stew at his place.

"What happened today?" She quickly sliced a loaf of bread and brought it to the table. Rees pulled out her chair before sitting down himself.

"Richard is still missing and I haven't been able to talk to him yet. Besides Richard, Nate had a daughter, Grace. I met her. She looks exactly like Nate. And there's a little boy named Ben. About three, I would guess, and still in skirts." He looked up at Lydia, his eyes resting fondly upon her. "Perhaps the marriage was happy once."

Lydia raised a dubious eyebrow.

"And I met the constable."

"Ah, the drunken lout described by Mr. Potter," she said.

Rees didn't miss her sarcasm. "Yes. Except, he's not a drunken lout—well, not as he was described to me. In fact, I suspect he's much sharper than people believe. Mrs. Bowditch kept back some information. . . ." He heard his voice rise with simmering anger and inhaled a deep calming breath.

"Information that made Richard appear guilty, no doubt," Lydia said. "She would, though, wouldn't she?"

"Maybe," Rees said. Molly Bowditch had not helped her cause by doing so. With a effort, he pushed all thoughts of the murder to the back of his mind. "And what's been happening here?"

"David is thinking of planting rye next year," Lydia said, twisting her hands together.

Rees contemplated her expression thoughtfully. "What else?" He knew something weighed upon her.

"Tomorrow is market day." She hesitated and then blurted, "I plan to go with David and sell my honey and eggs. The hens are laying well. . . ."

Rees said nothing. He didn't want her to go to market—well, he didn't mind if she sold her honey and eggs with the other farmwives, but he didn't want the good folk of Dugard to see her with either David or Rees himself and assume they were a couple. He knew Dugard and he knew how tongues would wag. The old biddies would have him wed to Lydia in the time it took for the story to fly around town. Although it shamed him to admit it, that fear also underlay his reluctance to hire kitchen help. Someone like Mary Martha would chatter out everything she knew. He wanted to wed Lydia, someday, in a future he couldn't yet visualize, but he would not be forced.

Lydia looked at him and smiled faintly, reading his thoughts without difficulty. "If anyone asks, we'll tell the truth, that I am your housekeeper."

Rees frowned. "Our finances are not so poor you need to sell anything at market," he said. "I still have the money I made last year. And, as soon as I set up my loom, I'll begin weaving again. I'm certain to be offered more work than I can handle."

Lydia's bereft expression made Rees feel both guilty and cruel. "In Zion, my Sisters always surrounded me. And although we spoke little, I knew they were there. Here I'm always alone. Except for David. And you." For several minutes they sat in silence. Then Lydia jumped to her feet and began stirring up the fire.

"You're going to do it anyway," Rees said, staring at the stubborn set of her shoulders.

She turned, her eyes sparkling defiantly. "Yes. Why not? After all, I am only your housekeeper."

Rees jerked back, his cheeks stinging as though she'd slapped him. "All right," he said after he'd caught his breath. "I'll drive you and David into Dugard."

"Are you certain? After all, people might see us together."

"Yes. I need to stop in Dugard and talk to a few people anyway. Besides," he said, looking for the bright side, "Potter already knows you as my housekeeper." Lydia's mouth twitched down unhappily. Rees did not know how to correct his thoughtless comment without making it worse. "I'll speak to David," he said, rising to his feet.

"Speak to me about what?" David came out of the mudroom. Lydia uttered a squeak of dismay. Mud from the yard coated his boots and smelled strongly of cow.

"Finding a girl to help Lydia Jane. What are you doing in the house so early?"

"Most of the lads helping me have to be home in time to finish their own milking," David said with a twist of his lips.

He looked at Lydia uncertainly. She nodded. "I'll put on my

boots." And when Rees stared at her in surprise, she added, "I'm not too fine a lady to milk. And David needs the help."

And how clever of Lydia to offer it, Rees thought. Working with David would go a long way toward overcoming his reservations about her place in their lives. "I'll help, too," Rees said, wondering what would happen if she returned to Zion. Would David feel abandoned all over again? Or would he be glad? Rees wished he'd considered David's reactions when he'd invited Lydia to Dugard, but it was too late now.

"Thank you," David said in surprise. "We'll finish all the more quickly."

Lydia disappeared into the mudroom to slip on her clogs. Abandoning his stew, Rees followed them out of the house and to the barns. Although David and Lydia did not speak, their silence was one of joined purpose. Rees didn't like it. He wanted them to be friendly, yes, but not enjoy a relationship of their own. What if he didn't wed Lydia? Or worse, what if he did? When he started traveling, it would be like leaving Dolly behind all over again.

Rees rose before dawn on Saturday, but David was awake before him. He'd already packed a large basket filled with jugs of honey and several crates of eggs into the wagon. He was standing by the wagon holding a table, Dolly's table, when his father joined him in the yard. Rees looked at the table and the rough chair that accompanied it. "Mother's table . . ." David said. "I wasn't sure. . . ."

Rees nodded. He remembered building them for Dolly to display the cheeses, as well as the milk and butter she sold. Although most of the farms hereabouts kept cattle, Dolly had treated her cows almost like pets, and in response they had given such sweet creamy milk, Dolly's cheese and butter had been famous. Rees remembered teasing her that she loved her herd more than she did him.

"I don't think your mother would mind," Rees said.

"She really is gone," David said, his eyes glistening with tears.

Rees put his arm around his son's shoulder. David knew his mother had passed away. But at the sight of her table and her chair, he felt the cutting pain of her loss, fresh and immediate, all over again. "Not completely," Rees said. "Not as long as we remember her."

"And now Miss Lydia . . ."

Rees struggled to think of something comforting to say that would not be disloyal to either woman. "No one will ever replace your mother," he said. "Ever. But she would not want either of us to live in misery. You know that. She would want us to be happy. . . ." As he spoke, he realized that although he had intended to comfort David, he was also comforting himself.

David pondered his father's words for a moment and then heaved a sigh. "She wouldn't mind if Miss Lydia used her table and chair, would she?"

"No," Rees said.

David nodded and picked up the table.

"Breakfast," Lydia announced from the porch. "Just oatmeal and coffee, I'm afraid."

David gave the rough wood a curious little pat before positioning it in the wagon. Rees placed the chair in after it and clapped a hand on David's shoulder. "She would be proud of you," he said as they walked to the house.

They set out for town as soon as breakfast was done and dawn edged the horizon with pink. A cavalcade of wagons already lumbered toward town, and by sunrise when Rees reached Dugard's outskirts, the congestion was too great to allow entrance onto Market Street. Rees turned Bessie and joined a line of wagons going around to the east and entering town by way of Water Street. Rees pulled into the yard by Isaac's smithy and jumped out. David grabbed the table and set off at a run for the space his mother had long ago claimed as her own. Rees followed with the chair and the basket of honey.

By the time he found David, he'd erected the table and stood at guard. "I'll get the eggs and Lydia," said his son, and hared off again. Rees deposited the basket of honey and set up the chair. Then he stood awkwardly by the table, certain that the farmers and their wives were staring at him. But when he looked around, everyone seemed busy and he caught no stray glances.

When he finally saw David and Lydia approaching, Rees stood aside. Although Lydia cast him a quick glance, she did not speak. As she and David spread out the jugs of honey and a crate of eggs, Rees began walking away from them, toward the Contented Rooster.

It was once a dark and dirty tavern on the shores of Dugard Pond, but Jack and Susannah Anderson had transformed it into an airy and popular coffeehouse. Today, market day, the line stretched out the door and to the lane in front.

"Rees!" The shout spun the weaver around. Samuel Prentiss, Rees's brother-in-law, pushed his way through the crowds toward him. "I thought you might be here, selling the harvest your sister and I produced with our toil."

"There isn't enough of it to sell," Rees said. "I may have to purchase hay and corn for the winter."

"You stole that farm from us, and now my children will starve." Sam thrust his face belligerently into Rees's.

"I took back what was mine," Rees said, stepping back from Sam's pungent breath. "And you and Caro could have remained, managing the farm and living on the harvests as well as on the money I gave you from my weaving, if only you hadn't pushed David out. He is heir to that farm, not a servant."

"He's a spoiled brat. And that farm belonged to Caro's parents as well as yours," Sam said. "She has as much right to it as you do."

"Except that Dolly and I paid some to my parents for it," Rees retorted. "And I was left it in my father's will when he passed on. Caro's portion bought you a small holding; what happened to that?" An ugly flush rose into Sam's cheeks and drained away leaving his face dead white.

Rees, who remembered Sam's temper from his boyhood, adjusted his stance, just in case Sam rushed him. But Prentiss looked at the excited and attentive crowd and instead whirled around and fled. In the space of a few heartbeats, he disappeared into the throng.

If Sam was here, then probably Caroline was, too. Rees looked around for her but didn't see her. For the first time, he wondered what her life was like with Sam Prentiss. Consciously relaxing his fists, Rees started walking again to the Rooster. But his racing pulse did not slow for several minutes, and by then he had joined the queue into the coffeehouse.

"What was all the shouting about?" asked the sunburned fellow ahead of him. "I couldn't see anything."

"Oh, just an argument," Rees said with a shrug. He hadn't expected his first meeting with Caroline and her husband to go well, but Sam's violent belligerence surprised him.

The farmer in front of the first fellow turned around. Although in homespun, the linsey-woolsey had been dyed a dark blue. "Will?" Rees looked at the man without recognition. "Adam Barlow." Rees stared in amazement. This grizzled fellow with the paunch was the elfin Adam? "I heard you were back. Are you planning to settle down on the farm now?"

"For a little while," Rees said. "Nice to see you again."

As the line moved inside, other men recognized him and he developed a rhythm. "Yes, I'm back for a little while. I still weave. No, I don't plan to sell the farm; my son is managing it right now."

He was relieved when, on some unseen signal, everyone else cleared out. He found a table and sat down. Jack Jr., as lanky and towheaded as his father had been at that age, brought him a slice of Sally Lunn bread. "Coffee?"

"Please."

"I'll tell my parents you're here."

A few minutes later, Susannah hurried out. Her curly hair sprang out from under her cap in tight ringlets. "Willie," she cried, scurrying across the floor. "How nice to see you again." Rising to his feet, Rees gestured her to a seat at the table. Dimpling up at him, she sat down, saying, "Are your ears burning? Everyone is talking about you. You're studying Nate's death, I hear." Rees stared at her in consternation. She smiled mockingly. "This is a small town, remember? Not much goes on that we don't hear about."

Rees offered her a sickly smile and replied with as much gallantry as he could muster. "I knew I should apply to you and Jack for answers."

As he spoke, Jack came out of the back, his belly straining against his apron. An old schoolmate, although a few years older, the lanky boy Rees once knew had matured into a balding, self-confident businessman. "Do you and Suze have a few moments to speak to me?"

"Of course. None of us wants a killer running loose."

Rees eyed his old friend with interest. "You didn't like Nate, if I recall, "

"You recall correctly," Jack said with a nod. "He exhibited a sweeter side to you. But you didn't live in town, and you missed a lot of school. You never saw him bully the smaller boys."

Rees said nothing. He *had* seen that side. He recalled many a fistfight with Nate, who would fling himself upon Rees in a sudden frenzy. But even as a boy, Rees had been taller and stronger than most, and Nate always lost to him. "Did he bully his family?" he asked, although he recalled no bruises or marks upon Molly or the children.

"I don't know." Jack looked at his wife. "Do the women talk?"

Rees smiled at Susannah, who was frowning at her husband. "I hope so," he said. Female observation and discussion had helped him in the past more times than he could count.

"With maturity came a certain steadiness," she said. "He was almost too benign. Many of us thought Richard could use a firmer hand."

"Who would want to murder him?"

"Other than Richard?" Susannah asked with a smile.

"No one," said Jack. "Everyone. He was tough in business but reclusive. Even I, who grew up with him, always felt I didn't know him well." Susannah nodded.

"And Richard?" Rees said. "What do you think of him?"

Jack and Susannah exchanged a long look. "I wouldn't want to accuse him of murdering his father," Jack finally admitted.

His wife nodded in agreement. "But he was a bully, too," Susannah said. "Jack Jr. used to come home covered with bruises."

"Like father, like son," Jack murmured.

"I'm looking for the boy now," Rees said. "I want to talk to him before the constable jails him."

Both Jack and Susannah shook their heads. "We haven't seen him," Jack said.

"I thought he might be with Augustus," Rees said.

"You know about Augie?" Susannah said in surprise.

"I know a little. He's Rachel's boy and grew up with Richard. 'Closer than brothers,' that's what I was told."

"Augie *is* a nice boy," Susannah said. "He attended school for a little while. Jack Jr. liked him."

Jack frowned darkly. "Until some of our more enlightened men wanted him removed," he said. "They didn't want their children attending school with a 'darky.'"

"It was sad. Augie really had more potential as a scholar than Richard," Susannah agreed.

"But Nate apprenticed him to Isaacs," Jack said, jerking his head toward the street outside.

Susannah leaned forward. "He might know where Richard hides," she agreed. "Augie is probably Richard's only true friend." Rees looked at her, catching something in her voice. They'd come through the grades together, and in some ways he knew her better than he knew either of his sisters. She was keeping something back.

"What else?" he asked.

"Tell him," said Jack.

"Well, it is commonly believed the two boys are not just as close as brothers but *are* brothers. Sons of Nate, you know." Rees thought of Rachel and nodded. Of course the boys were brothers. "Nate never denied it," Susannah said. "You must have noticed Molly's antipathy toward Rachel."

Rees nodded. "Molly makes no effort to hide it." And Suze didn't disguise her dislike of Molly. "How old is Augustus? Is he the same age as Richard?"

"No. Augie is the older, by a few years." She paused and then went on in a rush. "Rachel delivered Augie not quite eight months after Nate purchased her."

"Rachel didn't say," Rees said.

"Of course not," Susannah said tartly. "You're a man; a white man. You need a woman's touch in a matter of such delicacy. And it won't be me," she said, seeing the question forming on his lips.

They sat in silence. Rees pondered his next line of inquiry. "Where would Richard go for refuge? Does he have any friends besides Augie?"

"Well," Susannah said after a moment's thought, "Richard is courting Elizabeth Carleton. James's daughter," she added for Rees's benefit.

"He's married?" Rees asked in surprise, recalling the doughy boy he'd known.

"Yes. He brought a wife home from London. Charlotte is a daughter of minor nobility and is said to want titles for her daughters." Susannah pursed her lips in disapproval. "We Colonials aren't well bred, you know."

"Not Richard, then," Rees said.

"Huh. Nate fancied himself local aristocracy," Jack said, "and I expect Richard imbibed that arrogance with his morning cider."

Rees considered that. "I didn't even know James had come home from London," he said. He clearly remembered the circumstances surrounding Carleton's move to London, since he'd caused it. At eleven, James had been an insufferable little prig and a Tory while Rees was already a staunch patriot. He had thrashed James into swearing fealty to the Continental Congress. Henry Carleton, nicknamed King because of his arrogant manner, promptly sent servants after Rees to administer a severe beating. He wouldn't yield even then, bloodying a few noses with his own flying fists. His defiance won him the status of hero, and the other children took revenge upon James in a myriad of petty ways. King Carleton sent his son to England to complete his schooling, and Rees hadn't seen him since.

"I thought James would stay in England forever," he muttered.

"King Carleton, when faced with losing his properties, turned his coat," Susannah said. "James came home a few times for visits—"

"Summoned home by his father," Jack interjected. "In fact, King sent Nate to England to fetch him."

"Nate? They loathed each other. Why did Carleton choose Nate?" Rees asked incredulously.

Jack shrugged. "I don't know. But Nate appeared to be on good terms with the old man. And with James."

"Better than good terms," Susannah said, "James Carleton is—was Nate's closest friend."

"James finally returned permanently six or seven years ago, just before his father's final illness and death. Anyway, Elizabeth is James's eldest daughter and, I believe, the heir to all the Carleton properties."

"I can't conceive of King Carleton allowing his granddaughter to consort with riffraff like Nate Bowditch's son," Rees murmured. "And the James I remember wouldn't either. He detested Nate."

Susannah threw Rees the same scornful glance she'd employed when they were students together and he needed help with a math problem. "Elizabeth and Richard are meeting on the sly, of course, trying to keep the connection a secret."

"How do you know?" her husband asked.

"They were seen. King Carleton gobbled up a dozen or more of the small farms hereabouts. Memories are long, and there's always someone wanting to serve him an ill turn."

Rees nodded. He'd known several families who had lost their land to Carleton and as a consequence became renters or, worse, homeless.

"Women's chatter." Jack growled.

"I would warn James," Susannah said, ignoring her husband, "but I know he won't listen. I'm so thankful Leah and Hannah are too young to attract Richard's attention."

"I'd kill him if he interfered with either," Jack said. The absence of bluster made his threat all the more chilling.

"But Nate knew Richard was courting," Rees said, recalling one of Molly's statements. "He didn't approve."

Susannah's eyebrows went up, and her mouth rounded: the very picture of surprise. "Why would Nate object? He should be jumping for joy. The Carletons are the largest landowners in the county."

"And Nate isn't far behind now," Jack said. "My God, if the two heirs marry, they'll *own* the county."

"Nate?" Rees looked at Jack in surprise. "The son of a farmer? How did he acquire the cash? Certainly not from weaving?" He'd wondered about the new farm but thought maybe Molly's portion explained the sudden wealth. Although her father was only a cobbler, so that couldn't be the answer.

"I don't know. A good businessman, I suppose," Jack said with a shrug.

"Nate and James, friends? How can that be?" Rees asked, unable to absorb this unexpected news.

"They were business partners first," Jack said.

"Anyway, it was you James hated," Susannah said. "You bested him in everything. And everyone liked you, besides."

Rees shook his head in disbelief. And now he must reacquaint himself with his old nemesis. Did James resemble his lean silver-haired father or was he portly and content? Try as he might, Rees couldn't envision James as anything but a plump dark-haired boy with the pallor of someone who rarely saw the sun.

"Everyone wondered about the sudden connection between Nate and Mr. Henry Carleton," Susannah said. "Especially when Nate bought the new farm and rented the old to Thomas."

Rees's mind veered into a different direction. "Could Richard be staying with Thomas? He is the boy's uncle. . . ."

Susannah and Jack looked at each other. "Doubtful," Jack said.

Susannah nodded in agreement. "The relationship between Thomas and Nate did not improve as they grew into manhood."

"Besides, Thomas numbers three daughters in his large brood," Jack added, lumbering to his feet. "Excuse me. Customers." Three women, townsfolk by the look of their fashionable gowns and extravagant hats, paused inside the door. Jack bustled over, smiling, and gestured them to a table by the front windows. Another lady was sipping coffee there, and as her friends approached she took out a deck of cards from her reticule.

"Those ladies come regularly," Susannah said, also pushing back her chair. "I believe they wish their husbands to remain ignorant of their pastime. Now, to my duties."

Rees jumped up, bowing as she hurried away. But he sat down again to ponder what he'd been told. James Carleton back in Dugard? How surprising. And his daughter and Nate's son together? Now, that was a connection Rees could never have imagined. Fascinating, but of no help in discovering Augustus's whereabouts. Rees drained his cup, threw a ha'penny onto the table, and left.

Chapter Six

Once outside, he crossed the road and went down Wheeler's Way. Although the yard was on the opposite side of the stable wall, he could hear the sounds of horses; Wheeler's stalls must be full today. A short walk brought him to Isaacs's smithy, cheek by jowl next to the gunsmith. Several horses were tied up outside, and a crowd of men stood in the doorway laughing and smoking. Rees brushed past them and stepped inside.

The short, grizzled Isaacs hurried to him. "What may I help you with, Mr. Rees?"

"Nothing. I want to speak to him." Rees nodded at the young man wielding the hammer. He was lighter skinned than Rachel, but possessed of her long lithe legs and arms and thick eyelashes. His heavy prognathic jaw and full lips kept him from a girlish beauty. Except for the leather apron protecting his chest, he was naked to the waist and streaming with sweat.

"We're very busy today, as you can see," Isaacs said, gesturing to the waiting horses.

Rees glanced at them. Besides the horseshoes and various farming implements, Augustus must also be working on the barrels and other metal parts to some rifles. "I daresay he can take a short break, can't he?"

Isaacs looked at Rees thoughtfully.

"Very well. For you. Your father was one of my best customers."

Rees raised his eyes to Augustus. Although the young man must have heard them, he gave no sign. The hammer continued to come down, *clang, clang,* on the shoe, without breaking rhythm.

"Augustus," Rees said. The young man flicked an antagonistic glance at the weaver and continued hammering. "Augustus!" Rees bellowed. Still, the pounding did not cease. The weaver approached the anvil. "I'm looking for Richard," he said quietly. "But I can shout out my questions and everyone can hear our business if you wish."

Augustus looked at him with dislike and stilled the hammer. After grabbing a towel from a nearby rail, he wiped himself down and stepped through a side door into the smithy yard. A sickly maple provided some shade, dappling the hides of the two farm cobs tied to it. Stables formed a back wall, adjoining the garden wall of Isaacs's cottage.

Augustus lifted a dipper of water from the barrel under the tree and drank deeply before speaking. "I left that house when I was twelve," he said, sitting down upon the bench. "I don't even visit my mother. Why do you think I know anything about Richard?" His instant protestation immediately persuaded Rees that Augustus knew exactly where Richard had gone to ground.

"Because you grew up with him. Because you're as close as brothers. And because he has no one else." Augustus looked at the sky and said nothing. "I'm trying to help him," Rees said. "I'm not convinced he's guilty. But before I can determine his innocence, and before I can fight for him, I must speak to him."

Augustus's gaze swept around the stable yard. "I live in the loft of Isaacs's house, above his family. I couldn't hide Richard if I wanted to," he said. Rees eyed the boy skeptically. Although the lad's exact words might be true, Rees heard an evasion. "But I'll send word if I see Richard." Augustus jumped to his feet. "Break's over." He hurried into the smith and a moment later the relentless pounding began again.

Rees stood there burning with frustration. *Damn kids!* But as he turned to walk away, he noticed the windows lining the wall just under the stable roof. The loft would make a fine hiding place. Then he glanced at the men outside in the lane and saw Isaacs watching him from the smithy door. Rees knew he couldn't investigate right now. But first thing tomorrow morning, when most good people were in church, he would return and explore the loft and the area more completely.

He cut through the alley by Wheeler's, plunging into the crowds of farmers thronging Market Street. With his height, and with David's, Rees could see his son standing on the other side of the street. David's head swiveled from side to side as he searched for his father.

Rees waved and, began shoving through the congestion, cut across toward the table. The back of his neck began to tingle. He stopped, his eyes darting from side to side, but he saw nothing. He spun around.

His sister Caroline, almost unidentifiable in her broad-brimmed straw hat, stood not twenty feet from him. Although he couldn't see her face, her proud carriage and the arrogant tilt of her chin made her easily recognizable. "Caro?" Attempting a cautious smile—she was, after all, his baby sister—he stepped toward her.

She tipped her head back and stared balefully at him from under the broad brim before spinning around and fleeing into the crowd. "Caro, wait." Rees expected to hear her calling for her husband but didn't. He thrust his way through the crowd after her, but she had disappeared. Rees stopped and stared around him, searching the faces. Regret swept through him, an ache far more painful than he expected. This might be his only chance to make things right between them.

Finally accepting she was gone Rees turned and retraced his steps to join David. "Did you see your aunt Caroline?"

"No. She won't speak to me anyway." David handed the empty basket to Lydia. Her cheeks and hands exhibited the scarlet flush of sunburn. "I took most of the crates to the wagon already. Will you take the table?"

Rees nodded. "You two go on," he said, horribly conscious of the curious eyes all around them. "I'll meet you. . . ." He waited until they'd disappeared around the corner of Market and Church Streets before hoisting up the table and following.

Many farmers were abandoning their stalls. Like Lydia, they'd sold their wares and now streamed toward their wagons. Rees knew that once he passed this first row of vendors—some with carts displaying their produce, others with wheelbarrows—the crowd would thin. But trying to push through the humanity crushed in around him was like walking through molasses: slow and tiresome. Rees used the table to open a path.

"Rees. Oh, Rees." From his position on the elevated wooden sidewalk, Caldwell gestured to him. By sidestepping a few steps, Rees managed to reach the sidewalk and step up. "See the slave catchers?"

"Slave catchers? How can you tell?" Rees looked all around but didn't see anything unusual. Few farmers in Maine owned slaves. However, escaped slaves sometimes made their way to Dugard. Since the Fugitive Slave Act of 1793 permitted their recapture into perpetuity, slave takers were sometimes seen in town.

Caldwell pointed at two men. A thick black mustache distinguished the older of the two, but the younger man seemed little more than a boy. Their linen suits were almost as dirty as Caldwell's shirt. They traveled in a small empty circle as the townspeople pushed away from them in revulsion. "They were watching Marsh."

"But Marsh is free," Rees objected.

Caldwell threw him a scornful glance. "Do you think that matters? They won't go south empty handed." He sighed. "We better get the word out; all the blacks should stay hidden until I can move these fellows along."

"Are there any escapees here?" Rees asked in a low voice.

Caldwell shook his head. "None that I know of. But not everyone tells me either."

"Aren't the catchers supposed to bring their captive in front of a magistrate?" Rees asked, watching the men tack from side to side, their eyes constantly moving.

"A legal provision regularly flouted. Anyway, the current magistrate on circuit is Cornelius Hansen."

"Piggy Hansen?" Rees cried, aghast.

"I see you know the gentleman," Caldwell said.

"He was a cruel bully as a boy," Rees said.

"He hasn't changed much," Caldwell said. He and Rees exchanged a glance of understanding. "Of course, Marsh is probably safe, if the catchers take that step. Judge Hansen and his wife were good friends with Nate Bowditch, and I believe Molly still socializes with Mrs. Hansen."

Rees stared at Caldwell in shock. As a boy, Nate regularly thrashed Piggy. "So, where is Marsh?" he asked.

Caldwell smiled. "He left rather hastily. I am sorry to report that the crowd surrounding him prevented the catchers from following him. I told him to inform his mistress and suggested she might want to make other arrangements for market day, at least until they're gone."

He and Rees shared a grin. "Good," Rees said.

"Planning to have a picnic?" Caldwell asked, gesturing to the table and laughing at his wit.

"Market day," Rees said, grunting and jerking the table to his shoulder. Since the crowd here was marginally thinner, he was able to push through it. He finally reached the corner of Market and Church. A left onto Church and another left onto Wheeler's Way. Rees finally reached the wagon.

"That took longer than I expected," David said.

"Too many people," Rees said, and climbed into the seat.

Lydia and David spent the ride home congratulating each other on a successful day. Rees was happy for them, he was, but he was also aware of something different about their relationship. As though they were joined in some purpose. As though the first barricades were up against him. He could feel himself stiffening into granite, putting up his defenses. He was not surprised when, at the close of dinner, David said, "I want to discuss something with you, Father."

"Father? That sounds serious."

"I've found someone to help Lydia." He paused, waiting for his father's explosion.

But Rees was looking at Lydia, whose expression of hope, anxiety, and belligerence tugged at him. "Who is it?" he said in a resigned voice.

"Abigail Jane, Mary Martha's sister," David said.

Lydia clenched her hands together in an agony of hope.

Rees gritted his teeth. "Mary Martha can talk the hind leg off a donkey," he said, shaking his head.

"Abby isn't like that. She doesn't talk. Well, she does, but she doesn't chatter like her sister. We would all prefer that." Anger throbbed through Rees's temples and he didn't dare speak. "Lydia doesn't want her reputation compromised by gossip any more than you do," David added.

Rees turned to stare at her.

She met his gaze. "Although I want another woman by me, I don't want the townsfolk believing I share your bed," she said. "I too would prefer employing someone who keeps her own counsel. David assures me this Abigail is the girl."

Rees heard Lydia refer to David with a shock of exclusion. He shook his head.

"Mother was often lonely," David said. "She concealed it from you. And you never questioned it. She grew up here and she saw her parents and her brothers and sisters and a whole skein of cousins almost daily. And I still heard her sometimes, crying at night."

Rees swallowed. "She—she did? She never said."

"Lydia has no one but us." He continued to contemplate his father until Rees felt like a worm on the end of a hook, squirming and unable to break free. Wasn't it his job to protect Lydia? Not David's.

He dragged his gaze to Lydia and said, "You'll hire someone even if I say no, won't you?"

She didn't try to soften her response. "Yes. Eventually. But I'd much rather share this decision with you." With David's accusation reverberating in his ears, Rees did not want to argue.

David looked from Lydia to Rees and back again. "I have chores," he said, rising to his feet. As David walked into the mudroom, throwing a final glance at his father, Rees turned to Lydia.

"I followed you here for a better life, " she said, raising her chin.

"I want you to stay," he admitted.

She nodded. "You have memories of Dolly," she said. "Just

as I have memories of Charles. I understand. I accept that. For now."

She might still return to the Shakers, Rees thought, his stomach lurching. He sat at the table watching her as she stirred up the fire under the water heating in the kettle. She was smiling and he longed to put his arms around her and kiss the delicate nape of her neck. But he didn't have the right, by his own choice. Finally he rose to his feet and followed David outside.

Chapter Seven

Rees drove into town the next morning in the midst of church traffic, farmers and families in their Sunday best. Although baptized and confirmed into the stone Anglican church in town, he maintained his skepticism of all things religious. His mother would be horrified.

Buggies and carriages clogged Church Street, Market Street, and all the lanes around. Rees finally parked in the yard behind Potter's establishment and walked the distance to Wheeler's Way. The door into the blacksmith's was shut and locked. He should have thought of that. Cursing himself for a fool, Rees hauled himself over the fence. All was silent. He knew someone would be here; the horses in their stalls must be tended whether Sunday or no, and he saw fresh water in the trough. As quietly as possible, he eased into the stable. He heard voices in the loft. He climbed the ladder, praying that the shuffling of hooves and odd whinny would cover any sound that he might make. The roof captured and held the heat, so with each rung up, the temperature noticeably increased.

He paused at the top of the ladder and peered into the sun-spotted gloom. Straw had been piled in one corner and a pallet stretched out upon it. Augustus sat with his back to Rees, facing a lanky dark-haired boy. He did not resemble Molly Bowditch, but Rees would have recognized him as Augustus's brother anywhere. Both shared that heavy jaw and full sensual lips.

"I don't trust him," Richard said flatly. "He's one of Caldwell's, I know it."

"He was your father's best friend," Augustus argued. "And your mother hired him. And he told me he doesn't automatically assume you're guilty."

Richard, his expression agonized, looked at his brother and shook his head.

Augustus believes Richard's guilty, Rees thought, shifting his weight as he leaned forward for a better view. The ladder shrieked in protest.

Richard looked up, his brown eyes lighting upon the unwanted visitor. "He followed you!" he shouted accusingly, jumping to his feet. He glanced wildly around him for a way out and suddenly threw himself off the loft to the hay bales below.

"Wait, wait!" Rees called after him. "Richard. I just want to talk to you." He began scrambling down the ladder, but by the time he reached the stable floor, Richard had disappeared through the door. Although Rees ran into the yard and looked all around, he knew he was too late. Still, he had to try. Climbing the fence to the alley, he glanced in both directions. Nothing but a faint haze of dust. Rees trotted north to Water Street. Even the Contented Rooster was closed now, at least until dinnertime. And he saw no sign of Richard. *Damn!* Turning around, he started back to the smithy. He planned to say a few choice words to Augustus.

But Augustus, who'd also jumped the fence to follow his brother, was caught in the tight grip of the two slave takers. He'd put up a fight; his nose streamed blood and an ugly gash went from eyebrow to cheek around his left eye. But he'd been unable to vanquish the two other men. Now they dragged him toward the horses tethered at the end of the street.

Without a moment's thought, Rees steamed toward them, shouting. "Let him go! Let him go!" They speeded up into a clumsy trot, Augustus fighting their hold.

Unencumbered, Rees caught up to them. He grabbed the older of the two catchers and, spinning him around, hit him with all his strength. The catcher released his hold upon the prisoner and dropped to the ground like a felled tree. Augustus wrenched himself out of the other's grip and pushed the young man away. The young catcher reached into his pocket. Rees didn't know if he'd pull out a pistol or a knife or something innocuous; he didn't pause to find out. He hit the boy as well and watched him drop. Panting, shaking his stinging hand, Rees stepped back.

Running feet pounded up behind him and as Caldwell's penetrating odor ballooned around the combatants, he pushed Augustus backwards. One of the deputies, a tavern rat from the Bull from the look of him, stood over the older of the two men. Caldwell held a flintlock pistol.

"I have a description," the older catcher cried. He pulled a paper from his pocket and brandished it.

Caldwell snatched it out of his hands, skimmed it, and handed it to Rees.

He read aloud, "Five dollars reward. Ran away from subscriber about six weeks ago. Understands blacksmithing. Mulatto about five feet nine inches tall, thirty years of age, and greatly addicted to drink. Answers to the name Hercules." He looked at the man and said angrily, "This boy is not even twenty. And he was born here."

"We want to see a magistrate," the catcher retorted. "By the

Act of 1793—" He sounded as though he were repeating a lesson drilled into him. Rees suspected neither of these men could read.

"Is that why you were dragging Augie down the street, because you were bringing him to a magistrate?" Caldwell asked. "And on a Sunday, too."

"You calling me a liar?" the catcher bellowed.

"I'll call you worse if you don't get out of town," Caldwell said. "I've known this lad since he was born. You're lucky I don't jail you for kidnapping."

The older fellow, lanky and almost as tall as Rees, hesitated. Then he smiled, gap-toothed, and pulled himself upright. "Sorry. We made a mistake. Sorry." He pulled his companion up and they began walking away.

Rees touched Augustus, who was trembling with terror, on the shoulder.

"I won't lay money on them leaving," Caldwell said, staring after the two men as they hurried toward their horses. "You were lucky Mr. Rees happened along, Augustus." Then he turned to Rees in puzzlement. "Why were you here?"

"I thought Augustus might know more about Richard than he claimed," Rees said, not altogether truthfully. He fixed a stern eye upon the lad. "And indeed I found him in Richard's company."

Caldwell turned to glare at Augustus. "You lied to me, boy." Augustus didn't speak, but his expression was defeated. "I think a day or two in jail will be just the thing. It'll teach you not to lie to the law."

Augustus threw Rees a pleading look. "I'm innocent. Why should I go to jail?"

"It's not safe for you to stay here, not until those damn

crackers go home," he said, not unkindly. "I hope it won't be for more than a day or two."

Caldwell nodded at Rees. "Yes. I'll release him when those catchers leave town. Now, for jail."

"First," Rees said, tipping the boy's face up so he could see the cut, "let's stop and see if Dr. Wrothman is around. This cut looks ugly."

Caldwell glanced at Augie and nodded. "Very well."

Rees kept a tight grip upon Augustus's arm as he followed the constable north through town. The doctor lived on the outskirts, not in a fine mansion but a stout house with at least two floors. An ell to one side boasted its own door, and as they approached the door opened, and Dr. Wrothman stepped out.

He stopped short when he saw Augustus. "What happened?"

"The slave takers caught him," Caldwell said. "There was a scuffle. . . ."

"I should say so," Wrothman said. He paused on the step, and Rees wondered if he were trying to decide whether or not to treat the lad.

"I don't want blood all over my jail," Caldwell said.

Wrothman looked at the blood and pulled a face. He opened his door and ushered them in. Caldwell sat down and averted his face from the operation, but Rees stepped up to the table. He wanted to keep an eye, and a quick hand, on the boy, but also he wanted to question the good doctor without Molly nearby.

"You think I killed your friend, don't you?" Wrothman said as he washed the blood from the gash.

"Did you?" Rees asked.

"Of course not."

"You had good reason." Rees glanced quickly at Augustus and did not continue.

Wrothman smiled. "Did I? Maybe. He should have paid more attention to his wife. But I didn't do it. I couldn't. I was twenty miles west of here, delivering a baby." He cut his eyes toward Augustus. "The Collier baby. You know Enoch Collier, don't you?"

Augie nodded. "Doesn't he already have five or six kids?"

"Seven. It's eight now." He leaned forward to dab at the cut.

Augie pushed his hand away. "Stings."

"I'll be happy to give you the direction, if you like." The doctor looked at Rees with a smug expression. Rees knew the doctor must have done exactly as he said to look so confident. But that didn't mean Wrothman hadn't conjured some other method of murdering his mistress's husband.

"Thank you. I'll take it," Rees said, just to see if any slight discomfort crossed the doctor's face. But he maintained his arrogant smile as he tied a linen strip over Augustus's wound. As Rees joined the constable, and they escorted Augustus back into the sunshine, Rees said, "I'd like to smack that grin right off Wrothman's face."

"I doubt you'll be offered a chance," Caldwell said in amusement. "He's entirely too sure of himself."

Although Augustus scowled furiously, he did not protest as they marched him the three streets over to the jail. Rees held the boy as Caldwell fetched a large key from his desk in the middle of the main room. Then they hustled Augustus into one of the two cells and Caldwell locked the barred door. Augustus rattled it a few times before turning to the bench and subsiding upon it.

"See? I told you. Local boy hears more," Caldwell said to Rees as he dropped the key back into his drawer.

Rees sat down in the chair by the desk and looked around. Since his childhood, the jail had been rebuilt: larger and of fine chestnut wood. He rose to his feet and ran his hand over the smoothly planed wall. Sometimes he regretted not apprenticing with a carpenter; he loved working with wood. Then he looked at the desk, now stained with white rings and the blackened marks left by burning cigars, and shuddered to see such careless damage.

"I'm sure you know many things I don't," he said. "I'll check on the boy tomorrow." Turning to the cell, he shouted at Augustus, "The constable will make sure you have food and water!" He raised his brows at Caldwell. When the constable sighed and frowned in reluctance, Rees fumbled in his pocket for a few coins.

Caldwell nodded, more eagerly this time, and put his hand out. "You know," he said as he clutched his fingers around the money, "it will prove expensive to keep him here for longer than a day or two."

"You can't release him too soon. I don't think any of us want to see him dragged south," Rees protested.

"We need to find him a safer billet." Caldwell looked at Rees sternly.

"I'll give it some thought," he promised, although he couldn't think of a safer place than the jail.

"Join me for a drink at the Bull?" Caldwell stood up.

Rees hesitated and then nodded. "Very well."

Caldwell carefully closed and locked the office door behind him and they crossed the street to the tavern.

Since today was Sunday, and midday, few men stood at the bar. Caldwell ordered a whiskey, Rees ale. It was thin and sour, without the flavor of Marsh's home-brewed.

"So, where do you think Richard Bowditch has gone now?" Caldwell asked, swiping his tongue around his mouth to suck up any stray drops.

Rees shrugged. "I don't know. He doesn't have anyone else," he said. Anyone but Elizabeth Carleton; the thought popped into his mind.

Caldwell glanced at him. "You won't lie to me, now, will you, Rees?"

"If I discover something definite, I promise I will tell you." A door at the back opened and four men stepped out, wreathed in smoke.

As Rees glanced at them, recognizing George Potter and someone he thought must be Piggy Hansen, Sam Prentiss detached himself from the group. "What are you doing here?" he snarled, bearing down upon Rees.

"Come on, Sam," said Hansen. Formerly a plump boy, he had matured into a corpulent man with thinning hair.

"You had beginners' luck today," said the fourth man. Rees caught a confused impression of breeches and a scarlet waistcoat before the dark-haired gentleman disappeared through the door.

Piggy Hansen shot Rees a curious glance but didn't immediately recognize him and joined his companion outside on West Street.

Potter nodded at Rees, his expression self-conscious, and said to Sam, "Go home to your wife. You've got good news for a change."

Rees, who simply could not credit his friend's evident friendship with Sam Prentiss, stared at Potter in dismay. The lawyer grasped Sam's arm and with a faint shrug of apology shepherded him out the door. Rees turned to look at Caldwell.

"I guess they couldn't find a fourth," Caldwell said. "Your friend Nate Bowditch usually made up that quartet." He drained the remainder of his whiskey. "They didn't play here, either. Although no one knew the exact location of their games, I'm guessing they played in your friend's cottage."

"Who was the gentleman in the scarlet waistcoat?" Rees asked. Nate with Piggy Hansen? What had happened to his old friend?

"You didn't recognize him?" Caldwell smiled mockingly at his companion. "I suppose I do know more than you do. That was James Carleton."

Rees stared at Caldwell incredulously, and then his eyes rose to the open door and the street outside. James Carleton? And Sam Prentiss? That was even more surprising than Carleton's friendship with Nate. Rees decided he would ride to the Carleton mansion tomorrow and speak to James Carleton and also to his eldest daughter if possible.

With the end of church services, people crowded into the streets. *Oh no,* Rees thought, watching them pile into their buggies and wagons. Sure enough, when he entered the traffic, he found himself mired in a slow-moving stream of vehicles and so didn't arrive home until almost dinnertime. When Bessie trotted up the drive, Rees saw an unfamiliar buggy parked by the porch. Company and someone who didn't plan to stay long; their gray mare was still hitched to the wagon. Regarding the unfamiliar buggy with disfavor, for he was tired, hungry, and irritable, Rees quickly unharnessed Bessie and released her into the field before trudging into the house.

He found everyone seated in the front parlor. The last time he met company in this room, he'd ordered Sam and Caroline off the farm. Even now, that memory made him flinch.

The stolid farmer in his plain-cut black suit rose to his feet. "Mr. and Mrs. Bristol," David said. Mr. Bristol had put aside his flat-brimmed hat, revealing a shock of graying hair. His sun-burned face and neck betrayed long days spent in the fields.

"Will Rees." He nodded at the plump matron sitting next to her husband. She smiled in return, her red hair and freckles and wide smile reminiscent of Mary Martha.

"Cake?" Lydia offered. "Coffee?" Rees shook his head. The litter of empty plates and cups upon the tea cart told Rees that the Bristols had been here for some time.

"Forgive me for arriving late," Rees said, shooting his son an angry glare.

"They wished to meet you," David said. "And Lydia, of course. And I thought you would want to meet Abigail."

Directing another frown at his son, Rees inspected the wench sitting between her parents. A mere slip of a girl, and a pale shadow of her ebullient sister, Abigail sat quietly with her hands folded in her lap. Unlike her sister's fiery mop, Abby's hair was tow colored and straight, and still plaited into two skinny braids. A few freckles dusted her nose, but otherwise her skin was porcelain. A milk-and-water miss, Rees thought, with nothing interesting about her.

Mrs. Bristol's anxious glance darted from Rees to Lydia and back again. "Abby speaks little," Mrs. Bristol said.

"I am well used to silence and comfortable with it," Lydia replied.

"I daresay you must be," Mr. Bristol said, eyeing the linen square covering Lydia's bright hair. His round blue eyes, so like Mary Martha's, moved to Rees.

"How old is she?" Rees asked, eyeing the girl's skinny arms.

"Rising thirteen" Mrs. Bristol said.

"Your housekeeper will find my daughter well versed in all the housewifely arts," Mr. Bristol said, "and far stronger than she first appears."

Rees glanced at the girl once again and surprised her as she threw a quick flashing glance at him. Although her eyes were gray, there was nothing plain or simple about the steely look she gave him. Rees eyed her more searchingly this time, noting the hard muscles in those skinny arms and the expressive mouth. Despite her quiet nature, she might very well hold her own in this opinionated family.

"What do you say?" he asked Lydia.

"Can she begin tomorrow?"

Rees and Mr. Bristol haggled over the wage, finally settling on a few pennies each day. She would arrive at six, but leave by three so as to be home in time to help her mother with supper and milking.

With handshakes all around, the Bristols prepared to depart. "Bye, Abby," David said. "See you tomorrow." Her smile illuminated her pale face, and when she looked at him, her eyes sparkled with excitement. Rees and Lydia exchanged worried looks.

"Still waters indeed," he murmured.

As Lydia wheeled the tea cart out of the parlor, David leaned back in his chair with a smug grin. "I knew Lydia would like her," he said.

Rees jumped to his feet and snatched his son out of his chair so fast, David gasped. "Don't ever do that to me again," Rees said. "No warning. I just walked into it."

David gaped at him in astonishment. "When I saw Mr. Bristol at the market and suggested employing Abby, he said not without meeting you. I didn't think you would mind—"

"This is still my farm," Rees said through gritted teeth.

David flung his father's hand from him. "It's only mine, is it, when you're gone? When you take off, then I can run the farm as I please? But I'm just a child when you return?"

Rees stared into his son's angry face. "But you are a child," he protested, shocked into calmness by David's fury.

"Not anymore. I've been doing a man's work for years. And this farm, you promised it to me."

"Of course," Rees began. "When I die—"

"Or do you intend to break your promise to me as you did to Mother?"

Rees examined the contorted face of his son. "I never broke a promise to your mother," he said, his voice cracking. "Never."

"Didn't you swear you'd give up the road when she quickened with another child?"

"I did. And—"

"She was pregnant when she died of the illness you brought home with you. Why didn't you stay home when you knew another child grew within her?"

Rees struggled to catch his breath. "I—I would have, when I'd earned enough money."

"And Lydia, she followed you expecting marriage. You've broken that promise also."

"I never promised her anything," Rees cried. He stopped short, realizing Lydia was standing in the doorway listening to them.

She marched into the parlor, the red flush in her cheeks the only sign of her emotion. "This is a discussion that should end now," she said.

"I'm sorry," Rees said to David. "Your mother understood; I need to travel for work. The money I make weaving helps support this farm."

"Then why didn't you take me with you?" David bellowed, tears streaming down his cheeks. Rees shrugged helplessly, aware that this quarrel had left the original shores and drifted far out to sea. "You could have taken me with you when Mother died. . . ."

"Come outside now," Lydia said, drawing David away. The

lad towered over her; she barely topped his shoulder, but right now he looked like a little boy. "I'll help you milk." Biting her lip, she put her hand on the boy's elbow and urged him from the room.

Rees stared after them. He felt excluded from the connection forming between them—nay, not excluded but ostracized. His initial anger drained away, leaving him tired and very sad. He remembered David's birth and infancy and the soft coppery hair that covered his little skull like down. When Rees had dragged his lips over the silky strands, the sweet fragrant scent of baby enveloped him. It was the happiest time of his life. But that little boy was gone and he'd missed all the growing. A man called David with Rees's red hair and Dolly's gray eyes stood in that boy's place. "I'm sorry, David," he cried after him. "I'm sorry." But neither David nor Lydia turned around.

Chapter Eight

Rees climbed the stairs to the second floor and his loom, taking refuge from his regrets in the familiar tasks. Quickly attaching front and back beams, he inserted the comblike reed into its slot and arranged the heddles on the sheds. He took the chained warp off the board and tied it to the back beam. He began threading the heddles, calmed by the tedious and repetitive chore.

A soft tap upon the door startled him, returning him to an awareness of his surroundings. By the golden light streaming through the window, Rees guessed the time to be early afternoon. He was very hungry. He turned to see Lydia, standing outside.

"Dinner is on the table," she said. "Or do you want a plate in here?"

For one brief second, Rees considered taking the coward's way out, but he would have to face his son sometime. "I'll come down," he said, pushing the bench backwards. He shook out his stiff legs.

"Don't be hard on David," she said, watching him. "In some ways, he's older than his years, but in others he's still a boy." A boy with an absent father. She didn't say that, but Rees heard it all the same.

"I'm a factor, that's what I do," he said.

"You could choose to set up a shop here," Lydia suggested. "In Dugard. But I know you won't. You were born under the traveling foot quilt, and the road is in your blood."

"Even the Shakers travel to sell their goods," he said, knowing he sounded defensive. She nodded in acknowledgment. But Rees traveled much more. He knew it but didn't think he could explain the attraction of leaving everything familiar behind and finding the new and different. After a while, the same recycled conversations, the same histories, the same people—no matter how loved—suffocated him.

"Don't worry about your quarrel with David," she said, turning to descend the stairs. "Sometimes a festering boil must be lanced to start the healing."

"I expect this particular boil will require lancing several times," he said dryly, following her into the hall.

She moved lightly down the steps. "And your investigation? How is that proceeding?"

"Not well," he said. "Dr. Wrothman, who has the best reason for wanting Nate dead outside of Richard, apparently was miles away. Could he have hired someone, that's the question. And Richard? Well, I still haven't spoken to him. I know he was in the weaving house and something happened between him and Nate. But the situation is so much more complicated than it first appeared."

Lydia nodded. "It always is, isn't it?" Then she turned to look at him. "You aren't persuaded of his guilt."

"No, I'm not. Although everyone, including Augustus, assumes he is the killer. It just doesn't feel right."

"He did run," Lydia pointed out.

"Yes. He's scared. I'm sure of that. But several people at the

Bowditch farm lied to me, or lied by omission, and as a consequence, I trust none of them."

"I could help you with that," Lydia said in a low voice.

Rees shook his head. "I want to speak to Richard and interpret his story myself." And he must study the man Nate had become. The descriptions of him sounded like a different person from the boy Rees remembered. That boy hated slavery, but the man he'd become owned slaves and, in fact, had fathered a son with one of them. He'd become a card player and a gambler. And although always secretive, one might now describe him as reclusive. Why? Rees realized Lydia had turned to stare curiously at him. "What?"

"I asked what do you plan to do next?"

"Well, I hear Richard is courting Elizabeth Carleton, James Carleton's daughter, and Nate wasn't happy about it," Rees said. Although he planned to speak to George Potter also as soon as he could, he didn't feel comfortable confiding that to Lydia, since she knew him. "I don't believe James Carleton knows of the connection between the children. Probably he wouldn't approve either. I don't know. James Carleton and Nate Bowditch became friendlier as men, but they were sworn enemies as boys. In any case, I plan to ride out to the Carleton estate tomorrow and talk to James. And to his daughter if possible."

"How very *Romeo and Juliet*," Lydia said.

"What do you mean?" Rees asked.

"It's a play about two warring families and their children who fall in love anyway."

"Ahh. Well, I don't have the benefit of a classical education," Rees said. "Did they kill their fathers?"

"No. Themselves. Suicide pact," she clarified when Rees stared at her.

"Themselves? Although patricide is a terrible crime, it makes more sense to me than suicide."

"My governess would be horrified to hear you," Lydia said, preceding Rees down the stairs.

When Rees arrived at the Potter residence the following morning, he found the entire family still at breakfast. Sally hesitated to invite the unexpected visitor inside, but her father, rolling down his sleeves, joined her at the door. "Go back to the kitchen, Sally," he said. "I'll take Mr. Rees upstairs to my office."

Neither one spoke as they climbed the stairs. Potter shut the door behind them and burst into speech. "It's not what you think, Will."

"Cards with Sam Prentiss?" Rees asked, glaring at his friend.

"I only played with the club once in a while and for small stakes; my wife would skin me alive otherwise." Rees did not soften. "Nate usually made up the fourth. Although Sam was invited to join the club occasionally, this was my very first time playing opposite him."

Rees considered this. "But Nate played often?"

"I believe so. Almost every week. He and James Carleton, Cornelius Hansen when he was in town, sometimes Reverend Sperling."

"I wish you'd told me," Rees said peevishly. "This explains some of the connection between Nate and James."

"I believe their connection formed the root of this group, rather than otherwise," Potter said. "I didn't want to tell you. I didn't participate very often—they played for high stakes, and I knew you would disapprove. In some ways, you hark back to our Puritan ancestors."

"I'm surprised Nate could keep up with such wealthy company," Rees said. Although still shocked, he reminded himself he wasn't Potter's mother.

"Nate usually won," Potter said dryly. "Besides, you must have already realized that he did very well for himself. All that property, a new and expansive farm . . ."

"Yes. He did so well, I find it curious. How did the son of a poor farmer become so wealthy?" Potter shrugged. And Rees, who thought he did not entirely trust his old friend anymore, did not pursue that topic. "I apologize for interrupting your breakfast. I left home early, as I have several errands in town."

"I'm glad we cleared the air," Potter said, stretching out his hand.

Rees hesitated and then shook and departed, smiling genially. But his smile dropped away as he climbed into his wagon. Cards and gambling? Disgusting. He urged Bessie into a rapid trot, northwest, to the Carleton farm. The changes in the people he once knew continued to surprise and shock him.

Even as a boy, Rees had not visited Carleton Hall more than two or three times, and then always in the company of his father. Pausing at the end of the long drive leading up to the house, Rees recalled his final visit. His father intended to remonstrate with King Carleton for ordering his servants to beat his son. They'd walked up the drive together, his father smelling powerfully of whiskey and tobacco, and his fingers black with ink. No amount of scrubbing could wash that ingrained ink away. Rees, who knew even at eleven that he disappointed his father in choosing weaving instead of printing as a profession, could feel him trembling. Carleton allowed them in, but before the elder Rees spoke more than a few words, King went after him with his cane. White hair flying, he whaled about him with the oak stick, and Rees and his father fled. Rees sighed, only now understanding the depth of his father's humiliation.

He urged Bessie forward. The trees appeared thicker and denser than he remembered, and the leafy branches woven together overhead completely occluded the sky. A lone figure on horseback trotted toward Rees. James Carleton. Seated astride a beautiful chestnut gelding with a white stocking upon the left hind leg, James wore a tall black hat and a bright yellow coat. His riding boots, polished to a mirror shine, reflected the sun in bright flashes. Rees pulled Bessie to a stop and waited, his heart beginning to thunder in his chest.

"Well, if it isn't Will Rees," James sneered. "When I saw you at the Bull, I wondered how long it would take you to visit me."

Rees inspected his boyhood nemesis. The boy he remembered was still recognizable in the man, although his plumpness had become a portly gravitas. His full lips, fleshy and sensual in his father, looked feminine and weak on James and softened the heavy jaw. The arrogance Rees recalled now presented as bluster. Or a mask for something else. Fear, maybe?

"Still a model of sartorial elegance," Carleton mocked. Under his canary-colored jacket, he wore nankeen breeches tucked into those astonishing glossy boots.

"And you are a fashion plate," Rees said, eyeing the pale blue waistcoat with its thickly embroidered fantastical birds and flowers. He himself cared little for clothes, as long as they were clean and mended. His breeches were old and comfortable, and his homespun jacket and stockings recently laundered. Lydia had even pressed his linen shirt. "I prefer more important pursuits."

James smiled. "Ah, the same old Will. I'm glad to see that some people remain exactly as one remembers them."

"You were not so witty as a boy," Rees said, surprised by the adroit insult.

"I assume you are calling upon me to discuss Nate's death. And what a tragedy that was." Carleton's face crumpled. "I'll miss him. I could talk to him."

"Talk to him? About what?" Rees asked. Nate had spent his boyhood chasing James and calling him names.

"We enjoyed our time together in London," James said with a smirk.

"I know you gambled together," Rees said.

"And I had every reason for wanting him alive." James sighed.

Carleton's subdued passion surprised Rees. He could almost believe James cared about Nate.

"But, as you can see, I'm on my way into town and don't have time to meet with you. Permit me to save you some time. I didn't kill him. Why would I? I had no reason to. We were good friends. And I can't imagine who might have killed him, except I'm certain Richard is not the guilty party." He clucked to his mount, but Rees held up his hand.

"Wait. You truly don't believe the boy is guilty?"

"I'd lay my life on his innocence,," Carleton said. "They were devoted to one another."

"You knew them well, then?" Rees could hardly credit this friendship.

"Of course. We met often, Nate and I. Like I said, we were friends. I've known Richard since he was born."

"I understand you have a daughter Richard's age?" Rees said, trying to wrest control of this interview from James.

"I have three daughters. My eldest is a year or two younger than Richard. But what does she have to do with this? She barely knows the boy. She's been away at school for several years."

"A connection between the two largest landowners . . . ," Rees suggested. *James doesn't know*, he thought. *How can he not know?*

Carleton smiled. "I would not object. But it is my wife's fondest wish that Elizabeth—in fact, all of my daughters—experience a season in London. I fear no local sprig could compete with that." James chuckled. "Well, it was a pleasure meeting you again, Will. Please stop by again." With a flick of the reins, James steered his chestnut around Rees and his wagon. But before he galloped away, he turned back and shouted over his shoulder, "Ask your brother-in-law! Sam had a good reason for wishing Nate dead." And then he was off, disappearing in a cloud of dust.

"Sam Prentiss," Rees said in astonishment. Well, he knew Sam's temper from the past, but a close connection between the two men surprised him. And the prospect of questioning Sam, especially now, sent a nervous shock of dismay through Rees.

He planned to stop at the Bowditch farm and so headed due south on a smaller and less traveled lane. It bisected acres of lush Carleton fields. Occasionally, in the distance, Rees spotted an abandoned house, evidence of King Carleton's land grab. Rees wondered what had happened to the families who'd been forced out of those houses. He'd known some of the children in school; were they still around, married with farms and families of their own, or had the parents taken them west to the frontier?

Abruptly the fields went from planted to fallow, meadows thick with daisies and goldenrod. Left untilled for a few years, these parcels were no longer fields and, if the number of saplings were any indication, would soon revert to forest. Now, why had Carleton abandoned these plots?

And that question brought Rees full circle, back to his old enemy. He replayed his earlier meeting with James, the first in almost twenty years. Carleton had been more than rude and unmannerly, surprisingly so. He hadn't asked Rees any questions about his return to Dugard or even attempted polite small talk.

In fact, his demeanor and eagerness to escape solidified Rees's initial impression: Carleton was afraid. But of what? Rees? Some secret that pertained to Nate's death?

James Carleton clearly demanded more attention.

About twenty minutes later, Rees reached Nate's property; he knew it by the worked fields full of laborers harvesting the crops. Several minutes more and he approached the crossroad that ran east to Dugard. Straight ahead he saw the front of Nate's fine brick house. Rees did not turn into the main drive but continued to the back entrance. He felt more comfortable parking his wagon here. He tied up Bessie to the rail and went in search of Fred Salley, the hand who had witnessed Richard's flight from the cottage.

He asked the first laborer he saw for Mr. Salley. The man jerked his thumb at the barns and continued walking. Rees asked twice more before he found the man in the tack room. Although Rees had pictured a young man, little more than a boy, with red hair and freckles, the man he met was a laborer, a grizzled old veteran of a lifetime spent wandering on the roads. He now walked with the awkward jerky gait of a rheumatism sufferer, and Rees understood how he had fetched up on the shores of Nate's farm.

"Mr. Salley?" Rees asked. The man looked up. "I spoke with the constable. He told me you saw Richard Bowditch leaving the cottage the night before Nate's body was discovered."

"You ain't telling me you're helping Caldwell," the man replied skeptically.

"I am," Rees said. "Did you see the lad?"

"It ain't no secret. He come out, runnin' like the Devil himself was after him. . . ." He stopped.

"I already have a witness to that," Rees said. "And to the . . . the stains upon his shirt."

Salley stared at him. "You heard about the blood? The mistress didn't want me talking about it."

"You're sure it was blood?"

"Course I'm sure. He passed within two feet of me. And I know blood when I sees it."

Rees nodded slowly. "Describe exactly what you saw, if you please."

"The blood was sprayed down his right arm. Little bit on his chest. And a stain on his belly, like he took his father's head in his lap."

Rees stared over Salley's head, thinking. For the first time, he considered the bruising around Nate's nose. Had Richard held his father's nose closed and smothered him to make sure of his death? "What were you doing in front of the cottage?" Rees asked after a brief silence.

The man's eyes slid away. "Well, I warn't in front. More like going down the lane. Mr. Bowditch didn't like me to take the shortcut to the road, but my legs ain't so good anymore. I was just starting down the hill. . . ."

"And?"

"And nothing." Salley looked at him in disgust. "He was arguing with someone," he said. "Mr. Bowditch, I mean. Even before Richard went in. I heard the raised voices from the hill."

"Who was it?"

"Don't know. Then Richard went in from the road and there was more arguing. I figured I had a few minutes." He paused. Rees nodded in encouragement. "I was just at the bottom of the hill when the boy ran out. I jumped to the side, into the weeds there and Richard ran right by me. You know?"

Rees turned Salley's statement over in his mind. Someone

had been in the cottage before Richard, and maybe after as well unless he fled through the back door. "Anything else?"

"I went on down. Didn't see nothing else," he said.

"Why didn't you call Marsh or someone?"

"Well, it wasn't my business, was it? And if Mr. Bowditch was inside, well, he'd turn me off for sure. I been warned before, you see. So I kept going, just as fast as these tired old legs could carry me."

"And did Richard see you?" Rees asked.

Salley pondered a moment. "I'm not sure. I don't think so. It was getting dark. He never looked my way. And I sure didn't call out to him. Why would I do that?"

"Why indeed," Rees agreed. "Thank you, Mr. Salley." He started away but realized he still did not know why Salley had traveled past the cabin. "Why were you going past the cottage? Why take that route?"

The hand looked at him in surprise. "You go past the cottage and through the trees and you get to the main road. Cuts off a good mile or more. Easy," the hand said.

Rees realized with a start that Nate had a private entrance to the cottage. He could have come and gone as he pleased. So could anyone, including the murderer.

"Did you see anyone else when you left, maybe riding down the road?"

Salley shook his head. "A couple of horses in the lay-by. Richard's gelding, Marsh's gray cob, and one other—nothing else."

"Marsh's horse? You're sure?" Rees asked.

Salley nodded. "He tied the gray there when he was on his way out."

Rees considered that. Marsh was supposed to be gone. Everyone told Rees Marsh had been gone. "Who owned the other horse? Do you know?"

Salley shook his head. "But that lay-by isn't a secret. Sometimes the local farmers tie up their horses there."

"Thank you," Rees said. He would have to examine the lay-by to be certain, but he could already guess how easy it might be for someone to visit the cottage with no one in the house the wiser. Did Molly know of it and of the quartet of men who met to play cards at the cottage?

"I won't be turned off, will I?" Salley asked, his wrinkled face anxious.

"Not on account of me."

Abandoning the hand to his tack mending, Rees left the barn. He walked slowly back to the house. The number of men in Nate's circle must be enormous: customers, servants, casual help. Usually, though, friends and family were the more likely culprits, and that brought Rees full circle back to family and help. What about Marsh? Although several people had told Rees Marsh was away visiting his sister, Salley had just identified Marsh's horse. That meant that at the time of Nate's murder, the servant was still present on the property. Could he be the man overheard arguing with Nate? Maybe Nate had just demanded too much and Marsh had snapped?

As Rees crossed the lane and approached the back of the house, Marsh himself popped out of the door. Rees looked at him speculatively. "The mistress wants to speak to you," Marsh said. Sweaty and hot, he still wore his apron and carried a rag in his hand. He must have been watching for Rees, and Rees wondered if Molly—who of course could not be expected to call after him herself—had interrupted Marsh and compelled him to leave his own duties. Of course she had. Molly was too conscious of her own consequence to do otherwise.

Chapter Nine

The small sitting room at the front of the house was as different from Nate's messy office as it could be. No expense had been spared in furnishing this, Molly's boudoir. The graceful furniture had probably been imported from England; Rees did not know furniture. But he knew textiles and the silk covering the chairs and swathing the windows were imported from China. A delicate porcelain bowl brought back from the orient occupied pride of place on a marble-topped table. Molly was playing a musical instrument that resembled a harpsichord but sounded different, even to Rees's untrained ear, and the tinkling sounds of some piece filled the air.

She turned from the keyboard to look at him. "Do you enjoy music, Mr. Rees?" He shrugged. "I imported this pianoforte from Europe; it is the latest thing."

Rees looked at the instrument. Gold leaf decorated the sage green body, and it appeared both delicate and heavy. He could not even hazard a guess at the expense necessary for transporting this instrument but knew it must be significant.

"Oh, I am so pleased with you," Molly said. After jumping to her feet, she crossed the room to a delicate writing desk and extracted a small sack that jingled enticingly. "Dr. Wrothman brought me the good news. You've already caught the villain who murdered my dear husband." She held out the leather bag.

Rees regarded her in surprise. "He is mistaken. I haven't."

"Augustus is in jail, is he not?"

"Yes, he is. But not for—"

"Of course he's guilty. Now Richard can come home."

"I'm not certain Augustus is," Rees said. "Why would he murder Nate?"

"You must know the boy was raised here," she said, regarding him from blue eyes as piercing as rapier points and about as warm.

"Treated as a son," Rees said.

Sudden humiliated tears filled her eyes. "He is Nate's son," she cried. "By that . . . that woman downstairs. So you see, Mr. Rees, that Augustus could desire Nate's death for all of the reasons ascribed to Richard."

"Except that Augustus wasn't seen running away with blood on his shirt," Rees said, his voice cold. "And, by all accounts, he hasn't come home in years."

"He could have been sneaking into that weaver's cottage, with none of us knowing," Molly retorted.

She's talking about the lay-by, Rees realized.

"Anyway, I know Nate visited that boy in town. We can't know what arguments occurred." She thrust the bag at him. "Take your payment, Mr. Rees. Your investigation is over."

Rees put his hands behind his back. "The killer is still not identified." She stared at him. "Look, the murderer may not be either Richard or Augustus. Nate had another life, other than the one you witnessed on this farm. Customers and friends . . ."

He watched the anger run out of her, leaving her pale and tired. "He did little weaving anymore," she said, subsiding upon her couch. She sounded bone weary and Rees felt a flash of unexpected sympathy for her. "He preferred playing with his powders and roots. He was looking for the perfect red, the perfect green, or something like."

"Did he buy someone's farm and cause bitter feelings?"

"No. He acquired land from the Carletons, that's all I know. Quite a bit from King Carleton. But Nate rented a lot of it. He said he had enough." She uttered a humorless bark of laughter. "I was a widow, Mr. Rees, long before my husband died."

Rees nodded. "Was there anyone you know of that visited Nate regularly?" She shook her head. He rubbed his nose, contemplating the secluded cottage and the card players who met there in private. Maybe she didn't know about them; Rees wasn't the only one who didn't know Nate very well.

"I just want my son home," Molly said suddenly, her eyes brimming with tears. She tried to wipe them away with the lacy scrap of a handkerchief, and Rees, although he knew she was manipulative and not always kind, felt sorry for her. "Everyone blames my boy. . . ."

"We'll find the murderer," he promised. "I'll expand my search. Nate's office, maybe there's something in there."

"I looked. I found nothing." She sighed in defeat.

"Correspondence?" Rees asked.

"Nothing useful. Come and I'll show you. Maybe your eyes will find something. . . ." She rose to her feet, her filmy lawn gown swirling around her. Rees rose as well and together they walked down the hall to Nate's office.

As soon as Molly opened the door, Rees understood why they had not met in here; the results of her searching were obvious. Nate's ledgers covered every surface, and the desk drawers hung open. He involuntarily glanced at Molly.

"I thought I might find a will," she said in a small voice.

"George says he doesn't have it. Of course, Richard will inherit as the eldest son. But I thought Nate would set aside a portion for Grace at the very least. . . ." Rees moved toward the desk and picked up the top ledger. A large *D* marked the front in Nate's fine copperplate hand. When Rees skimmed through the pages, he saw entries for indigo and cochineal as well as for items he did not recognize; copper-based chemicals with sulfate and arsenite and carbonate in the names. A letter from a Mr. Scheele offering directions on the use of these products fell from between the leaves of the ledger.

Another book listed sales and purchases of farm items: corn to Mr. Pennington and hay from Mr. Jensen. Every line bore a small but definite *M*. Rees pointed it out to Molly.

"That is Marsh's mark," she said. She added in response to Rees's interrogative expression, "Nate trusted Marsh completely."

"He's literate?" Rees's voice squeaked in surprise. He'd wager that more than half the white farmers' daughters hereabouts could not read.

"I believe he worked as someone's secretary once . . . ," Molly said vaguely. "He knew how to read and write when he came to work here."

Rees picked up a third ledger, this one marked with an *H*. It included the people employed upon the farm, and their rate of pay. "Are all the ledgers like these?"

"Yes. Everything to do with the running of the farm. Nothing personal." She looked around the room, exhaling with frustration.

Rees sat down at the desk and began pulling out drawers at random: ink blocks, quills, and a penknife. A short letter relating to the sale of a colt. And then, tucked into the back of the central drawer, a scrap of paper torn from a larger sheet with a name: *Cornelius Lattimore, New Winstead.* "Do you know who this might be?" Rees asked.

Molly glanced at it and shook her head. "I've never seen or heard that name before. And look, it's not in Nate's hand."

Rees reexamined the note. No, the careful hand did not belong to Nate. After studying the signature, he dropped the paper back into the drawer and stared around, mirroring Molly's frustration. Nate must have a will; he was too responsible to shirk that task. So where was it?

Rees's stomach growled, suddenly and embarrassingly loud. "I'll think on this," he promised.

Molly, who'd politely affected not to notice the belly rumble, said, "Would you like to stay for dinner?" She did not sound enthusiastic.

"Thank you, no," he said. He wanted to spend no more time in Molly's company. "I have other errands . . . ," he said, a sop to her feelings. "I'll show myself out."

She nodded, brushing ineffectually at the dirt streaks on her gown.

He left the room wondering why Nate had wed Molly, a fashion plate and social butterfly: exactly the sort of woman he had always professed to despise. Rees would have thought his old friend would prefer a farmer's wife, a woman well used to hard work and not above milking her own cows. But then Nate had grown into a very different man than Rees would have expected. And he and Molly had succeeded in producing three children together, so Rees wanted to believe they'd been happy together.

Chapter Ten

The road into Dugard passed close by the jail, and Rees, with Augustus already on his mind, decided to stop and look in on the boy. When he entered the jail, the sweet scent of bacon reminded him of his hunger.

The constable looked up from his own plate. "Ah, Rees, your friend Mrs. Anderson just left. She brought some dinner for me and Augustus."

"My next stop will be the Contented Rooster," Rees said. His stomach rumbled, demanding sustenance, and Caldwell held out a strip of bacon. Rees looked at the dirty fingers holding the meat and said, "Thank you, no. I'll have my own dinner soon." He walked the few steps to the cell and stared in at the lad sitting inside. His dinner looked untouched. "How are you?" Rees asked Augustus. No answer. "Don't worry, lad. We'll get you out of here." The young man looked up, his expression agonized, but he still said nothing. "I am helping you," Rees said. Still no response. "I'll return soon." Feeling helpless, he walked back into the main room. Caldwell was scrubbing his plate with a thick slice of freshly baked bread.

"You done?" He jerked his head at the cell. Rees nodded. "Good. I've got something to show you." He rose to his feet in a billow of stink and gestured Rees to the door. They crossed the dirt street toward Dolan's furniture shop. The sound of running water intensified and Rees could smell freshly cut wood. But Caldwell did not enter the shop; he gestured instead to a cluster of thick shrubbery. In the dust underneath, partly obliterated by heavy boots, lay a small cigar. Rees looked at Caldwell in dismay. "I saw the light last night," the constable said.

"The slave catchers?"

"I think so, yes. Unless your friend Judge Hansen was lurking here under the shrubbery. So I asked at the Bull. Stupid fools been hanging around. But not where I can find them."

"I suppose they don't want to take their case to Piggy," Rees said.

"Huh. They don't know him. He'd turn the boy over in a heartbeat, just because he could. You have to get Augustus out of here, Rees. And soon. He's not guilty of anything that we know of, and now we need to protect him until I can find those catchers and get them out of town."

"And take Augustus where? I can't let him go back to the smithy; they'll snatch him right out of there."

Caldwell nodded. "I know. But you've got to think of something. I'll stand guard tonight, but we need a more permanent solution."

"Tomorrow or the next day," Rees promised, throwing a final searching glance at the tracks underneath the shrubs. He started across the road but turned back. "Would the men at the Bull tell you if Wrothman hired them to kill Nate?"

"You still think the doctor killed him?" Caldwell asked in surprise. Rees shrugged. "Course those scum wouldn't tell me. But I'll keep my ears open. If there's anything to find, I'll find it."

Rees nodded his thanks and returned to his wagon. He drove north to Water Street and the Contented Rooster. A snapping breeze blew off Dugard Pond, and all the windows in the coffeehouse were open to catch the gusts. Although it was warm today, Rees, and everyone else in town, knew this unseasonable summery weather could not last.

Inside the coffeehouse, the air smelled enticingly of coffee and cinnamon cake and roast beef. On a Monday, and still early, there were only a few tables occupied. Rees headed for the back table between the fireplace, the decorative screen hiding the empty interior, and the window from which he could watch the road outside. Jack Jr. brought fresh bread and suggested the beef. But it was Susannah who brought out the plate. The sight of the beef swimming in its pool of gravy and the mound of potatoes flooded Rees's mouth with water again. He wanted to fall upon his plate like the starving man he was, but it would be impolite to eat in front of Susannah. He forced a smile and tried not to wish her away.

"Rumor has it that you arrested Augie," she said. Rees nodded. "He didn't do it."

"I—we, Caldwell and I, put Augustus into the jail for his own safety," Rees said. "We caught two slave catchers trying to wrestle him away, presumably to sell him down South."

Susannah sat down in the chair opposite. "I hope the constable is trying to expel them from the village. It seems to me they should be in jail, not Augie."

"You know him, then? And well?"

"Of course. He lives and works just across Water Street. He comes in sometimes for a meal or two."

Rees put down his fork. "What was his relationship with his father?"

"Nate? Fine, I suppose. Somewhat constrained. Augustus didn't like being a bastard. But Nate visited his son from time to time when he came to town." She leaned across the table. "Few people in town will believe that lad guilty of murder. We all know him too well."

Rees thought of the scutching knife. Augustus could easily lift the wooden blade and batter his father and certainly had the strength to hold Nate's nose closed. But was the constraint between father and son enough of a reason? Rees saw this murder as one of rage, and Augie's feelings didn't seem strong enough. Still, he knew better than to dismiss the boy on that account.

"And Richard?" Rees asked.

"He went to school in Boston, so we don't know him as well." Susannah chose to misunderstand the question. Rees frowned at her. "He was always a tearaway, even as a little boy. Like Nate. Remember when he turned Johnson's pigs loose and herded them down Main Street?"

Rees nodded. He'd helped recapture the pigs. Nate's idea had seemed funny in the beginning, but scraping up pig excrement had cured Rees's laughter. "Do you remember when Nate collected all the church candles into one pile and lit them all?"

Susannah nodded. "It took days to clean up the wax."

"He hated Father Easton," Rees said. After a particularly bad beating at his father's hands, Nate had run to the church for refuge. Easton had instructed the boy to be obedient to his father, and reminded him of his father's right to correct him with the rod, before returning Nate to Mr. Bowditch.

"Maybe some of the farmers who don't know Augie as well will assume he's guilty, just because he's the son of a slave, but ask anyone here in Dugard. We won't believe it."

"But Richard might be guilty?"

"Doubtful," she replied, her voice curt.

"And Molly, what do you think of her?" He knew Susannah didn't like the other woman and wondered what she would say.

Some of the fire went out from Susannah's eyes and she

hesitated. "Well, I certainly don't believe she killed her husband," she said. "But I don't know her very well."

Rees directed a skeptical frown at her. "She's almost exactly your age, Suze."

"But we were never friendly. She acted like a boy when she was little. A dirty little urchin in dirty britches. And then, when she turned thirteen or fourteen, she became a flirtatious minx." Realizing her voice had risen, she stopped talking and bit her lip. "But here I am, chattering and keeping you from your dinner." She jumped to her feet and fled back to the kitchen.

Rees gaped after her, startled. A very outspoken woman, Suze didn't usually exercise such restraint over her tongue. And she must know that Rees, a friend since childhood, would guess her true feelings. So why then not admit what she felt? Suze must be embarrassed about something to do with Molly; Rees could think of no other reason. He spared a few moments pondering that conundrum and then he pushed all thoughts of Nate and his wife and family from his mind and fell to his dinner.

A thick slab of bread made short work of the gravy remaining on his plate and Rees sat back with a satisfied sigh. The cook for the Contented Rooster cooked like an angel.

The door opened and Potter entered. He looked around and then, spotting Rees, hurried over. "I thought I'd find you here," he said.

Rees sipped his coffee without speaking. After some of his discoveries regarding Potter, Rees felt a certain amount of skittishness about his old friend.

"I need to speak to you. I had a visit from an old friend of yours a while ago."

"Who is that?" Rees asked without interest.

"James Carleton. What did you say to him that frightened him so much?"

"Frightened him?" Rees's voice rose into a shout. "I didn't say anything. . . . I barely managed two words."

Potter pulled out a chair and sat down. "He claims you exhibited an inappropriate interest in his daughters."

"Did he?" Rees sipped his coffee, using the time to think. "Now, that is interesting. I mentioned Elizabeth and her connection to Richard. Why would that unnerve James?" Potter shrugged. "And I asked him about Nate. He boasted of their friendship."

Potter leaned across the table. "Be careful, Will. Although James is a much gentler soul than his father, he is still a powerful man. I don't need to remind you that the Carleton family is the closest thing we have to local aristocracy."

Rees scowled. "I thought this new country was supposed to move beyond that," he said. But of course it hadn't. He recalled his time on the frontier, where the small distillers battled the forces of money and power and, ultimately, the federal government. "He's hiding something," he said, knowing it was true as soon as he vocalized it.

"Something about Nate?" Potter asked.

Rees deliberated, reluctant to confide too much. "I don't know. Maybe. I'm still trying to accept this odd friendship. They loathed each other as boys." That was common knowledge.

"We all grew up, Will. James and Nate found they had more in common than not."

"Found when they were in England together," Rees said sourly. "Why did King Carleton send Nate after James?" Spotting Jack Jr., Rees gestured for more coffee and some of that fragrant cinnamon cake.

"I don't know. Not for certain. But Nate bought land from King Carleton and they were involved in a few business deals.

Nate was one of the few willing to stand up to Mr. Carleton. And of course Nate and James are—were of an age. So, when James refused to return home, his father asked Nate to go after him. Nate always did. Not once but several times. James kept running back to London. Somewhere along the line, James and Nate became friends."

"I wonder what happened in London," Rees said, rubbing his nose thoughtfully. Something bonded James and Nate together, that was clear.

"No one knows. They never spoke of it. But many things have changed since you first joined the Army. When we were boys, Nate would have bullied me but for you, but he and I became good friends. You just missed it all."

Rees stared at him. "I've come home since several times."

"Yes, but for how long? A few months here and there? When Dolly was still alive you stayed on the farm, and when she passed on, you barely came home at all." Rees could not protest; Potter spoke only the truth. "You and Nate were alike in that, although he at least remained physically in the area. But he mostly kept himself to himself. I don't know what Molly would have done without Marsh."

Rees thought about Marsh. "He behaves like a mother hen. How long ago did Nate hire him? He did hire him, yes?"

"Yes, from Rhode Island, I believe. Nate hired him about twelve, thirteen years ago, when Grace was about two I think, and then quickly relinquished all the care of the farm to him."

Rees knew Nate had not wanted to be a farmer; they'd been united in that. But Nate hadn't wanted to be a weaver either. His dream had been to attend Harvard, a dream his father would have denied him even if they'd had the money. "Well, I still plan to speak to James, whether he likes it or no. If he's guilty of Nate's death, I'll discover it." Potter threw him a glance in which skepticism and anxious warning were mingled. "And somehow I'll talk to Elizabeth Carleton," Rees added. "She surely knows more about Richard than anyone."

"I wouldn't give a farthing for your chance of succeeding in that," Potter said. "Those girls are carefully protected, not only by James but by Mrs. Carleton as well. Have you met Charlotte?" Rees shook his head. "She seems as delicate as a Dresden shepherdess but is blessed with a core of steel. My Nell has felt the rough edge of her tongue once or twice. That aristocratic sneering snobbery, you know."

"I'm duly warned," Rees said. He disliked the woman already, just on the strength of Potter's description.

"She's really the reason the Carleton and the Bowditch families didn't socialize; Mrs. Carleton despised Molly as a 'jumped-up bootmaker's daughter.'"

"She's living in the wrong country," Rees said.

"Most of what passes as 'society' in Dugard is more tolerant," Potter agreed with a nod. "According to Nell, Mrs. Hansen, Piggy's wife, and Molly are great friends. But then, most of them are from farming stock. Charlotte doesn't think much of them either." Potter stood up, turning his fine tall hat in his hands. "Just be careful, Will," he said, and turned to leave.

Chapter Eleven

With his belly full, and somewhat more in charity with his old friend Potter, Rees sat for a few more minutes before quitting the coffeehouse. He climbed into his wagon and, within the hour, was pulling up the drive to his farm. He unhitched Bessie and fed and watered her and released her into the paddock. David was tending to the cattle in the meadow at the paddock's back, and when he took off his hat to wave, his hair blazed fiery bright as a new penny. Rees waved back.

When he went inside, he found the kitchen empty but very hot and steamy. It was laundry day and water bubbled noisily in the copper kettle over the flames. The remains of a pickup dinner, just bread and cheese, littered the table. Hearing voices out back, Rees poked his head through the open door. While Abigail scrubbed ferociously at a linen garment on a washboard, Lydia spread body linen across the shrubbery to dry. Her rolled sleeves bared slender arms, and exertion had loosened the pins in her hair so that her dark red hair uncoiled down her back. Rees thought he had never seen anyone so beautiful. He sat down upon the top step to watch her.

She didn't realize he was there until she turned. "I didn't expect you home for dinner," she said. "Have you eaten?" She started toward him.

As she ran up the back steps, Rees put out an arm to stop her. "You look tired and hot," he said. "Sit down and rest."

Lydia sat down beside him but jumped to her feet almost immediately and ran to help Abigail with the heavy basket of wet linen. For several minutes the two women draped the clothing over the bushes in a companionable silence. Abby dealt with the last two shirts while Lydia rejoined Rees. "Are you home for the afternoon?"

"Yes." He nodded at the girl arranging a wet shirt upon a tree branch. "The laundry on her first day?"

"I thought I should begin as I mean to continue. How was your morning?"

"Puzzling. Disturbing." Rees shook his head. "The town seems the same, but it is so different. The people are different. Nate bullied both James Carleton and George Potter when we were boys. But they became great friends. And Molly is not at all the kind of wife I would have expected Nate to choose. And then there's Rachel. . . ."

"It sounds like Nate became someone other than your boyhood friend," Lydia said. "Do you believe either of those men killed Nate?"

"I have no reason now. James sounded surprisingly sorrowful. Anyway, Nate's murder appears to have been committed out of fury. That speaks of passion, and I didn't see that in James. Not this time, anyway. And although Dr. Wrothman certainly had good reason to want his rival dead, it appears he was elsewhere at the time." Rees turned to Lydia. "Augustus was estranged from his father, but I'm not sure he could slip onto the farm without *someone* seeing him. The only person who had the passion and the physical strength and was also witnessed in the cottage at the proper time is Richard."

She slanted a glance at him. "You don't want Richard to be guilty, do you?"

Rees considered her statement and then admitted in a rush, "Nate suffered enough at the hands of his father. He shouldn't have been murdered by his son."

Lydia, looking at him quizzically, waited to see if Rees would say anything further. When he didn't break his glum silence, she said, "Will, I had a thought, if Richard struck his father and stained his shirt with blood, where's the shirt?" Rees turned to look at her. "I'm thinking it might be in the laundry." He stared at her, his morose expression lightening into excitement.

"Along with Nate's apron," he said. Lydia nodded. Rees wanted to hug her but settled for a smile. "Thank you. Thank you."

She beamed. "You're welcome."

"Lydia . . ." Taking a deep breath, he spoke quickly. "I told you Augustus is in jail? Caldwell wants me to move him. I thought I'd bring him here. For a little while."

"You what?' She leaned toward him and folded her arms across her indigo-skirted knees. "Are you sure that's wise?"

Rees shrugged. "I doubt he's a murderer." He turned to look her in the eyes. "I can't abandon him in Dugard, where the slave catchers might take him."

"Of course not." An expression of shame crossed her face. "No, I don't want that either."

"He and David know one another, so I expect that will help." He paused. Her frozen expression conveyed her uncertainty, but she did not speak. After a brief pause, Rees said, "There is something very wrong at Nate's farm."

"What do you mean?"

"Secrets. Too many secrets. Everyone has secrets." When

Lydia looked at him questioningly, he gathered his thoughts together. "The weaver's cottage is secluded from the rest of the farm, and the farmhand told me there's a secret entrance. Well, not secret since a number of people know about it. But Nate didn't want anyone to use it. And there's nothing in his office except ledgers: no correspondence or anything personal. And no will."

"Not everyone sees the need for a will," Lydia said. "Besides, Mr. Potter—"

"No," he interrupted, "George Potter doesn't have it. At least that's what Molly told me. I'll ask him myself, of course. But Nate was too careful to ignore that responsibility."

"Molly," she repeated in an odd voice.

"I don't care for her overmuch," Rees said, missing her expression, "and I don't understand why Nate married her. She seems so unlike the type of wife he would choose."

"You don't really know Nate either, though, do you?" Lydia said. "You've said, more times than I can count, that the man was not the boy you remembered." Rees said nothing, stung by the truth of that. "And I think you should not dismiss Molly as a possible murderer. She had more reason than anyone to kill your friend. She was jealous of Rachel and she has a new romance with Dr. Wrothman. . . ."

"Maybe not that new," Rees said, thinking of the three-year-old Ben. "Well, I doubt she has the strength to lift the scutching knife and hammer at Nate with it, even if she was the person Mr. Salley heard arguing with Nate. But perhaps a more compelling argument against her involvement is financial: How will she live as a widow? This is why seeing Nate's will is critical. Did he leave her a pension? Did he leave everything to Richard, who will now be responsible for his mother until, or if, she remarries? Nate's death leaves Molly without an English penny to her name." Lydia nodded in reluctant agreement. "But I do agree Molly has the passion for murder. If it were Rachel's body discovered . . ."

"Well, then," Lydia said, "Nate put his private information somewhere else. And although Mrs. Bowditch may not know where that is, I'm certain she knows more than she is telling you."

Rees nodded. With that, he must agree. "I'm returning to the Bowditch farm tomorrow. Nate spent most of his time in that weaver's cottage. If he concealed his papers anywhere on that farm, it would be in that shed." He exhaled in frustration. "And I still haven't had the chance for a thorough search. Marsh is determined to prevent me from visiting the cottage alone." He smiled at her. "But I'll speak to the laundress tomorrow."

She did not return his smile this time and plucked at her skirt nervously. "I'd like to go with you." He stared at her in dismay. "Mary Martha told Abby Marsh is taking on some temporary help. Mrs. Bowditch is planning a memorial service for Nate on Sunday, and I—"

"No."

"I can help you, as I did in Zion by listening to the women. . . ."

"No," he said more emphatically. "I don't want your help." She glared at him in furious disappointment. He added more gently, "It's not that I don't need you, but it's too dangerous. Someone murdered Nate, and right now the most likely person is Richard Bowditch. You'll be walking into the lion's den."

"There was a killer at Zion, too," she said, keeping her voice low with an effort. "I can help."

"Absolutely not."

"Let me understand," Lydia said, struggling to maintain a low and even pitch. "You'll bring Augustus, a possible murderer, here. But I am not to work in the kitchen at the Bowditch farm because his brother might be guilty?"

Rees turned his irritated gaze upon her. Of course, his reasoning was far more complicated, involving his pride and his desire to prevent anyone from knowing of the connection between himself and Lydia, at least for now. With a quick angry frown, she jumped to her feet and went inside. When Rees looked up, he found Abby staring at him. She immediately turned her gaze away from him. Scowling, he followed Lydia into the kitchen. But she turned her face away from him, and after a hesitation he went upstairs. He sat down to finish threading the heddles. If he made an unnecessary amount of noise, no one seemed to notice.

The emotional hum generated by his argument with Lydia, and the question that had reminded Rees of Nate's childhood, turned his thoughts to the very first time he saw Nate as just another child and not the bully he avoided in school. He'd been eight, Nate nine. They'd been sent outside to play while Rees's mother visited with Mrs. Bowditch. Rees, wary, had followed the older boy to the barn.

"You like school?" Nate asked.

"I guess," Rees said. He was hesitant, cautious: he knew Nate as a bully and was prepared to defend himself should he be attacked.

Instead Nate directed him to a convenient hay bale. "Watch this." He unearthed a calico skirt, faded, dirty, and reduced to rags, and slung it around his narrow boy hips. He added a battered bonnet and said in a falsetto mimicry of Miss Shore, "Now, Will, you must never say 'bastard.'"

His impersonation was so accurate, Rees began laughing in spite of himself. Nate turned his back and mimed writing upon an invisible board. "Take out your slates, class. . . ." He swung his hips with a little hitch at the end, exactly like Miss Shore. Rees laughed harder. Nate began flouncing around the barn floor, squeaking out instructions exactly like Miss Shore, exaggerating her phrasing and mannerisms until Rees had laughed himself off the hay bale onto the floor.

"What are you doing in here?" Mr. Bowditch stormed into the barn and backhanded Nate onto the floor. "You've got the evil in you." He kicked Nate. Rees lay on the floor, frozen with terror.

He could hear Nate crying, pleading, "I'll be good."

"You'll never be good. Just good for nothing . . ." Rees heard the brutal slap.

Pulling himself out of his stupor, he scrambled to his knees and peered over the hay bale. Nate was curled into a ball on the floor, his arms folded over his head; Rees could see the blood running from his nose and split lip.

"I'll teach you. . . ." The drunken man turned to hunt for a weapon, and his hand caught up an axe handle, thick and strong.

Without even knowing how, Rees found himself on his feet and staggering toward the other boy. "No. No!" he screamed. "Stop. You're killing him. Stop."

"You want some of this, too? . . ." Mr. Bowditch turned with the handle raised. But before he could bring it down upon Rees, Mrs. Bowditch ran through the barn door and flung herself between them, grabbing the handle.

She hung on to the handle with all her strength, her knuckles whitening. "Go to your mother!" she ordered Rees. He turned to flee, but paused by Nate.

"Come on," he said, and reached out to grab him.

Nate, crying hard and covered with blood and straw, took Rees's hand and limped after him. He moved stiffly and Rees could see the bruises already darkening his face and arms.

Rees ran straight to his mother, dragging Nate behind him. "We've got to help him."

But she shook her head. "This is for the Bowditch family. We don't interfere. . . ." It was the first time his mother disappointed him.

"I'll be all right," Nate said, squaring his shoulders. "He does this all the time. I . . . got caught off guard, that's all." Moving quickly, despite his obvious pain, he shot across the lane and disappeared into the cornfield.

When Rees saw him again at market a few weeks later, most of the cuts had scabbed over. But, although he immediately approached Rees, greeting him like his best friend, he didn't refer to the scene in the barn at all. And Rees was too embarrassed to mention it. So, although the incident bonded the two boys together, they never discussed it again.

Rees shuddered, shaking off the uncomfortably vivid memory. He did not like thinking of it, even now, almost thirty years later. As an adult, he knew the covert conversations between his parents concerned the beating. As a child, though, it had seemed that no one was doing anything to protect Nate. It was the first time he realized his parents could not help, impotent in this case. But he also learned that they were not the harsh figures he'd always believed them. Although his father whipped him from time to time, he never did so, not even for the worst infractions, with that red-hot murderous fury.

Realizing he'd been sitting in frozen stillness with a sley hook in his hand, Rees bent forward once again to his chore. He still didn't understand why Mr. Bowditch had hated his son so. But Nate had proved his father wrong after all. He'd made good, all right, becoming one of the largest landowners in the county. Rees wished the old man had lived long enough to see the success his son had become.

Chapter Twelve

Rees knew Lydia was still annoyed with him when he went downstairs for breakfast the next morning and found no one. Not even David. Coffee kept warm upon the hob, and leftover mush, rather crusty and overcooked, remained in the spider. He poured some honey on it and ate it standing up by the hearth. Wagon wheels outside heralded Abigail's arrival, and when she came in he was drinking his coffee. She said nothing as she hung her bonnet on the peg and set the flatirons by the fire to warm. Rees drained his mug, nodded at her, and departed.

As he drove through Dugard, he decided to stop at the jail, see how Augustus fared, and tell Caldwell he'd rescue Augustus tonight. But before then, Rees thought he would stop at Brown's cobbler shop. Molly's brother Billy had taken it over upon the death of his father. When he stepped inside, he was assailed by the smell of leather. Shoes of all types were piled on the shelves behind the cobbler, even a few ladies' slippers, but most of the footwear made here was stout shoes and boots.

Rees remembered Billy as a square-built boy with a shock of dark hair. The man was still solidly built, but his hair had mostly disappeared and the strands remaining were shot with gray. "Will Rees, as I live and breathe," Billy said, wiping his greasy hands on his apron. "I heard you were back in Dugard."

Rees reached out and grasped the other man's hand, slick and gritty at once. "Yes. For a little while."

"Ah. Still working as a factor, then?"

"Yes. And now I'm looking into Nate Bowditch's death."

"George Potter told me." Billy sighed. "I don't know what the world is coming to."

"Do you have any idea who might have wanted to kill him?"

"Other than my nephew, you mean?" Billy replied drily. "No." He sighed. "The truth is, Will, I see my sister very little. She feels she is better than a cobbler's family."

"You and Nate used to fight all the time?"

"Sure, when we were boys. He always had to win. He had to ride harder, win every fistfight, every game of marbles . . . but he grew into a good man."

There it was again, that distance between what Rees remembered and the situation now. "Did you ever see Nate?"

"I saw him far more often than my sister. He regularly stopped in when he came to town. Fact is, when I ran into a patch of trouble, he helped me out." He looked around his shop.

"There's no one, outside of Richard, that might want Nate dead?" Rees sounded despairing, even to himself.

"Well, he didn't get along with Thomas, I don't know why. And Nate and James Carleton were fast friends up until a month or so ago. You'd have to talk to James about that. . . ."

"Father?" A boy of about twelve cannonballed into the store from a door in the back.

"My eldest," Billy said to Rees. "And this is David's father."

The boy looked at Rees and smiled. "I used to see David in school. Is he coming back?" His voice broke into soprano and dropped again and he went scarlet.

"I hope so," Rees said. "I'll tell him you asked after him." He returned to his wagon, thinking. James Carleton and Thomas Bowditch; the conversation kept returning to them.

The constable sat in his usual place, at his desk, and Rees wondered if he lived at the jail.

The remains of a hearty breakfast had been pushed to one side, and the sweet smell of cider dampened the stink of an unwashed body and dirty clothes.

"I spoke to Mr. Collier," Caldwell said, motioning Rees to sit by the desk. "He confirmed Dr. Wrothman's story."

"How can Collier be sure?" Rees asked. Maybe Wrothman paid him?

"Because Wrothman was there three days. Mrs. Collier had trouble this time, so Wrothman stayed. He was just washing up when one of the hands arrived to call him to the Bowditch farm, the body of Nate Bowditch having just been discovered. That's one reason Jeb Collier remembers it so well."

"Damn," Rees muttered.

"Well, he could still have paid one of the drifters that come through the Bull," Caldwell said. "I haven't heard anything yet."

Rees looked at the constable, knowing he didn't expect to either.

"And the boy?" Caldwell tipped his head at the jail cell.

"I'll come for him after dark tonight," Rees said.

"Good." Caldwell rose to his feet. "Come around midnight; everyone will be asleep by then." He guided Rees through what had been the previous constable's office. A rough pallet made an untidy heap in one corner, and Rees knew his suspicion had been correct: Caldwell slept here. The constable opened a back door into a narrow alley between the jail and a high stone wall. "Park the wagon here," he said.

Rees looked around him. The Bull sat across the street, slightly north, and the wall hid everything of the house on the other side but the top-floor windows. He nodded; this was as private as it could be. "This is good," he said.

"I'll be here," Caldwell said unnecessarily. "You going to talk to the boy?"

Nodding, Rees stepped back inside and went through the building to the cell. Augustus was huddled in a ball in the corner. "Hello," Rees said.

Augustus looked up, his expression dull with misery. "Why are you helping me now?" he asked. "This is your fault. If you hadn't come after Richard, I wouldn't be here."

"Your father was my best friend," Rees said. "Besides, I only wanted to speak with your brother. And now even more so." He paused. Augustus's burst of anger was spent, and he regarded Rees in silence. "I'm taking you home, to my farm, until the slave catchers are gone."

"Aren't you afraid I'm a murderer?" Augustus asked in a nasty voice.

"Are you?"

"Of course not. I haven't visited the farm in years, and the last time I saw only Marsh."

"Marsh?"

"Of course. He is more of a father to me than the—the . . ." The boy struggled and finally settled upon, ". . . master. To both Richard and me." The boy rose to his feet and approached the bars. "Why would I kill the master?"

"Because Richard inherits," Caldwell interjected from behind Rees.

"And what good would that do me?" Augustus cried with a

flash of spirit. "I'm a slave's bastard; I couldn't inherit if the whole pack of them died."

Rees regarded the dark face thoughtfully. "That is certainly true. But your relationship with Nate was a lot closer than master to servant, wasn't it? He was seen visiting you at the smithy."

Augustus hesitated for so long, Rees thought he would not speak. "Yes," he said at last. "He often came to see me when he had business in town." He grimaced. "He didn't want her to know."

"Her? His wife?" Rees asked.

"Who else?"

"But he acknowledged you as his son?" Augustus nodded this time with reluctance. "I suppose you could have borrowed a horse from the smithy, ridden out to the farm, and slipped into the cottage to murder your father," Rees said.

"Of course not," Augustus said, his voice shaking with passion. "I wouldn't do that. He was good to me. And anyway, I wouldn't have time. Mr. Isaacs keeps me busy, dawn to dusk."

"I believe you," Rees said. "But you'd better be a little more cooperative. You'd make a handy scapegoat." Augustus digested this and nodded. "Did you ever see your father meeting anyone?"

"Everyone." Augustus smiled. "He had business dealings with half the men in town. I often saw him meet Mr. Potter or Mr. Carleton, as they were special friends of his, but he frequently met others as well."

"Did you see any arguments or disagreements?"

"Sometimes. But they always shook hands afterwards. . . ." He hesitated and then added, "I had no reason to murder my father, Mr. Rees. He was always good to me."

"I see." But Augustus clearly resented his place in Nate's family. Enough to kill? Rees thought not, but he'd been wrong before. "Until tonight, then."

"What do you think?" Caldwell asked as they walked away.

"He's right about not inheriting."

"Anger can drive a man mad," Caldwell said. "A momentary rage has murdered more than one man."

"Indeed. I just don't see that fire burning inside Augustus's belly."

"So far, most of the town agrees with you," Caldwell said with a nod. "But if Nate's murderer isn't identified soon, Augustus might hang for it. The black son . . . a much more palatable choice than Richard."

Rees nodded in unhappy agreement.

At least Augustus would be safe for a time, Rees thought as he climbed into his wagon. Enough time, he hoped, to find Nate's killer. He turned around and directed Bessie west. This time, though, he did not take the road that ran by Nate's farm. Instead, he drove down the more southerly route toward the farm on which his old friend had grown up. It was time to talk to Thomas.

The route out to the old Bowditch farm was as familiar to Rees as his name. He must have walked or ridden this road a thousand times. But even here he saw differences. Silas Bowditch's horses had been nags, gaunt and overworked. The horses Rees saw now were plump beauties. Well, Thomas had always loved horses, and now he could indulge himself. The fields were productive and well cared for, not the ragged half-weedy meadows of the indifferent farmer.

When he reached the dirt lane leading up to the house, Rees's heart began to pound. His body remembered Silas Bowditch. He urged Bessie forward in a slow walk. Odd, he thought. He was older now than Mr. Bowditch had been then, and taller and stronger, too, but his childhood memories made him shiver.

He rounded a curve and saw the house for the first time, experiencing a moment of disorientation. It was the same, but not the same. The original structure remained but had been relegated to the back with a neat two-story clapboard now attached to the front. As Rees approached the door, Thomas and at least two of his sons followed by a hand or two began running toward him. Rees pulled Bessie up a few feet from the steps and jumped down to wait for his old childhood friend.

Before Thomas reached him, a woman with a baby on her hip stepped through the front door and paused on the porch. A toddler, sucking upon his two middle fingers, clung to her skirt. She regarded Rees warily. "Can I help you?"

"I'm waiting for Tom," Rees said, gesturing to the men hurrying toward them. He stepped forward, his arms outstretched. "Tom? It's Will, Will Rees."

"I recognized you." Tom ran forward. He wasn't smiling, and before Rees had time to react, a whirlwind of punches descended upon him. "It was your fault!" screamed the man, his fist connecting with Rees's head and knocking him sideways. "You turned my brother—" Another punch sent Rees reeling. But when Tom flung himself at the weaver a third time, he was ready.

Grasping the other man in a bear hug that effectively trapped his arms, he lifted Tom so only his toes touched the earth. "Settle down!" Rees roared. When last he saw Tom, he'd been still a boy, barely into his teens. "What's the matter with you?"

"Let me down," Tom said in a muffled voice as his wife and sons rushed to his side.

"I will when you calm down," Rees said. "I don't want to hurt you."

"Very well."

Cautiously Rees released his grip and Tom dropped to the

ground and staggered. Then he jumped back, into the protective circle of his family, and glowered balefully at his visitor. Rees regarded Tom in silence. Although he had the Bowditch eyes, that deep navy blue, and the same cleft in his chin as Nate, Tom's hair was a lighter brown and his features more angular.

"I haven't seen you for almost twenty years," Rees said. "What's wrong with you? Did I torment you when we were boys?"

"It's what you did to Nate," Tom cried. But his passion had diminished. His wife put a hand upon his wrist. After a moment, he became aware of the audience behind him. He turned and ordered his sons and the field hands back to work.

"And what was that?" Rees asked, bewildered. "We didn't part on the best of terms, I admit."

"You must know," Tom cried, staring at him.

Rees shrugged helplessly, wondering at Tom's hostility. "I will regret to the end of days that I didn't mend our quarrel. But I am making amends; I'm searching for the villain who murdered your brother."

Tom grinned without amusement. "I should have known my brother's death would bring you back," he said. He was no longer convinced of Rees's guilt; now he just wished it to be true.

"I thought Richard murdered his father," Mrs. Bowditch said in astonishment.

"That remains to be determined," Rees said. "Do you think Richard is guilty?"

Husband and wife exchanged a glance. "No," said Thomas. "We know Richard well and don't believe it." But his wife did not speak and she frowned.

Rees looked at her. "And you? What do you think?"

She glanced at her husband and then her gaze dropped. "It's hard to believe," she said in a quiet voice.

"He's not here, if that's your next question," Thomas said.

"Would you tell me if he was?"

"Why are you even meddling in this?" Thomas asked.

"I've had some experience with this type of tragedy," Rees said. "During the War. And Molly Bowditch, your brother's wife, hired me to look into it."

Mrs. Bowditch's lip curled, and Tom spit upon the ground. "She wants you to clear Richard's name," he said.

"Probably. But you said you don't believe in his guilt either."

"Ask your questions, then," Tom snapped.

Rees eyed him. "I apologize for interrupting your work," he said, "but I thought you would be as interested in identifying Nate's murderer as I am."

Thomas's eyes dropped. "Of course I am," he said. "Although Nate and I didn't get along, I loved him. But I won't accuse my nephew either."

"Then tell me what you think," Rees said.

After several seconds of silence, Tom brushed back his hair from his damp forehead and said, "You'd better come inside."

Rees followed them up the stairs and into the kitchen. Two girls, one about David's age, were chopping vegetables at the table. Mrs. Bowditch shooed them outside. The older girl cast a curious glance at Rees but quickly followed her sister. Rees guessed they found few opportunities for play.

"You must remember how we fought?" Tom said, sitting down at the scrubbed farm table.

"Yes," Rees said. "But often brothers grow closer as they age."

"Tell him the truth," his wife said as she sliced cake onto a plate.

"Do you know Nate rented this farm to me?" Tom did not wait for Rees's nod. "I have something in Nate's hand leaving this land to me. But not a will. Just a—a note, like. Nate refused to put it in his will or write out a contract. And now that harridan of a wife refuses to accept the note. She claims that Richard, as Nate's eldest son, inherits everything."

"It is a sad comment on human nature," Thomas's wife said, "when a man cuts his own brother out of inheriting the family farm. Nate owns—owned so much. Why couldn't he allow us the use of this farm upon his death?"

"You might be in the will," Rees said. Was it possible Thomas killed his brother for this farm?

"And she without a farming bone in her body!" Thomas's wife said.

"And Richard?" Rees asked. "Why do you believe he isn't a murderer?"

Thomas shrugged.

"The boy has a temper," said Mrs. Bowditch.

"But he doesn't have the stomach for it," Tom said. "Did you talk to Augustus? He's the closest thing to a friend Richard has." His wife made a moue of distaste. "Marsh virtually raised the two of them."

Rees nodded. "So I understand." He paused and then added in a burst of candor, "Why wouldn't you protect your nephew if it came to it? Weren't you close to Richard?"

"When he was a boy, he was here all the time," Tom said. "Both him and Grace. Well, we still see her regularly. But Richard? No."

"Why not?" Rees asked.

Thomas stirred slightly but did not speak, leaving his wife to tell the tale. "He became . . . flirtatious with my girls. I hoped that family feeling would prevent Richard from . . ." She paused. Rees nodded to show his understanding. "Anyway, Tom caught the boy kissing my Anne in the barn. He's not welcome anymore."

"When was that?" Rees asked.

"A few months ago," she replied, glancing at her husband for confirmation.

"Maybe six to eight weeks ago," Thomas said. "He changed about that time, I'm not sure why. He was very angry with his father." Now he paused.

"What did Nate say when you told him about Anne?" Rees asked.

"That Richard was sowing his wild oats," he replied briefly, his eyes settling upon his wife. Rees knew Thomas was holding something back, and knew as well that he would not confide the truth in his wife's presence. "Anyway, Richard has not visited us since. So you see, we would not hide him here."

They sat in silence, each busy with their own thoughts. Rees could think of no more questions, and anyway Lydia was probably wondering where he was. Rising to his feet, he thanked Mrs. Bowditch with a bow.

"I'll walk you to the door," Thomas said, also standing up.

"Dinner will be ready soon," his wife said.

Tom nodded. "I'll fetch the boys."

He paused upon the step and the two men silently shook hands. As Rees turned toward his wagon, Thomas said, "You came home so infrequently. I know my brother missed you, but you never visited him."

Rees turned. "We . . . quarreled," he said.

Thomas searched Rees's face as though trying to dig out the memory. "I see," he said finally. "Are you home for good now?"

"I'm still a traveling weaver," Rees said.

"But you own a farm," Thomas argued. "Why would you choose to leave everyone you love, everyone you know, behind?"

That's why, Rees thought. When he looked at many of his childhood acquaintances, he saw the child they'd been behind the adult mask, and he suspected they saw his young self in him. But he was no longer the little scrapper who jumped into a fight at the drop of a hat, the tearaway at the heart of every spot of trouble. The beast, that temper he regularly had cause to regret, was under better control now. Dolly had begun his change, and all the subsequent years on the road had schooled him into someone different. But as long as he lived in Dugard, those who knew him as a child would always expect him to be that angry boy.

"Weaving is all I know," Rees said. It was not an answer and he knew it.

Tom nodded, understanding what Rees really meant. "Nate took a long time to settle, too," he said. "He went to Boston and New York and even London."

"Yes, Nate went to fetch James Carleton," Rees said, relaxing now that the conversation was no longer about him.

Thomas grinned. "Nate remarked one time that James risked Hellfire. Not sure what he meant, but I know he gambled deep."

"I wondered about the connection between Nate and Carleton," Rees said. "Remember? He bullied James mercilessly. How did they become friends?"

"I don't know. First Nate became an associate of King Carleton. Money and success followed. I always thought it was a more sophisticated form of bullying. After a while I felt that I didn't know him at all."

"I know," Rees said sadly.

The two men stood in silence, reflecting upon the boy they'd both loved and the man he'd become. Then, with a curt wave, Tom turned and trotted back to the fields. Rees watched him go, wondering if any of the secrets Thomas kept to protect his brother had resulted instead in his murder.

"Mr. Rees?" A shy light voice broke into his thoughts. He

turned to see the older of the girls, fair-haired like her mother but with Thomas's blue eyes.

"Which daughter are you?"

"Flora." She clenched her hands together. "I'm in school with David. Will you tell him hello for me?"

"I will," Rees said, with a smile.

"Maybe, when you call upon us again, you'll bring him?"

"Perhaps," Rees said.

"Flora." Her mother's voice carried clearly to the yard. "Where is that girl?"

Flora quickly bobbed a curtsey and fled.

Still amused, Rees clambered into his wagon and turned Bessie in the wide arc to face the road. David would be happy in Dugard. Like Nate, he would have his choice of girls.

Rees's smile faded. Nate so dominated his thoughts right now that Rees almost expected him to haul himself into the wagon seat and cry, "Hey, Will, let's go fishing." Sudden grief brought burning tears to Rees's eyes, and he pulled over at the end of the lane. He wiped his eyes with a grubby handkerchief. "What the Hell happened to you, Nate?" he said aloud. What had happened to that laughing boy?

Chapter Thirteen

As he drove out to the road and turned Bessie's head toward Nate's farm, Rees replayed his visit with Tom. Had he told the truth about Richard, or had family feeling trumped other concerns? Regretfully Rees concluded that Tom had been truthful: Richard wasn't staying with his uncle. So, where was that elusive lad? He'd proved surprisingly successful at escaping Rees's attention.

Then, as Rees turned the wagon west, his thoughts turned to Tom's behavior—the wild anger, the conflicted affection he still felt for his brother—and he wondered what had happened between them. The break between them seemed to stem from something more serious than normal sibling conflict.

Rees turned west at the junction of the lane with the main road. Although today was only Tuesday, the traffic traveling east into town seemed unusually heavy. One of the vehicles, a fine carriage, he recognized from the Bowditch farm. Although Rees could not see Molly within the shadows, he certainly knew Fred Salley, who sat in the box. The groom acknowledged Rees with a brief nod but was far too conscious of his own consequence to do more than that.

Rees usually drove the back road, not this main thorough-fare. When he passed a small but thick copse of trees, he wondered if they screened the lay-by described by Mr. Salley. If so, the weaver's cottage must be close by, completely hidden by vegetation from casual traffic and yet with its own entrance. Rees almost turned around to look for it, but the morning was rapidly disappearing before him. Anyway, he would find it much simpler to mark the location from the cottage first. No doubt the card players were all familiar with that entrance, he thought sourly.

He pulled round to the back drive and parked in his usual spot. A quick look through the kitchen door showed him a hive of activity, Rachel and several other women rushing around, preparing dinner. As his shadow fell through the door, Mary Martha looked up. "I'm just looking for the laundry," Rees said.

"Summer kitchen," Rachel said, dropping her wooden spoon and approaching him eagerly. "That brick building across the road." And then, looking at Rees curiously, she added, "Why?" He could almost see Mary Martha's ears flapping.

"I want to talk to the laundress for a moment," he said, purposely vague.

"Is Juniper there?" Mary Martha asked. She couldn't help herself; she had to jump into the conversation.

"Yes," Rachel said. With a nod of thanks, he turned away. "Mr. Rees. Wait." Rachel took a few steps after him. But Mary Martha ran up behind her. With a frustrated groan, Rachel said to Rees, "Will you stop back in the kitchen before you go?"

"Of course," he said. She went back inside. Rees started down the lane, toward the path that ran behind the barn along the pond to the laundry house. He paused at the crest of the hill, contemplating at the cottage and wondering if he should grab this opportunity to search. As he hesitated, Marsh came out the front door. Rees promptly turned down the footpath, so quickly, he thought Marsh could not have seen him. He didn't want Marsh to know how curious he was still about the cottage and how determined to conduct a thorough search.

The narrow path ran behind the barn toward a small brick structure sitting on the banks of the pond. Rees didn't blame Rachel from returning to the regular kitchen as soon as she could. The summer kitchen was far away from the house and in a valley. Carrying food to the house must be difficult.

He paused at the door and looked around him. Drying laundry festooned the trees and bushes around him, and he could smell the hot steamy smell of washing. When he looked over his shoulder, he could just see a corner of the weaver's cottage through the pointed evergreens and the maples and oaks beside them. Some of the leaves already blushed pink and yellow; fall was fast approaching. That window above the sugar maple was the one by Nate's bed, and as Rees fixed his gaze upon it he caught a flicker of movement.

"I don't often see visitors down here." The voice took Rees by surprise and he turned to look at the laundress. A heavyset black woman, familiar to him from her shifts in the kitchen, Juniper motioned him into the laundry, where she was aggressively ironing wrinkled linen. Since this was Tuesday, most of the copper kettles were empty and stacked on one wall. But the fire was blazing and flatirons were lined up in a row on the hearth to heat. "Whatever are you doing here, Mr. Rees?"

"I'm looking for the shirt Richard was wearing the day his father died."

She eyed him anxiously. "It's stained with blood, Mr. Rees." She bit her lip.

Rees nodded. "I know. That is why I want to see it." She looked at him carefully, to see if he was serious, before waddling to a basket by the wall. She rummaged through the linen, treating Rees to a view of her tow-covered broad backside before coming up with a white shirt. The brownish stains speckling the right sleeve and belly were clearly visible.

"Do you think the lad murdered his father?" she asked.

"That's what I'm trying to find out," Rees said. "He might be innocent, but right now Augustus is in jail for it and if I don't find the guilty man, he will catch the blame."

She nodded, her eyes filling with tears, and handed Rees the shirt. He shook it out so he could inspect the stains more easily.

A large stain over the belly, exactly where Mr. Salley said it would be. Solid brown stained the right cuff, diminishing to a spray of dots that crept up the shoulder and down the right front. Exactly what one would expect if Richard had struck his father once or twice. "There's not enough blood," Rees mumbled. "Is this the only shirt?"

"Not the only shirt," she replied dryly, "but the only one with bloodstains, yes."

"Did you see anything else unusual?" Rees asked, hearing the desperation in his voice. She thought and turned again to rummage through a basket. This time she offered him a shawl knitted from many bright strands of yarn. "Rachel's shawl?"

She nodded. "Rachel would never bring it up to the house. The mistress is that jealous. . . ."

"Marsh was looking for this." A closer examination revealed faint smudged bloody fingerprints down the front edge. "Do you know who might have taken this out of the cottage?" Rees looked at Juniper, catching a fleeting worry speeding across her face before her expression went blank. She shook her head. "Anything else?" Rees asked. "Rags, maybe?"

Looking surprised, Juniper turned and fetched a rag with a swirly brown stain. "How did you know? This came down covered with vomit. . . ."

Rees took it from her. Mary Martha said Nate had tried to

clean up after himself. He would have been alive then. Someone had entered the cottage after and put this into the laundry. Had that person also murdered Nate?

"Who sent this down?" he asked.

She shrugged. "It came in a basket from the cottage."

"It's not dyed green," Rees muttered. Green had splashed Nate's shirt and the floor.

"I don't wash anything dyed," Juniper said. "Marsh washes all that nasty dyed stuff."

"But you knew the rags came from the cottage?"

"I regularly get rags, especially after the master—" She stopped abruptly.

She knows about the card players, Rees thought as he stared at her. "After the master has company?"

She nodded. "Well, there's wine and all," she said. "Some of the gentlemen drink too much. And the drinks get spilled, so there's table linens—"

"How often did they meet?" Rees asked roughly.

"I don't know. Marsh might. I got something to wash only once or twice a month."

Marsh again. Rees stared unseeingly at the brick wall over Juniper's head.

"I hope I haven't gotten the young master in trouble," she said. "He isn't wicked, you know. He's just a boy. High spirited."

Rees nodded without speaking and left. From the laundry door he stared up at the cottage window. Nothing moved. He climbed the hill and looked down again at the cottage. It appeared quiet, empty and almost abandoned. Yet again he considered running down and searching the place, but he suspected Marsh would come looking for him. Instead, he trotted down the overgrown lane toward the trees. Wheeled traffic had cut grooves into the mud and with the recent summery heat, the ruts were now as hard as stone. The lane narrowed to a worn footpath that cut left, toward the trees at the edge of the flax field. He followed it into the woods and through to a disguised clearing where the scars of wheels and many piles of horse droppings indicated heavy use. A thick screen of trees and underbrush shielded this small area from the main road. Rees understood why Fred, and probably the other hands who relied upon shank's mare to reach their homes, preferred this route; it would be a much shorter walk to Dugard, especially if no one offered a ride.

He shook his head. Was it only the card players who used this secret way or others? And what other skeletons would he discover in Nate's closet?

With a final glance around, Rees retraced his steps through the tree break. As he started up the overgrown lane toward the hill, Marsh, Munch at his heels, appeared at the top of the slope. Although the dark face remained empty of emotion, his tense shoulders looked angry. Rees was glad he hadn't gone into the cottage; Marsh would surely have followed.

In silence he trailed Marsh to the kitchen. Rachel must have been waiting for him; she popped out of the kitchen as soon as he stepped into the yard. Marsh threw Rees a glance and went inside. "Augustus?" Rachel whispered.

"He's safe," Rees replied.

"Still in jail?"

"For the time being." Rees said. He considered sharing his plan for Augustus's escape but decided against it. He doubted Rachel could hide her joy at his escape, and anyway one of the women helping in the kitchen came outside just then.

"Rachel?"

Rees's gaze, which had passed over the woman without really noticing her, snapped back at the sound of her voice. Lydia?

"Yes?" Rachel turned. Lydia's nervous gaze fastened upon Rees. "Did you need something?" Rachel asked with some impatience.

Lydia dragged her eyes from Rees. "The large bread bowl?"

"Ask Mary Martha." Sensing the sudden undercurrent, she turned to Rees and she said, "Our new kitchen maid." Rees nodded, staring at Lydia. "We took on some additional help, at least until after the memorial service." He found himself incapable of speech.

Lydia smiled up at him. "Mr. Rees," she said with the amount of interest appropriate to a first meeting.

If Rees had been younger, he probably would have exploded. But now, older and a little more thoughtful, his consciousness of Rachel's curious gaze kept him still. Several seconds went by. Lydia's smile wavered and Rachel cleared her throat. Rees squawked some kind of greeting and inclined his head. Then the moment was past. Lydia nodded politely in farewell and returned to the kitchen with the other women.

Rees turned to Rachel. "Don't worry. I will keep Augustus safe." He began walking up the slope toward his wagon, unaware of the curious glance she threw after him. He climbed into it and started down the lane just as though his day had not been turned upside down. But as he steered Bessie onto the Dugard road, the dizzying shock began to fade and he became conscious only of the fury building inside him. Didn't she know she had put herself into danger? As well as imperiled his investigation?

He drove home rapidly, pushing Bessie into a steady canter. At first enraged only with Lydia, he realized as he reconsidered the situation that David must have played a part in this as well. Besides the wagon, Rees owned only a buggy, and if Lydia had driven herself, he would surely have noticed its absence in the barn. So, someone had driven her and that someone must be Rees's son.

David was working in the barn when Rees rolled up the drive and he came out when he heard the sound of wheels. Recognizing his father's furious expression, David paused a few feet away and waited in silence for the storm to break.

Rees jumped down from the wagon. "Why did you drive Lydia to the Bowditch farm?" Although he attempted to speak calmly, his voice rose into a roar as he unleashed his fury at Lydia toward his son.

"She would have driven herself," David said. "You should know that about her."

"Why didn't you restrain her?" Rees demanded, knowing he was being unreasonable but too angry to care.

"How? By tying her down?" David shook his head. "It wouldn't have worked. Lydia is like Mother in that." He paused and when he spoke again his voice trembled. "Mother hated being left alone all the time, but she at least had family and friends around her. Lydia needs the company of other women."

"I see," Rees said. "This is revenge. When you are a man you'll understand how important it is to earn a living, to support your family."

"I do understand," David retorted, his own voice rising. He paced a few steps. "I saw Uncle Sam. He wasted money and sold the livestock to make it up. If it hadn't been for the money you brought home, every cow, every sheep would have been sold and my uncle's creditors might still have taken the farm. So don't tell me I don't understand. I'm old enough to know you had to travel, old enough to appreciate the brass you brought back for us. But to be gone a year or more? Was that necessary? No. You didn't return, because you didn't wish to."

"That's not true!" Rees shouted, knowing David spoke only the truth. "I'm not a farmer—"

"You were a husband and a father." David cut him off without mercy. "Or did you forget that?" He turned on his heel and walked away.

Rees glared after him. How could he describe the choking smothering feeling that swept over him when he considered the prospect of staying on the farm? Day after day, week after week, month after month, with nothing to show for it but a bent back and dirt ingrained into his callused hands. "I feel trapped," he said. David didn't turn around.

Rees stamped into the house. Abigail, her face reddened by the heat, was ironing. She looked up as he entered and just as quickly looked away. Rees knew she'd heard the raised voices outside. And she probably agreed with David and Lydia. Rees tramped angrily upstairs to his loom. He threw the shuttle a few times and noticed his hands were trembling. A few more passes and his shakiness diminished. He began to regret losing his temper with David, but his anger at Lydia did not fade.

The Bristol wagon came for Abigail, and her high voice floated up to the open chamber window and into Rees's ears. The lower burr of David saying farewell was audible, too, but less distinct. Although Rees couldn't hear the words, there was something in the boy's voice that betrayed David's growing attachment to Abby. Rees sighed. Another problem. The wheels creaked away, and shortly after Rees's buggy rolled down the drive. Now that David was gone, Rees went downstairs to see if there was any dinner left in the larder. He ate cold chicken standing up, washed his hands, and returned to his loom. But he couldn't concentrate. All his being listened for the sound of the buggy's return, and yet when he heard the vehicle trundling up the drive he couldn't force himself to go downstairs and face Lydia.

Her light step tapped upon the stairs and he felt her presence behind him but he did not turn. "I know you're angry," she said. "You might as well scold me. I know that's what you've been waiting for."

"Why did you hire on at the Bowditch farm? Especially after I asked you not to," he demanded, spinning around. "Isn't there enough work for you here?"

She lifted her chin, and he could see her considering and discarding several responses. "I want to help you," she said. "And you didn't ask, you commanded—"

"I don't want you threatened!"

"But you think nothing of bringing Augustus, a possible murderer, to the farm?" she said with a flash of temper.

"I don't think he—"

"Fortunately, David agrees that Augustus could not possibly be a killer, else I should be worried."

"You discussed this with David?" Rees's voice rose until it squeaked.

"We discussed it, yes. I tried to talk it over with you, but you were too busy being king." Tears pricked at her eyes but she scrubbed them angrily away. "Your concern is not for my safety. You're afraid someone will discover the connection between us. Well, no one will. Because there is none. I am not your wife, nor your sister nor even your cousin. I'm only a housekeeper. And, as such, you have no authority over me."

"But I do," he said, knowing as soon as the words flew out of his mouth, they were a mistake.

Her mouth twisted. "No, you don't. I think you're scared. You know I'll hear more than you will. I learned something

already; everyone liked Nate. No one cares much for his wife."
When Rees did not speak, she added, "I was your partner in
Zion. I want only to be your partner again."

"Why didn't you tell me you were planning this?" Rees said.
He sounded hurt even to himself.

Lydia examined his expression and heaved a sigh. "I see. You
feel betrayed. Perhaps I should have said something. Only telling you would have felt too much like asking permission. And
you would have refused it, playing the lord and master." She
smiled without humor. "Then I would have done it anyway.
Even if I were your wife and you forbade me. I want to be your
helpmeet, not your servant, not someone inferior."

"I only want to protect you."

"From what? Living?" She looked away from him. "What do
you want, Will? A docile dependent woman? Someone who
makes you feel strong in comparison? I expected more from you."
She turned around and ran down the stairs, leaving Rees staring
after her in dismay.

He turned back to his loom. For the next hour and more he
wove, but he ripped out his rows as often as he put them in.
Lydia's words echoed in his head, painful in their truth. Why
was he behaving so much like his father? The memories of his
mother surrendering over and over to her drunken spouse still
made him cringe. And, if he were honest, he loved Lydia's feisti-
ness. Of course, it scared him, too. Didn't she know she could
be putting herself in danger? Realizing he'd stopped weaving, the
shuttle lifted motionless in his hand, he began working again.
But his punishing thoughts continued.

He went down for supper, expecting to mend the relation-
ships with Lydia and David by apologizing. Instead, he ate
alone. Lydia put cheese and bread upon the table but did not
stay to eat. And his son, with a dark look at his father, made a

sandwich and went back out to evening chores. Or maybe he just wanted to avoid his father's presence. Feeling like a pariah, and knowing some of it was his fault, Rees went back upstairs. He feared he was too upset to sleep before Augustus's jailbreak tonight.

Chapter Fourteen

When Rees went downstairs just before midnight, both David and Lydia were waiting in the kitchen. "What are you doing here?" he asked in surprise.

"You don't think I'd allow you rescue Augustus on your own," David said. "I've harnessed Amos to the buggy. Your wagon and Bessie are too recognizable. Augie can lie down between the seats, out of sight, until we're clear."

Rees began shaking his head. "I don't want to involve either or you in this."

"I'll be involved no matter what," David said. "Besides," he added after a beat, "I thought Caldwell was in this with you."

"He is," Rees agreed.

He hesitated thinking. Augustus would probably feel more comfortable if David were there. "Very well." He caught David's annoyed expression and was prepared to bellow. But he stopped, recalling several of his son's earlier statements, and really looked at his boy. At fourteen and already almost his father's height, David was just a few years shy of manhood. And marriage. And babies of his own. Dear Lord, Rees would be a grandfather! "But you don't need to ask permission," he said, astonishment coloring his words. "You're old enough to make your own decisions. . . ."

David, mouth open, ready to argue, paused, his smile stretching across his face.

"And I'll have hot food waiting," Lydia said. "No doubt the young man will be hungry."

Although it was past eleven at night, and as dark as the inside of a kettle, Rees no longer felt tired. Instead excitement burned through him, buzzing him into alertness. By the light of a candle, he and David went out to the buggy. David had already lit the lanterns hanging on either side of the horse and by that pale golden light they climbed up to the seat and started out for town. Amos stepped out right smartly, and Rees watched his son handle the reins with firm control.

"I couldn't handle the ribbons better myself," he said.

David ducked his head in pleased surprise.

They stopped a few blocks away from the jail and wrapped Amos's hooves in rags to muffle the sound of hoofbeats. David blew out the lanterns. Except for the three-quarter moon and a scattering of stars, all was dark. Rees's eyes slowly adjusted to the dim gray world.

Caldwell was waiting for them. As soon as they pulled into the alley, he opened the back door and beckoned them inside with one small burning candle. Rees felt his way through the small musty chamber and into the darkness of the main room. He heard Augustus move but didn't dare proceed into the blackness. Caldwell brushed by him, the candle illuminating a small circle around him, and started for the cells, jingling his keys. "If you run," he warned Augustus, "or turn out to be your father's murderer, I swear I'll hunt you down and kill you myself."

"I'm not. And I won't run," Augustus said. "Anyway, there's nowhere for me to go."

The constable unlocked the door. Augustus darted out as though he thought they might change their minds. When he saw

David, he relaxed. Smiling, David clapped the other lad's shoulder. "You're safe now."

Rees, hearing some heavy breathing, looked over into the next cell. He could just dimly see a shock of white hair. "Who's that?"

"Just some drifter," Caldwell said. "He got liquored up at the Bull. Come on." They hurried to the back and he threw open the door. David had cleverly angled the buggy so the escapee could climb in on the sheltered side, invisible from the street. As Augustus scrambled over the step and disappeared between the seats, Caldwell said to Rees, "No lights leaving the jail. And you're responsible if he runs."

"You make sure those slave takers leave town."

"It'll be easier now that I'm not guarding the jail."

Rees grunted and climbed into the buggy. He suspected Caldwell, instead of hunting the slave catchers, would be propping up the bar at the tavern.

David scrambled into the driver's seat and they started off. Even without the lanterns, Rees felt that everyone must be aware of them and know what they were doing; every muffled hoofbeat sounded to him like a pistol shot.

"I won't run," Augustus said from his position on the buggy floor. "I promise. Where would I go? The catchers almost caught me here—and in Dugard. I at least have friends and family."

Rees nodded and turned around, struck pensive. Where he saw confinement, Augustus saw protection. He would not ever enjoy the freedom Rees experienced: that of jumping into the wagon and driving away for parts unknown.

David halted on the outskirts of Dugard and lit the lanterns. The sudden flare of light sprang forward onto the road in golden circles.

"Thank you," Rees said, turning toward his son.

Only David's profile, outlined in the golden lantern light, was truly visible. Smiling at his father, he said, "Augie, do you know how to milk?"

"I have milked," Augustus said, pulling himself up into a rear buggy seat. "A few times, as a boy. But not recently . . ."

"You'll become an expert," David promised with a grin.

"What about Abigail?" Rees asked suddenly. "How can we keep her from knowing about him?" He jerked his head at Augie.

"Don't trouble yourself," David said. "I'll tell her. We won't be able to keep it a secret anyway. Not from her. But she won't say anything, that I promise."

His confident statement made Rees wonder if his earlier reflections about David's marriage had been prescient.

They sped through the darkness at a rapid trot, arriving home in the early hours of the morning. Candlelight shone through the windows, and as Amos clip-clopped up the drive, Lydia came out upon the porch with a lantern. Augustus climbed down but froze, staring shyly at the ground.

"Come on, lad," Rees said, gesturing at the steps in invitation.

"Go on," David said, grasping Amos's bridle and hauling him toward the barn. Augustus followed Rees into the house.

Lydia had set up a big wash pan before the fire. She gestured to the gently steaming water in the tub. "Bath first? Or supper?"

"Bath I think. The constable did feed me. . . ."

"Of course he wouldn't think a bath was important," Rees said with a wry grin.

"I'll leave the supper on the table," Lydia said. "And here are some clean clothes—borrowed from David, so they'll be too large." She picked up one of the candles. "I'll bid you good night." She smiled at Augustus and disappeared through the back door.

Rees could see the bright spark of her candle flame dancing

down the slope to the cottage. Tomorrow he would speak to her; no more time should pass before he made everything right with her. "I'm going to bed as well," he said, suddenly achingly tired. "David, you should retire, too."

"I will," he said. "The cows will want milking in only a few hours." Turning to their visitor, he said, "Come with me and I'll show you where to sleep."

Augustus, who had the expression of someone stunned into compliance, rose to his feet and followed David up the stairs. Rees plodded after them. He washed his face and hands to the low mutter of their conversation and lowered himself into bed with a groan of relief. He went to sleep so quickly and so soundly, he didn't hear Augustus thud back downstairs to the kitchen.

He overslept the following morning and clumped peevishly downstairs. Abigail paused in her ironing. She moved the spider to the fire and dropped in some bacon to fry. "David told me about Augie," she said, pouring him a mug of coffee. "Don't worry. I'll say nothing. Not even to my parents."

Frowning, Rees sat down and stirred milk and sugar into the brew. "Where is our guest?" he asked.

"Still sleeping. David decided to allow Augie one morning before rousing him for chores."

Huh, so David had wasted no time telling Abby about their guest. And Rees knew David was gone, driving Lydia to the Bowditch farm. Wishing they had listened to his objections, he put down his spoon with unnecessary force.

Abby glanced at his expression, and as soon as she put his fried bacon and bread in front of him, retreated to the far end of the kitchen.

He left for the farm as well, immediately after breakfast. This time he took the fork that led to the lay-by off the road and parked Bessie and the wagon at the end, under the shadow of the trees. He found the path and walked through the tree break to the meadow beyond. His heart speeded up when he reached the fields, but he saw no one. Nothing moved. Taking in a deep breath, he sprinted toward the cottage door. He whipped through it and shut it quietly but firmly behind him.

When he entered the room on the right, he stepped into quiet. He looked around. Although empty, the cottage did not appear abandoned. Marsh had removed the pot hanging over the fireplace and swept the hearth clean. And crumbs of food scattered the table as though he had snacked here but been called away before cleanup.

Rees walked into the weaving room. It betrayed evidence of a hasty search. The books in the bookcase were no longer arranged evenly, spine out, in alphabetical order, and everything had been removed from the small desk. Marsh, for certain. If anything, such as the will, had been hidden in this room, he would surely have found it.

Rees suspected Nate would have hidden something personal upstairs anyway. He took the stairs two at a time. Shifting motes of dust hung in the sun and furred the floor. Rees could still see his tracks from his last visit, faint now with a layer of dust, and a set of fresh tracks laying over them. Most of the old clothes hanging by the chimney had been torn down and the chamber pot had been emptied and cleaned. As expected, the cedar blanket chest at the foot of the bed held only bedding; Rees went through it just to make sure. Nothing. Puffing in frustration, he looked around. Where else? The dye room? He turned and started down the stairs, but he paused a few steps down and glanced around the room one last time. This time he saw another chest under the bed. After running back up the steps and circling the bed, he dropped to his knees. The wood screeched when he dragged the trunk across the floor. He thought at first that the top was locked and it may have been, but as he wrestled with it, the old wood, rotted by damp and alternating cycles of hot and cold, dry and wet, splintered apart in his hands.

He knew instantly he had found Nate's treasures. Two collections of letters, one tied with a faded blue ribbon, a handful of chits—IOUs, with Piggy Hansen's scrawl upon the top one and a yellowed poster underneath those. But Rees forgot all about the papers, unconsciously shoving them into his pockets when he saw the collection of artifacts underneath.

Wild roses, withered and brown but still recognizable, were carefully wrapped in linen and nestled up against an oddly shaped rock shot with veins of quartz. Next to that was a necklace, the beads on the cord crudely whittled. Rees remembered carving them for Nate's birthday. The other two items were mementos from an abortive journey he and Nate had embarked upon as boys.

Rees had started it, running away from his father, who insisted he work in both the fields and the printer's shop. He stopped at the Bowditch farm and shouted down Nate, who, beaten by his father on a regular basis, was only too glad to join him. Other than a block of cheese Rees had wrapped in a rag, they carried no supplies but they headed west confidently. Not far outside of town, they stopped at a pond, a pond Rees suspected, that probably lay upon Nate's current property, and went swimming. Rees had found the rock in the pond and pocketed it. Afterwards, during their explorations, Nate fell into a hedge of wild roses and had to be disentangled from the thorns, bravely suffering the cuts of a thousand thorns. Rees had cut himself in the rescue and they'd mingled blood, promising to be blood brothers forever. Then they'd started out again. Not more than a mile later, Constable Franklin caught them both. He brought them home, knowing they would both be whipped within an inch of their lives.

Rees suddenly became aware of frenzied barking outside. Munch! Dropping the items into the trunk, he started for the window. Marsh was running down the slope. "Oh damn!" Rees muttered. He hurried back to the bed and shoved the trunk under it. Then he fled down the stairs, slipping and almost falling. But when Marsh opened the door and came in, he found Rees in the weaving room, looking around at the looms in assumed perplexity.

"What are you doing here?" Marsh demanded with none of the subservience he was expected to show a white man.

"Nothing," Rees said. "Just looking around."

Marsh took in a deep breath, his furious eyes sliding away from Rees. "I'll be happy to accompany you the next time you want to visit the cottage. This was Nate's . . . He was a very private person. . . . Does the mistress know you're here?" Rees listened to Marsh trying to divert attention from his anger and recover his mask, but Rees knew the man now.

"Of course," he lied with a smile. Marsh was looking for something hidden in the cottage. If he found it, whatever it was, Rees knew he would never see it. Casting about for a neutral topic, he said, "I examined Nate's ledgers and saw entries for materials I did not recognize. Dyes and such. Mrs. Bowditch suggested I speak with you. As the expert."

Marsh looked at him in surprise. "Did she now? How much about dyeing do you know?"

"Very little," Rees said truthfully. "I've seen indigo preparation, of course. And I have some passing knowledge of madder."

"The roots, the berries, and the leaves of many plants produce color. Onionskins simmered in an iron pot will dye cloth
brown, as do coffee and tea. Sometimes yellow flowers will yield
yellow. I've tried using rose petals to produce pink. But most of
the dyes made from these common sources rapidly fade in sunlight or after washing."

"Not indigo," Rees said.

"No. Indigo produces that wonderful blue without any help.
But you must know how expensive indigo is. Even the indigo
produced in South Carolina." Beckoning Rees with his dark
fingers, he went down the hall to the kitchen. He crossed to the
prickly plant on the windowsill and brushed his fingers over the
white film. But, when he showed Rees the result, it was not
powder as Rees supposed but tiny squirming insects. Marsh
crushed them between his fingers, producing a dark red fluid.
"Spanish red, cochineal. The dye used to color the Roman
pope's robes. This plant grows in Mexico and South America. It
does not grow well here; I'm not sure why not. Believe me, I
tried." He stepped around Rees and threw open the door into
the dye room.

A flood of pungent musty air rushed out, setting Rees
coughing.

Marsh went on through and opened the back door. "Do you
see those samples?" He pointed to the strips of red cloth hanging from the rail, right next to several strips of green, tinted in
hues ranging from pale celery to emerald. "You see that bright
scarlet? That's cochineal. The rosier pink next to it is madder
root. Sometimes madder will yield a bright red, too, but cochineal is much better."

"And that?" Rees asked, pointing to a burgundy strip, the
color of fine wine.

"From a Peruvian berry." Marsh sighed. "Expensive to import. And we tried to duplicate the results with pokeberry, but although the original color is a beautiful dark reddish burgundy, it fades immediately."

"Nate was trying to produce Spanish red, emerald green, some of these intense colors much more cheaply," Rees said.

Marsh nodded. "And the most difficult color of all to produce is green, especially that intense emerald." Marsh pointed at a bale of withering leaves. "That is chilla, from the Andes Mountains. That makes a nice green with copper carbonate, but the leaves only grow at a certain altitude in the mountains. And it does not surrender the same intensity as Scheele's green. Have you heard of Scheele's green?"

"I saw correspondence from a Mr. Scheele in Nate's desk," Rees said.

"Yes. Nate was in communication with Mr. Scheele. He invented that bright green, made of copper arsenite. I've heard President Washington had two rooms decorated in that color."

"And that?" Rees asked, pointing to the pale celery green.

"That's from lily of the valley. But I wouldn't recommend using that if I were you; that plant is extremely poisonous."

"Hmmm. And the yellow?" Rees asked.

Marsh opened his mouth to answer but then, recollecting the time and place, stopped. "May we continue this conversation at a later time? The memorial service for the master is absorbing all of my energy right now."

"Of course," Rees said with a bow. "But I hope to continue it. Dyes are more interesting than I thought."

"I'll look forward to it—after the memorial. Grace is working extremely hard on it, helping us in the kitchen, and she often asks my advice."

"And how does Molly feel about that?" Rees asked, flicking a look at the other man. "Her daughter, in the kitchen?"

Marsh smiled without humor. "She's isn't happy about it, but Grace is just as strong willed as her mother and she wants to do this. Besides, keeping busy is how she deals with her grief." As he talked, he urged Rees toward the front door.

Rees stopped, just a little rebellious at being herded, and glanced around. "You're fond of Grace."

"I'm fond of all of Nate's children," Marsh replied promptly, shouldering the other man forward. This time Rees acquiesced; he knew he'd return to the cottage, and soon, despite Marsh.

They climbed the slope to the house, Rees quickly falling behind the other man's long-legged stride. Even from the top of the slope, he could see the activity inside the kitchen. With dinnertime approaching, in addition to the upcoming memorial reception, the kitchen staff must work at full speed. He imagined he could see Lydia's square white cap inside and craned his neck.

Rachel saw him and hurried out, wiping her wet hands on a towel. "Mr. Rees. Stay for dinner?" She looked at him with an anxious smile and leaned ever so slightly forward. "Augustus?"

"He's safe. He . . ." Realizing all at once that Marsh was regarding him with interest, Rees closed his mouth. He didn't think Marsh would betray Augustus but couldn't be sure. The fewer people who knew Augustus's secret location, the better.

Rachel scowled at Marsh and with a reluctant glance he retreated into the kitchen. Rachel turned back to Rees. "Some of Master Nate's things are still downstairs," she said, her gaze hot and fierce. "Perhaps you should collect them."

"Perhaps I should," he agreed. He followed Rachel through the kitchen downstairs to the cellar. The door to the small room in which Nate had lain was open and Rees went straight to it. In the dim light he could see something lying on the floor but he couldn't tell if it was the canvas shroud or something else.

"Mr. Rees."

He turned with a start, knocking his head on the lintel. Nude to the waist, her breasts completely exposed, Rachel stood close behind him. Rees backed up until he was pressed against the table. "Please, Mr. Rees," she whispered, "save my son. I have no money to offer you. . . ." Taking his hand, she pulled it toward one of her naked breasts.

For a moment Rees surrendered to lust, but jerked his hand back before he touched her. "No," he said. "I mean, I will help Augustus. He's safe. But you mustn't—"

A slight sound at the door brought his head up and his gaze locked with Lydia's shocked and horrified stare. Betrayal, anger, and a horrible crushing hurt contorted her features. Tears overflowed her eyes and began spilling down her cheeks. "Lydia." Rees breathed. Rachel whirled, holding her bodice over her naked breasts, as Lydia fled up the stairs. "No. Lydia, wait!" Rees shouted, starting forward. He pushed past Rachel so violently, he almost knocked her over. "I already promised your son I would do all I could to free him, and I will. This isn't necessary."

Rachel lowered her eyes, humiliated, but she spoke from relief. "I should have known you are as Master Nate was." Rees barely heard her. He hurried up the stairs, out from the kitchen, and down the road to catch up with Lydia.

He saw her indigo skirts disappearing behind the barn as she ran, without bonnet or basket, toward the laundry room. Dust puffed up from her flying feet and hung in the air; if it didn't rain soon, all the crops would burn up in the fields and everyone would go hungry. "Lydia!" he cried after her. "Lydia, wait!" She neither slowed nor turned around. Rees ran after her, his long legs eating up the distance between them. "Lydia, please."

Juniper stepped out of the laundry and, shading her eyes, watching the running woman and the man pursuing her. She held out her arms to catch Lydia and threw Rees such a baleful glare, he jolted to a stop. Burning with frustration, he watched the laundress wrap the sobbing woman in her arms and hustle her to safety in the laundry.

"Damn," Rees muttered. Now when would he find an opportunity to make things right? Would it even be possible?

Chapter Fifteen

Rees couldn't go home; he couldn't. But he couldn't stay here either. He knew everyone was staring at him, wondering what had happened. Certainly neither of the women would explain and he couldn't either. Fuming, he spun around and started down the lane toward the lay-by. He wanted to go into the cottage and finish his search of that mysterious trunk, but he knew Marsh would be on his trail in a few minutes. Of course, Marsh's desperate effort to bar Rees from searching the cottage only made him more determined to know what the servant wanted to keep hidden. Tomorrow Rees would arrive here even earlier.

He turned his wagon toward Dugard and the Contented Rooster. Dinnertime was fast approaching and with only a few slices of bacon and bread for breakfast, Rees's stomach growled demandingly. He sat at his usual small table by the window, his thoughts still scattered by the anger and shame that burned like banked coals, ready to burst into flame at a moment's notice. Jack Jr. brought a cup of coffee and withdrew silently, after one fleeting glance at Rees's grim expression.

He gazed unseeingly out the window, trying to think around the emotion that blazed inside him.

Susannah approached carrying a plate of apple cake. "More questions?" She smiled at him.

"Not today," Rees said.

She inspected his expression. "You look as though you lost your last friend," she said.

"I don't want to talk about it," he said.

"What's bothering you? I know that look. Remember when Nate decided he preferred Ernest Bridge to you?" Rees managed a smile.

"I was all of eight or nine, I think."

"Nate was angry at you for something and wanted to punish you." She paused. "He could be cruel." Rees nodded and sighed. With one final anxious look in his direction, Susannah departed, her skirts whispering. Rees was left in solitude to reflect upon his sins.

When he reached home several hours later, Abigail was alone in the kitchen. She turned with a bright and very strange smile. He knew immediately Lydia was home and visibly upset. "Where's Miss Farrell?" he asked.

"Down by the bees."

Of course: she had gone to the bees for comfort. Rees turned and went out the back door, walking down the slope to the cottage. He spotted her from the hill's crest, her white linen cap moving among the boxes lined up in the shade of the oak trees, and knew when she had seen him by her sudden stillness. He paused a few feet away.

"Lydia," he said. "You completely misread the situation."

"Misread? Am I to doubt my own eyes?" She turned toward him. Her face was so swollen with crying, she was unrecognizable. "How can anyone misread an unclothed woman?"

"You don't understand. She offered herself to me in payment for helping her son. I declined. I would never accept such an offer."

"I— When I saw her with you, I felt I understood why you were so passionate I not work there. You wanted to hide your connection to Rachel."

"You should know me better. I would never take advantage of anyone weaker than myself. Even as a boy, I didn't."

"I'm certain you could find an argument that would allow such congress," Lydia said bitterly, "especially if you desired her."

"If I loved her, perhaps," Rees admitted, "but I barely know her." He paused, peering into her face and hoping for a sign of softening. "Lydia, I remained alone for eight years after Dolly's death. I could not betray her, and I'd watched her coffin go into the ground."

"But we don't even have an understanding," she said. Rees stared at her and as the fear of losing her took hold, a proposal of marriage trembled on his tongue. "Don't ask me to marry you, not now," she said, reading his intent. "I will refuse, knowing you offered only from fear." Slapped by the rebuff, Rees stepped back. Lydia took in a deep breath. "I'll listen," she said. "I know Rachel is desperately worried about her son."

"Yes," Rees said eagerly. "She's a slave. She owns nothing but desperately wants to protect her child. So, she tried to pay for my help in a different coin. I assured her I was already rescuing Augustus." He paused and then added, "In any case, I suspect she must know our secret now. She saw me hare out of the kitchen after you." Lydia slanted a glance at him, and for the first time her body relaxed. "I doubt she'll betray us," he added, "but I'll speak to her."

She shook her head at him, her expression stern. "No," she said, "I will." She started up the slope to the cottage. When

Rees turned to follow her, she held up her hand to stop him. "I need time to think."

"Nothing happened . . . ," he protested once again.

She looked at him, her eyes troubled. She didn't smile or frown; she just regarded him in silence. Then she turned and walked away. This time Rees made no attempt to follow. Cautiously hopeful that she would accept his explanation and turn sweet, he walked back to the house.

He did not realize he had taken the letters from Nate's trunk and stuffed them into his pocket until he was getting undressed for bed that night. When he took off his coat and went to hang it on the chair, he heard the crackle of paper. *What the—?* He pulled out the wad of paper and looked at it in dismay. He must have pushed them into his pocket when he heard Munch barking, an action so automatic, he had not been aware of it. He untied the blue ribbon and pulled a letter out of the packet at random. The first paragraph made him squirm in embarrassment; these were love letters. And from Molly, if the definite *M* at the bottom was any indication. Rees hastily bundled them back together and tossed them onto the bedside table.

The second packet, comprising three documents, appeared more promising. All were signed *Cornelius Lattimore, Esquire, New Winstead,* the same name Rees had found in Nate's desk. He held them to the candle to better read the script. In beautiful flowing copperplate, the first responded to an inquiry, apparently from Nate, expressing a willingness to meet in the near future. The second set a date and time and referred to previously mailed directions. The final document was an invoice for services rendered. With a sudden flare of excitement, Rees reread the third communication. Although nothing indicated the exact kind of services, he'd wager his soul that these had been legal services. And if that were true, what kind of legal services had they been? And did George Potter know?

Rees refolded the documents and put them upon the table. These provided a new path to explore and one he was certain would lead to some answers. How soon could he travel to New Winstead? In a more hopeful frame of mind than he had been for some time, he washed his face and hands and went to bed, putting an end to a very long and eventful day. He hoped tomorrow would be less exhausting.

A thunderous knocking woke Rees. He sat up and looked around, muzzy with sleep. The sky outside the window was still black, sprinkled with stars, and he thought it could not be earlier than three o'clock in the morning. The knocking came again, followed by an unfamiliar voice calling his name. Rees went to the window and threw it up, pushing his head out into the fine drizzle. "I'll be down!" he shouted. "Stop that noise." He saw movement but could not recognize the visitor. Rees pulled on his breeches and slid his bare feet into his shoes and tiptoed quietly into the hall. Although he hoped David had not been disturbed, he met his son also creeping downstairs.

"I'm sorry," Rees said.

"Might as well get an early start," David said. "The cows will be demanding my attention in an hour anyway."

They descended the stairs to the kitchen in the dark. The fire had been banked; David stirred it up and by its reddish light Rees lit a candle and went to answer the door. He did not recognize the man outside.

"Caldwell says come now," the man said, his voice hoarse. Now Rees realized this was one of the tavern rats from the Bull. "The jail is on fire."

"What?"

"Hurry." As the deputy turned back to his nag, Rees closed the door and ran into the kitchen.

"I've got to go," he said. "Now. The jail is on fire." He raced upstairs and finished dressing. By the time he returned to the kitchen, coffee perked over the fire and David was gone. Rees gobbled down a heel of stale bread and drank a cup of weak coffee before running outside. David was just finishing harnessing Bessie to the wagon. Grateful, Rees hugged his son, surprising both of them with this unusual physical demonstration, and jumped up into the damp seat.

He'd barely reached the outskirts of town when he smelled the stink of wet ashes. He drove as rapidly as he dared through the dark streets to the jail. Despite the early hour, people and vehicles clogged the street around the burning structure. The roof was already gone.

"Dear God," Rees muttered in a shocked whisper, staring at the charred timbers and soot-darkened stone walls.

"They say the man inside burned to death," said the man standing next to him.

Rees felt an icy chill crawl down his spine. If he had hesitated only one day . . . In a daze, he pushed through the crowd of gawkers to the space in front of the jail. Caldwell turned, ready to shout, but when he saw Rees he dropped his sooty hand. Black coated his face, and the acrid stink of burning completely submerged his body odor.

"When did it start?"

"Close around midnight, I think. I was at the Bull. I went over about ten. Didn't want to change my routine, you know. By the time I came back for bed, the blaze had already taken hold." He turned to look at Rees. "It would have been far worse if not for the mist."

"This is attempted murder," Rees said in a low voice. "Someone wanted to make sure Augustus didn't survive his time in jail."

"It is murder. That drifter? He was still inside." Caldwell gestured to a dirty sheet shrouding a still form behind him. A boot, with the sole completely worn through, protruded from the linen. "A man innocent of everything but drinking too much." Caldwell's voice caught. "The smoke got him. I couldn't get to the cells."

Rees growled inarticulately. "Even a guilty man doesn't deserve this kind of death." Caldwell nodded in agreement. Rees cast one more glance at the smoking pile of blackened stones and charred timbers and turned away in disgust. "Did anyone see anything?"

"A woman, up with her new baby. She said she saw a boy hanging around here. A few minutes later, she smelled smoke."

Rees cast Caldwell a questioning look. "Richard, do you think?" he asked.

Caldwell nodded. "Who else? The only other boy I thought it might be is that young slave catcher. Frustrated maybe since they couldn't get to Augustus. But that seemed far-fetched."

Rees nodded in agreement. "Does Potter know?"

"Probably," Caldwell said. "If he's awake, that is. No one is talking about anything else."

Rees looked at the western sky. The first pale gray lit the horizon, diffused by fog. "I'll wager he's awake now," he said. "I'm certain one visitor after another has been knocking on his door." He began walking toward his wagon and after a brief hesitation the constable fell into step with him. They did not speak as he drove to the center of town and Potter's office. Rees was grappling with the wickedness behind the arson and accompanying murder. No doubt Caldwell was doing the same.

Despite the early hour, the streets of Dugard were busy. The fire had awakened many townspeople who had elected not to return to their beds. The congestion forced Rees to park in the alley behind the lawyer's establishment. When he and Caldwell climbed down from the wagon, Potter, dressed only in shirt and breeches, appeared at the top of the back stairs. "Why would anyone want to hurt that boy?" he said in distress.

"He wasn't in the jail," Rees said. "I moved him out a day or two ago."

Potter's mouth rounded in surprise. "You both better come upstairs," he said. "I'll see about some breakfast."

As Rees and Caldwell went down the hall to the stairs and up, Potter disappeared into the kitchen. A few minutes later, he joined his visitors in his office, casually dressed in his waistcoat but not his jacket. "Start at the beginning," he said.

"You know about the slave catchers," Caldwell said. "Slippery bastards. I knew they were still in town, but I could never find them. And they showed much too much interest in that boy Augustus."

"So I moved him out," Rees said. "But no one but us knew that, so I think we can safely assume the fire was set to kill him."

"The fire was set on that side of the jail," Caldwell said, nodding his head in agreement. "The roof is gone, but the walls on the office side are barely touched."

Potter shook his head in distress. "And the blaze, how did it start?" he asked.

"I don't know exactly," Caldwell said. "My first guess? Someone set a fire against the wall outside and tossed a burning tallow-soaked rag up to the roof."

Potter looked ill. "Why Augie?" he asked. "Did he know something?"

"What? He never went home," Rees said.

"Wait," Caldwell argued, his thought running in a different track. "Maybe he did. And there are only two people Augustus will lie for: his mother and his brother."

"Not true," Rees said. "He's fond of Marsh, too."

"Marsh?" Caldwell said, nodding in excitement.

"I would hate to think Marsh murdered Nate," Potter said. "Nate trusted him like a brother."

"And I can't see him threatening Augustus," Rees said. "He treats that boy, and Richard and Grace, like his own." He knew by the look Caldwell shot him that he did not accept that argument. "Besides, no one saw him in town, even assuming he could leave the farm unnoticed."

Caldwell nodded slowly, in reluctant agreement. "That's true. He would be difficult to miss."

"So, are we back to Richard?" Potter asked with a sigh. Rees and Caldwell exchanged a glance of unhappy concord. "But why would he kill Augustus?"

"It could be someone else," Rees said, trying to imagine another possibility. "Someone's convinced he's guilty and decided to take justice in his own hands."

Potter nodded. "Not everyone is willing to believe him innocent and his white brother guilty."

"Scapegoat," Caldwell agreed. "Dead, he can't refute the claim he's guilty."

"I suggest we keep Augustus's whereabouts secret for now," Rees said. "Let everyone believe he burned to death in the jail. It's the only way to keep him safe." Looking at the other men, he added firmly, "I believe we should also keep in mind the women involved and include both Rachel and Molly Bowditch as possible killers."

Caldwell shook his head in immediate refusal. "I can't see a woman battering Nat to death. He was a big man, almost as big as you," he said nodding at Rees, "and both women are small and delicate."

"Molly?" Potter cried at the same moment. "Of course, she's not a murderer. She hired you to find the truth, remember?"

"She hired me to free her son," Rees corrected him. "And once she felt I'd succeeded, she had no more need of me. Indeed, my suggestion that Augustus might be innocent brought on a fit of temper. And Rachel also has a son at risk." Recalling the scene at the Bowditch farm, he added in a low voice, "She, too, will do almost anything to protect her child."

"Mr. Rees is correct." A light female voice came from the door. Mrs. Potter, struggling with a heavy tray, tried to nudge the door wider with her foot. Both Caldwell and Rees leaped to their feet. Caldwell, the closer man to the door, quickly thrust it back. Rees lifted the heavy tray from Mrs. Potter's hands and carried it to her husband's desk.

"Really," Potter said, glaring at his wife, "I don't think women's chatter should be any part of this discussion."

Rees, who frequently found women's gossip a source of important information, shook his head at the other man. "What's your opinion, Mrs. Potter?" he asked her courteously.

"Molly's always been a little too fond of other people's husbands," Mrs. Potter said, shooting a sour look at her husband. "But she won't share anything she sees as her own. She's always been like that, even as a little girl. She resents Augustus and his place as her husband's bastard son. Would she throw him to the lions to save Richard? Without a moment's thought."

"But she is but a weak woman," her husband objected. "Too weak to bludgeon a man to death."

Mrs. Potter cast him a scornful glance. "We are all of us stronger than we let on, George. To protect my children, I would strangle a wolf bare-handed."

With a final nod, she withdrew. Potter, flushed with embarrassment, turned to his two guests. "You must forgive her. She's never liked Molly—"

"No forgiveness necessary," Rees said. "And I think she's entirely correct. I'll leave both Molly Bowditch and Rachel on my list of possible murderers. After all," he added with a flash of dark humor, "who has more reason to hate and kill a husband than his wife? Or a mistress?"

"That's why I am not married," Caldwell said, baring his rotting teeth in a grin.

Rees helped himself to a cup of coffee, so strong and so black, it looked like ink. Just the way he liked it. He dropped in two lumps of sugar and poured in cream until the color more closely resembled buckskin. While he prepared his coffee, Caldwell fell upon the cake like a starving man, liberally strewing crumbs over his grubby shirt and buff coat.

"Did anyone see anything?" Potter asked, but not as though he believed it possible.

Caldwell and Rees exchanged a glance. "I spoke to the neighbors. Not really."

Rees nodded in agreement. The young mother had seen a boy, but Rees concurred with Caldwell's decision to keep her report to themselves, at least for now.

Chapter Sixteen

It was midmorning, but still cool and foggy, by the time Rees and Caldwell left Potter's office. As the constable started back to the jail, Rees walked the two blocks to the Contented Rooster. The morning rush must be over and he hoped to find time to talk to Jack and Susannah before dinnertime.

Although not packed, the establishment still hummed with activity. But the two proprietors sat comfortably at a table in the back, enjoying cake and coffee. "Do you mind if I join you?" Rees asked, looming up beside them.

"More questions?" Susannah asked.

Pulling up a chair, Rees sat down. "More like your opinions," he said.

"Gossip," Jack muttered disdainfully.

"Not exactly," Rees said, putting out a hand to forestall the other man's departure. "Did you hear about the jail?"

"Of course. No one's talking about anything else," Jack said.

Susannah leaned forward, her expression one of alarm. "Is it about Augustus? Did that poor boy burn to death?" Sorrow contorted her face.

"Augustus?" Jack repeated, aghast. "Was he—?"

"You don't listen," Susannah said in fond reproof.

"Well, he was in the jail," Rees said, trying to decide how much to admit.

Susannah inspected Rees's expression and then she relaxed, smiling. "Don't worry, Will. Jack doesn't listen and I will certainly keep any secret you decide to share." Rees nodded but continued to hesitate. A secret shared by two was usually a secret no longer. Susannah put her hand over his. "Augustus was not in the jail, was he?"

"I took him home," Rees admitted.

"Good. Of course, he had nothing to do with his father's death," she said. "He's always been gentle."

"He seems so. I'm not sure what to believe anymore." He sighed. "The stories I hear of Nate don't mesh with the lad I recall. I mean, friends with King Carleton? That man was as nasty as they come." Susannah shrugged. "But why then would Nate refuse to bless a marriage between Richard and Elizabeth? "

"I wonder if that is due to the enmity between the two wives," Susannah said. "Charlotte Carleton pays little attention to us lesser mortals. And Molly—" The easy atmosphere shifted subtly to one of tension. Susannah added acerbically, "I will only say that she prefers men and pays little attention to her fellow females." She glanced at her husband. He shifted uncomfortably and would not meet his wife's gaze.

Rees stared at both of them. "I see," he said, not seeing at all. "She has a reputation, then?"

"Even James Carleton was rumored to be one of her conquests," Susannah said with a nod. "I never believed it, though. They met only briefly when he returned home for a visit. Then he was off for England again and shortly after, Molly married Nate."

"They met at the Carletons' annual Christmas party," Jack

interjected abruptly. "That was when Mrs. Carleton still lived here, before she took her daughters to England to join her son. She threw open the big house for a party every year."

"Even we were invited to those," Susannah said. "But once Charlotte arrived here—well, I haven't seen the inside of that house since and I believe the same is true of Molly."

"How did Nate feel about this?" Rees asked. It was a bitter pill to realize he could not guess how his boyhood friend, closer than a brother, would feel.

Susannah and Jack glanced at each other. "I doubt he cared," she said. "He maintained his business relationship with Henry Carleton, and then James after that."

"Nate, well, he kept to himself," Jack added. "Molly seemed to settle down and concentrate upon raising Richard. A few years later, Grace came along and then Ben, so I assume they were happy enough."

"Any rumors?" Rees asked. Jack shook his head, but Susannah pushed out her lips in a self-conscious moue. "Suze?"

"Well, Dr. Wrothman spends a lot of time at the farm," she said.

Jack frowned. "And that is sheer speculation," he said, stirring restlessly. "For all we know, there is no truth at all to any of those scandalous whispers. And now I must return to my duties. It's more work for us since our cook disappeared. . . ."

"We think she ran off to get married," Susannah explained, also rising to her feet. "I do wish she'd said something. . . ."

Rees remained in his seat as Susannah and Jack returned to their customers. He drained his cup in one draft, frustration mixing with regret. He just didn't know enough about Nate, not anymore. The boy Rees remembered had become a stranger and he could not guess whom Nate had angered so greatly that they battered him to death.

Suddenly aware of Susannah's ferocious glare, Rees shot to his feet. It was approaching midday and dinnertime, and she wanted this table for paying customers. Throwing a penny on the table to appease her, he left the coffeehouse, thinking hard as he tramped to his wagon. James Carleton was at the center of this mystery, and he was afraid. It was time to press him for answers. And that Mr. Lattimore, whose letters Rees had found in the trunk, certainly knew some of Nate's secrets. He must be found and questioned. But today Rees would get to the bottom of the trunk under Nate's bed.

Rees turned his wagon west, toward the Bowditch farm.

Although he spent most of the drive to the cottage cocooned in fog, by the time he reached Nate's farm, the gray shroud had finally begun to thin. He pulled into the hidden clearing, tethered Bessie to a tree and picked up Rachel's shawl, now rather dirty and battered from its time in the wagon bed. He would leave it in the cottage. He plunged into the trees. Droplets of water filmed the leaves, and the rocks underfoot were slick with moisture. When he stepped out of the break, the weaver's cottage was visible but dreamlike in its diaphanous coat of vapor.

As Rees started across the meadow, the window in the front room flew up and a musket barrel stabbed out. Warned by the sound of the window sliding up the casement, he threw himself to one side just as the musket discharged. He felt the sting of the ball as it sliced through his left arm. Blood immediately darkened his coat sleeve. Spurred by anger and, yes, fear, too, and unaware of the pain, Rees jumped to his feet and began running toward the house. He did not go through the front door but around the side. Just as he expected, the shooter had torn out the back door and was running down the slope toward the pond. Richard Bowditch. Rees put on a burst of speed and flung himself forward, tackling the slighter figure and bearing him to the ground with his greater weight. Richard, his expression terrified, clawed furiously at the bigger man.

"You foolish boy!" Rees grasped Richard's hands and pinned him to the ground. "I'm not going to hurt you. Why did you shoot me? Does Marsh know you're hiding here? Does your mother?" Of course they did. Panting, and with his wound beginning to sting, Rees relaxed and let his weight hold the boy down.

"He's been shot!" Marsh shouted, thudding up behind Rees and clutching at his shoulders. Rees released his grip on Richard and allowed himself to be tugged away. The boy did not move. He remained on the ground, trying to catch his breath.

"What are you doing to my son?" Molly screamed.

"Trying to save his fool life," Rees said angrily, looking up. "He can't run and hide forever."

Lydia, Rachel, and Mary Martha, clustered together in the cottage door, were brushed aside like flies as Molly Bowditch raced toward her son. "Leave him alone."

Rees snapped, "Do you want to see your son hanged? This isn't just about clearing Richard's name, you know. Until we identify Nate's killer, everyone who might be guilty will be suspected of the murder. And right now, Richard is the primary suspect. Someone who thinks he is guilty, or has an itchy trigger finger, or is drunk and angry, or there's no one else will go after Richard. He will make a handy target. Is that what you want?"

Molly blanched. Richard scrambled to his feet and rushed to her side. "Augie is in jail," she protested, grasping her son's arm. "He's guilty—"

"And the jail burned down last night," Rees said. Rachel uttered an involuntary scream. "Why is your son running away from me? Is he guilty? If so, you'd better counsel him to flee to the frontier. He won't be safe anywhere in Dugard."

Molly's hand crept up to her mouth.

"Is this necessary?" Richard demanded, glancing anxiously at his mother.

"And I need to speak to you," Rees said.

Molly's furious glare could have peeled bark. "He is not his father's killer," she protested.

"I want to speak to you now," Rees said to Richard. "By to-morrow you'll be gone again."

"I won't run," Richard said, raising his eyes to meet the Rees's gaze. "I give you my word." Rees inspected the young man's expression. Richard managed a lopsided smile. "I'm tired of running."

"Go home. Tend to your wound." Molly said, turning to Rees. "My son gave his word. . . ."

"Very well," Rees said in assent. His wound was beginning to burn like a stripe of fire. "But I will return tomorrow. And I'll bring the constable."

"Return to your duties, all of you," Molly commanded, ges-turing at the other women. She linked arms with her son and they disappeared into the cottage. Rachel, after casting an anx-ious glance at Rees, reluctantly followed them and, after a stern frown from Marsh, the others joined her. Only Lydia did not move.

"Miss Farrell," Marsh said. Reluctantly she trailed Rachel into the cottage.

Marsh put one bluish-tinted hand upon Rees's right shoul-der. "Come up to the kitchen," he said. "I'll dress your wound."

"A moment," Rees said. "I have Rachel's shawl."

"Rachel's shawl?" Marsh repeated as they walked around the cottage.

"I must have dropped it."

"Where did you find it?" Marsh asked

"Juniper said it came down with the soiled body linen," Rees said. He pointed to the bright garment lying upon the grass.

"How did it find its way into the laundry?" Marsh wondered as he hurried forward to pick it up. His dark fingers smoothed the trailing yarn. "Rachel won't be pleased to see this damage. She'll have to knit it all again. . . ."

Rees said nothing. The pain from his wound now radiated down his arm to his elbow and hand.

Marsh glanced at him and at the blood soaking his jacket. "Go to the kitchen. I'll patch you up. I just want to put this inside. . . ."

Rees trudged up the dry lane. Although he'd been shot during the War, he did not remember the wound hurting quite so much as this. Hard to believe a small metal ball that struck him such a glancing blow could cause such pain.

When Marsh rejoined him and they walked up the slope, Rees felt every footfall throbbing through his arm. Marsh glanced at him and took his right elbow. "You're as white as a sheet," he said. Rees nodded. He felt hot, too, and perspiration ran down his face in a stream.

Rachel had already put a roll of linen strips and a basin on the table. As Marsh took the basin to the barrel to fill it, Rees collapsed heavily in the chair. Lydia brought over a cup of coffee, liberally sugared and floating with cream. "Drink this," she said. "It will make you feel better."

"Rachel," Rees whispered to the cook, "Augustus is with me. Don't worry." Rachel gasped but she dared not vent her emotions by speaking. Instead, as Marsh approached, she spun around to the fireplace, stirring up the flames through a haze of happy tears.

First Rees's coat had to come off. Marsh helped Lydia pull the right sleeve down, Rees biting the inside of his cheek as the other sleeve dragged painfully over the wound. That was the worst of it; Marsh eased the left sleeve down and dropped the coat on the floor to reveal the bloody shirtsleeve. Lydia cut away the soft worn linen and then carefully bathed the wound free of blood.

"The ball just grazed you," Marsh said. "It'll be stiff for a while but you should be fine in a few days."

Rees managed a faint smile. "You can look at it tomorrow when I visit."

Lydia unwound a strip of linen and wrapped it around Rees's arm. "You aren't going to be able to manage the reins home," she said.

"Maybe this is a message," Marsh said. "It's time to let sleeping dogs lie."

Rees glared at the other man. "No. I meant what I told Mrs. Bowditch. Richard will never lose the taint of suspicion. Maybe he is the killer, but if he isn't, he needs to be declared innocent."

"Are you sure this isn't about revenge?" Marsh asked. Rees looked into the other man's dark eyes. Marsh did not look away.

"It's about justice. You were fond of Nate. Don't you want to see his killer caught? And you're fond of Richard and Augustus. Surely you want them freed of suspicion?" Marsh didn't say anything immediately, but Rees could see words trembling on his tongue. "What?"

"Your investigation seems to be stirring up the mud," Marsh said.

Rees nodded. "I warned both your mistress and Mr. Potter that once I begin looking into a murder, I do not stop until I find the answer. Usually that results in stirring up a lot of mud."

His expression troubled, Marsh said no more.

"You can't drive yourself home," Lydia said, more insistently. She looked at Marsh. "Can we spare a groom?"

"I doubt the mistress will permit that," he said.

She nodded and threw the linen roll to the table. "In that case, I'll drive him to Dugard."

Both the men regarded her, appalled.

"Of course you can't," Marsh said.

"I can manage myself," Rees said at the same moment.

Lydia said nothing. She collected her bonnet from the hook and put it on. As she walked to the door, she picked up Rees's jacket. When he did not immediately follow, she said, "Shall we go?"

Marsh looked at Rees. He shrugged and, after struggling to his feet, followed her.

Neither one spoke as they descended the hill, Rees because he felt shaky. Lydia looked around curiously as they traversed the tree break but didn't comment.

She went to the passenger side and held out her arm, ready to assist Rees into the seat. He ignored her and hauled himself into the driver seat with his good arm. He picked up the reins.

"You aren't able to drive home," she insisted.

"I'm fine," Rees said curtly, discovering his left arm had no strength. Cursing his choice of Amos this morning instead of Bessie, who was a sweet-tempered and biddable mare, Rees looped the reins around his right hand. He slapped them down and Amos jolted forward into a walk. Rees didn't dare go any faster. The tendons on the back of his hand and the muscles in his forearm and biceps were already beginning to ache with the strain.

"Will, you are injured. And you aren't a boy anymore. Please, allow me to take the reins." Lydia said with an audible exasperation.

Rees shook his head.

They continued on at a walk. The slow pace offered Rees the

opportunity for some hard thinking. Richard certainly behaved like a guilty man. So why didn't it feel right? Well, for one thing, he thought, answering his own question, Marsh had secrets of his own. And he was a strong healthy man with connections to the Bowditch family. And he'd lied about visiting his sister at the time of Nate's murder.

"Did you speak to Rachel?" Rees asked Lydia, his thoughts veering in another direction.

"I had to, didn't I?" She cast him a sardonic glance. "I told her you and I were friends and swore her to secrecy." She paused and then added slowly, "I believe that helped rather than hurt. She felt comfortable talking to me then. She apologized and assured me she . . . she only wants to protect her son."

Rees caught the hesitation and looked at her, wondering what Lydia had chosen to keep from him. "And?"

"Rachel was frank about the estrangement between herself and her son. Augustus has never forgiven her for not accepting Nate's offer to free her." Lydia drew her brows together. "I don't think he knows the whole story. Rachel wants to remain as she is."

"Maybe Marsh has something to do with that," Rees suggested. "They work closely together—"

Lydia shook her head. "I believe Marsh is already married. No, Rachel is afraid of something. I don't know what, but even living at the beck and call of Mrs. Bowditch is better than leaving the safety of the farm and her kitchen."

"You met Mrs. Bowditch?"

"We spoke for only a few moments," Lydia said carefully. "I saw her for too short a time to develop an impression."

"Ahh. You didn't like her," Rees said. He pulled Amos to a stop. He had to rest his right arm. The muscles were beginning to cramp and his hand trembled from the effort of gripping the reins.

"You're behaving foolishly," Lydia scolded. "Let me drive for a while."

Rees imagined his arrival in Dugard with a woman holding the reins and shook his head once more.

"I'll change places with you before we reach the town," Lydia insisted. "You can drive in, if you must. But at least let me offer you a few moments' rest."

Rees looked at her. She met his gaze, her dark blue eyes stern. Finally he nodded. He tried to climb down, but his right arm was too tired to hold his weight and he half fell into the dust. Lydia slid over and picked up the reins. He struggled a little to climb into the seat but once his foot was on the step, he used his powerful legs to push himself up. With a slap of the leather ribbons upon Amos's withers, they started off once again.

"You've driven yourself before," Rees said, watching her hands.

"Not a wagon, a curricle," she admitted. "And not often. I'm more experienced riding a horse. . . ."

He nodded, thinking that he should be more used to the double nature of women. He knew, better than most men, that the females in one's life were not the frail sex. Pressed by exigency, they could be as strong and as courageous as any man, able to jump in and do a man's work when necessary. It was just difficult for a man to accept that *his* woman, the woman he loved, did not need to rely upon him completely.

"Did you know Richard was hiding in the cottage?" Lydia asked him now, breaking into his thoughts.

"No. I had another purpose. Did you?"

"Of course not, else I would have told you. I suspect only Mrs. Bowditch knew. And maybe Marsh."

That made sense, Rees thought.

"Do you think Richard killed his father?" Lydia asked.

"I don't know." Rees said with a sigh. "All of the evidence points to him, and God knows he thought he had reason. Caldwell assumes that, because he ran, he's guilty. But he didn't run far. This is what I don't understand. If he is guilty, why not deny it in court and take his chances? I doubt he'd ever see the business end of a rope. Nobody's eager to send the son of a large and wealthy landowner to the gallows."

Lydia looked at him, startled. "You're right, of course," she said.

"Richard claims he's innocent. Maybe he is."

"We're missing something."

Rees, noticing the plural, smiled at her and shook his head, ruefully this time. How quickly she had put herself into partnership.

Lydia pulled over in the outskirts of town, and she and Rees switched places. He knew it was a mistake as soon as they'd traveled a few feet. His right forearm and hand, already tired from the previous stretch, began to burn and tremble. He said nothing. Although his world narrowed to the reins in front of him and the fire racing up and down his arm, he vowed to make it into town.

Chapter Seventeen

He managed to drive the half mile or so to the remains of the jail, pulling to a stop with an involuntary groan of relief. Releasing the reins sent a shock of pain through his clenched hand, quickly followed by an intense tingling as the blood began to flow once again.

The smell of smoke and burning still lingered in the air. Lydia regarded the soot-streaked ruin, the jail cells open to the sky, in horrified dismay. "Thank the Lord you rescued Augustus," she said.

"A drifter died in the other cell," Rees said, "so this is still murder."

Caldwell, walking around and around the destruction, saw them and ambled over to the wagon. He cast a curious glance at Lydia, but most of his attention focused upon Rees. "What in Hell happened to you!" the constable exclaimed.

"Richard shot me," Rees said, climbing down very slowly and painfully from the seat.

"What?"

"He was hiding in the weaver's cottage. When I approached it, he shot me. I suppose he was scared."

"Well, I'll go right out there and arrest that boy," Caldwell said.

"And where will you put him? You have no jail. I told him and his mother we'd go out tomorrow morning and talk to him together."

"You think he'll wait for you?" Caldwell asked with a mocking chuckle. "I swear, he'd be in the next state by then."

"He gave his word."

"And you believed him? You're soft on him. He was seen both entering and leaving the cottage within a few minutes of his father's death."

"I don't doubt he struck his father, but he didn't have enough time to beat him to death."

"He could have returned later," Caldwell said.

Rees nodded reluctantly. "True. But so could someone else." He looked at the constable, wondering if he knew of the lay-by. Probably not.

"You'd better get home," Caldwell said, offering his arm to assist Rees into the wagon seat. His powerful odor on top of the pain made Rees retch, throwing up his breakfast into the muddy street. Lydia jumped down and together she and Caldwell shoved Rees up into the wagon seat. Rees saw her nostrils clench, and she backed away from the constable as rapidly as she could.

Once she was back onto the seat, the constable slapped Amos on the rump and the gelding jumped forward, almost toppling Rees to the ground. He threw his weight backwards, pulling on the reins with all his strength. Amos slowed to a walk. Rees could feel the slow crawl of blood leaking out from underneath the bandage on his left arm.

Lydia's scared and angry expression said everything as she climbed down and circled around the wagon to the driver seat. Rees moved over enough to allow her to climb up. She took the reins from his hand and slapped them down upon the gelding's back. Amos broke into a trot. Rees gasped as the jolting gait of the horse sent a throb of pain into his arm with every step, but he refused to complain.

After an eternity of pounding, the churned dirt of the turn into the drive appeared before them. Rees's right arm was almost too tired to hold on. Amos lurched to a stop in front of the farmhouse. Lydia climbed down and sped around the wagon to help Rees dismount. He leaned upon her more than he wished and still hit the ground with a thud. He groaned. The front door slammed and Abby came out upon the porch. Uttering a squeak of consternation, she ran down the steps and put his right arm across her skinny shoulders. Rees could feel the wiry strength in her body.

"What happened, Miss Lydia?"

"Richard Bowditch shot him."

"Just a flesh wound," Rees grunted.

Together the two women got him into the chair in the kitchen. While Abby swung the teakettle over the fire, Lydia hurried into the larder to fetch her medical supplies. She laid out scissors, linen strips, and a basin. Snipping through the now blood-sodden bandage, she bent forward to examine the wound. "This looks nice and clean," she said. "I think it is overuse that started the bleeding again."

Rees said nothing. All he could think of just then was her sweet scent of lavender and honey. His entire body flushed with heat as the pain retreated before his desire. He dared not speak.

Abby poured steaming water into the basin and Lydia threw a selection of dried leaves into it. A sharp acrid odor filled the air. Wetting a rag in the solution, she gently began cleaning the bloody gash. "So far, it is not suppurating," she said, adding in annoyance, "What was that boy thinking?"

Rees shook his head.

"Dinner will be ready soon," Abby said.

"Sit in the parlor for a few moments and rest," Lydia commanded.

Rees nodded obediently. The wound and the harrowing journey home had worn him down to the nubbin. Lydia helped him rise but he lumbered into the parlor under his own power. Subsiding upon the horsehair sofa with a groan, he allowed his eyes to close.

Rees awoke late in the afternoon. For a moment, still caught in a confused dream in which Philip, the Iroquois guide he'd known in the Continental Army, wore Nate's apron, Rees did not know where he was. He'd fallen sideways and now his neck hurt. But someone had removed his shoes and covered him with a light summer quilt. He sat up, the movement sending a throb of pain through his injured arm. Although a little woozy from sleeping in the afternoon, he did feel better. He flexed his right hand. The muscles ached all the way to his shoulder; his uninjured arm, in fact, hurt more than the one with the gunshot wound. He slipped his feet into his shoes and walked into the kitchen.

Humming a Shaker hymn, Lydia was sorting the laundry. Although some clothing had been ironed, Rees noticed that almost a full basket remained. She smiled at him. "You're awake sooner than I expected," she said.

Rees sat down at the table. "I'm starving," he said.

"You missed dinner," she said, moving the piles of clean linens from the kitchen table.

"What did you give me?"

"A drop or two of laudanum." She paused. "You needed the sleep."

Although irked by her duplicity, he couldn't argue with the result. "Where's the girl?"

"Helping David milk." Lydia went to the larder and brought out a loaf of chewy fresh baked bread and a piece of cold egg pie. "I'm more than pleased with her," she added as she stirred up the fire and pushed the kettle over the flames.

"And Augustus?"

"With David and Abby." She paused, the poker hanging from her hand. "Apparently he did not remember the way of it and had to be retaught."

"That's good. I'll be no good for milking for several days," Rees said.

Lydia smiled. "Don't worry, we'll manage." Dropping the poker, she took a cream-colored envelope down from the gray stone mantel. "This was delivered today." As Rees broke the seal, she said, "The boy who delivered it said it is an invitation to the memorial service."

Rees skimmed the page inside. Nate's memorial would be held at St. John's Church at ten thirty, at the end of the regular seven o'clock Sunday service, with dinner to follow at the Bowditch farm.

"Will you attend?" Lydia asked.

"Of course. I owe it to Nate." And, with Marsh busy with so many guests, Rees would have a perfect opportunity to search the wooden chest under the bed. And return Molly's love letters to it. Rising to his feet, he added, "I will check on the kids. One of the Bristols should be arriving soon for Abby."

He could hear Abby's high-pitched laughter as soon as he stepped out of the house. He walked quickly toward the barn and peered inside. From his position by the door, David was hidden behind the stall wall. But Rees could see Abby perched upon the stool, her hands expertly pulling at the cow's teats. The hissing stream of milk into the bucket never faltered. She did not rest her head against the cow's flank but kept her face turned toward David, directing all her attention to him. Augustus might as well have been invisible. David, bantering with the girl, regularly directed comments to the other lad but Augustus answered in monosyllables. Rees suspected Augustus wished he were anywhere but in the barn with the other two. Rees understood. The courtship dance was both embarrassing and irritating to the excluded.

As he retreated from the barn and started back to the house, he realized he and David would have to talk.

Pain woke Rees several times during the night when he rolled onto his wounded arm. When he climbed out of bed he knew he would not be able to drive himself to the Bowditch farm today. Oh, the lips of the wound stung and the area around the injury burned! Although the sympathetic pain down his forearm had disappeared, he found he couldn't lift his left arm above his waist.

When he went downstairs, Lydia was waiting for him, a basin of warm water and a fresh roll of linen before her. "David harnessed Bessie to the buggy for you," she said, cutting away the bandage. "And I'll drive you to Dugard." She leaned forward and inspected the wound. "This looks better, although it's still seeping a little. Does it hurt?" Rees nodded. She painted it with some herbal concoction before winding another bandage over it. The pain diminished slightly.

When he finished breakfast they hurried outside. Augustus waited by the buggy, stroking Bessie's nose. Rees looked at the sky, glad to accept that vehicle today. Gray clouds clotted the western sky like heavy cream. Although rain wasn't falling yet, he expected showers within the hour.

"Are you any closer to finding the man who murdered my father?" Augustus asked as he offered his arm to help Rees up to the step. When Rees glanced over, Augustus managed a lopsided smile and said, "I don't care only for myself. I know I didn't kill him, but I want the person responsible found and punished."

Rees did not answer until he was secure in the seat and Lydia had joined him and taken hold of the reins. "I'm sorry, lad," he said. "I'm still working on it." He hesitated, wondering if he should tell Augustus about the jail, but decided it would be too cruel. "You told me you never visited your father at the farm. Is that true?"

Augustus nodded. "Completely. I knew Mrs. Bowditch didn't want me there."

"And you're estranged from your mother?"

"My father offered to free her, as he did me. She refused. Refused!" His voice rose with his outrage. "What's wrong with her that she should prefer servitude?"

"I don't know," Rees said, glancing at Lydia. "But I'm sure she has her reasons." Life could be so much clearer to the young, without the nuance of experience. "Maybe she was in love with your father. Or maybe she had a frightening experience with slave catchers." Augustus stared at Rees, the suggestion, and the revelation that followed it, sending a ripple of horrified under-standing across his face. "Don't worry, I'll let you know when I learn something."

Lydia looked at Rees and smacked the reins lightly on Bessie's back. They started forward, Bessie's gait smoother than Amos's rough trot. Lydia kept the mare moving at a steady pace and they arrived in Dugard in reasonable time. Caldwell was waiting for them outside the jail's blackened skeleton. Although he seemed surprised to see Lydia in the driver's seat, he said nothing. But he walked around and indicated that she should remove herself to the back. He jumped up and took the reins.

"Bessie is a gentle mare," Rees said, "with a soft mouth." Caldwell threw him an annoyed look and responded by slapping the reins down upon the horse's withers. She jumped forward and they careened west on Church Street. Rees clutched at the wagon side with his good hand. "Slow down, man," he cried. The constable did not reply and kept Bessie at a rapid trot the entire distance to the Bowditch property. By the time they reached the front door, Bessie's muzzle was flecked with foam.

A familiar buggy and horse were already there, pulled to one side, but Rees didn't have time to examine them. Marsh came out to the porch. "Mrs. Bowditch has been looking out for you for at least an hour."

"We are here now," he said, hearing the reproof in Marsh's voice. He climbed down very carefully. Lydia followed, and Marsh looked at her in surprise. He glanced at Rees with surmise.

"She drove him into town," Caldwell said. "He had to protect his wound, the wound your young master inflicted upon him."

"Of course," Marsh said with a bow.

"Please see that Bessie is cooled down and watered," Rees asked. "The constable pushed her hard." Rees detected a scornful gleam in Marsh's dark eyes before he hid his expression with another bow.

"Certainly. Mrs. Bowditch and Master Richard are waiting for you in the office," he said.

"Nate let him get away with thinking he's a white man's equal." Caldwell said when he offered to assist Lydia to the ground. Refusing his hand, she jumped down. "You've got to keep his kind in their places."

"From the stories I've heard," Rees said, not bothering to disguise his disgust, "Nate handed off his responsibilities to Marsh. Without him, this farm would be neither productive nor economical."

"And that was his mistake," Caldwell retorted.

Lydia looked at Rees and shook her head in warning. So he did not reply, although several arguments trembled upon his tongue. They entered the house in silence, Lydia promptly disappearing to the kitchen.

"They're waiting in Master Nate's office," Marsh said, assuming a subservience that was foreign to the man Rees knew. He couldn't bear to watch.

They walked the few steps toward the office, and Rees held up his hand for silence. He could hear the subdued murmur of Molly Bowditch's voice and paused by the door to listen.

"This is important," Molly was saying to her son. "Remember what I told you. . . ." Richard made a small sound of protest, his gaze lighting upon the door. Molly whirled. "Come in, Mr. Rees." she said, her tone neither gracious nor inviting. Rees stepped into view. Both Mother and son stared at him, both nervous although Molly's trepidation was mixed with belligerence. Seen together, they looked nothing alike. Richard's coloring was darker and his eyes were brown rather than blue.

And George Potter, his expression self-conscious, stood protectively behind them both.

"We'd like to speak to Richard alone, please," Rees said, gesturing the constable forward.

"No," she said. "With me and Mr. Potter or not at all."

"With all due respect," Rees said, bowing, "Richard is a man and no longer requires the shelter of his mother's skirts."

The fear and anger upon Molly's face congealed into fury. She did not move. But Richard smiled.

"Please, Mama," he said. "Mr. Rees is correct. I am a man and well able to fight my own battles. I would prefer it if you and Mr. Potter waited outside."

Molly turned to glare at her son, her eyes full of resentment, and then she rose stiffly to her feet and stalked out. Her delicate muslin gown fluttered enticingly around her and Caldwell turned to watch her go. Rees was more interested in Potter. The lawyer scurried out without glancing at the other men.

Rees sat down in the chair across from Richard but he said nothing until Caldwell pulled up a chair beside him. "Do you believe Augustus guilty of your father's murder?" Rees asked.

Richard's lips began to tremble and he shook his head. "No. Augie wouldn't hurt a fly. And he never came back home."

"Never?" Caldwell asked, leaning forward.

Richard shook his head. "Not that I knew of. Especially when I was at school. I wasn't here for Augie and he wouldn't visit his mother. He's been angry at her for years."

"What did you argue with your father about?" Caldwell demanded.

Richard hesitated for several seconds. "I wasn't the only one who fought with him," he burst out at last. "Everybody did. The man wouldn't see reason."

Rees recalled Mr. Salley's statement. "Did you hear him arguing with someone before you went into the cottage?"

Richard hesitated. He didn't want to admit that he had and Rees wondered why. "Yes," the lad said at last. "I heard raised voices as I came up the path. But nobody was inside. So I don't know who it was."

And that was a lie if Rees had ever heard one.

"Were there horses in the lay-by when you came through it?"

Richard hesitated. "Yes," he said slowly.

"Describe them."

"A chestnut."

"Do you know who owns that horse?"

"Don't know," Richard said indifferently. And that might be the truth.

"Is this important?" Caldwell asked. "Do you know how many chestnuts there are in Dugard? Scores."

"You didn't see an old gray?" Rees fixed his gaze sternly upon the boy.

"No," Richard said defiantly.

Another lie. Rees smiled; clearly Richard recognized Marsh's mount. "Man or woman?" Rees asked. "Who argued with your father—man or woman?"

Richard rolled his eyes. "Man, of course." Then he clamped his lips tightly together. Rees didn't think he would get anything more about that from him, not at the moment anyway. But he could easily guess whom Richard overheard arguing with his father: Marsh.

"What did you and your father argue about?" Caldwell asked, directing a glare at Rees. "This time."

"I want to get married," Richard said. "He doesn't like the girl. I don't know why."

Rees waited to see if Caldwell would speak. Did the constable even know about Elizabeth Carleton?

"Why not?" Caldwell asked.

"He said I'm too young. That's a lie, of course. He was only a year or two older when he married my mother." Richard shrugged. "So, we've been arguing for months."

"You went into the cottage," Rees said. "And you began arguing?"

Richard scowled. "Well, sort of. He was already angry, you see. He told me he couldn't speak to me now. I . . . insisted. He said I couldn't marry Elizabeth, and that was final." He twisted his hands together and Rees noticed the bitten nails, right down to the quick.

"And then what?"

Richard wrung his hands. Although he kept his head lowered, Rees saw the tears filling his eyes. "I lost my temper. I picked up the scutching knife and I hit him and blood flew out of his head and he fell down." Richard shuddered. "He was groaning. And I ran."

"How many times did you hit him?" Caldwell asked.

"Once or twice."

"What did you do then?" Rees asked. He was trying to reserve judgment, but this looked bad for the boy.

"He called out to me. I knelt beside him and I could see he was hurt. But when he looked up at me, his eyes opened and he spoke to me."

"Did you put his head into your lap?" Rees asked.

Richard stared at him in surprise. "How did you know that?'

"What did you do then?"

"I ran home. I swear he was still alive when I left the cottage." Richard looked up at Rees. "You've got to believe me. I didn't kill him."

"Did you see anyone as you were running away?" Rees asked.

Richard shook his head. "Only Mr. Salley, coming down from the barn."

"If you're not guilty," Caldwell said in a cold voice, "why did you run?"

"You think I'm a murderer," Richard said.

"Until you prove otherwise," the constable said.

"Why didn't you come to me, Richard?" Rees asked. "Your mother hired me to prove your innocence. I just wanted to ask a few questions."

Richard looked at Rees in silence. When he finally spoke his voice was pitched so low, Rees could hardly hear it. "She thinks I'm guilty, Mr. Rees. She says she believes I'm innocent, but she doesn't. Not really. I can see it in her eyes."

Rees could not reassure the boy. Molly might believe Richard was guilty and still fight for him like a bear for her cub. That was a terrible weight to put on someone.

"Well, Mr. Carleton believes you are innocent," Caldwell said.

Richard looked up. "He does?" He smiled, radiant with happiness. "I daresay I will be getting married, then."

"And Augustus?" Rees asked sternly. "You aren't going to let your brother assume your guilt, are you?"

"Of course not." Richard's gaze slid to the constable. "You know Augustus is innocent, don't you?" Now that he'd told his tale, he sat relaxed and at his ease.

"He might be the man you heard arguing with your father," Caldwell said. "But I admit, that doesn't seem likely." He heaved a heavy sigh. "I suppose we'll have to continue looking."

Rees looked at Richard. Since yesterday, when fear and panic had brought him to firing upon Rees, the boy had slept and bathed. He was now garbed in a fine coat and a white silk waistcoat. Silver buttons gleamed at the knees of his breeches. He looked a perfect young gentleman. "You know Kate is expecting your child," Rees said.

"She says so," Richard said indifferently. Rees did not look away, and under the weight of his disapproving regard, Richard blushed. "I never promised marriage," he said. "I only wanted to have some fun. And she never said different."

"When you are older and hopefully wiser," Rees said, thinking that that mark must be many years in the future, "you'll know that women look upon this 'fun' differently than we do. The price is much higher for them. And right now it looks as though you're leaving Kate to pay it alone."

"She's only a nursemaid," Richard said. He sounded like a sulky eight-year-old.

"He's answered all of your questions," Molly said, appearing at the door. "There is no more to be said." She hurried to her son's side.

Rees thought there was much more to be said. He would try to speak to the boy again, alone this time, without the constable, who was clearly James Carleton's man, or Richard's fiercely protective mother. "Very well," he said, bowing. "Until Sunday, then."

Molly nodded, her hand resting upon Richard's shoulder.

"Definitely the favored child," Caldwell said as they went into the hall.

"Indeed," Rees agreed. "What do you think? Guilty or innocent?"

Caldwell smiled sourly. "Oh, guilty for certain. But he has powerful connections. And there's enough doubt that he won't hang."

Rees shook his head. "What about the man arguing with Nate before Richard arrived?"

Caldwell looked at Rees sardonically. "If there was a man, which I doubt."

"It could have been one of the card players," Rees said.

"Don't tell me you think the boy is innocent?" Caldwell looked at Rees in disbelief.

Rees did not speak. God help him, he thought Richard might be.

"I wouldn't have thought you were so gullible." Caldwell shook his head incredulously.

"Gullible? I don't think so. I simply have too many questions. Yes, it looks bad for the boy, but guilty of murder? I am not convinced."

"Huh. Are we going back to town now?"

"Not yet. I want to speak to someone."

"Who? That beautiful Negress? Or that redheaded Shaker?"

Caldwell spoke with a faint leer. Rees looked at him, ready to smack the constable down if he made another such remark. Caldwell saw his expression and said quickly, "I'll wait by the wagon, then. Too many women down there, all chattering." He slouched out the front door, leaving a faint lingering taint behind him.

Rees waited until the constable had passed through the front door before turning back toward Nate's office. He paused in the doorway. "A word, please," Rees said, not caring that he'd interrupted the conversation between Molly Bowditch and George Potter. "I wonder, do you recognize the name Cornelius Lattimore?"

Potter stared off into space, his forehead wrinkled. "No," he said, "I don't. But the name does sound vaguely familiar, as though I've heard it in the past. Why? What importance is he to you?" He still could not meet Rees's eyes.

"None, that I know of," Rees said, not altogether truthfully.

"I'll ask my father," Potter said. "He knows all of the lawyers hereabouts."

"Thank you," Rees said in a chilly voice. This time he did cross the front hall and walked to the back of the house toward the kitchen stairs. He planned to assure Rachel of Augustus's safety, that was true, but his primary target was Lydia. Did she plan to return to town now or should Rees promise to send David after her?

Everyone looked up at him as he entered the kitchen, Lydia with some wariness. When he approached her, the glances directed at them told him that the women at least knew of the connection between them. "The constable is driving me back to Dugard," he said. She did not speak, but her gaze shot to his wounded arm. "I believe I can make it home from there. Someone else will come for you." He hoped she would understand he meant David.

"Thank you, Mr. Rees," she said. But her effort to sound as though they were simply acquaintances failed; he knew that from the knowing smiles, even though no one looked at them directly. The cat was out of the bag, and he could now expect this juicy bit of gossip to make the rounds. As he left the kitchen by way of the outside door and climbed the hill, he wondered how he felt about it. He prodded his feelings and found to his surprise that he was not as unhappy as he'd expected. He didn't like the prospect of serving as the center of this gossip, but he'd become comfortable with thinking of himself and Lydia as a couple.

Chapter Eighteen

Caldwell and Rees passed almost the entire distance into town in silence. Finally the constable spoke. "What do you intend to do now?"

"What do you mean?"

"You've accomplished precisely what Mistress Molly asked of you: You've freed her son. Are you finished with your questions?"

Rees, whose thoughts were still focused upon Lydia, took a moment to switch back to Nate's murder. "No. I've spoken to Richard, but he hasn't been declared innocent, beyond a doubt. Do you imagine that because Richard's connections may save him from hanging, he won't spend the rest of his life under a cloud? You still think he's guilty. Unless I name the murderer, many people will always believe he's guilty. Not just him but Augustus, too. And he doesn't have Richard's social standing to protect him."

"Maybe Richard should live under a cloud," Caldwell said dryly. "He looks guilty to me."

"I still have questions, " Rees repeated. He thought he might stop by the Contented Rooster for a little chat with Susannah, and see what else she knew about James Carleton and about his daughter Elizabeth.

Caldwell drove the wagon to the coffeehouse and helped Rees

alight, but he declined to enter, preferring the rougher hospitality of the Bull. So Rees went in by himself, not displeased to question Jack and Susannah without the constable in attendance.

"What happened to you?" Susannah asked, pointing at his wounded arm. Rees glanced down at the bandage, visible under his linen shirt. The gash hurt and the scab pulled with motion, but he had successfully pushed the discomfort to the back of his mind.

"Richard Bowditch shot me. It's nothing."

"I daresay that's why there's blood on your sleeve," Jack said, coming up behind his wife. Rees glanced at the stain. It was already dry.

"More questions?" Susannah asked.

"Yes. I hardly know what to ask first," Rees said. Jack pulled out a chair for his wife and both of them sat down. "I spoke to Richard. He admitted to arguing with his father and striking him with the scutching knife."

"But you don't believe he's guilty," Susannah said softly, her eyes never leaving Rees's face.

"It just doesn't feel right," Rees said. "Several people heard Nate arguing with someone else." And if Dr. Wrothman did not have such a solid alibi, Rees would suspect he was the other man. "Richard might have interrupted him, whoever he is. He could have hidden upstairs and beaten Nate to death after Richard left. And of course, I am not certain of the identity of that man." Although Rees, suspecting it was Marsh, added quickly, "And the mystery man might be innocent as well."

"You've cast enough doubt on Richard's guilt that he won't hang," Jack said. "Surely you need do nothing else."

"Caldwell says he won't, not with his connections," Rees said glumly.

Susannah said nothing, but when Rees met her eyes he saw understanding and sympathy.

Three men, well-to-do farmers, appeared at the door and Jack heaved himself to his feet. As he hurried toward them, Susannah leaned across the table and said, "You know Caldwell is James Carleton's man?"

Rees nodded. "I know. In fact, let's talk about James. I know King Carleton hired Nate to fetch James back from London, not once but several times."

"James spent the entire War in London, carousing if the gossip is to be believed."

"Gambling away his patrimony?" Rees guessed. She shrugged. "Why Nate?"

"I don't know. I suspect only Mr. Carleton and Nate knew the answer to that question. But Nate went over at least four times, maybe five, to fetch the boy. James always fled back to London. Well, I suppose he can't be blamed; his mother and sisters were in London. Only his father remained here, and he was not a pleasant person even at the best of times. But when Nate went overseas for the last time, he returned with James's entire family, including his wife, Charlotte, and baby girl. Elizabeth."

"I see. So James and Nate became friends. And fellow card players. Did either one play deep? Especially James?"

"Not that we ever heard," Jack said, approaching the table and sitting down. "Of course, Carleton is as rich as Croesus and owns half the property around town. And Nate didn't do badly either."

"I don't think they played that often," Susannah said, frowning at her husband.

"We don't know that," Jack said. "They were here once or twice and at the Bull maybe once or twice. Who knows where they were otherwise?"

Rees considered the cottage. They could have played cards there every night with no one the wiser. "I'll ask Marsh," he said.

Jack rose to his feet again and looked pointedly at his wife. "We've got to get back to work. With our cook gone—"

"One last question." Rees drained his cup. "I don't remember Caldwell from school."

"His father came to Dugard as a laborer and then just remained here," Susannah replied. "He was about ten. I was older then, sixteen, so you were in the Army. His mother took in laundry to survive." She also stood up.

"Caldwell is younger than I am?" Rees asked in amazement.

Susannah nodded. "I always thought there was some mystery there. Cleanliness is still important to his mother." She met Rees's gaze. "And she continues to take in laundry even though Caldwell supports her."

Rees nodded. Some mystery there, indeed.

He threw a coin onto the table and walked out to his wagon. Buggies and wagons now occupied all the spaces around him. Climbing into the seat was a struggle but he managed. Since he was already parked on Water Street, he followed the road east out of town.

Tired out by Caldwell's snappy pace earlier, Bessie walked home and Rees was able to let the reins lie slack. He was grateful; the pace was gentle upon his wounded arm. She broke into an eager trot when they turned up the drive into the farm, but Rees let her have her head. David popped out of the barn when he heard the wagon wheels on the hardpan and ran to help.

Rees slept poorly Friday night; every time he rolled over, a burst of flame burned up his wounded arm. As a result, he overslept and when he finally went downstairs he found everyone gone, except for Abby. Lydia, of course, was at the Bowditch farm. "And David is at market," Abby said.

After breakfast, Rees went upstairs. His sore left arm couldn't throw the shuttle, but he could turn it and nudge it through the warp until his right hand grabbed it. Once he had a rhythm, and was able to weave fairly efficiently, he turned his thoughts from his personal concerns to Nate's death. Tomorrow, when he's at the Bowditch farm after the memorial service, he would speak again to Mr. Salley, the hand that had witnessed Richard fleeing from the cottage. Maybe he knew the owner of the chestnut. And also to Kate, the nursemaid. Had she seen anyone running from the cottage after Richard's departure? The killer might have been hiding up stairs while the drama played out in the kitchen below. Rees suspected he would have fled through the lay-by and ridden away, but Marsh, if he were the other man, might have gone to the house.

Of course, Rees intended to finish searching the trunk hidden under the bed. He suspected—was almost certain, in fact—that the item for which Marsh searched was hidden there. Richard's brief residence, and the upcoming memorial, prevented Marsh from searching for it, but after tomorrow he would have both time and opportunity. Rees must grab his chance now.

He turned his thoughts to Marsh. Could he be Nate's murderer? He'd assumed Marsh's innocence at first when everyone said he had gone to visit his sister, but now Rees knew the other man had been on the farm at that time after all. And he was probably the man with whom Nate had been arguing.

And the Carletons. Rees sighed. He didn't fancy another argument with James Carleton, and anyway he wasn't sure he could drive out to the estate. He moved his left arm experimentally. A shock of pain shot down his biceps. Maybe David would be willing to help? Oh, how Rees hated to be dependent.

"Mr. Rees." Abigail hesitated in the doorway. "You have a visitor. A Mr. Potter? I put him in the parlor."

Rees stood up so suddenly, the bench fell over, and ran downstairs.

George Potter had not seated himself. Instead he roamed around the perimeter of the room, examining the silhouettes upon the wall. In his black jacket and buff breeches, he looked like a townsman. But his waistcoat was plain linen and Rees suspected that in Potter's mind he was casually dressed.

"This is a surprise," Rees said.

Potter turned with a nervous smile. "It's market day. The street outside my office is congested with people. And the noise! I thought a quiet drive out to your farm would be just the thing."

"Hmm," Rees said dubiously. "Why are you really here?"

"You asked me for some information. Remember? Cornelius Lattimore?"

Inviting Potter to sit, Rees dropped into a chair. "You know who he is?"

"I asked my father. He knew. Mr. Lattimore is an attorney, practicing out of New Winstead."

"Of your father's generation, I suppose?" Rees asked. Potter nodded.

"Yes." He frowned. "Where did you hear the name? Was Nate planning on employing him?"

Abby's sudden entrance with a tray spared Rees from answering. He didn't know what he would say. Nate, after all, had not chosen to consult his friend George Potter. Abby offered Potter a cup, not one of the earthenware mug Rees used for every day but one of his mother's thin porcelain cups. Potter looked at it in surprise and then at the pound cake nestled on a china plate beside the teapot. Rees realized he would have ignored the duties of a host; he must remember to thank the girl.

When Abby withdrew, Potter turned to Rees and said, "Where's Miss Farrell?"

Rees didn't know what to say. Confess that she was working at the Bowditch farm? What would Potter think? That Rees couldn't support his family?

Potter watched the play of emotions speed across his friend's face and put down his teacup. "You know," he said, "no one will blame you for remarrying."

"What?" Rees stared at the other man in astonishment.

"How long has Dolly been gone? Six, seven years?"

"Almost eight." He cleared his throat. The sympathy upon Potter's face compelled Rees to look away.

"It's time, Will. I know you loved Dolly. But wedding vows say 'Until death do you part' for a reason."

"I don't want to talk about it."

"I've seen you look at Miss Farrell. You won't persuade me you don't desire her. Or is it that—well, she is a Shaker. I suppose she doesn't wish to wed." The pity with which he regarded Rees made him squirm.

"I said I don't want to talk about it," he repeated so loudly, Potter jumped. He glared at Rees. A cold silence settled around them. After a fleeting hesitation, Rees said, "Why were you at the Bowditch farm when I went to question Richard?"

Potter stiffened. "Molly came to me and asked me to be there. She's frightened for her son."

"Hmmm. How old were you when you married?" Rees asked.

"Twenty-two," Potter said in surprise.

"I was but eighteen. Richard is seventeen. In a few months,

he'll reach his majority. And he's looking to wed. I think Molly needs to stop sheltering her son behind her skirts." He wanted to ask Potter how his wife would feel about his friendship with Molly Bowditch but bit his tongue at the last minute.

"I don't think she should be blamed for wanting to protect her son from a murder charge," Potter said, rising to his feet. "Especially since she feels Caldwell will take the easy way out and hang the boy."

"Caldwell will not," Rees said. "Whatever he may personally feel, the constable doesn't believe Richard will even appear in court. What's more, James Carleton believes the boy is innocent. You're too close, George." He stopped himself from remarking upon Nate's choice of an out-of-town lawyer, but Potter understood.

"I suppose I'll see you in town," Potter said angrily, putting on his beaver hat. He walked quickly from the room. Rees followed him to the porch with some vague intention of calling after his old friend. But he didn't know what to say, and anyway Potter was already mounting his bay.

"I seem to be irritating everyone I meet," Rees said aloud. He lingered on the porch, looking at the first of the changing leaves. With the approach of late September, some of the overeager sugar maples had put on their autumn scarlet. Brown leaves, although not so many as would come, littered the driveway. Only a few weeks of good weather left before the cold grasped the farm in its icy fingers. Rees dreaded the coming of winter; he felt trapped after only a few weeks of cold and the enforced habitation inside.

The sound of hooves drew his attention and when he looked down at the road he saw dust. Potter must be returning. But instead of a lone horse, a buggy turned into the drive; David pulled up in front of the porch, arriving home much earlier than Rees expected. And Amos was lathered up and blowing hard. Augustus, who must have been keeping watch, ran out from the barn toward the horse. He uttered a short high-pitched cry of distress. Rees, who'd been wondering why David had not sprung from the seat as he usually did, raced down the steps.

David, leaning heavily upon Augustus's arm, climbed carefully down from the seat. He moved stiffly and when Rees raced around to the front, he saw bruises stippling David's jaw. His nose was still dribbling blood.

"What happened?" Rees cried.

"I'm all right. He took me by surprise," David said, wincing as he stepped gingerly down from the high step.

"Who took you by surprise?" Rees demanded. "Who?"

"Uncle Sam. He saw me at market. He went for me. Luckily, I'd already sold most of the eggs, so only a few were broken."

Rees regarded his son in growing anger. "He attacked you?"

"It wasn't that serious. Your friend Caldwell stepped in and arrested him." David smiled faintly. "Last I saw of my uncle, he was being dragged away—to the tack room at Wheeler's Livery, since there is no jail right now."

"Was he drunk?" Rees asked.

"No more than usual." David shook his head. "He really thinks this farm is his and he blames you for taking it away."

Rees said nothing. Ejecting his sister and her husband from the farm had been an ugly business and it hadn't ended. How long before Sam and Caro accepted the truth?

"Let's get him inside," Augie said, putting his shoulder under David's arm. Rees hastened to the other side and together they assisted the boy into the kitchen. Abigail immediately ran for the medical supplies. "I'll take care of Amos," Augustus said.

Rees said into the sudden and probably short-lived moment of privacy, "I'm sorry."

"This wasn't your fault." David collapsed into a kitchen chair with a huff of effort.

"Yes, it was. I should have paid more attention all along." Rees looked at his son in shame.

"Uncle Sam wasn't so bad before. He just got worse and worse, I don't know why." Perplexity creased David's brow.

"I'm sorry I blamed you for Lydia's decision. She's . . . strong-willed."

"I know you want to protect her. I understand." He looked over his father's head. When Rees turned, he saw Abigail waiting by the door with a basin of bandages. She smiled at David as though they two were the only ones in the room. "But Lydia won't allow that. No, that isn't right. It's not the caring that's behind the desire to protect, it's the restriction of her independence." He stopped, frustrated with his inability to fully describe Lydia's feelings.

"Making her an inferior," Rees said in understanding.

David nodded. "She thinks you're demeaning her." He paused. "I suppose I should have told you."

"You would have been caught in the middle," Rees said, not liking the picture he saw of himself. "You like her?"

"Yes," David said with a nod. "Mother would have approved. . . ." Unsettled by the approving inclusion of both Dolly and Lydia in one sentence, Rees said nothing.

Abby approached the table, subtly forcing Rees to move back. She began sponging away the blood from David's face, leaning closer to him than Rees thought necessary. And touching him with glancing pats and caresses. The connection between them was so intimate, Rees felt as though he were intruding. He backed away but did not dare leave the young people in the kitchen alone. He must somehow find an opportunity to talk to David.

And he must deal with Sam.

Chapter Nineteen

Rees went to the church on Sunday morning for Nate's memorial. But he froze outside, unable to pass through those double wooden doors. He hadn't been inside this small stone building since Dolly's service almost eight years ago. Recalling her funeral brought on a flood of strong feelings that rooted him to the courtyard outside, despite the curious and disapproving glances directed his way.

David and Lydia both had already gone inside. She hadn't come up to the house yesterday, upon her return from the Bowditch farm, and although they'd driven into Dugard this morning, David's presence had inhibited Rees from speaking openly. She, in turn, was polite but Rees felt her continuing reserve like a knife to the heart. Especially since she and David talked comfortably together, without restraint.

Muttering "ridiculous" to himself, Rees forced himself to walk up the stone path and pass through the front door. But he stopped in the vestibule, breathing hard, as guilt and grief crashed upon him.

"Are you all right?" Caldwell grasped Rees's arm, his penetrating body odor clearing Rees's head with a rush. He nodded and detached the constable's hand from his sleeve. But, although he moved forward, he went no farther than the back of the church, behind the hand-carved pews. All the seats were full and it looked as though most of the town had come to honor Nate. More were arriving; the throng pressed in around Rees, surging to the front and filling the space behind him. He did not possess the will to press through to the front.

Father Sperling, standing at the lectern in the front, burst into speech. He looked older and grayer than Rees remembered. His praise changed Nate into someone completely unfamiliar. Suddenly spinning around, Rees fought his way through the crowd and back into the crisp morning air. His heart pounded. Furiously he began pacing through the cemetery.

The graves in the churchyard belonged to the early settlers. Some of the families represented here had died out or moved on, and the names were unfamiliar, even to Rees. Both Dolly and his parents were buried in the family graveyard on the farm, with the other members of the Rees family. And where was Nate? Had Molly Bowditch buried him in the graveyard on the farm Thomas now worked, next to his parents?

Footsteps thudded up behind Rees. When he turned, he saw Caldwell hurrying up behind him. "Just making sure you're all right," Caldwell said, regarding the weaver in concern.

"Just thinking about death and funerals," Rees said.

Caldwell nodded. "My mother is still alive," he murmured. Since this was the first personal bit of information shared by the constable, Rees did not reveal his knowledge.

"She lives around here?"

"Down by the river. In the family hovel."

Rees tried to think of a question that didn't sound intrusive but before he could formulate one, the church doors opened and the first wave of mourners surged out; mostly townspeople and single men he didn't recognize. Businessmen maybe from neighboring towns? Was Cornelius Lattimore, the mysterious lawyer, among them? Rees scrutinized each face carefully as if he might guess.

Then Molly Bowditch and her children exited, blinking in the bright sun, and Rees directed all his attention to them. The widow made great play with her lacy handkerchief, mopping up a few delicate tears glittering like diamonds upon her porcelain cheeks.

Her children did not express their grief so attractively. Grace's sobbing was audible and her handkerchief too sodden to wipe away the tears streaming down her cheeks. Richard did not weep but his eyes were red and swollen and any effort to respond to condolences contorted his mouth into a silent scream of pain.

Both children fled to the protection of the carriage as soon as they could. Molly smiled bravely as she acknowledged the condolences offered her.

Then Thomas Bowditch and his family came out of the church. When he looked at his sister-in-law, he scowled with mingled fury and grief. Rees took two steps in Thomas's direction but paused, unwilling to intrude into what was clearly an emotional time. Thomas turned to his wife. She took his arm and they hurried out of the yard to their buggy. Rees doubted that branch of the Bowditch family would attend the memorial dinner—no matter how much they wished to honor Nate.

All the people employed at the Bowditch farm came out of the church in a group, Lydia among them, and were hustled to the waiting wagons. Of course, they must hasten back to the house and prepare for the arrival of the guests. Rees noticed that although Marsh was present, and assisting in dividing the help among the waiting wagons, Rachel was not. Molly Bowditch had been unable to resist that little bit of cruelty.

And now James Carleton, flanked by his family of women,

stepped through the church's wooden doors. Rees turned to look. Mrs. Carleton was as tiny and as pink and white and fair as a porcelain statuette, just as Potter said. Eschewing black, she wore a gray silk gown so pale, it was almost white and as luminescent as a pearl. It exactly matched James's waistcoat, although the pale silk of his garment was heavily embroidered in subtle shades of cream and gray. He wore a black coat and the matching black long trousers that were becoming so popular overseas.

Mrs. Carleton had passed her blond beauty on to the two eldest girls. The taller of the two, Richard's beloved, had also inherited her mother's dainty and regular features. Only her dark brown eyes and fleshy lips came from her father, and on her the rosy fullness beckoned a man with seductive promise. Elizabeth's younger sister was also blond, although her fair hair was a shade or two darker, and she appeared just old enough to put it up. She, too, was very pretty but a paler shadow of her beautiful older sister.

Only the youngest of the three resembled James. Dark-haired, stocky, and with that pugnacious outthrust jaw, she was the boy her father should have had. She scowled ferociously at everyone, already aware, at the tender age of eight, of her unfortunate appearance. Rees could just imagine all the comments she'd probably heard; people could be so heartless.

Richard peered through the carriage window, staring at Elizabeth longingly, and made as if to jump out. But the glance she returned, although it included longing and desire, was nuanced with uncertainty. James nodded at the lad but made a quick and furtive warning motion with his hand. And Mrs. Carleton, throwing a dark glance at Richard, grasped her daughter's arm and pulled her toward the elaborate Carleton carriage.

"Enjoying Dugard's own little *Romeo and Juliet* performance?" George Potter murmured into Rees's ear.

He jumped and whirled. "It's . . . interesting." He would not have understood Potter's allusion but for Lydia. "James seems not so opposed as Mrs. Carleton."

"She wants a title for her daughter," said Mrs. Potter with a scornful frown.

"And Elizabeth is so lovely, she may obtain one," Potter said. Rees nodded. "Will you be at the dinner?"

"Yes. I have a few more questions for the nursemaid and so on." Rees wished he did not wonder about his old friend's part in the web of Dugard society.

"I saw Miss Farrell in the wagon with the Bowditch help," Potter said with a knowing expression. Rees sighed and nodded. "I can't believe you're desperate for the few pennies she earns. Or did you send a Christian into the lion's den?"

"She chose to assist me," Rees said in an icy tone. "Insisted upon it, in fact. Please tell no one."

"Of course not," Potter agreed. "I wouldn't want to put her in any danger." He eyed the other man with some disapproval. "But I wonder that you permitted her to do this."

"If you knew her, you wouldn't," Rees said with a snort.

"We women are far more capable than you men believe," Mrs. Potter said, turning her clever eyes upon her husband. "I'd be interested in hearing how Miss Farrell fares. And what she thinks of Mrs. Bowditch. Ahh, there's my Sally," Mrs. Potter's gaze moved away from the men. "I must get home; I have children to feed." She nodded politely at Rees, admonished her husband not to stay too long, and darted down the walk toward home.

"I'll drive with you if I may," Potter said as David drove up to them. Rees hesitated. He no longer felt completely comfortable with Potter. The moment of silence rapidly became uncomfortable, and Rees nodded reluctantly.

Potter offered Rees an arm up. "How is your gunshot wound doing?" he asked.

Rees moved his arm back and forth experimentally. "It's still sore but much better. I think I'll be able to begin driving myself again soon."

Potter and David exchanged a look. "You don't want to rush it," the attorney said, clambering up the step and squeezing into the rear seat. No one suggested the six-foot plus Rees fold himself into the back.

"Exactly," David muttered as he grasped the reins. The resulting silence was awkward.

"There's been some vandalism at the smithy," Potter said. "Branding Augustus as the murderer."

Rees looked at the lawyer in horror. "But he grew up here," he protested. "And he's Nate's son."

"Some people will never be able to see beyond skin color," Potter said regretfully. "It's human nature. Fortunately, he's safe for now."

By the time they reached the Bowditch farm, the front drive and much of the yard were filled with buggies and wagons. No horses, though, and as they came to a stop Fred Salley appeared. "I'll park the buggy, if you don't mind," he said to Rees. "And your cattle'll be loosed in the paddock with the others."

Rees nodded and turning to Potter he said, "Go on in. I'll follow you directly." The lawyer looked surprised but obeyed. Rees waited until Potter was out of earshot before speaking. "Mr. Salley," he said, "the evening Master Nate was killed and you walked down through the lay-by to the road, you saw several horses."

"Richard's gelding, Marsh's gray nag, and a chestnut," Salley said with a nod.

"When we spoke before, you said it could be a farmer's nag. I wondered if you had discovered who owned it."

Salley shook his head but the movement stopped abruptly, and Rees realized the hand had thought of something. "Not a farmer's horse, a gentleman's."

"What did he look like? Did you recognize him?"

"Beautiful gelding, white stocking on his back rear foot," Salley said. "Don't know who he belongs to."

Rees remembered seeing a chestnut with a white stocking recently but couldn't recall where. "One of the gentlemen who played cards with Master Nate?"

"Maybe. They usually arrive after I've gone. And not Mr. Hansen, he drives a buggy. Too stout to ride a horse, you know," he said with a grin. "Not Mr. Potter's. He rides a bay. Nor Mr. Carleton's. He rides a wild black stallion called Lucifer. Saw that horse a few times when Mr. Carleton came to visit the master. None of us wanted to go near him."

"Thank you." Rees said. Deep in thought, he watched the groom unhitch the horses and lead them away. So, whose chestnut was it in the lay-by that day? Rees would wager his farm that the chestnut's owner had been in Nate's cottage. Had that man murdered Nate after Richard struck him and then fled?

After several minutes of thought, Rees filed away his questions and went up the steps into the house. The affluent members of Dugard society congregated in the emerald parlor. Rees hesitated by the door, watching Potter greet the men in a group that included Dr. Wrothman and Piggy Hansen. Now a magistrate, he looked like an older version of the boy Rees recalled: chubby and self-satisfied, his eyes buried in pillows of fat and his small red lips pursed together. But Rees didn't know most of the others and had no interest in making polite conversation with either Wrothman or Hansen. He slipped around them al-most furtively, searching for the widow and her children.

He found both Richard and Grace flanking their mother, Grace pinned to Molly's side by her mother's tight grip. The girl's eyes were still red, her skin was pale, and she looked worn out against her poorly dyed black frock. Richard nodded at Rees, his expression wary.

"Mr. Rees," Molly said.

"Your father would not want to see you so distraught," Rees said to Grace, taking her free hand gently into his large freckled paw. She looked at him, her eyes filling with tears.

"Exactly what I told her," Molly said irritably. "But she in-sisted upon wearing black. She looks like a crow." She twitched a fold of the streaky black gown in distaste. Rees suspected Grace had dyed her dress herself, yearning to honor her father with a clear proof of her grief.

"I miss him," she whispered, looking at Rees from Nate's blue eyes.

"I know," Rees said, his own eyes smarting. "I know you do." He pressed her hand and released it. "I'm looking for Kate."

"She's outside with Ben, under the tree—," she began.

"Why do you need to speak to her?" Richard interrupted indignantly. Rees did not reply. As he walked past the boy, Rees stared intently into Richard's face until he looked away. But he looked angry rather than ashamed.

Unwilling to run the gamut of the important men, the weaver hurried toward the back door. Jack and Susannah were standing just inside the parlor door; Susannah perched upon the edge of a chair. They looked uncomfortable.

"I didn't expect to see you here," Rees said, coming to a stop.

"We thought we should attend," Jack said.

"For Nate," Susannah added.

"Who's minding the coffeehouse?"

"We don't open until afternoon on Sundays," Jack said.

"If we open up at all today," Susannah said.

Rees looked at Jack for clarification.

"It's been a struggle since Ruth left," he said. "Suze is finding the cooking—" He considered and discarded several words. "—difficult."

"We knew she was stepping out with her young man," Susannah said. "Caleb Fields, one of the grooms at Wheeler's."

"Did you ask him what happened?" Rees asked.

Susannah lifted her shoulder in a ladylike shrug. "He's disappeared, too."

"We suspect they ran off together." Jack did not sound happy. "Now, with Suze doing the cooking, I'm very short in the dining room."

"We'll need someone in place by next Saturday," Susannah said. "We'll be very busy when the farmers come in for market. Yesterday was horrible without a cook."

"And there's always a stage coach Saturday afternoons," Jack said glumly. "Jack Jr. will have to put in more hours, I suppose."

"Surely there are other cooks," Rees said.

"Not like Ruth," Jack said.

Susannah suddenly leaned forward and said, "We heard a rumor Sam Prentiss attacked David?"

"That's true," Rees said. "David came home all bruised and bloody."

Susannah nodded. "You know he beats his family," she said.

Rees stared at her, aghast. "Are you sure?" The possibility had never occurred to him.

"He has that right," Jack said.

"You wouldn't dare strike me," Susannah said, casting him an ominous glance.

"And he's a regular at the Bull," Jack said, nodding reassuringly at his wife.

"I'm going to have to do something about Sam," Rees said. Too distressed to take a proper farewell, he drifted blindly outside into the sun. Was there anything he could do? And what did Caroline think?

Plank tables with benches crowded the kitchen yard; the help who would of course not sit down with their mistress and new master could still share in memorializing Nate. As Rees turned in from the road and started up the slope, Lydia and Marsh stepped out of the kitchen. Rees waved at Marsh, rather insistently, until the other man nodded in acknowledgment. Rees wanted to make certain Marsh noticed him as he climbed the slope to the front.

Avoiding the few small clusters of raucous men, and Munch busy begging treats, Rees found Kate and Ben on the other side of the smokehouse. In the ten days since Rees had spoken to Kate, her condition had become unmistakable. She looked up eagerly when she heard his footfall, her expression crumpling in disappointment when she saw him.

"I have another question," Rees said. She sighed and nodded. "After Richard ran home from the cottage, did you see anyone else?" Kate began shaking her head. "It would have been a while, maybe fifteen or twenty minutes later." Her head stilled suddenly.

"Someone," she admitted, "but I don't know who. It was dark by then. All I saw was white trousers. Dark jacket, I think. It was just a fleeting glance. . . ."

Rees nodded, exhaling slowly. The combination of Mr. Salley's and Kate's statements confirmed the presence of another man in the cottage. He looked around. Almost all the men wore white or yellow nankeen breeches with white stockings. And he thought he knew who that man might have been; Marsh, the trusted family servant. Who else could run up the slope from the cottage to the house except a resident, someone whom no one would notice or remark upon? Rees must get down to the weaver's house and search the trunk immediately.

To reach the cottage, Rees had to retrace his steps past the kitchen yard. He hugged the tree line. As he skulked past the yard, he saw Lydia, a large basket of bread upon her hip. She glanced up and caught his eyes but looked quickly away again as she deposited the basket upon the table and disappeared back into the shadowy kitchen.

No one else looked at Rees or saw him dart by. He considered striking through the tree break down to the cottage but abandoned that thought. The descent was steep, the footing uncertain, so he crossed to the road in full view of anyone who cared to look and hurried over the crest and down, his fast walk becoming a rapid trot. No one shouted after him or appeared behind him. Safe! Gasping in relief, Rees sprinted across the last leg and slipped into the cottage.

The air settled around him, close and still. And undisturbed—a quick glance around assured him of that. The spiny plant on the windowsill looked limp, although the powdery beetle coating appeared larger, as though it had spread. The back door to the dye room was open, and the peculiar mix of decaying vegetation and metallic chemicals greeted him as he walked toward the back hall. Although he hadn't intended to enter, he saw, hanging from the rope strung across the ceiling, two items of clothing: a woman's filmy dress and a man's canvas apron. Both were mottled with shades of green. And the man's apron— Rees entered the room to stare at it. It must be Nate's apron. Underlying the green was a smattering of other colors. And down the left side was a trail of muddy spots that Rees thought might be blood. A darker half moon of green went around the neckline. Had Nate been drinking the stuff? And how had the apron ended up in the dye pot?

Filing those questions away for further thought, Rees hurried from the room. He didn't know how much time he had before Marsh came looking for him but knew it wouldn't be very long. He ran up the stairs to the loft and to the far side of the bed. The trunk was still there and it did not look as though it had been disturbed since his last visit. Breathing a sigh of relief, Rees pulled it out. Within seconds he had the top pulled off and the contents laid bare.

He put the artifacts from Nate's childhood to one side. The next layer seemed to consist of paper, lots and lots of paper. Rees pulled out a handful of slips, most bearing jagged edges where they'd been torn from larger sheets. IOUs: gambling chits, and the first one on top signed by Piggy Hansen. His wavering signature—he was probably almost too drunk to write—verified a debt of twenty dollars to Nate Bowditch. The second and third also bore his signature and were of like amounts. Rees whistled soundlessly. Sixty dollars was a significant sum, more than most people earned annually. He quickly glanced through the other chits. One from George Potter, for five dollars and three from James Carleton totaling twenty dollars. When Rees examined them once again, he saw that they were all dated for the same Tuesday evenings. By this evidence, Nate did not lose often. But none of the sums, even Hansen's, were so great that they explained murder. Rees slipped them into his pocket for future study.

He pawed down to the next level. Here were deeds to various small properties, almost all purchased from James Carleton. He sat back on his heels, trying to envision the scope of the property Nate had owned at his death. Richard would be a wealthy man.

Rees put those aside and dug down to the next layer. His hand stilled as he carefully took the brown and crumbling newspaper from the box. Dated May 1779, the weekly was open to the advertisements and one in particular had been circled.

Twenty Dollars Reward. Run away from the subscriber a slave called Nacho, about twenty-one or twenty-two years old. Tall, his complexion inclining toward copper. Escaped from an indigo plantation and skilled at same so his hands exhibit a blue tint. Reasonable recompense for distance offered.

Rees read it twice. This must be the document Marsh appeared so desperate to recover.

A soft footfall attracted Rees's attention and he looked up. The servant stood upon the stairs, his expression one of terror. "Is this you?" Rees asked. Marsh hesitated, finally nodded. "Nate knew?"

"Obviously," Marsh said. He swallowed. "What are you going to do?"

"Nothing." Rees took the brittle and yellowing sheet from the trunk and extended it toward the other man. "As far as I'm concerned, you're free." Marsh sucked in his breath, the smooth mask he usually wore crumbling as he fought emotion. He crossed the floor and snatched the newspaper out of Rees's hand so rapidly, the paper dissolved, leaving a trail like bread crumbs across the planks. "But I want the truth."

Marsh met Rees's implacable expression and finally nodded, taking up a seat upon the top step. "Nate knew, of course," he said. "But you can imagine how Mistress Molly would react. . . ." Rees heard the unspoken words; Molly would sell him without hesitation if she knew. "Was there anything else important in the trunk?"

"You're welcome to look," Rees said, conscious of the IOUs in his pocket. "So, you were here the night Nate was killed."

Marsh nodded. "Yes. I stopped here before I went to Portland. I suspect someone else was here before me; I heard raised voices as I went down the hill, but Nate was alone when he opened the door to me."

"And you argued?"

"Yes. I couldn't understand why he forbade Richard to court Elizabeth Carleton." He paused and some remembered pain flashed across his face.

Rees waited. That wasn't all of it. When Marsh did not continue speaking, he said impatiently, "What else?"

"We argued about the dyeing." Marsh managed a faint smile. "An interest we shared, but for him, well, it had become all-consuming. He spent all his time down here at the cottage, ignoring his family and the farm."

"How did he react?" Rees asked. Nate had never appreciated anyone telling him what to do, and Marsh was just his servant.

"Why do you think we were arguing?" Marsh looked across the space separating him from Rees. "You must remember what he was like. Anyway, there was a pounding on the door and Richard's voice shouting outside. As he came in the front door, I went through the dye room and out. Richard was quarreling with his father about the exact same issue, Elizabeth Carleton. So I left."

Rees contemplated Marsh's account seeing several holes. "You didn't return after Richard left?"

Marsh shook his head. "No. Richard might have stayed there for an hour or more and I was already leaving late."

"And you didn't run back to the big house?"

"Why would I do that?" Marsh asked, shooting the other man a derisive glance.

Rees nodded slowly; he believed him. "Did you see any other horses in the lay-by?"

Marsh nodded in surprise. "How did you know that? I was too upset to remark upon it at the time, but there was a chestnut tied to a tree. Nice animal, well cared for and with a beautiful saddle." A short pause and then added in sudden understanding, "He probably belonged to the man I overheard with Nate."

"Who was it?" Rees asked, his words tripping over one another. That man could have waited until Richard left and then gone back inside and bludgeoned Nate to death. Probably did, in fact.

Marsh shrugged. "I didn't recognize the horse. Or the man's voice."

"I assume you knew all the men who played cards with Nate?"

"I served drinks," Marsh said with a nod. "I didn't participate, of course. Magistrates, lawyers, other men of means were the only ones invited."

"Dr. Wrothman?"

"Once or twice only. For obvious reasons." The servant's expression might almost be described as contemptuous.

"Does everyone know about the good doctor's connection with Mrs. Bowditch?"

"Not everyone. But those in the house . . ." Marsh met Rees's gaze. "Most of the servants knew. The mistress never troubled to hide it. . . ."

"The card players always met here?"

"No, but more often than not. This was the only place without intrusive wives or other witnesses."

"Could one of those men have stopped over? Been the man you heard arguing with Nate?"

"Possibly." Marsh nodded slowly. "I wouldn't know their horses, though. Except for James Carleton, who always rode a wild black stallion." Rees nodded, recalling other remarks to the same effect. "I doubt one of them is Nate's murderer," Marsh continued. "They were a friendly group and played for small sums. You must have found the chits."

Rees, choosing not to reply to Marsh's question, asked instead, "Did you always remain until the end of the evening?"

"No. Never. I made sure everyone had something to drink and then I left." He smiled a grim not-smile. "After all, I was expected to arise at dawn and begin upon my other duties."

Rees wondered if he would have to question Piggy Hansen as well as George Potter and James Carleton, a task he already dreaded. They sat in silence, Rees reflecting upon Nate. Hard to imagine Nate as a gambler, a successful one anyway. He'd always been generous with his possessions, sharing candy or a horse with equal graciousness.

"How long did you work for Nate?" Rees asked at last.

"Twelve years. He found me in Providence," Marsh said. "I was selling indigo, a few blocks of it, and some other dyestuffs. . . ."

No doubt stolen from his master, but Rees wasn't inclined to judge Marsh too harshly. A man had to live. "Nacho is an odd name," he said.

"Short for Ignacio. I grew up a slave in Mexico," Marsh said with a faint smile. "My father was apprenticed to an indigo dyer in Africa and carried his skills to his new master. I grew up around dyes, most particularly the cochineal beetle—" He stopped abruptly, hearing a sudden increase in the volume of voices from the house. "It's a long story and I'm too busy now to tell you the whole of it."

"Another time, then," Rees said. "You owe me that much."

"It isn't all that interesting," Marsh said.

"I'll decide that," Rees said. After all, at this point Marsh understood Nate far better than Rees. "I'm trusting you not to run."

"And where would I go? I have a home here. And I would never put my sister and her family into danger. . . ." Marsh jumped to his feet and started down the stairs. Rees shoved the trunk under the bed and followed the other man. By the time he went out, closing the front door behind him, Marsh was already almost at the top of the slope. He was moving fast, almost running, and Munch was tearing after him, barking in delight.

Rees started the climb more slowly, thinking hard. Marsh had several good reasons to murder Nate, not least the desire for freedom. But why then didn't he run? Instead, he stayed, fighting for Richard and his happiness and pouring drinks at the card games and dyeing. Was he afraid Richard would send the slave takers after him?

Rees was almost at the top when he realized that Marsh had mentioned the gambling IOUs. He must have seen them if he knew the amounts. And that meant he'd already searched the trunk. Surely he could have taken the newspaper at any time. So why hadn't he? Rees was missing something.

Chapter Twenty

A s Marsh headed into the kitchen, Rees went around the house and through the front door. The front hall was empty and when Rees went into the dining room he saw why: The food had been brought out and placed upon the long tables against the wall. Many, many dishes—the fruit of Rachel's labors these past few days. Most of the guests occupied the chairs around the three other walls and into the piece of the parlor visible through the connecting door. David sat alone, looking uncomfortable in his fine clothes and good shoes. Rees crossed the floor and pulled up an empty chair beside him.

"Where have you been?" David asked. He looked bored.

"I had a few people to speak to," Rees said. "Where's Mr. Potter?"

David shrugged. "I haven't seen him. Are you ready to leave?"

Rees looked at his son. Besides Grace and Richard, there were no people his age here, and besides this type of gathering was not at all his thing. "If we leave now," he said, "one of us will still have to return for Lydia."

"Fine," David said, jumping to his feet. "I'll do it."

"Let me find Mr. Potter," Rees said. "Perhaps he can find his own way back to town."

Potter was not far distant. Attracted by the loud roar of male laughter, Rees found him closeted with several other men in the smaller family dining room. Cigar smoke wreathed the air. These gentlemen seemed more interested in drinking spirits than in consuming food. Marsh was pouring whiskey with amazing speed and efficiency.

"Ah, Will," Potter said, taking the cigar from his mouth, "interested in a wee dram?"

"Thank you, no," Rees said, glancing around at the men surrounding him. Magistrates, lawyers, affluent landholders, even Dr. Wrothman: all the Dugard elite. Rees knew most of them, or at least he had when they were boys, and he hadn't thought much of some of them then. "I'll be taking David home. Will you be able to cadge a ride from one of these important gentlemen?"

Potter nodded. "Of course. Are you sure you won't stay a few moments?"

"No. Thank you."

"I heard you were back in town, Will." Magistrate Hansen advanced toward Rees, led by his protruding yellow silk waistcoated belly.

"Hello, Piggy," Rees said, just as if the past twenty years did not exist.

"As polite and charming as ever," Hansen replied, baring his teeth in a smile as artificial as he was.

Rees bowed. "Gentlemen," he said, and withdrew.

David's seat was empty except for a stack of dirty plates and cups. Muttering impatiently, Rees moved quickly toward the door into the parlor. As he reached it, James Carleton arrived. He swept into the emerald room with panache, as though he'd been here many times before, and shot unerringly toward Richard. The boy turned to him with a smile. Carleton whispered something to him; good news, Rees suspected. Richard beamed, joy drowning any sorrow he felt. Now, what could occasion such a response? Rees kept his eyes upon Richard even as James moved away to greet other guests. The lad tried to school his expression into neutrality, grief seemed beyond him right now, but a smile kept tugging at his lips. Curious.

Rees made his farewells to Molly, who scarcely seemed to recognize him, and retreated to the front porch. He did not see David anywhere. He walked around the house toward the kitchen—he refused to make polite conversation with anyone inside—and looked over the yard. The help: farmhands, grooms, Juniper the laundress either sat at the temporary tables or on the ground at the yard's edges. Caldwell ate at one table, a clear mark of a constable's low status. Rees waved, knowing he, too, would not have been invited into the house were it not for his privileged status as Nate's good friend. And even that might not have been enough if he hadn't owned a large farm of his own.

David suddenly appeared at the kitchen door, large basket in hand. Spotting his father, he wove through the mob in the yard and began climbing up the hill. "Leftovers," he explained. "I went to ask Lydia when she might be ready. She gave me this."

Lydia, huh? David was as comfortable with her now as with Abby. "And when will she be ready?" Rees asked.

"I'll fetch her when I finish the milking. Mr. Potter?"

"He'll find his own way."

Although they were ready to leave, Amos had to be collected from the paddock and hitched to the buggy, so it was twenty minutes and more before they started home. The basket of food sitting behind the seat released the enticing aromas of roast chicken and fresh bread. Rees, who hadn't eaten anything after the service, could think of nothing else. After a few miles he reached behind him and folded the linen napkin back. Working entirely by touch, he wrenched a chicken leg from carcass and turned around with a self-satisfied grin. David cast him a questioning look. "A working man's got to eat," Rees said, and bit down with pleasure.

By the time they pulled up to the house, the sun was beginning to sink. Rees guessed it was coming on to five o'clock or so. Augustus popped out of the barn and followed David, and the aromatic basket, into the house. "What's that?" he asked.

"Supper," Rees said. "Are you hungry?"

Augustus hesitated.

"Did you start the milking?" David asked.

Augustus nodded. "Almost done."

"Why don't you get a plate, then," David suggested, looking pleased. "I ate earlier. Maybe my father will join you." He eyed his father and added teasingly, "He's already begun, in fact."

"Respect your elders, boy," Rees responded. He began removing food from the basket: the remains of the chicken, and not much of that, an entire loaf of bread, sliced ham upon a plate and at the very bottom, most of an apple pie. Augustus stared at the food and then rushed to put a plate and fork on the table. David fetched a plate as well and helped himself to a piece of pie. Rees felt he must join them and try a little bit of the ham. Then all was silent except for the sound of chewing.

Rees knew Lydia would have scolded them for their poor manners.

When they pushed their plates away, nothing of the chicken remained but bones. Augustus, chasing the last of the piecrust around his plate with his fork, sighed, "Whatever you can say about my mother, she's a great cook."

"Indeed she is," Rees agreed, looking at his son. He hated to disturb the good feeling, but he knew he must speak to David about Abby. "David, I—" The sound of buggy wheels intruded into his tentative speech.

"It must be Miss Lydia," Augustus said.

"It can't be," David said, pointing at himself. "I should be leaving now."

"She would never accept a ride home," Rees agreed. "Augustus, out the back door. Now. Just in case." And as the boy fled to the back, Rees and David hurried down the hall toward the front. Before they reached the door, Caroline flung it open and plunged inside.

"Caroline," Rees said in astonishment. "What are you doing here?"

"Can't your sister visit you?" She moved forward, intending to brush past him on her course to the kitchen.

Rees thrust out his arm to bar her way. "Let's sit in the parlor," he suggested, mindful of Augustus sprinting out the back door. He stepped forward, forcing her to retreat, and opened the parlor door. "You're my guest." He knew she had something planned; that was how she operated, and his stomach tightened in nervous anticipation.

The parlor air smelled stale, but at least it was tidy and clean. Caroline glanced around, almost with a proprietary air, and seated herself in the upholstered chair once favored by their mother. Her nervous hands began pleating her skirt and Rees wondered if she was remembering their last meeting in this room. It had ended badly, with tears, anger, and her family evicted from the farm.

"I saw you at market," she said. Rees nodded. "I suppose you were helping David. He's gotten so tall." She paused, but Rees still said nothing.

Did she know of Sam's attack upon David?

She lifted her gaze. "You should know that Sam took both boys out of school; Charlie as well as David."

Rees looked back at her, trying to keep his face blank.

"I want to come home, Will. Just me and the children, not

Sam. Just for a little while." She clutched her hands so tightly together, the knuckles went white.

"What? Here? Now?" Caught off guard, Rees stumbled over his words. "But there's no room. . . ." Not with Augustus and Lydia living here.

"Why not? It's just you and David. I'm your sister, Will."

Rees almost reminded her of their previous meeting in this room. She hadn't been so quick to claim a relationship then. What was the matter with her? Caroline didn't plead, she commanded or wept and made a great play with her handkerchief. But, as he examined her expression, he saw she looked tired and frightened. "What's the matter, Caro? What happened?"

Tears filled her eyes. "We can stay in Grandmother's cottage. Just for a little while, Will. Please."

Rees regarded her silently, recalling Susannah's statement. "Is Sam hurting you, Caro?"

Anger, sorrow, and fear all passed through her expression. "I don't have anywhere else to go," she said abruptly. "Just for a little while," she whispered. "Please Will."

Rees remained silent as he thought about the space. Augustus would have to stay hidden, of course, at least for a little while. And he must discuss this with Lydia. And probably David as well; he had earned the right to express an opinion about this.

The tears in her eyes began spilling down her cheeks. "I can't believe you won't help your own sister," she wailed.

"I didn't say that," Rees said. "I just want to discuss it with David. . . ." Should he mention Lydia?

"Will. Will, look at this," Lydia called as she and David plunged through the front door. Caroline turned to Rees, her mouth open with astonishment.

"In here," he said as they walked past the door. "You're home early."

"I had a ride into Dugard. . . ." Her words trailed off as she saw Caroline. David appeared behind Lydia, another heavy basket, twin to the one Rees had brought home, in his arms.

Caroline stared at them, and then her furious gaze fixed upon her brother. "Now I understand," she said. "Of course there's no room. Your fancy woman lives here with you. Poor Dolly. She would be horrified." She rose to her feet and shook out her skirts. When she stalked toward the door, she brushed past Lydia as though she were invisible and spared only the slightest nod for David.

Rees knew with a sinking in his gut that his connection to Lydia was no longer even a half secret. But although he would have wished it were not Caroline who became the messenger, he was not upset to see the secret go public. The news had been slowly leaking out for some time now, and somewhere along the way he'd made his peace with it.

"Oh, dear," Lydia said. "I won't dare show my face in town."

"Did she apologize for Sam's attack upon me?" David asked sourly.

Rees shook his head. "No. She wants to bring the children here. . . . I think she's leaving Sam."

"I don't blame her," David said. "I saw Charlie. They're all living near the Bull—"

"Not on the farm?" Rees said in surprise.

"He lost it gambling a long time ago," David said, surprised in his turn. "I thought you knew."

"I thought they were renting it," Rees said. How could he have been so stupid? "What can we do?"

"We have Augie," David said, gesturing toward the back of the house. "We can't take her in. This is her problem," he added with the heartlessness of youth. He carried the heavy basket into the kitchen. In the sudden silence, Rees clearly heard the thud of the basket landing upon the table and the slam of the back door.

"Of course, you must do something," Lydia said. But Rees's interest in his sister had evaporated for the moment.

"Lydia . . . ," he began. She turned to look at him. But after all, Rees didn't know what to say. "I'm sorry" encompassed too much and at the same time wasn't enough. The silence stretched on and on. Rees realized Lydia, too, was holding her tongue, as afraid as he was of saying too much. The sound of David and Augustus slamming into the kitchen broke the moment. With a sigh, Rees bowed Lydia into the hall outside.

"I learned something that may be of use to you," she said, speaking quickly. "Rachel said—well, suggested, really—that Nate wasn't Augustus's father."

"What? But he has to be. If he isn't, who is?"

Lydia shrugged. "She wouldn't say."

"I'll talk to her myself tomorrow," Rees said.

"I'll see you there, then," Lydia said. She went into the kitchen. Rees followed her, shutting the parlor door behind him. He'd wasted his opportunity to speak to Lydia in private.

After supper that night, while Lydia cleaned the kitchen, Rees grabbed his chance to to talk to his son. He asked David to join him in the parlor. Looking startled and a little worried, the boy followed him into the dark room. Rees lit the candles on the mantel and, in the flickering light, turned to gaze at his son. David's eyes slid away from his father's as he tried to figure out what he had done lately. "You're not in trouble," Rees said quickly. "I just, ah . . ." As David looked at him in perplexity, Rees took a short walk in the shadows. "You like Lydia?" Rees took the coward's way out and slid away from the questions he wanted to ask.

"Yes," David said cautiously, seating himself. "She's . . . nice. Are you marrying her?"

"What? No! I mean, well, not right away. Would you mind?"

"Of course not. It's time," he said, sounding surprisingly adult. "But you didn't bring me in here to talk about Lydia, then, did you?"

Rees took another turn into the darkness. "You know," he said, throwing himself into a chair, "Richard Bowditch is expecting a baby."

"He is?" David sounded confused.

"He . . . Kate, the nursemaid . . ." Rees realized perspiration was streaming down his face and the small of his back. "I know you and Abby . . ." Even in the dim half light, Rees could see a fiery blush spread across his son's face. By now, Rees felt as though he might be blushing, too.

"It's not like that," David said. "I would never . . . I'm not like Richard."

"No, you're not," Rees agreed. "You would always do the right thing." Such as marrying the mother of his child. Rees didn't want to say David was too young to marry, although that is what he thought. Voicing it would inflame David, lighting him up like a candle. Instead Rees said, "Do you want to marry Abby? Now, I mean?" David's mouth opened and rounded into an O. "Just be careful. I know, sometimes, there's a slip between a lip and a cup."

David leaped up and fled. Rees heard the front door slam and the thud of David's boots as he ran for the barn. As for Rees, well, he couldn't stand at all. His legs were trembling. Talking to David had been one of the hardest, and most embarrassing, things he had ever done.

Chapter Twenty-one

When he went downstairs the next morning, only Abigail was in the kitchen. David's empty bowl still sat upon the table, clean of mush. Relieved, for he could only imagine how awkward the next meeting between them would be, Rees carried the bowl to the dishpan. As he helped himself to mush and coffee, Abby picked up her broom and went upstairs to begin on the bedrooms. Rees sat down. Despite his busy thoughts, the kitchen felt empty without Lydia and David. Rees scraped his bowl clean and left as soon as he could.

Augustus helped him harness Bessie to the wagon, and Rees climbed into the seat. Despite some residual stiffness in his left arm, and a twinge of pain at every bump, he was able to manage the reins. He drove slowly but steadily to the Bowditch farm and pulled up to the back door. Marsh answered the knock.

"Let's go to the cottage," Rees said. "We can talk there."

"Very well," he said in resignation, coming onto the porch and shutting the door behind him.

As they started down the road, Munch appeared from the shrubbery and trotted after them. He followed them into the cottage, where he collapsed in front of the hearth with a sigh. Rees sat down at the table by the window and, when Marsh remained standing, pointed to the bench across from him. Marsh sat down. He moved stiffly, and when Rees looked at him carefully he realized how much effort Marsh was expending to control his emotions.

Marsh caught his glance. "I don't know how my history will help you find Nate's killer," he said.

"Perhaps," Rees said. "Perhaps not." He waited.

"As I told you, I was born into slavery in Mexico on a cochineal plantation. My master traveled regularly to other parts of the Spanish Empire; that's how I knew about the chilla leaves from Peru. The native population uses them to make a green dye."

"Then your master sold you to an indigo plantation in South Carolina?"

"Yes." Marsh nodded. "When I was sixteen." He hesitated and then added, "I ran away a few years later. Came north."

"How soon after that did you meet Nate Bowditch?"

"Not long. I brought indigo to Providence. Also a bag of logwood shavings—"

"And Nate, once he learned of your specialized knowledge, hired you to work for him?"

"Yes." Marsh smiled faintly. "He knew even more about dyestuffs than I did."

Rees let the silence lengthen before speaking. "I want to know what you argued about with Nate." Marsh was quiet for so long, Rees thought he would not answer. "It wasn't only about Richard, was it? Or about dyeing?"

"No." Marsh exhaled. "Partly. I couldn't understand why he refused to encourage the boy's happiness. But . . ." He ran down.

"Yes."

"You don't know what he was like. Nate was obsessed with finding the perfect dyes, cheaper and better than everything we already know. Now, I mean before he died, he focused on green. But, I promise you, when he solved that conundrum, it would be red. Or blue. He searched for dyes we could obtain from sources here, not imported fustic or logwood. He spent every day, every minute of every day, here in this cottage. He paid no attention to the farm, to his family, to—" He stopped short.

"To what?"

"To anything. So we argued." He hesitated and then admitted, "I punched him. In the face."

Rees thought of the bruise upon Nate's cheek and nodded. "And then Richard arrived."

"He didn't kill his father."

"How do you know? You left, didn't you? That's what you said."

"I just know. He wouldn't."

"And you saw no one else?"

"No. Just the horse. As I told you."

"And you went to your sister's? In Portland?" When Marsh did not immediately respond, Rees fixed him with a fierce glare. "The truth, Marsh."

"She's not my sister, she's my wife," he suddenly burst out. Rees felt his mouth drop open. "Yes, I see your question. Why doesn't she live here, with me? She wouldn't come. My South Carolina master forced us to wed, to produce more slaves, you see."

Rees saw. He would have run, too. "Children?"

"Three. None of mine, but I help her support them. It's the least I can do," he added, so softly Rees could barely hear him.

"Did you kill Nate, Marsh?"

"Of course not. I would never . . ." Emotion choked him. Rees waited for the other man to compose himself. Finally Marsh said, "I should return to my duties."

"I want to speak briefly with Rachel," Rees said, also rising to his feet. Marsh bobbed his head in acquiescence.

They walked silently up the slope, Munch at their heels. Both men passed through the kitchen, but as Marsh continued to the back stairs Rees paused. Only Mary Martha and Lydia were inside today, both washing dishes but without the frenzy of the previous week. "I'm looking for Rachel," Rees said.

"In the dining room," Mary Martha said. "The little one. The company left a bit of a mess. . . ."

Rees nodded his thanks and went up the stairs. As soon as he approached the family dining room he smelled stale smoke and whiskey. He peered through the door. Ash covered the table and the floor and dirty glasses littered every surface. Rachel, moving slowly with fatigue, was piling glasses and dishes into a basket. She looked up at him, seeing something in his eyes that forced her to step back.

"You haven't told me everything," Rees said. Rachel swallowed nervously. "Was Nate Augustus's father?" Rachel opened her mouth to say yes but at the last moment could not speak the lie. Finally she lowered her eyes and shook her head. "Who was it?" Rees asked. No answer. "Rachel," he said.

She choked back a sob. "This has nothing to do with the master's death," she said.

"We can't know that," Rees said gently. "Who, Rachel? No one can harm you now."

"King Carleton."

Rees stared at her in shock and then, as the news sank in, he knew it was true. Of course, King Carleton always took what he wanted. "Did Nate know?"

"Yes. I told him immediately. But it made no difference. He still treated Augustus like his own." She paused and then added in a soft voice, "No one knew. Not even Master Carleton. He sold me before I began to show. I barely knew I was expecting myself. And everyone assumed the baby was Nate's and he never told them different. He was a good man."

"Yes," Rees said. Unbelievably good to accept another man's child as his own. Nate must have had a compelling reason. His mind whirling, Rees headed to his wagon in a daze.

By the time he reached Dugard, dark clouds were scudding across the sky and the first fat drops of rain had begun to fall. He didn't think he would make it home before the storm hit in earnest. Anyway he didn't want to go home. Only the silent Abby would be in the kitchen when Rees wanted to share his amazement and his new questions with Lydia.

He turned the wagon north, toward the Contented Rooster. The street out front was empty except for a few people running for shelter. He went down the drive and parked Bessie and the wagon under a tree. The wind was whipping the pewter water in Dugard Pond into whitecaps. Suddenly the skies opened and a deluge began. The wind blew the rain sideways, and leaves and other debris spun sluggishly down the street. Rees sprinted for the front door.

The coffeehouse was almost empty. A fire snapped on the hearth, a cozy counterpoint to the rain outside. Rees threw himself into a chair in the back corner near the fireplace.

Jack approached with a smile. "I heard a rumor. . . ."

Rees turned astonished eyes toward the other man. "Already?" But he'd just spoken to Rachel.

"Oh, Caroline wasted no time in spreading the news," Jack said.

"Caroline? Wait, what?" Rees tried to pull his scattered thoughts together. "What does Caroline have to do with anything?"

"She claims you have your mistress at the farm," Susannah said, scurrying across the floor with cups of coffee. A pitcher of cream and a dish of fat sugar chunks followed.

Jack pulled over a chair. "She says you have a woman living with you."

Rees regarded Jack sourly. "I'm sure she did not describe Lydia so kindly."

"Is that true?" asked Susannah.

"My sister wanted to move in," he said, so furious, he spat out the words. "My housekeeper lives in my grandmother's cottage. Augie—" He stopped short. Susannah offered him a small smile. "She can't stay with me now, can she? She isn't my mistress. She's a . . ." He paused. Could Lydia still be considered a Shaker when she no longer lived in a Shaker community and had been expelled from it, in fact? "I told Caro I needed time to make arrangements."

Both of Rees's companions regarded him with varying degrees of interest. Then Susannah said, "I expect Caroline is desperate."

Rees nodded. "I know he beats her," he said. Under Susannah's gaze, he felt the hot flush of shame spread over his body.

"When he loses at the gambling table, he takes it out on his family," Jack replied with a humorless chuckle. "And he almost always loses. Where do you think your land and your livestock went?"

Rees squirmed. "That's why she was at the farm," he admitted in a low voice. "She wanted to bring the children and stay for a while."

Susannah leaned toward Rees. "Your sister Phoebe and her husband moved to Rumford and your parents and grandparents are dead. Caroline is your younger sister and she and those kids have no one else."

"I didn't refuse her," he said. "I just wanted some time to figure it out. . . ." Realizing his protest sounded uncomfortably like whining, he shut up.

Susannah sat back, her expression no less stern. "Have you spoken to James Carleton yet?"

"I drove out there and he was leaving. Then Richard shot me—"

"A little ashamed for the Hell you and Nate put James through as boys?" Susannah asked shrewdly.

Rees did not reply. James had been a bookish boy, preferring to settle down with his Latin schoolwork to tramping around outside. His quiet nature and solitary habits especially seemed to irritate Nate, who never let an opportunity to torture the boy pass. "Why did Nate bully James so much?" he asked now.

"You knew Nate better than anyone," Jack replied. "You should know." Rees shook his head.

"It's just that, well, Elizabeth Carleton is at the center of this, isn't she?" Susannah said, pursuing her own thoughts. "If Nate hadn't forbidden the courtship, the two young people might already be married with a baby on the way. And Nate still alive."

"It couldn't be that simple," Rees said.

"Well, no. But James and Nate were better than good friends. So why did Nate refuse to allow his son to wed James's daughter? James might know. And he probably has other information—" She stopped so suddenly, Rees looked at her suspiciously.

"Women's gossip," Jack said, his voice laden with scorn.

"Please, Suze," Rees said.

She sighed. "King Carleton had an eye for a beautiful woman," she said.

"This is news?" Rees said, disappointed.

"Rumors," Jack said.

"What about Hannah Bishop?' Susannah asked, irritated. "And Leah McKinney?"

"They *claim* he fathered their children," her husband argued. "We don't know that's true."

"He sent the girls to school," Susannah said. "That's corroboration if I ever heard it."

Rees said nothing as he pondered the discussion. Rachel had named King Carleton as Augustus's father, and Rees believed her. Knowing there were others only confirmed her story. In fact, he now remembered Dolly waxing outraged about King Carleton's larks all over town. He looked at Susannah. "What do you know?"

"I heard that King Carleton and his daughter-in-law—," Susannah admitted as Jack lunged to his feet and stomped away.

Rees gaped at her. "Charlotte Carleton?" She nodded. "Does James know?" She shrugged. He moved his wounded arm experimentally. Although it ached a little, it itched now more than it hurt. "I'll drive out right now." He drained his cup.

"Will?" She hesitated, looking up at him. "You don't seem surprised?"

"I heard this from someone else."

"Rachel. It must be." He said nothing, but Susannah nodded as though he'd admitted everything. "Of course. A lovely young girl in that household? It would have been like putting a lamb between a lion's paws. What about Augie?"

"Please, don't say anything to anyone," Rees said, leaning across the table. She nodded. He looked at her carefully. Something about the set of her shoulders and tight mouth suggested another secret. "King Carleton went after you, too, didn't he?"

"Me and everyone else. For six months, I was a prisoner in my father's house, afraid to show my face before he was on to someone else. And I had a father and brothers to protect me. Do you know, King Carleton tried to bribe my father, threatening him and offering him money at the same time? I know my father was frightened. My mother wanted to send me to her sister's in Boston. So, what chance did Rachel have? Fortunately for all of us, Mr. Carleton's interest never lasted very long. When he fell ill in '89, every woman in town breathed a sigh of relief."

"No help from the constable? Or from the magistrates?"

She shook her head. "Most of them owed him money or were involved in business deals with him. I was fortunate in that as well. My father was of sober temperament with no vices, and he owned his own shop."

Pity and anger curdled Rees's belly and he pushed away his plate. What were the common working men and their daughters to do against the wealth and power of King Carleton?

"And Jack doesn't know?"

"He wouldn't believe me anyway," Susannah said with a touch of bitterness.

"Mother?" Jack Jr. appeared at the kitchen door. Although opened for only a few seconds, the bitter stink of burning seeped into the common room. Uttering a cry of dismay, Susannah jumped to her feet and ran toward the back.

Rees looked through the window. Although the rain had diminished to a drizzle, it looked cold and wet outside. A drive to the Carleton estate would not be pleasant, but since Dugard was more than halfway it made sense to do it now—especially since tomorrow he must drive to New Winstead and find Cornelius Lattimore.

Rees dropped a penny onto the table and went outside to collect his horse and wagon from the yard. The storm had brought in cooler temperatures, and everything was dark with moisture, the air heavy with a thick mist that muffled all sounds. But the wind was whipping the clouds into rags, and as Rees started west on Water Street a ray of sun peeked through. He found himself thinking of secrets and how far people were willing to go to keep them hidden. But was making a bastard on a slave woman enough of a secret? Not for King Carleton. Unless . . . Rees suddenly wondered about the paternity of Elizabeth's younger sisters.

And Elizabeth. If she were at the center as Susannah suggested, why, that gave James as many reasons to murder Nate as Richard had. James claimed he was in favor of the match, but it wouldn't be the first time he'd lied to Rees. Or maybe James was furiously insulted at Nate's slight. Either way, he had as powerful a reason to murder Nate as Richard. Rees snapped the whip and Bessie broke into a canter.

By the time he reached the Carleton estate, the sun was out although the air remained cool. He parked Bessie in front and regarded the mansion. An addition had been added to the imposing brick structure built by King Carleton and a circular drive laid out in place of the narrow lane. Rees saw several new outbuildings as well, mostly stables; and in the yard to the side grooms were busily exercising one horse after another. One groom was struggling with the excitable black horse and from the animal's wildly rolling eyes, failing in his efforts to calm him. That must be the wild black stallion described by Fred Salley.

Rees pounded upon the front door. A man—so much shorter than Rees, he had to tip his head back—opened the door. Except for his white shirt and stockings, the servant was dressed entirely in black. He examined Rees disapprovingly, his eyes lingering particularly on the old much-patched linen coat.

"Mr. Carleton, please," Rees said.

"Mr. Carleton is not at home," the servant said in the clipped tones of the upper-class servant.

"Hmmm. Tell Jimmy, Will Rees is here to see him."

"I told you—" Before the refusal was out of his mouth, Rees brushed past him and into the house.

It had been many years since he'd set foot in this house, and he'd never been on this side. The back door must now be buried inside the addition. Rees paused, looking down the long hall to the staircase at the end in consternation. Several doors opened off this hall, and he could not even guess which one he would need. The servant took advantage of Rees's sudden hesitation and almost pushed him into a small sitting room on the left.

"I'll inform Mrs. Carleton of your arrival," he said.

Rees stopped inside the door, not daring to go any farther with his muddy shoes. A fine Chinese carpet covered the floor, and the delicate furniture around it appeared too frail to hold his weight. The walls were covered in a bright paper, Chinese again. Rees removed his shoes and padded into the room. A door located in the back wall gave access to the next room; when Rees tried it, he discovered it was locked. Heavy silk drapes covered the window next to the fireplace. He tweaked them away and peered outside. A long porch stretched across this side of the house. And at one end, in a pale pink gown and with her hat in the chair beside her, sat Elizabeth Carleton. Rees glanced around but saw no entry to the porch, so he threw up the window sash and squeezed his large body through the opening.

Elizabeth turned to stare at him in surprise. She held an open book upon her lap but was not reading. "Who are you?"

"I'm Will Rees," he said.

She smiled. "Oh, Richard spoke of you." Shrill screaming erupting from the lawn below drew her to the porch rail. "Stop fighting!" she shouted to her sisters.

"I wanted to ask you a few questions," Rees said, inspecting her carefully. She smiled at him, her full lips soft and pink. "If you don't mind, that is."

"I don't mind. Richard said you might. Anyway, I want to thank you for demonstrating his innocence. As soon as you determine his father's murderer, we'll marry."

"You will?" Rees couldn't keep the astonishment from his voice.

"Oh yes. My father has given permission. Only Mr. Bowditch did not favor the marriage." Her face clouded. "I thought he liked me, but he would never agree to the union."

"I understand your mother is not enthusiastic either," Rees said.

Elizabeth laughed. "That's true, but that is only because she wants me to marry a title. I prefer to wed Richard and I will." Her soft brown eyes hardened with determination.

King Carleton, it seemed, had passed his insistence upon having his own way down to his granddaughter.

"How long have you been seeing Richard?"

"Just since I came home from school." She smiled shyly.

"And how old are you?"

"Sixteen. My father took me out of school a little early. He held a ball to welcome me home. Richard attended and as soon as we saw one another, we knew we were meant to be together."

From his advanced age of thirty-six, Rees could only try to remember what such certainty felt like.

"He began courting me." Remembered pain shadowed her expression. "And when his father discovered it, he forbade us to see one another. Richard didn't want to deceive his father, but it was necessary."

"Your father did not protest?"

"No. He encouraged it, from the very beginning." She smiled reminiscently.

"And Mr. Bowditch never told Richard why he did not approve?"

"No." Tears gathered in her eyes. "He just didn't like me."

Rees could not believe Nate's reaction was so simple. "The night Mr. Bowditch was . . ." He didn't continue, unable to find a word that did not sound too harsh in the face of this pink and white perfection.

"Richard was with me. We met at an abandoned house. He left me about five, and went home, determined to persuade his father to approve our union."

"You've been meeting him since, haven't you?"

Although she didn't reply, her self-conscious expression told Rees the truth. No wonder no one had found the boy. He'd been moving from cottage to cottage on the Carleton estates.

A sudden hard slap cracked through the air, sharp as a pistol shot, and someone began to wail. Leaping to her feet, Elizabeth sped to the porch rail. "I'm going to tell," cried the younger girl in the piping treble of a child. Rees peered over Elizabeth's shoulder. Her sisters had been playing bowls and disagreed over something. Now the younger girl's cheek bore a bright red handprint.

"Really, Sofia," Elizabeth cried. "You're almost a young lady. You should know better."

"But she said I—"

"I don't want to hear it," Elizabeth said. "You both know better. Lawks, what are you going to do when I'm no longer here to separate you?"

"That won't be for many years," Sofia declared.

"Sooner than you think," Elizabeth said with a secret smile.

"Both of you, come up here right now. Mother would be so disappointed to see you quarrelling. And the grass is too wet anyway. Look at the hems of your gowns."

As the two girls shrieked their protests, Rees said good-bye and climbed back through the window into the morning room. No one seemed to have detected his absence. He sat gingerly upon the settee but within a few minutes he jumped to his feet again. No refreshments beckoned him—and, in fact, if that arrogant servant had come in and found him missing, a great hue and cry would certainly have gone up. He'd been forgotten.

Chapter Twenty-two

Rees slipped on his shoes and stepped out into the hall. He looked around at the doors and the stairs at the other end. Where to go? He began walking down the hall, his feet silent upon the carpet.

He glanced through the open doors as he passed them and saw no one but maids too busy to notice him. None were fitted out as offices: a large parlor decorated again with chinoiserie; a dining room with a table and chairs for twelve; and at the back, another small sitting room, this time in shades of blue. Mrs. Carleton owned the first floor.

Rees looked at the stairs. King Carleton's office had been located on the second floor; it made sense that James used it now. Rees climbed the stairs and turned left, toward the side of the house where he thought the office might be located. Everything looked different and very confusing. At the end of the hall and up a small flight of steps was another door. Loud and angry voices penetrated through it to the hall outside.

"I don't care what . . . reasoning . . . Elizabeth . . . marry a title."

"But Richard . . . large landowner . . . maintain . . . ruin." James's low rumble caused Rees to strain to hear.

"Then I'll take the girls to London. . . ." Charlotte's knife-edged voice sliced through her husband's bass. Rees paused. Should he knock? Suddenly the door was wrenched open and Mrs. Carleton stormed out. Scowling ferociously, she brushed past him as though he were invisible.

James hesitated in the door. "Charlotte, please." Today his waistcoat matched his wife's pale blue gown. He glared at Rees. "What do you want?"

"Just to talk to you for a few moments," Rees said, his voice soothing. "Women, huh?"

"Indeed." James glared after his diminutive spouse, his expression mutinous. He was terrified of her.

Not surprising, Rees decided, since the dainty appealing package disguised a stiletto.

Carleton turned and stomped into his office. "What do you want?" he snarled as Rees hurried after him. "I didn't murder Nate. Why would I? We were friends. Good friends."

"That friendship puzzles me," Rees said, sitting down in a scarred chair.

James put his booted feet upon his desk. He wore riding boots again, but these were old, battered, and hard used. "Make yourself at home," he grunted sarcastically. But when he pulled the green glass bottle of whiskey from his drawer, he brought out two glasses. "I don't know why you should be puzzled," he said as he poured. He drained his glass, not his first by the look of it, and poured another. "You were gone. And Nate and I had much in common." He threw back the second whiskey and shuddered. "More than you can imagine."

"You played cards," Rees said, stung by James's claim to Nate's friendship.

"So? We played often. Usually Corny Hansen joined us, and sometimes George Potter."

"And you lost. I found a chit for twenty dollars."

James stared at him, perspiration beading his forehead. "Nate was a lucky devil, that's true, but I certainly didn't kill him over twenty dollars."

Rees deflated. Put like that, even the suggestion sounded ridiculous. Carleton's waistcoat cost more than that. "You played at the cottage?"

"Usually, yes. At the table in front of that diseased plant. I don't know what Potter told his wife, but Charlotte—" He stopped abruptly.

No question who ruled the roost in this household. "Did anyone lose heavily?"

"Not really," James said with a shrug. He poured another glass of whiskey, his trembling hands spilling the amber fluid upon the desk.

"You better ease off," Rees said.

"Don't you start now," James said, tossing the whiskey back with a defiant flick of his wrist. "I get enough of that from my wife."

"Does she know about Augustus?"

"Augustus? Augustus who?" James stared at Rees in perplexity.

"The blacksmith in town. Son of Rachel, the cook for Nate."

"What does he have to do with anything?"

"He's your half brother."

James burst out into a loud guffaw. "He is? Well, damn." He continued to glance at Rees. "But it makes sense. How well do you remember my father?"

"I remember our fight," Rees said carefully.

Carleton nodded. "You probably won't believe this, but I fared worse than you did. First you beat me and then my father horsewhipped me for losing and sent me away to London." A reminiscent smile tugged at the corners of his mouth. "Of course,

I loved it in London so he did me a good turn without realizing it. Never wanted to come home." Swinging his feet off the desk, he leaned forward. "My father hated losers. I was a great disappointment to him. He expected to have everything he wanted. I have bastard sisters all over town, probably all over the state. First time I heard of a brother, though."

"You never guessed about Augustus?" Rees asked.

James shook his head. "None of us knew. I'm sure my father didn't either. By his lights, he was honorable. He married the girls off and if that failed paid for the schooling for their children."

"No doubt he felt that unnecessary for a slave," Rees said with a frown.

"He would have taken an interest in a boy," James said. The laughter died suddenly from his eyes. "Nate thought that lad was his. He was proud of him. I'm glad he never had to know the truth. . . ."

Rees said nothing. Rachel said she had told Nate, so he had known the truth. He'd chosen to keep it a secret from everyone. Even James. He and Nate had not been as good friends as he thought.

James suddenly chuckled again. "I understand now. You thought I might have murdered Nate to keep that secret safe? Really, Will, how foolish. Why would I care? And my father, if he knew, everyone would know. He had that damn-your-eyes attitude and cared nothing for public opinion."

"And Charlotte?" Rees demanded, knowing his question was cruel.

James looked at him. "You heard that foul rumor linking my father and my wife? Even King Carleton would not go that far." He laughed. "Anyway, it wasn't my father who got himself murdered. It was Nate. Maybe it's his secrets you should be uncovering." His loud mocking laughter brought on a fit of coughing.

Rees rose to his feet. "What secrets?" he asked James.

"You're sticking your nose into everything; you find out." He added nastily, "I see you and Nate weren't such good friends after all. Now get out before I have you thrown out."

Rees looked at James's hand, trembling next to the bell rope, and left. But as he climbed into his wagon and turned Bessie toward home, he realized that James Carleton, for all his laughter and his mockery, was terrified.

Lydia did not return until midafternoon, and when she came inside and hung her bonnet on the hook she moved slowly with fatigue. Rees stirred up the fire and pushed the kettle over the flame. "Would you like a cup of tea?" he asked.

"Thank you, yes," she said, looking at him in surprise. "Did you speak to Rachel?"

"Yes," he said, turning to look at her. Something was wrong, he could feel it. "Augustus's father was not Nate; it was King Carleton. But it's a dead end. James didn't know it, but he didn't care either. He laughed me out of the room." Realizing he was rambling, Rees stopped talking. He and Lydia were alone and for the first time in many days there was no crisis. This might be his best chance to make things right with her. "You must know there's nothing between Rachel and me?"

She inclined her head but said, "And what is between you and me, Will?"

He stared at her, his stomach clenching. "I thought . . . you needed time, too. Didn't you? Because of Charles?"

"Yes. I needed some time to accept Charles's murder." She looked up at him, her eyes filling with tears. "But Will, I followed you here. And I've been waiting . . . through everything. Surely that must reveal my feelings."

He experienced a sudden awful premonition. "Don't go back to Zion. Please."

"Why not? This arrangement suits you. But me? I want to be your equal partner, a wife, not a housekeeper."

"Then let's get married," he blurted.

She shook her head at him. "And then what?" She sighed. "I don't want a proposal made from fear. Nor do I want a husband who behaves like my master. I was never very good at obedience, even when I belonged to the Shakers."

"I want to marry you. I love you. I'm . . . just not sure I'm ready. Not yet." Rees paced a lap in front of the fireplace, trying to release some of his emotion.

"I understand," she said. "You still love Dolly. I daresay you'll never love anyone as much as you love her."

Rees couldn't look at her. "That's not it," he said hoarsely.

"Of course it is."

"No. You don't understand. I didn't love her. I grew fond of her, that's true. But I didn't love her. And I was the one who killed her."

The silence seemed to extend into eternity. Finally Lydia swallowed and said in a whisper, "What do you mean?"

"I was home, wounded. Nate was already married and with a little boy, Richard. We argued, something trivial, no doubt. I barely remember. Anyway, I wanted to show him I could find a girl of my own and I knew Dolly was interested so . . ." He couldn't look at Lydia. "I was a boy and I behaved like a boy. When I came home again a few months later, David was on the way and Dolly and I wed." He peeked at Lydia. Emotions— surprise, disappointment, relief—all spun rapidly across her face.

"What about Nate?"

"I never spoke to him again." He forced a laugh. "Nate always thought he knew best. When we were apprentices together,

I wanted to court and marry Mr. Stewart's daughter. Nate talked me out of it." He paused. Lydia waited in silence for him to continue. "Dolly deserved a better man," Rees said at last. "I never stayed home. Well, I couldn't if I were to earn our bread. But I wouldn't have anyway. I'm a wanderer. . . ."

"David tells me his mother was happy," Lydia said. "Most of the time."

Rees shook his head. When he looked at her, his eyes were liquid with unshed tears. "You don't understand. It's my fault she died, she and our unborn babe. I brought back the sickness that took her." He heard Lydia inhale and waited for the storm to break: a storm of disgust and hatred.

"So now you're God?"

"Huh? What?"

"Are you now taking on God's work as your own? He has the power of life and death. Not you."

"But I brought the sickness home."

"Neither you nor David succumbed." Lydia suddenly leaned forward and put her hand upon his. Physical contact with her was so rare, and now so unexpected, that Rees felt a shock of heat burn through him. "It wasn't your time. God chooses when to invite us into His House; not you." Withdrawing her hand, Lydia said with a smile, "Not everything is your responsibility, Will Rees. And you tried to do the right thing, even if you were not the kind of husband you wished to be. From what I've heard about your Dolly, she knew that."

Rees felt the knot he'd carried inside him for so many years loosen.

"That's why you didn't come home for years at a time?" Lydia murmured. "The farm reminds you of Dolly."

Rees nodded. "She loved the farm, loved the work. I can hardly set foot in the barn without remembering her there." He smiled through a haze of tears. "She spent a lot of time in the barn, fussing with her cows." He sucked in a breath, hating the quaver in his voice. "She'd always say the same thing: 'Hello, Willie, visiting the cowherd.' And I'd always say yes."

Lydia remained briefly silent; then she leaned forward and clasped his hand. "You have nothing over which to reproach yourself. Although your marriage may have begun, well, not so propitiately as you would have liked, you grew to love Dolly and she loved you, too. She was taken home young, but she enjoyed a good life while she lived here. None of us can hope for more. You know that."

Rees nodded. Turning his hand over, he clenched her hand tightly in his. "And you—what do you know?" he asked, his chest aching with his captured breath.

"I know I don't expect you to stay home all the time. You aren't a farmer and probably will never want to be. But I would expect you to come home to me. I would expect to be your only woman. And I would expect to be your partner, equal in every way. Equal as the women are in the Shakers. Not someone you treat with the condescending protectiveness of a child."

"I'm certain if I backslide, you'll remind me," Rees said with a sudden grin.

She smiled in return, but her words were serious. "I don't want to feel Dolly's ghost standing between us."

"She doesn't. Not for me, anyway," he said, thinking of David. "I choose you, Lydia."

Now her smile was genuine. "We'll talk more, Will," she said as rose to her feet. "But David will be in soon. And the water will boil away if we leave it much longer."

"I'm making the tea for you," Rees said, pulling down the tin. "Sit down." He wanted to continue this conversation, but besides David's incipient arrival, he could see Lydia needed some time to ponder his revelation.

She obeyed. After a moment's uncomfortable silence, she said, "Why, do you think, did Nate encourage the fiction that Augustus was his son?"

"I don't know. Not from a desire to have a son, since he has one of his own." He paused. "What is your opinion of Richard? You know him now, better than I do."

"He's spoiled," she said. "Mrs. Bowditch reserves all her affection for him. He feels he is entitled to whatever he desires. I suspect Nate's refusal to countenance his marriage to Elizabeth Carleton was the very first time he was ever denied anything." Lydia's forehead crinkled in thought. "But I don't see Richard as capable of murder. He is essentially soft."

Rees nodded. "I agree."

"I think Mrs. Bowditch resented Nate's affection for Augustus. Not so much for herself—she sees him as a threat to Richard."

"So why did Rachel keep his parentage a secret? Molly treated her poorly for many years, and for no reason. Yet Rachel preferred to keep silent and suffer her mistress's punishment."

"She was afraid," Lydia said.

Rees paused, the teapot held aloft. "Of what? Surely she was safe at the Bowditch farm?"

"Why indeed?" Lydia rushed forward to rescue the teapot and transfer it to the table.

"Why what?" asked David, entering silently in stocking feet.

"Nothing," Rees responded promptly. Lydia made a half gesture warning him to silence, but it was too late. "It's a private matter—"

"Private. You mean for adults." David shook his head, his

eyes narrowing with fury. "Private. Don't I do a man's work? Why do you persist in treating me like a child?" He stamped out, slamming the door behind him.

Rees looked at Lydia and sighed. "I've tried to remember he isn't a little boy, really I have. But we can't tell him this. . . ."

"I know. But he just wants to be included with us, the adults. Now he feels betrayed by both of us." She sighed. "And this is so ugly." Laying a hand on Rees's wrist, she said, "Go after him. Explain as much as you feel you can."

"But what shall I say?"

"You'll know. It's not the secret that's important to him. He wants to feel we include him and trust him, that's all."

Rees turned his arm over and, taking her small callused hand into his, he gave it a squeeze. "I want . . . We'll talk again later." He rose to his feet and with a final glance at Lydia, he went after David.

Considering what he might say to smooth the troubled waters, Rees tracked his son to the barn. Of course. Like his mother, David found solace in the farm. When Rees peered cautiously through the door, he saw both David and Augustus at the back. David held a pitchfork as though he planned to throw the hay into a stack. But instead of working he was ranting.

"He never paid any attention to me," he said. "He dropped me off at my aunt's and took off, not bothering to return for months at a time. Even years. And now, when I'm running the farm like a man, doing a man's work, he treats me like a five-year-old." With a mighty heave, he tossed a particularly large forkful of hay on top of the pile.

"I think your father is a good man," Augustus said, his voice soft. "He married your mother, didn't he? I wish my father had wed my mother. And when he traveled, he worked and brought home money to support you. He didn't just abandon you; he left you with relatives. His sister. He didn't know she would mistreat you, did he?"

David turned to look at the other boy. "Well, she didn't exactly mistreat me," he admitted. "Charley, my cousin, and I were treated the same. Sort of. And it wasn't her so much as my uncle."

"I wish I had an aunt and uncle," Augustus said, even more softly. "And cousins. Not just a half brother who inherits everything and only treats me like family when it suits him. Besides, your father is dealing in other people's secrets. My mother's for one. *I* don't even know everything about her. It's not that he doesn't want to tell you, but he shouldn't."

David said nothing. Slowly he picked up the pitchfork and began to toss hay. Rees quietly withdrew. He owed Augustus a big thank-you.

Chapter Twenty-three

Rees arose with David the following morning, before 4 A.M., since he planned to leave immediately for New Winstead. Lydia had coffee perking on the hob. As she poured out a cup, she and Rees shared an intimate smile. Rees ate his breakfast, last night's biscuits soaked in honey, and went outside. Bessie was already hitched to the wagon: David's apology. Rees, who thought he owed David an apology as well, looked around for his son, but he was already somewhere else and busy with chores.

The journey south to New Winstead took almost three hours. Rees had never visited this town, a somewhat larger community than Dugard and lying closer to the line of their parent state of Massachusetts. He drove in slowly and pulled into the yard of the first livery stable he saw. Since he could not guess how long his search for, and hopefully meeting with, Mr. Lattimore would take, he thought the tuppence for stabling Bessie well spent.

When the groom, a gangly fellow with unkempt fair hair and a gap between his front teeth, appeared to take the reins, Rees stayed him with a question. "Do you know a Mr. Cornelius Lattimore?"

"Mr. Lattimore? Sure. But you got a bit of a walk."

"I need to stretch my legs." True enough. At thirty-six, he

felt his knees stiffening after more than an hour of sitting. "Where is his office?"

"Walk straight until you reach Oak Street. You're going to want to go right. Across from the village green turn left. You'll see Mr. Garrett the tailor on the corner. Walk another block and turn right. Brick house."

Rees nodded his thanks and began walking. He walked through the center of town and out again, heading into a neighborhood of tree-lined streets. Rees, who had a long stride, took twenty minutes to reach the brick house described by the groom.

The large house was set a distance back from the road. Rees crossed the walk and went up the stairs to the porch. A matronly woman opened the door to his knock. "Yes?"

"Is Mr. Lattimore available?"

"Is he expecting you?" Rees heard the implied reproof.

"No. I've come from a distance, from Dugard," he said.

"He's eating his breakfast." She kept her hand upon the door.

"I'll wait until he finishes his meal." Rees could be stubborn, too.

She hesitated, thinking, and finally stood back. "Come in. I'll inform Mr. Lattimore of your arrival. Please sit down." She directed his attention to a chair by the front door. "Whom shall I say is calling?"

"William Rees. It is in regard to Nathaniel Bowditch." He didn't know if Nate's name would trigger a response but knew his own would not, and when her eyes flickered with Nate's name Rees knew he was right.

She hurried away. Rees sat down gingerly, unsure if the chair was sturdy enough to support his weight, and looked around. Pocket doors closed off the two rooms to his left, and a narrow staircase on the right rose to the second floor. The servant had hurried toward the back of the hall and disappeared through the door facing Rees. She reappeared through it very suddenly.

"Come with me, Mr. Rees," she said, sliding back the rear doors and gesturing him into a book-lined room. Another door in the back wall led to a small office lined with more books. "Mr. Lattimore will join you here shortly." She pointed him to the chair across from the desk and withdrew. Rees sat down. This small narrow office looked as though it had been carved from the larger room outside. She returned with sliced cake and tea, just as a spare older gentleman in a blue jacket and buff breeches appeared.

He paused by the door, waiting for his housekeeper to withdraw and inspecting Rees in silence. Rees turned to regard this gentleman as well. His clothing was old-fashioned but of excellent quality. A few gray strands of hair striped his bald pate and he bore the bony desiccated appearance of an abstemious Puritan. His brown eyes scrutinized Rees with interest, but he did not speak until he sat down behind his desk.

"How did you find my name, Mr. Rees?" he asked.

"I found it in Nate Bowditch's desk," Rees said.

"I see. From your appearance here, I deduce he has passed on."

"Murdered." Rees found himself adopting Mr. Lattimore's laconic style of speech. "How did you know he died?"

Mr. Lattimore permitted himself a small smile. "Mr. Bowditch knew he was ill and suspected that he might not have much time remaining to him. In fact, your name is not unfamiliar to me. He mentioned you once or twice."

Rees shivered. For the first time he wondered if Nate, knowing his life was in danger, had planned to involve his boyhood friend in the investigation. After all these years, Nate had turned to the one person he knew he could still trust. Rees turned his head to hide the moisture in his eyes but didn't fool Mr. Lattimore, who pushed a handkerchief into Rees's hand.

"Are you an attorney?" Rees asked. He had always found attorneys helpful.

"I am. Silas Potter sent Mr. Bowditch to me to draw up his will and hold for safe keeping some other items." Again a slight smile. "He hoped you would be the one to collect them."

"I see." Rees knew George Potter would be hurt by Nate's defection but understood all too clearly why he'd chosen an attorney outside of Dugard's society.

"Now that I know of Mr. Bowditch's death, I will arrange a reading of the will," Mr. Lattimore said. "I daresay Silas Potter will allow me to use his office for the purpose; I see no point in compelling all of those identified in the will to travel from Dugard to New Winstead." He paused and added, "I hope you know I can say nothing until then."

Rees nodded. He knew Mr. Lattimore would refuse to share the particulars of the will. He sipped his tea, although he didn't care for that beverage, to give himself time to think.

Mr. Lattimore came to some decision. "Today is Tuesday. If you will carry a message to Mr. Silas Potter, perhaps we can arrange the reading for Thursday."

"That will be helpful," Rees said in relief.

"And I have a number of documents Mr. Bowditch left with me for safekeeping. He asked me to surrender them to someone trustworthy. He mentioned your name particularly." He pulled a rough tow sack from his drawer and handed it over the desk. "And this accompanies whatever is in the bag." Lattimore drew a large map case from beside his bookcase.

Rees pulled the drawstring. Inside were several rough squares of paper torn from a larger sheet. They looked familiar, and his fingers itched to pull out those scraps. But he did not want to examine them in front of the lawyer. "Did you look inside?" Rees asked.

"I did not." Mr. Lattimore offered Rees a chilly smile. "Of course not. I hope you will eventually share their contents with me. I am . . . curious." His expression clouded. "Nate promised to return with more items to safeguard, but he never did."

"When was that?" Rees asked.

"A few weeks ago. No longer than that."

"That is right before he was murdered." Now Rees could barely restrain his curiosity, and his fingers began to knead the bag.

"Please, inspect them if you wish," Mr. Lattimore said, removing a sheet of parchment from his desk and dipping his quill into an inkstand. "I must write a request to Mr. Potter anyway."

Rees pulled out a handful of the paper scraps and began unfolding them one by one. For a moment there was no sound but the scratching of the pen upon the paper. "What the—?" These scraps were the companions to the gambling chits Rees had found in the trunk, only there were many more in the sack and most of them were signed by James Carleton. Rees pulled the case over and untied the string. Some of the large sheets inside were maps, but they were accompanied by deeds. Many deeds. The earliest, signed by Henry Meacham Carleton, known to all as King, began in the late 1780s. Rees guessed this was the method by which Carleton had paid Nate for dragging James back from London; the sums paid for the properties were unusually reasonable.

Although King Carleton's signature sprawled across the early documents, all the subsequent deeds bore James's signature. Rees quickly added up the sums owed by James to Nate in his head; the few scraps in his hand alone totaled over two hundred dollars. With the number of chits still to be counted, well, Rees thought the grand total must be several thousand dollars. And a quick inspection of the faded maps indicated that Nate already owned most of the Carleton estate. Now this was a secret worth murdering for. Rees sank back against the chair's back, overcome with horrified dismay.

"Not what you expected?" Mr. Lattimore asked, noting Rees's stunned expression.

"No. I'm . . . surprised." Surprise didn't seem a strong enough word for the emotions churning through Rees's gut. "But this is very helpful. I believe I know now who murdered my friend." The depth of his regret startled him. He and James had never been friends, probably never would be, but they'd been boys together. And James had suffered at the hands of his father as much as, if not more than, everyone else. "And I'm sorry."

Mr. Lattimore nodded. "People are never quite what you expect, are they?" He sanded his letter and blew gently upon it. "Here. Take this. Tell Silas that if Thursday is not convenient, to send word. Otherwise, I shall deliver myself to his office at two o'clock that afternoon."

With a nod, Rees shook the letter to remove the final bits of dust and folded it into thirds. He stowed it carefully inside his jacket. "It's been a pleasure meeting you, Mr. Lattimore."

"I've included a list of those individuals I expect to attend," Mr. Lattimore said. "You are among them, Mr. Rees, so I look forward to renewing our acquaintance."

Rees, startled that Nate had included him, extended his hand. "Good-bye Mr. Lattimore."

Rees got on the road immediately and started the long drive home to Dugard, his thoughts in a whirl. Now he knew James Carleton's secret: his gambling, an addiction that had cost him most of the property left him by his father, all of it lost to Nate, the "lucky devil." Already facing financial ruin, Carleton would almost certainly lose his family and most of his friends as well if the truth escaped. That was a secret many men would protect at any cost. Rees needed to speak to James again.

Once in Dugard, Rees drove straight to George Potter's office. Although he did not relish telling his old friend that Nate had chosen an attorney from another town, Potter would have to know. Rees, fingering the letter in his pocket, thought he might as well get that chore over with.

Sally Potter showed Rees upstairs to her father's office. George, who'd been working in his shirtsleeves, hastily shrugged into his coat. "Will," he said in surprise. And then, catching Rees's expression, "What's wrong?"

"I know where Nate's will is."

"Where?"

"He retained a lawyer in New Winstead, that gentleman Cornelius Lattimore. And in fact, Mr. Lattimore offered to read the will here, in Dugard, at your father's office."

"My father no longer keeps an office," Potter said, struggling to absorb this shock.

"I thought I might at least inform your father of Mr. Lattimore's intentions," Rees said.

"Why did Nate go to New Winstead?" Potter asked, sounding both hurt and annoyed. "He was my friend."

Rees said nothing. He agreed with Nate's judgment in this case. George Potter, friend to James Carleton as well as to Nate, and fellow card player, could not be trusted to keep silent. At best.

"I'll tell my father," Potter said.

"I have a letter." Rees extracted it from his pocket and held it out.

Potter took it, his expression sour. "We'll have to meet here," he said. "I'll surrender my office for this occasion." He did not sound gracious.

"I'm sure Nate had his reasons for choosing Mr. Lattimore," Rees said. "Maybe you're mentioned in his will."

Potter threw him a skeptical look. "And why would I be? Especially since we were not the comrades I thought we were."

"Now I'm going to the Contented Rooster for some dinner. The taverns I passed in New Winstead did not appeal." Potter snorted. Rees withdrew, leaving his disgruntled friend turning the letter over and over in his hands.

The coffeehouse was nearly empty, but then it was almost two and late for dinner. When his beef stew arrived, however, he revised his reasons for the poor custom. It was not so toothsome as he expected; the beef tough and stringy, the potatoes slightly scorched. Jack Jr. confided that his mother was finding the cooking a bit of a struggle. But at least the food was hot and the coffee was excellent as usual. As Rees drank the last of his cup, an urchin with dirty face and hands and broken boots came inside to find him.

"Mr. Potter sent me with a message," he told Rees. "He spoke to his father and they'll be in attendance on Thursday when the other gentleman arrives."

"Very good," Rees said, handing over a farthing. George Potter would have typically delivered the message himself, and the fact that he did not indicated how very angry and hurt he was. Rees hoped he would be less upset when they all met for the reading of the will.

He stopped by the kitchen door and peeked in to greet Susannah. She paused to say good-bye, her hair flying around in a halo and her right hand wearing a mitten of linen strips. "Burned myself," she said, wiping her left elbow across her forehead. "I've always shared the cooking, but I never realized how much Ruth did. I vow, Will, if Ruth returns, I'll double her pay."

Rees looked at her sympathetically. He doubted Ruth would

return, and although he wouldn't swear to it, he suspected the slave catchers had taken her. He'd heard nothing of them for the last few days. He should ask Caldwell if they'd disappeared from the Bull; no doubt he had stopped searching for them long ago.

"Do you know anyone willing to cook for us?"

Rees shook his head and turned to go. He would not mention this opportunity to Lydia, just in case she took it into her head to accept.

After supper, he spread the deeds and the few maps out upon the kitchen table. Lydia took the sack of chits and began removing them, one by one, adding up the amounts for James Carleton in her head.

"The total is two thousand five hundred twenty-one dollars and sixty-five cents," she said at last.

"How much?" Rees's voice rose to a squeak in astonishment.

"Two thousand five hundred twenty-one dollars and sixty-five cents," she repeated. "I know. I couldn't believe it either. I added it up twice. And if I'm off by a penny or two, it is still a great sum."

Rees looked at the maps and deeds spread out before him. "And these documents disclose all the property that went to Nate from the Carletons."

"Was the elder Mr. Carleton a gambler, too?"

"I don't think so. I never heard anything." Rees looked up at Lydia and added, "Of course, I never heard anything about James either."

"Why don't we sort out all the deeds signed by Mr. Carleton the elder and see what's left."

Rees thought that a good suggestion and carefully extracted

the deeds with King Carleton's characteristic bold scrawl. There were only a few. And here was the deed to the Prentiss farm, signed over by Samuel Prentiss.

"Is something the matter?" Lydia asked.

Rees put that deed with King Carleton's. "No." He quickly riffled through the remainder; all bore James's more tentative signature. "It looks as though he paid off his debts to Nate with the more outlying properties first."

"Is there any land left?"

Rees shook his head. "I don't know; I don't have a map of the entire Carleton estate. I recognize many of these farms, though, as those King Carleton took away from some small landholders." Now Rees understood why so many of those outlying fields were untilled. Carleton no longer owned them, and Nate hadn't bothered. Did Marsh know about them? "James may still own the original Carleton property."

"Not if he paid these," Lydia said, holding up a fistful of paper. "I wonder if he could even hold on to the house, these debts are so substantial."

"Tomorrow I'll speak to James Carleton once again," Rees said. He knew that even if James confessed, there was little likelihood of judgment. But murder could not go ignored.

At that moment, David entered the kitchen. He'd taken off his boots upon the back porch and he padded into the kitchen in his stocking feet. He looked curiously at the stacks of paper on the table but said nothing. Since his outburst, and Augustus's advice, he'd been trying to behave with careful rectitude. Rees hated to see the pall his son's restraint threw upon him. But this time his curiosity proved too strong; he peered over Lydia's shoulder. "What are those?" She tried to cover the chits but didn't move quickly enough. David whistled soundlessly. "I guess the rumors are true," he said.

Rees regarded his son in surprise. "What rumors?"

"Elizabeth was taken out of school early," David said. "I heard some gossip at market. Wondering, you know, if her father was having money problems."

Rees nodded. She'd said something about that when they'd spoken, but he hadn't paid attention. "What else?"

"Well, Mr. Carleton's problems are bad enough that the shopkeepers don't want to extend credit for seeds or feed. And Mr. Duncan, the tailor, said Mr. Carleton owes him for two waistcoats."

"And each of them costing a year's pay for the average working man," Lydia said, not even trying to hide her disapproval.

"I wish I'd known that before," Rees said. Although, without the gambling chits in hand, he would not have realized the magnitude of the problem. "Thank you, David."

"I helped you?" David asked tentatively.

"Yes, you certainly did," Rees said, smiling. David returned that smile, his entire face aglow.

Chapter Twenty-four

Rees overslept the next morning, and by the time he went downstairs Lydia had mush and coffee prepared. She smiled at him and he thought how wonderful it was to see her there in his kitchen. She poured him a mug of coffee and placed it before him as he sat down. Humming, and for the moment content, Rees chipped a chunk from the sugar cone and dropped it in. Cream followed, lightening his brew to caramel, the exact color of Augustus's skin. Rees took his first sip, holding it in his mouth to savor it.

"You'd better come now, Dad," David said, plunging through the back door. "We have a problem."

Dad? Rees put his cup upon the table. "What happened?"

"You need to come with me." David looked both angry and sad.

Rees followed his son to the stable. Since all the horses were running loose in the paddock, the stable should have been empty. David pushed his father inside and pointed to the back. With a testy sigh—*Why all the mystery?*—Rees walked toward the rear wall, peering into the stalls, until he reached the final one. He stared at his sister in shock. Caroline, flanked by her three children, looked up at him from their nest in the straw. All of them were dirty and furred with chaff.

"I didn't know where else to go," she whispered. A large bruise purpled her left cheek, and blood from her split lip stained the collar of her dress. Charlie, her eldest, cradled his left arm as though it hurt him.

"Oh, Caro," Rees said, moving forward to lift her upright. "What happened? Was it Sam?"

She nodded and began to sob. He looked at the children. The youngest, Georgina, leaned against her mother in white-faced exhaustion. Purple fingermarks circled her delicate wrist like a bracelet. "Come inside," Rees said, trying to keep the burn of his increasing anger from his voice. "Oh, I am so sorry. I meant to deal with this and got busy and— Come inside and we'll have breakfast."

As Charlie and Georgina stepped out of the stall, Gwendolyn was revealed, huddled in the hay at the very back. "I'm very hungry," she whispered, her eyes huge in her pale face.

Shedding straw with each step, the small party left the barn and crossed the road to the farmhouse. Lydia, who had followed Rees as far as the back porch, understood the situation immediately and quickly darted inside. When they entered the kitchen, they found four additional bowls full of mush waiting upon the table and a cup of coffee poured for Caroline. She was so distraught, she did not push it away in disgust; she disliked coffee as much as her brother enjoyed it.

"What happened?" Rees asked, sipping his now lukewarm brew.

Lydia cast a quick warning look at the children, but Caro said, "They saw the whole thing." She paused, watching her children fall hungrily upon the food. "I asked him, as nicely as I could, not to go to the Bull." She drew in a shaky breath. "He used to hit me once or twice, but since we moved to town—"

"Why didn't you tell me?" Rees asked.

Caro shrugged. "What could you do?" She shook her head. "It wasn't so terrible before. But now, we're so close to the Bull. He doesn't play every night, but we have so little . . . I don't know what we're going to do." The knuckles of the hand clutching the cup went white.

Rees thought of the deed to the Prentiss farm in the case almost within reach of his hand but held his tongue. Offering it now to Caroline, even if it were his to offer, would simply give Sam something else to lose.

"He's begun striking the children with anything that comes to hand. Yesterday he struck Charles with a poker when he tried to protect me. And he slapped the baby. . . ." Caro bent her head over Georgina in an agony of grief and shame. Rees knew that his sister would never have confided this to him if it were not for her desire to protect her children.

"How did you come here?"

"We walked. We left last night, after dark."

Lydia and Rees exchanged a glance. "They'll have to stay at the cottage," she said. "It has the most room." Rees nodded reluctantly.

Caroline, sensing their intimacy, scowled. "And where will you sleep?" she asked Lydia with her usual venom. "As if I need to ask." Lydia looked at Rees.

He rubbed his nose, thinking. "We'll have to set up a bed in the master bedroom," he said.

"Oh, and now you'll tell me *you* aren't sleeping there," Caro said, the nasty tenor of her voice instantly reminding Rees of his childhood.

"I'm sleeping in the same room I had as a boy," Rees said. "I set up my loom in the large room. . . ." He wanted to say more, but the presence of the children, and of Abigail who'd just arrived, restrained him. He turned to Lydia. "The hives?"

She smiled as though she knew exactly what he was thinking. "A few stings and the children will avoid them," she said. "The bees are not as tolerant of ill-temper as we are."

Rees glanced at his sister to see if she'd felt the jab, but she was intent upon her bowl of oatmeal. Her expression had settled into its usual discontented creases. He wished he didn't feel so conflicted about her; his initial pity was already mixed with frustration and resentment at being dragged into her domestic drama again.

Lydia nodded at Rees. "I know you have some important errands today. Abby and I can resolve this little tempest. Go on."

With a sigh of relief, he abandoned the problem to her capable hands and hurried out to harness Bessie to the wagon. Although it was past seven thirty, he hoped he would reach the Carleton home in time. A good steward of his property would already be out riding the fields but James, Rees guessed, would not be that responsible.

He bypassed Dugard and reached the estate midmorning. This time he paid particular attention to the fields. As he'd recalled, the more outlying properties lay fallow. Now he knew why.

With the approach of October, the maples lining the Carleton drive were turning orange and scarlet. Some had begun dropping their leaves, and the sun, still warm, shone through the bare branches. Rees sighed, dreading the approach of winter. At least he would keep busy weaving this winter. He expected to receive a lot of customers with Nate's death, Dugard now had no local weaver.

He looped Bessie's reins around the rail, telling the ragged boy who arrived to take the mare that only a pail of water would be necessary. He didn't expect to stay long.

He knocked on the door. To his surprise, Elizabeth opened it. Rees, who'd been expecting an argument with the jumped-up servant, was thrown and didn't at first notice her tear-filled eyes. "What's the matter?" he asked in concern.

"Nothing important," she said. "I don't want to inflict my problems upon you."

"Obviously something important," Rees said. "You've been weeping."

She nodded, several fat tears rolling down her cheeks. "My parents have been fighting for three days," she said in a hushed whisper. "Richard asked me to marry him, and my father gave his blessing. But my mother . . ." Fresh tears welled up into her eyes.

"She refuses?"

"Yes. She has set her heart on a title. She doesn't care that I love Richard."

Rees patted her clumsily on the shoulder. "I'm sorry. Where is your father now?"

"In his office. He's always in his office." She gulped and shuddered.

"I know the way." Rees hurried down the hall and took the stairs at the other end two at a time. He knocked on the office door.

"Who is it?" James shouted. Without replying, Rees went in. "What are you doing here? I don't want to see you today."

Rees sat down in the chair and regarded his boyhood nemesis. His waistcoat was pale yellow silk, embroidered in a darker yellow. Would Mrs. Carleton be wearing yellow today or another color to clearly indicate the rift between husband and wife? "You lied to me." Rees said.

"No, I didn't," James protested automatically. But his shoulders tensed. "About what?"

"You owed Nate a lot of money. I know, I have the chits in my possession."

"They aren't yours. You need to give them to me."

"I believe they'll go into the estate," Rees said. "Yes, Nate did have a will. The reading is tomorrow at two. Richard will be a very wealthy man. I know; I've seen the deeds."

All the blood drained from James's face and he looked ill. "I would have won it all back if Nate was still alive," he said.

Rees doubted that but he did not argue. "Is that why you want your daughter to marry Nate's son? To recover your land?" As a relative, James would have pressured Nate—although Rees doubted that would have succeeded. "Now that Nate is dead, you believe you could persuade Richard to give you back your land. . . ." James's silence admitted it.

"Was your father also a gambler?"

"No. His weakness was women—girls, really. As you know. He couldn't leave them alone. He didn't understand the lure of the game. When my debts became too high, he sent Nate after me in London. Nate asked to be paid in land, not money."

"So, you've been gambling a long time."

James smiled with a queer kind of pride. "I was a member of the Hellfire Club. But the cards don't always love me."

Rees thought of the deeds and the chits, and disappointment in Nate swelled within him. He would not have expected his old friend to take advantage of another man's weakness. "And Nate has been gambling with you since you returned?"

"No." James shook his head. "He refused at first." His mouth curled into a gloating smile. "His weakness was a far greater sin." Rees clenched his hands into fists and kept silent with an effort. James laughed. "My father was on his deathbed and Nate felt it was time for me to take on 'adult responsibilities.' But other men were eager to play cards with me. Your own brother-in-law, Willie. I do believe he gambled with your farm." He chuckled.

Right now, Rees didn't know which man he wanted to hit first: Sam or James. After several deep breaths, he asked, "So how did Nate end up with the deed to Sam's farm?"

"Oh, he lost it before he went to manage your farm. Funny, Sam didn't play often, and he won sometimes. But that evening he had such a run of bad luck. Almost like he was being punished."

And maybe he was. Rees wondered if Nate cheated. "Is that why you killed Nate? Because you owed him so much money?"

James's eyes bugged out of his head. He leaped to his feet and began shouting, "I didn't kill him. Of course I didn't. Why would I? I want his son to marry my daughter."

"Your path to your economic recovery," Rees said sarcastically.

James squirmed. "Don't judge."

"It was a connection Nate refused. In fact, if I understand it correctly, he was adamantly opposed."

"He would have come around. The two children love one another."

"You can't even persuade your wife," Rees pointed out.

"You can't prove I was at the weaving cottage that night," James said, turning cunning. "Several men owe Nate money, not just me. Sam Prentiss, and Corny Hansen to name just two."

"But they didn't owe Nate such a great sum," Rees said.

"You're really stupid, you know that?" James said. "Haring around looking at everybody else. Always the admired one. Even my father respected you. You fought back. But you know nothing about this. Nothing about Nate." He paused.

Rees stared at James. That was the second time James had referred to some secret he knew. Rees had dismissed it the first time, but now . . .

James broke into Rees's thoughts. "It's time for you to leave. Don't visit me again."

Rees rose and stamped out of the house, not because he was obedient or frightened of James but because he had nothing further to say. Not yet, anyway. He climbed into the wagon and started back to town, replaying the conversation in his head. Although Rees wanted to believe James was lying, he couldn't. He thought James really did know something, something about Nate, and just couldn't help gloating about it. Especially to Rees, the farmer's son who always bested him. The intensity of James's jealousy was sobering.

There still was no proof Carleton had been at the cottage that day. That astonishing debt provided a good reason for murder, but it didn't prove James had actually done it.

And he had sounded sincere when he swore he had not killed Nate. If that were true, and Rees reluctantly believed it, then he still did not know the identity of Nate's killer.

As the wagon trundled toward town, Rees realized there was something more. Someone had told Rees something important. Who was it? Someone at the Bowditch farm? It was something that had to do with James, but cudgel his brain as hard as he could, Rees could not call it to mind. It had not seemed important at the time, and he had not noted it.

He paused in Dugard, pulling up in front of the ruined jail. Caldwell was nowhere about, and with a sigh Rees crossed the street to the Bull.

The constable leaned on the bar. He looked up in surprise. "Why, Mr. Rees, it's been several days since I've seen you." He motioned Rees to an empty table. "This is what passes for my office these days."

"Where do you put the lawbreakers?"

"In the tack room at Wheeler's. Last man I had inside was your brother-in-law," Caldwell said. "He went after some poor farmer, thinking he was you. Be careful, he's half-mad with anger and drink. Now he claims you've stolen his family."

"I found my sister and her brood hiding in the stable," Rees said. "They walked to the farm from town. Caro's face is all bruised and Charlie's arm is broken. You can tell Sam from me that if he sets one foot on my property, I'll shoot to kill."

Caldwell looked at Rees. "You better be sure he isn't sneaking up behind you. In his current mood, he's dangerous."

"Sam won't dare trouble me," Rees said.

Caldwell shook his head uneasily but didn't press the point. "How's the boy?" he asked, lowering his voice.

"Fine. No trouble that I can see. David likes him."

"Mr. Isaacs has a new apprentice." Caldwell paused. "He's threatening to accuse Augustus of running away—"

"Oh Lord! He knows Augustus was in danger."

Caldwell shrugged. "Best thing for the boy is to have someone buy out his term." Rees didn't reply. He felt as though dependents were attaching themselves to him like burrs. "Did you come here to talk about the fugitive?"

"In a sense. Have you seen the slave takers recently?"

"Not for several days." Caldwell looked at Rees in surprise. "Why?"

"Just wondering if it's safe for Augustus to return to town." He paused. "Have you heard about Ruth, the Andersons' cook?"

"Miss Susannah told me Ruth ran off to get married." Caldwell met Rees's gaze. "You think those Southern crackers took her?"

"Makes sense, doesn't it? She disappeared right around the time I took Augustus out of jail."

Caldwell pursed his lips and nodded. "Unfortunately, yes. Have you suggested this to Mrs. Anderson?"

Rees shook his head. "I don't know, exactly, and I think Susannah would rather believe Ruth ran off to marry."

Caldwell nodded. "Care for a drink?"

Rees shook his head. "I'm going to the Contented Rooster for something to eat." He started for the door but turned back. "Did you ever join Sam Prentiss and the others who played cards?"

Caldwell shook his head. "Not me. I work too hard for my few pennies to piss them away over a few squares of pasteboard. Besides, I don't have anything to gamble with." He paused and then said, "Anyway, most of the gamblers were the rich men in town. They wouldn't spit on me, forget about playing cards. And they usually played somewhere secret, not at the Bull."

Rees nodded and went out to his wagon. He wondered what Caldwell would say if he knew that James Carleton was in danger of losing everything over those squares of "pasteboard."

Again the coffeehouse was empty and Rees had his pick of tables. He chose his usual table between the fireplace and window. Jack Jr. brought him coffee with sugar and cream and a short wait Susannah sped out of the kitchen with a basket of fresh Sally Lunn bread. Although her flyaway hair was neatly coiffed under her cap, linen still swaddled her right hand and she looked anxious.

"More questions?" she asked.

"Not today," Rees said, helping himself to a slice of the bread and slathering it with butter. "What's the matter?"

She gestured around the coffeehouse. "Isn't it obvious? I just don't cook as well as Ruth."

"This is good," Rees said, waving the bread at her. But he did not tell the entire truth; the bread was neither as light nor as tasty as Ruth's.

Susannah smiled without humor. "You're a good friend, Will." After a pause, she said, "I heard a rumor that Nate retained another lawyer for his will."

Rees nodded. "The reading is tomorrow."

"Do you think it will help you find his murderer?"

"No, I . . ." Rees almost told her about James Carleton but stopped himself just in time. "Nate was a different person than the boy I remember," he said instead, thinking that saying it shouldn't hurt so much.

Susannah smiled. "We all grow up, Will. Nate made a success of himself, and I fancy he was happy with his life. I'm glad you like the Sally Lunn." She turned and dashed away.

Rees chewed automatically, his thoughts turning to Nate. Had he been happy? It certainly did not appear that he'd been content. And someone somewhere had hated him enough to kill him; Rees still didn't know who.

Chapter Twenty-five

The afternoon flew by in a flurry of shifting furniture and bedding between the house and the cottage. Moving Lydia's few bit and pieces took only one trip, but shifting the heavy loom to one corner to clear a space for the bed ate up over an hour. Both David and Rees struggled with it.

But by nightfall, everyone had a bed to sleep in or, in the case of the three Prentiss children, pallets on the floor. Lydia and Abby had put on a nourishing soup for dinner and when the girl left at three, the cauldron was bubbling over the fire and a large pan of corn bread waited to go into the oven.

Rees came down the stairs from the master bedroom to find the table set for seven. Only Lydia and Caroline remained in the kitchen. The older boys were still finishing chores, and the younger girls were playing quietly in the parlor, their voices rising and falling contentedly. "Why isn't there a plate for Augustus?" Rees asked.

"I can't believe you expect me to sit down at table with one of those people," Caro said with a sniff.

Rees turned to his sister, his mouth opening to shoot her some crushing remark. But Lydia jumped in before him. "Augie elected to eat after we finish," she said. "For tonight, anyway. Tomorrow he will sit down to breakfast and the other meals with us as usual."

"He will not," Caro said, straightening up from her position by the fire. "I won't allow it."

"You won't allow it?" Rees repeated.

"Since you and your children will be eating your meals down at the cottage," Lydia said, her voice calm but with a hint of iron, "I don't understand why you care."

"We'll be eating here, of course," Caro said. She looked at Lydia with disdain. "You and the other girl are working for my brother; it won't be much trouble to add me and my children."

Rees ignored Lydia's warning glance and shouted, "That is my future wife, Caro! She will be the mistress of this house, not you."

In the sudden silence, the bubble and pop of the soup sounded as loud as a fusillade of shots. Rees didn't know where those words had come from and for a moment he wished he could take them back. But Lydia was beaming with joy and he knew he couldn't wipe that astonished happiness from her face.

He glanced at Caro, expecting some nasty remark, but she stunned him. "Well, it's about time," she said. "All these years mooning after Dolly. A wonderful woman to be sure, but no longer among us. It's time for you to remarry and settle down." Rees was too staggered to speak.

Lydia moved forward. "I hope we shall become as close as sisters," she said, although her expression was wary. Caroline stared at Lydia and suddenly burst into deep chest grinding sobs.

Rees stared at her. His sister never wept, and certainly not with such abandon. "You're safe here," he said. She nodded but the weeping didn't cease.

Lydia fetched a cup of coffee and helped the sobbing woman into a chair at the table.

Caro struggled to control herself. When she calmed enough

to sip her coffee, she said, "When is the date of the wedding?" Although her voice trembled, she strove to sound as usual.

"We haven't selected one," Lydia said.

"I thought Christmastime," Rees said at the exact same moment.

Caro managed a chuckle. "Very well." She dashed the tears from her eyes and although she didn't rise to help Lydia finish dinner, she made no further criticisms. The next awkward moment came from David.

"How long is she staying here?" he asked, tipping his head in Caroline's direction.

"Manners," Rees said in reproof.

David looked at his father. "How can you side with her?" he said fiercely.

"I'm not—," Rees began.

"Until we find a safe place for them," Lydia said at the same moment. She drew David aside and spoke to him in a low voice, so low, Rees heard only a few words. "Difficult" was repeated several times but "Christian charity" was spoken with emphasis. David cast Caroline a dark glance but said no more.

Caro did not offer to help with the dishes either and Rees did not suggest it. As his sister and her children walked down to the cottage and David and Augustus retreated upstairs, the kitchen cleared, offering him his first private moments with Lydia all day.

She turned to look at him, the dishrag dripping water onto the floor. "Are you sure you want to marry me?"

"Are you sure you want to say yes and marry me and my overbearing family?"

"Yes." She smiled. "If you promise to mend your ways." Rees put out his arms. When she did not immediately react, he feared she would not accept his invitation but then she rushed forward, enveloping him in her scent of lavender and honey. Their first kiss was tentative and they broke apart immediately. Anyone might come upon them here in the kitchen and their passion for one another was too private, and still too fragile, to risk the intrusion of another person.

"You know what kind of man I am," Rees said. "I'm a wanderer; I'll never stay home all the time. But I will always return to you, securing our future with the money I've made as a weaver. And I'll always be faithful."

"I know," Lydia said with a smile. She moved away, keeping herself busy washing dishes. "And I will be your partner." She looked at him questioningly, checking her statement.

"You will be my partner," he agreed.

She smiled at him, radiant with joy. "So, did anything of note transpire in your conversation with James Carleton?"

"He swore he didn't murder Nate," Rees said. "I believe him, although I wish I didn't. And he didn't deny losing most of the property at cards. He claimed he wanted to marry his daughter to Richard Bowditch for that reason, to regain the property for his family."

Lydia poured soapy water into the soup pot. "That makes sense," she said. "What exactly did he say?"

Rees tried to repeat the exact sequence of his conversation with James, Lydia listening intently. "I made a hash of that, didn't I?" he asked.

"He never said he wasn't at the cottage that night," Lydia pointed out. "He just said you couldn't prove it. Perhaps he was there and he saw something."

"More likely he's lying."

"You know him far better than I do. Will he come after you

now, and try to silence you?" She turned to look at him her fore-head creased with worry. "I don't want to become an early widow." She smiled at him but he saw the anxiety behind it.

"That's a good question," Rees said. "But no, he won't. I mean, I suppose it's possible but I can't see it of James. His father, now I could see him as a murderer. But James . . . no. He went to England during the Revolutionary War; I doubt he even owns a gun." His words slowed as he realized what he was saying. If that were true, how could he believe James murdered Nate?

Lydia realized it, too. She turned to face him. "He doesn't sound a likely murderer."

"He had good reason."

Lydia threw him a skeptical glance. "Several people had good reason."

Rees nodded, thinking. "Why hasn't anyone else come after me?"

"Maybe he can't?"

Rees pondered. "Marsh?"

"Yes, like Marsh, who is kept busy until almost midnight and arises again at dawn. But I won't believe it of him. He is a good man, Will."

"Maybe James simply lost his temper and lashed out? But he doesn't own a murderer's heart—"

"Or a gun," Lydia put in.

"—and can't bring himself to menace someone else? Even me."

"Then what about the burning of the jail? That was clearly intended to kill Augustus," Lydia objected. "And did Marsh even know about Augustus?"

"He said not." He sighed. "Caldwell blames the slave catchers."

"Maybe he's right?"

"Maybe. But I refuse to believe in such coincidence." Was he back to Richard? Or was it still about James? Or someone else entirely? "Maybe James is right and I am stupid," Rees said.

Lydia turned a flicked the dish towel at him. "Stop. Stop right now. You'll see the way of it."

Rees nodded, his thoughts turning to Nate and the secrets he carried.

After dinner on Thursday, Augustus and Rees set off for Dugard. Like Rees, Augustus appeared on Mr. Lattimore's list and Rees decided that should not surprise him. After all, everyone thought of the lad as Nate's son, probably even Nate. Lydia, who joined David and Abby on the front porch to see the two men off, returned inside as soon as Rees climbed into the buggy and picked up the reins. But Rees noticed that David and Abigail remained outside, standing shoulder to shoulder, already a couple despite their youth. When he caught David's gaze, the lad stared back defiantly.

Rees twisted to look at Augustus, who had chosen to sit in the backseat, where the buggy walls hid him from view, and said, "Are you set?" Augustus nodded. He looked queasy with trepidation. "It'll be fine," Rees said, trying to reassure him. But the lad did not look comforted.

They arrived in Dugard just before one thirty and Rees, as he planned, pulled his buggy into the back alley behind George Potter's office. There was a little space remaining out front but the weaver didn't even consider stopping there; he suspected there were people in town who still believed Augustus was the guilty party, and so Rees wanted to sneak him up the back stairs unseen.

Molly Bowditch and her two eldest children were already

there, seated on the side of the room opposite the door. Their position told Rees they'd arrived first. Both Richard and Grace looked resigned, but Molly, lovely in pale gray with a lavender pelisse and matching bonnet, glowed with excitement. George Potter sat next to them, his sulky expression resting upon Mr. Lattimore, who'd captured the chair at the desk.

Thomas Bowditch and his wife sat in the opposite corner, as far as they could get from Nate's wife and still sit in the same room. Marsh and Rachel stood in back of the chairs, lined up in front of the windows that looked down upon Main Street.

When Molly saw Rees and Augustus, she leaped to her feet with a little scream. Both Rachel and Marsh looked at the door and Rachel rushed to her son's side. "I've been so worried." She clung to him, tears filling her eyes. Augustus, looking embarrassed, patted her shoulder awkwardly. Richard rose to his feet, shaking off his mother's hand, and went to embrace his brother.

"Now that everyone is here," Mr. Lattimore said, looking up from the papers upon his desk, "I'll begin."

"No. What are they doing here?" Molly said, gesturing disdainfully at Marsh, Rachel, and Augustus.

"They are named in the Last Will and Testament of Nathaniel Bowditch," Mr. Lattimore said. If he expected to crush Molly into silence, he failed.

"They have no rights . . . ," she began. This time the attorney just looked at her with stern impatience and she subsided.

"I will begin with the smaller bequests," he said when the rustle of soft breathing faded. "He leaves a sum of two hundred dollars to my good friend and companion Marshall Thompson." Rees gasped; two hundred dollars was an enormous sum. He looked over at Marsh, but his dark face did not reveal his emotions. Molly, however, glared at Marsh and seemed ready to burst into speech. Mr. Lattimore turned his steely gaze upon her. When she thought better of speaking and settled silently into her chair, the attorney continued. "I give the farm left me by my father to my brother, Thomas Bowditch, to own free and clear of all debt." As Mrs. Bowditch burst into excited sobs, Mr. Lattimore looked up at Tom. "Nate asked me to tell you that your father always wanted you to have the farm." Tom rubbed his eyes, too overcome to speak.

"That should belong to Richard," Molly declared.

Rees, who knew how wealthy his boyhood friend had been by the time of his death, frowned at her.

"Rachel: I give you your freedom. No person should be sold or be forced to serve another as a slave."

She and Molly gasped in concert, Rachel looking both alarmed and frightened.

"To Augustus, the son of my heart, I leave the sum of one hundred dollars. I hope this will prove sufficient to purchase the remainder of your contract and the smithy from Mr. Isaacs."

"No," Molly cried. "This is outrageous. These sums will beggar me."

"Of course you may contest the will," Mr. Lattimore said, his mouth pursing as though he'd bitten into a lemon. "Or rather, Richard may contest the will; that is his right." His gaze rested upon the young man. Richard nodded but not as though he cared very much. An involuntary smile tugged at his lips, immediately suppressed, but breaking out once again.

Rees stared at that puzzling grin. What was wrong with the boy?

"Now we come to the substance of the document." Mr. Lattimore looked around the room. "To my daughter, Grace, I leave my farm, bordered on the northern side by the Rumford road, on the south by . . ."

Rees stopped listening. Except for Molly's disgraceful behavior, the will presented nothing unusual at all. He focused his entire concentration upon Molly Bowditch. Her disbelief and horror had now segued into fury. Jumping to her feet, she began screaming. "What about Richard, his eldest son? What about me? And Ben?"

Mr. Lattimore ceased speaking. He looked at her with scornful impatience. "Mrs. Bowditch, if you do not cease interrupting, I will ask Mr. Potter to remove you, and one of your children can inform you of the will's contents."

Trembling, she returned to her seat. But her ashen cheeks and glittering tear-filled eyes promised another outburst. Grace sat in rigid silence. Richard patted his mother's wrist.

Mr. Lattimore continued the description of the farm, his words providing a backdrop to Rees's thoughts. But the mention of Richard's name jolted him to attention. "To Richard, I leave all of the property I obtained from Mr. James Carleton, to do with as he chooses. I ask my friend, William Rees, to ensure this transfer of property takes place. He may determine the disposition of the other properties won at the card table as he sees fit. I rely upon his good judgment and sense of fair play to decide in the best interests of all. To compensate him for his time I leave all of my looms, any linen or wool waiting to be woven, all of my dyes, and the sum of fifty dollars."

"What other properties?" Molly asked, staring around her. "What card games?" She looked at Potter. He shrugged, his eyes sliding away from hers. She turned to Mr. Lattimore. "What about me? "

He looked down at the parchment in front of him. "Ah, here is the phrase that refers to you. The care of my widow and her son, Benjamin, shall be the responsibility of her son, Richard."

So, Nate knew about Dr. Wrothman, Rees thought.

"He made me a pauper? A dependent?" Molly could scarcely force out the words.

"I'm sorry," Mr. Lattimore said. "Of course, this is not so unusual a provision; many widows are left in the care of their sons. And Ben, well, your husband was persuaded that he was not Ben's father."

"But I took care of everything while he played with his leaves and powders!" Molly screamed. "I suffered the presence of his mistress . . ." She flung her hand at Rachel. "Gave her room in my home. Well, let Rachel live without my help. You're free now, don't return to my house."

"That's Grace's house now," Mr. Lattimore said, his dry words somehow sounding cruel.

"But where will I go?" Rachel quavered.

"I don't care. I vow, if I see you there, I will have you shot you on sight."

"Excuse me," Mr. Lattimore said. "But Mrs. Bowditch, you do not own Rachel."

"Don't worry," Rees said to Rachel. "I have somewhere for you to go."

"Of course, she must return to the farm," Grace said. "It is her home."

"It will never work," Rees said, knowing he spoke the truth. Molly would torture Rachel without mercy.

"Please, allow her to collect her things," Potter said, gazing at Molly in disbelief.

"She owns nothing that my husband did not pay for." Molly tossed her head, the short soft brown waves a shiny nimbus. "She deserves nothing further from us."

"Mother," Richard said in gentle reproof.

"Don't 'Mother' me." She turned on him, outraged. "I will not allow it. I will not." She fixed her fiery gaze first upon her son and then upon her daughter and their protests withered. She rose to her feet. "Come, Richard—come, Grace."

Grace turned a glance of abject apology upon Rachel and reluctantly followed her mother from the room.

Rees shook his head regretfully. So, that was how it would be; Molly would play the tune and Richard would dance to it. But he couldn't entirely blame her for her anger. She was a proud woman and had just been thoroughly humiliated.

"I didn't realize Molly possessed such a temper," Potter said in amazement.

"I'll wager your wife knew," Rees said, scornfully.

"What am I going to do?" Rachel wailed.

"You'll live with me," Augustus said. "When I'm settled—"

"I have a more immediate solution," Rees said. "If she won't object to a short walk with me? I believe the Andersons will employ her."

Rachel looked at Marsh, her expression beseeching. He in turn stared searchingly into Rees's face. "It's all right," he said at last. "Go with him, Rachel. It will be all right. I trust Mr. Rees."

"You have what you need to fulfill Mr. Bowditch's commission," Mr. Lattimore said to Rees. "If you have any further questions, you know where my office is. And I shall correspond regularly with Mr. Potter."

"Very good," Rees said. He looked at Augustus. "I'll return very soon."

"Don't concern yourself over me," Augustus said. "I plan on visiting my old master, Mr. Isaacs." He grinned. "Wheeler's is just across the street. I believe I can find my way to the farm on my own."

"Don't assume, because you are now a man of property, that you are safe," Rees warned him. "There are almost certainly people who believe you guilty of your father's murder."

Some of the sparkle vanished from Augustus's eyes. "I'll be careful."

Rees nodded and held the door open for Rachel. "Don't be frightened," he said. "I know you'll be happy with my solution."

He offered her his arm, but she declined. As they walked through Dugard, she kept her head lowered, but her eyes darted from side to side. She was as timid as a bird, ready to take flight at any perceived threat. And Rees himself noticed a few astonished glances shot at him and his surprising companion.

He paused in front of the Contented Rooster. "The coffeehouse?" she said, her voice cracking with shock. Rees nodded and held the gate open. Now Rachel grasped his arm, gripping it like a lifeline, as they entered.

They stepped into the shadowy interior. Jack Jr. looked up from stirring up the fire. "Will you run and get your mother for me?" Rees said. Jack glanced at Rachel and shot off at top speed. Rees offered Rachel a chair but she refused with a tiny shake of her head and kept to her feet.

Susannah came out of the kitchen at a run. "Come in," she cried. "Come in." She stared at Rachel with a mixture of curiosity and excitement. "And who might this be?"

"This is Rachel," Rees said. "She was the cook for the Bowditch family. You've eaten her food, at Nate's memorial? I thought, since you need a cook . . ."

Susannah nodded and began to smile, her gaze never shifting from Rachel. "Please, sit. Let me fetch Jack." She insisted upon seeing them comfortably seated before speeding off once again.

Rachel looked at the fire snapping on the hearth, at the few men drinking coffee and eating cake at the tables and then at Rees. "What are we doing here?"

"They need a cook. You need a position. It seemed a good fit to me." Rachel stared at him, looked as though she might speak, and then tears sprang into her eyes. "They're good people," Rees said reassuringly. "You'll be safe here. And Augustus will be right across the road." He paused as Jack Jr. came out with coffee and tea and a plate of apple cake. Rees offered some to Rachel, but she shook her head, clenching her hands together so tightly, the knuckles paled. He helped himself.

He had eaten almost all the cake when Susannah and Jack finally appeared. They pulled up chairs to the table. Both the Andersons looked at Rachel curiously. She kept her eyes lowered, breathing rapidly with anxiety

"You did the cooking for the memorial dinner?" Jack rumbled. Rachel nodded. "Baking also?" She nodded again. Jack turned to his wife and they exchanged a glance.

"How is it that you're not working for Mrs. Bowditch?" Susannah asked.

"The master's will freed me," she replied in a low voice. "Mrs. Bowditch threw me off the property."

When both Andersons looked at Rees, he nodded in corroboration. "Not that she had that right," he said.

"Would you be willing to work for us?" Jack rumbled. "At least for a week or so, to see how it goes?"

"My husband is telling you he doesn't like my baking," Susannah said, smiling at Rachel.

"She means *she* doesn't like her baking," Jack said.

"I don't care for baking, that is true," Susannah agreed.

Rees sneaked a glance at Rachel. She was staring at the Andersons in amazement.

"The cakes I ate at the memorial dinner were excellent," Jack said.

"All my cooking is excellent," Rachel said, attempting to join the banter. When both Jack and Susannah laughed, her rigid shoulders relaxed slightly.

"Did you taste the apple cake?" Jack asked. Rachel looked at him and then cautiously ate a tiny morsel brought to her lips by the caramel-colored fingers.

"Be honest, pray," Susannah said.

"It's very good," Rachel said. Rees could see she was shading the truth.

"But yours is better?" Jack asked hopefully.

Rachel slanted a look at first Susannah and then Jack from under her lashes and nodded. "Mine is much better," she said.

"When can you begin?" Susannah asked.

"Right now," Rees said. He directed a pointed glance at Susannah. "Molly lost her temper. She didn't care for the provisions of Nate's will and Rachel caught that anger. She is not allowed even to return to the farm for her clothing."

Susannah nodded in understanding. "Ruth left some things upstairs." She jumped to her feet. "Come with me, Rachel, and I'll show you to your room."

Rachel darted a look of disbelieving joy at Rees and rose to follow her new mistress. Rees watched them cross the floor with the happy sense that this time something had worked for the best.

"I think we owe you dinner," Jack said. "I don't mind telling you, Suze had been struggling with the cooking."

Rees smiled. "Maybe tomorrow. Caroline arrived with the three children this morning."

Jack looked up in alarm. "Be careful, Will. Sam is not a man to cross."

Rees snorted in dismissal. "I'll see you tomorrow."

Chapter Twenty-six

When Rees arrived home, he found everything quiet and only Abby in the kitchen. Even the air was still. She gestured to the backyard. When he stepped out the back door, he saw Lydia down by the cottage, her gown a dark burgundy contrast to the white of her hives. Even from the hilltop he could see the sparkle of her hair against the cap. Inhaling a deep breath, he started down the hill. He knew she saw him approaching by the quick sideways glance, but she did not speak.

"They seem to be doing well," he said, pausing a distance away. Protected from the sun by a large oak, the hives were lined up in two rows, the landing pads out toward the kitchen garden and the southern fields.

Lydia nodded. "They survived the journey well and throve," she said. "It's time to take some of the honey and the combs. Winter is coming and soon they'll be sleeping." She turned to Rees. "And what happened at the reading of the will?"

"Nate freed Rachel and Molly Bowditch threw her off the farm."

Lydia shook her head regretfully. "That awful jealousy," she murmured. "And there's no reason for it."

"I took Rachel to the Contented Rooster and she'll be working for them," Rees said. "Jack invited me to dinner tomorrow, in thanks. I'd like you to accompany me."

Lydia looked at him in astonishment, her hands tugging at her skirt. "Do you know what you're suggesting?"

"I do." He grinned at her. "We won't have to post the banns; everyone in town will know in a few hours. Easier all around." When she didn't speak, he added anxiously, "Will you?"

"If you're sure? Yes, of course." She smiled and approached him, her step light. Rees held out his arm.

Rees began to regret his impulsive invitation as soon as he and Lydia, wearing her best dress, drove out of the drive. By the time they reached Dugard his heart was thudding. They drove the length of the town, from the southeastern tip to the coffee-house located in the center of northernmost Water Street, and Rees felt as though every single person they passed watched them. When he glanced at Lydia she was hanging on to the wagon for dear life, her mouth clenched into a tight line. She turned her head and smiled at him, a small uncertain smile that faded as quickly as it had come.

"It will be all right." Rees reassured both of them. "It will be all right."

He helped her alight from the wagon, her body trembling so powerfully, he could feel her shaking, and offered her his arm.

"Come in, come in," Susannah cried as she flung open the door. She must have been watching for Rees, but she focused all her attention now about Lydia. Her eyes rested with curiosity and surprise upon the white linen square occluding Lydia's dark red hair. "And who is this?"

"Lydia Jane Farrell," Rees said.

"I am very pleased to meet you," Susannah said, her bright blue-eyed gaze lingering upon that piece of linen. "Come in, please." She stepped aside, motion them toward Rees's favorite table by the window.

Lydia clutched at Rees's arm, her fingers digging painfully into the muscle. But she held her head high as they progressed through the room. It was dinnertime and busier than Rees had seen it lately. Several of the men nodded at him, curious, but the women stared avidly only at Lydia. Embarrassed color rose into her cheeks.

"I'll fetch Jack," Susannah said. But he, too, must have been waiting because, as she stepped toward the kitchen, he appeared with a tray with two cups, a teapot and a coffeepot.

He fumbled them onto the table, flicking his interested gaze at Lydia, and said, "Rachel wants to stop over also and greet you both. She's wonderful, by the way."

Rees nodded, bereft of speech. This had not been a good idea; he and Lydia were the cynosures of all eyes.

"And when is the wedding?" Susannah asked. When Rees looked at her in surprise, she said, "Really, Will, you would never introduce a woman to the entire town in this fashion unless you planned to marry."

"Christmas, I think," he said, glancing at Lydia for her approval.

Susannah said to Lydia, "Don't allow this rascal to string you along. I've known him all my life. He's a good man, born under the wandering foot maybe, but reliable and honest. And it's long past time that he remarried." Lydia smiled. Susannah looked over at Rees, who was standing in an uncomfortable silence.

"Listen to you rattling on," Jack said. "Let our old friend sit down and eat his dinner with his future wife."

Susannah nodded at Rees. "Of course. We prepared a wonderful ham today. Would you both care for ham?"

Rees nodded. He would have accepted a plateful of dirt just to shift everyone's attention away from him and Lydia. Very conscious of his manners, he held her chair. She was aware of everyone's gaze as well; she sat down and folded her hands daintily in her lap. When he seated himself across the table from her, he said, "I'm sorry. Putting you in this position was poor judgment on my part."

Lydia smiled. "After this nothing else will be difficult. But it will be a pleasure to eat something else besides my own cooking."

Rees sat back in his chair, relaxing, and very grateful that Lydia was not one of those picky hysterical women. Susannah hurried out with the first course, a salad of fresh garden greens. Rees spread his linen napkin across his lap and picked up his fork.

An hour later, after a fine and very substantial dinner, Rees sat back replete. He could not finish the apple tart sitting before him, although it was delicious. Lydia, more sensible, had satisfied herself with a cup of tea.

"I daresay it's time to go home," Rees said without moving. Lydia nodded and took a sip from her cup.

The door slammed open and Caldwell, his rusty black cloak flapping, hurried inside. "Rees. Rees," he cried. "Thank the Lord I found you."

"Yes," Rees said, a premonition dropping his heart to his feet.

"I thought you would want to hear this. Both James Carleton and Richard Bowditch have been shot."

Rees stood up so suddenly, his chair crashed to the floor. "What? Where? That's not possible. Was it a duel?"

"Don't know. Dr. Wrothman left for the scene and I thought you might . . ." Noticing Lydia, he paused.

Rees was already moving toward the constable but suddenly recollecting his companion, he stopped and turned back to her.

She smiled. "Go on. I'll find my own way home."

"We'll make sure she reaches the farm," Susannah said. Rees realized both she and Jack had come out from the back.

"I'll take her," Jack promised.

"Are they seriously hurt?" Susannah asked Caldwell.

He shrugged. "I won't know until I see for myself."

Rees shot an apologetic glance at Lydia and hurried forward. "We'll take my wagon," he said. "It's just outside."

"Follow Water Street to the end," Caldwell said as they climbed in.

"Where are we going?"

"A farm sold to Henry Carleton many years ago," Caldwell replied. "The fields were planted for the first time this year. Some of the hands harvesting the barley heard the shots." He glanced at his companion. "Both Richard Carleton and James Bowditch would have died for certain if the men hadn't been working close by."

"The hands see anyone?"

"Nah. The shooter didn't pass them. At least that's what they said."

"Do Mrs. Bowditch and Mrs. Carleton know yet?"

"Don't know. I sent a deputy to inform Mrs. Bowditch, but I assumed one of the hands would run and tell Mrs. Carleton." Caldwell sighed. "I really don't know any more. I wouldn't know that much but one of the hands came into the Bull." He glanced at Rees. "He was distraught, I suppose. I stopped at Dr. Wrothman's office to let him know and was heading out myself when one of the local boys said he saw you going into the coffee-house."

Rees nodded, his thoughts in turmoil. These shootings could

not be a coincidence, but he could not understand how they fit with Nate's murder.

Forty minutes later, they reached the lane leading to the old farmhouse. Several fields lay fallow and thick with goldenrod before they reached the barley. The tiny house—more of a shack, really—was weathered a dark gray. Both windows were gone, presumably removed for the glass, and the front steps were rotten. Rees spotted several weak places in the roof and suspected a heavy snow would bring the whole thing crashing down. A buggy and a wagon were drawn up to the steps. Rees pulled Bessie up beside the other vehicles and he and the constable climbed down. They jumped over the rotting steps and hurried inside.

Both the wounded men were lying upon the floor, scarlet blood dyeing the wooden planks around them. Dr. Wrothman knelt beside Richard, leaning over the gaping wound in his left shoulder blade. He did not move. And Rees hoped the boy was unconscious and not dead.

Rees knelt beside Carleton. Blood from the wound in his arm stained his fine yellow silk waistcoat. He was awake, his eyes glittering with pain. Rees cut off Carleton's coat sleeve and bent over the wound. It looked as though the ball had passed through his arm; by the size of the hole in his triceps the projectile had apparently gone all the way through. Rees looked at the positions of these two men. Richard lay on his belly and Carleton on his back. It appeared as though they'd been shooting at each other and Richard had turned to run. Were they dueling over Elizabeth? But the girl claimed her father supported this connection.

Rees untucked his shirt and tore a long strip from the bottom to use as a bandage. Although he hadn't dressed a wound for many years, he'd done hundreds of field dressings during the

War for Independence and his hands remembered how. Groaning, Carleton opened his eyes.

"I'll need to take this boy to town," Dr. Wrothman said. "This ball must be removed. . . ."

"No!" Molly's shrill scream made both the doctor and Rees jump. She ran into the abandoned house and tried to fling herself upon her son.

Dr. Wrothman caught her and shook her. "Molly. Molly, you'll injure him further. Stop."

"I must bring him home," she said, struggling in his arms. "Care for him."

"Molly. Listen to me. I must remove the ball. If I leave it in there, he could die from septicemia."

"Then you'll follow us home and perform the surgery there," she cried fiercely. With tears streaking her face and her mussed gown and that short hair, she could have been a woman recently freed from the tumbrel on its way to the guillotine. Rees pitied her.

Dr. Wrothman glanced over at James Carleton and rose slowly to his feet, his knees audibly creaking. He inspected Rees's bandage and nodded. "If you and the constable wouldn't mind taking Mr. Carleton home? Richard is much more seriously injured."

"Of course," Rees said.

"That's a good dressing," Wrothman added, turning to meet Rees's gaze. "Some skills are never lost, are they?"

Rees shook his head. "I'm sorry I still need to know it," he said.

Dr. Wrothman, Marsh, Rees, and one of the hands in his battered homespun carried the unconscious Richard down the steps. Navigating the rotten steps took a few minutes and Rees used that time to examine Richard's wound. The ball had shattered the bone, and the blood still oozing from the wound was mixed with a dark substance. Gunpowder. Carleton had been very close to Richard. Why had they chosen to duel inside? That didn't make sense. And who owned dueling pistols? James?

Once they got Richard down the steps without too much jostling, they laid him in the back of Molly's wagon. Someone had thought ahead; quilts padded the bottom, and Molly threw another over her son. Marsh and the hand sat in the back with Richard to hold him as steady as they could and Molly climbed up into the seat. She picked up the reins, too concerned for her son to care about the picture she made, and they set off. Rees watched her in approval, admiring her skill as she tried to balance speed with a smooth ride.

"I'll come by the Carleton home as soon as I've finished with Richard," Wrothman said as he jumped into his buggy. "The sooner I remove the ball, the better his chances of survival. After that, well, he's in God's hands."

"What were these men even doing here?" Rees asked.

"Maybe Carleton can tell you that," Wrothman said. "I asked Molly and she doesn't know why her son was here." He smacked the reins down hard upon his horse and they shot off in an explosion of dust.

Rees and Caldwell exchanged a glance and turned back to the house.

James had managed to lever himself into a sitting position. "You don't need to help me," he said. "I have a horse. Just give me a minute."

"That buggy outside isn't yours?" Rees asked. Carleton shook his head. Rees turned and hurried outside to the buggy, Caldwell at his heels. A valise had been strapped to the back. When Rees unstrapped it and examined its contents he saw fashionable expensive clothing: Richard's clothing.

"I fancy Richard was planning a journey," Caldwell said.

"Indeed," Rees agreed. "But why stop here?" Unless he'd planned to meet Elizabeth here?

"Carleton's horse is tethered at the back," the constable said, pointing.

Rees followed him around to the decaying lean-to at the back, instantly recognizing the beautiful chestnut with one white stocking as the animal described to him by Fred Salley. James had been at the cottage the day of Nate's murder!

"Carleton can't ride this animal," Caldwell said. "He's too fresh."

"We'll put Mr. Carleton into the buggy and tie the horse at the back," Rees said. Clucking at the gelding, Caldwell untied the reins from the rail and tugged the animal around toward the front of the house. Rees knelt and looked at the ground. The chestnut's prints were clear and obvious, very different from the other hoofprints marking the ground. Another horse had been tied here recently, a horse with one loose shoe. And underneath those prints were the hoofmarks of a third horse, a smaller animal that must be a lady's mount. Probably Elizabeth Carleton, Rees thought.

Whistling softly, he rose to his feet. Elizabeth and Richard must have been planning to run away together. So James Carleton followed his daughter. But why shoot the boy? Especially since Carleton favored the match?

As Rees walked toward the back door he spotted a thread caught in the splintered wood for the doorframe. Carefully he teased the fiber from its hook. Silk, yellow silk from James's waistcoat. Rees tucked it carefully into his pocket. He planned to have a serious discussion with James Carleton, and soon.

Together he and Caldwell supported Carleton to the buggy.

He argued with them and refused to climb in and fought them when they tried to force him. He grunted with pain as a sudden move wrenched his wound. "Don't struggle," Caldwell advised him, not without sympathy. "Your wound won't hurt as much if you don't fight us."

Realizing he was no match for two healthy uninjured men, he settled, reluctantly, and they crammed him inside. When he was safely stowed, Rees said, "I'll follow you in the wagon. You'll need my help at the other end." Caldwell nodded and whipped up the horse as Rees climbed into his wagon.

He kept well behind the buggy and the horse tied at the rear. Despite the dust that floated back at him, he appreciated this solitude. It offered him a chance to ponder the shootings in an abandoned house with the tracks of at least three horses at the back. Several additional questions had occurred to him, and Rees suspected Carleton could answer most of them. And where was Mrs. Carleton? She must not know of her husband's injury, or else she would surely hurry to him. When Rees had been the one shot, Lydia ran to his side.

No servant came to the door in answer to Caldwell's knock. Rees flung it open and entered, staggering under Carleton's weight. Nobody came to remonstrate with them. Rees kicked open the door into the small sitting room and manhandled the wounded man into the room and onto a fragile-looking couch.

"I'll go see if I can find anyone," Caldwell said to Rees, his eyebrows raised in some surprise. Rees nodded. Where was everybody? Inspiration struck him and he looked at James in sudden surmise.

"Leave me here," Carleton said. "I'm fine." Even his lips were white.

"You aren't fine," Rees said.

"I'm not dead."

"Don't you think your wife will want to know what happened to you?"

Carleton grinned humorlessly. "She's gone. She took the girls to London. And half the servants."

"Why?" But even as he asked the question, Rees knew. "She shot you? And Richard?"

Carleton shrugged. "She didn't mean to hit the boy. He was running out the front door with Elizabeth and she threatened him and told him to stop. She really wanted to shoot me, and after Richard fell, wounded, she turned the pistol on me."

"Dueling pistol?"

Carleton nodded. "From her father. Charlotte, well, she had her heart set on a title for each of the girls."

"To the point of killing someone?" Rees asked in astonishment. He found that hard to believe.

Carleton grinned, his smile bitter. "She's very much like my father. Determined to have her way." His eyes shifted away from Rees, and he admitted in shame, "He confided in her far more than he ever did in me, his own son."

Rees, whose thoughts tumbled over one another in such disordered speed he could scarcely decide which question to ask first, finally said, "Could she have killed Nate?"

Carleton snorted. "Why would she? She scarcely knew him. Besides, he was beaten with a scutching knife and you know how dainty she is. She wouldn't have the strength."

"You were at the cottage the night of his death," Rees said. "Don't deny it. The chestnut horse with the white stocking was seen in the lay-by."

Carleton stared to one side, his face working. Rees refused to help and sat in silence until James finally said, "Yes. I went to plead with Nate to allow the marriage between Richard and

Elizabeth. He knew why I was pushing the suit and he laughed at me. He said maybe we could talk about my debts and maybe, since we were long time friends, he would make an accommodation. But Richard and Elizabeth would never marry. He would see to that."

"But why?" Rees asked.

"I don't know. Anyway, he saw Marsh coming down the hill and I hurried upstairs to hide. They argued, too." Carleton grimaced. "I think Marsh is in love with Molly Bowditch."

"What?" Rees couldn't keep the disbelief from his voice.

"I know. Horrible. But I clearly heard the word 'love' and Marsh scolded Nate for not spending more time at the house. Anyway, he left because Richard arrived. The boy was furious; I heard that easily enough. He picked up the scutching knife, well, I didn't know what it was then, and *thwack*, *thwack*. As soon as Richard left, I hurried downstairs. Nate was alive, sitting on the floor by the table with a rag held to his head."

"So you knew Richard was innocent right from the beginning?"

"Yes, I knew," Carleton agreed with a nod. "And I knew you'd want to know why I was there if I told you what I overheard. But you know it now, anyway."

Rees nodded. "I do. You gambled away most of your property. What happened next?"

"I left. It was almost dark then and I thought I'd return when Nate wasn't so busy. I swear, one person after another visited him that day."

Rees sat back, thinking. "Did you see any other horses or buggies in the lay-by?"

"When I got there, an old gray was tied to a tree. But he was gone when I left."

"And Nate was injured but still alive?"

"Yes. He shouted at me and told me to get out. His wounds were bleeding terribly. . . ." James shuddered.

Rees eyed at the man across from him. He was back to the beginning if James was telling the truth. Unless Nate bled to death? But the wounds didn't look that serious. Or was James still lying? But why bother now that Rees knew his secret? "And what is Nate's secret?" he demanded.

"This is the cook," Caldwell said from the doorway. "She says Mr. Carleton and the girls have gone to London."

Rees nodded. "Yes, that is exactly what Mr. Carleton himself tells me."

"We'll look after the master, then," the cook said. A plump woman, she was breathing hard from her dash up the stairs.

"Dr. Wrothman will be along to look at the wound," Rees told her. He looked back at Carleton.

"Do you know Greek, Will?" James sneered, vindictive to the last.

"Did Mr. Carleton say anything else?" Caldwell said as they left the house.

"He assured me he didn't kill Nate," Rees said with a sour smile.

Caldwell sighed. "Nobody did, but the man still lies in a grave." He paused. "Well, I suppose I should return the buggy to the Bowditch farm."

"I want to do it," Rees said. "I want to walk the cottage once again." He looked at the constable. "I'll drive my wagon into town and leave it at Wheeler's. I'll meet you at the Bull, shall I? Pick up the buggy there."

"Very well," Caldwell agreed. He jumped up into the buggy seat and took off. Rees followed more slowly, his spinning thoughts finally beginning to settle into some kind of order. He knew he was finally beginning to understand.

Chapter Twenty-seven

By the time Rees arrived at the Bull, the line of empty glasses in front of the constable indicated many drinks. Caldwell flung back the most recent shot of whiskey and said, "What'll you have?"

"Beer." Rees had never developed a fondness for the rough whiskey burn. He looked around. Despite the time, midafternoon, customers thronged the Bull. Mostly men, but also one or two women. He carefully avoided looking at them. He didn't want to recognize them or, worse, have them recognize him.

"There he is, there's my brother-in-law." A heavy hand fell upon Rees's shoulder. He shook it off.

"Well, Sam." The buzz of conversation faded into silence.

"I want my wife."

Rees turned around. His brother-in-law stood just an inch or two shorter than Rees and, liquored up and angry, looked as dangerous as a bear. "You set one foot on my property, and I'll shoot you," Rees said.

Casting a quick glance at the men watching behind him, Sam said, "No, you won't. You're a woman-man, a weaver. You don't have the guts."

Rees shrugged. "I warned you." Now he looked at the men lined up behind him. "You all heard me."

"Go home," Caldwell told Sam. "Go home and sleep it off."

"Heard you're getting married again," Sam said. "Better keep this one on a tighter leash than Dolly. But a 'course you left her alone all the time, so what can you expect but one of King Carleton's bastards you're raising as your own. . . ." Rees hit him. He threw all his weight and strength into the punch, and Samuel dropped like a felled tree. After a second's shocked silence, the crowd burst into spontaneous applause. Rees, shaking his hand to ease the sting from his bruised knuckles, nodded at everyone and turned back to the bar.

"I think it's time for me to go," he said.

Caldwell nodded and drained his glass. "Don't take what he said too seriously. He's a troublemaker."

"I don't. And you wouldn't either if you knew Dolly. Besides, David looks exactly like me."

"Yes, he does," Caldwell agreed with a smile. "And that new Shaker girl looks like a good 'un." He clapped Rees on the back and followed him outside to the buggy. "I happened to think, how are you going to come back to Dugard? I'll follow you in your wagon in an hour or so. And," he added with a crafty smile, "you can confess what's going on in that mind of yours. You've figured something out, haven't you?"

"Some things," Rees said, "but not all. And sometimes just seeing the physical location helps jog something loose." He looked at the constable, weaving slightly as he stood before him. "I'll walk back; it's not that far. And don't worry; you'll know everything I know as soon as I'm sure."

Caldwell nodded. Rees climbed into the buggy and turned the mare west, toward the Bowditch farm.

He drove up to the back door as usual and turned the horse and vehicle over to a stable boy. The farm seemed so familiar now. He walked down to the kitchen. Juniper and Mary Martha were inside, and both looked up hopefully. "Will Rachel return, Mr. Rees?" Juniper asked.

"I doubt it," Rees said. "She's working at the Contented Rooster now."

Juniper frowned. "I'm not a cook," she declared. "I helped Rachel sometimes, that's all."

"Miss Lydia?" Mary Martha asked hopefully.

Rees shook his head. "Do either of you know where Marsh might be?"

"He was here a moment ago," Juniper said, looking around as though she expected Marsh to appear behind her.

"Where is that clear chicken broth I ordered for Master Richard?" Molly herself fluttered down the steps into the kitchen. "What are you doing here?" she demanded, walking forward. "I don't want you here. Get out."

"I brought back Richard's buggy," Rees said, biting the inside of his cheek so he wouldn't shout at her. "How is he?"

Her face crumpled. "Still unconscious," she said. Her hands clenched at the delicate fabric of her gown. "But the ball is out. Dr. Wrothman says . . . he says he thinks Richard will live. But he may have a frozen shoulder. If I find the man who shot my boy, I swear I will kill him myself."

"Mr. Rees?" Marsh stood just outside the kitchen door. Rees bowed to Molly and turned to the other man. "What are you doing here?"

"I just wanted to see the weaver's cottage again," Rees said. "Walk the property . . ." See how many lies he could uncover.

Wordlessly Marsh gestured to the lane leading down to the cottage. Together they tramped down the slope. Almost all the trees had turned now and several were already bare. Rees paused and stared toward the lay-by. The pines would continue to provide a screen but a much thinner one, and horses and wagons would be dimly visible from the road. Marsh lifted the latch and opened the door.

It no longer stank of mildew. Although the door to the dye room was open, the back door was as well and the fresh fall air swept through the house. Rees hesitated in the kitchen. Everything was tidy; the ashes swept from the hearth and the dye pot scrubbed but cobwebs festooned every corner and the cottage appeared long abandoned. Rees stared at the green stain on the floor in helpless grief before finally walking into the dye room. Rachel's shawl of many colors had been thrown upon the table. Rees picked it up. Knitted of yarns dyed many different colors, it was mostly shades of green with strands of indigo blue, scarlet, and yellow. The lady's frock and Nate's apron flapped above him.

"All of this belongs to you now," Marsh said from the kitchen.

Rees shook his head. "I am not a dyer. Besides, it still feels . . . it still belongs to Nate."

"When Nate was alive, this cottage was full of him. Now it just seems empty." Marsh sighed.

Rees turned around. "Molly must have found it very hard, knowing Nate preferred to live here."

Marsh nodded. "Very hard."

Rees brushed past him and went up the back stairs to the loft bedroom. He could easily imagine James Carleton cowering up here while all the action went on below. He heard Marsh's footfall behind him and turned. "Are you in love with Molly Bowditch?"

Marsh gasped and took several involuntary steps backwards. "Dear God, that would be worth my life. Of course not."

"But you argued with Nate, told him he should spend more time at the house?"

"Yes, I did. He spent all his time down here, obsessed with finding the perfect dyes. Sometimes he could be infuriating."

"I know," Rees said, remembering the many times a parent had been forced to separate them. "He always thought he was right. But I loved him anyway."

Sudden tears glittered in Marsh's eyes. "I know."

Rees glanced around one final time and went downstairs. James Carleton could be telling the truth, or at least part of it, but Rees felt he was no closer to the identity of the murderer. With a heavy heart he followed Marsh up the slope. Caldwell was already there, waiting in the wagon for him.

No opportunity for quiet reflection, or for discussing the case with Lydia, presented itself to him at home. Although all the children had been fed and sent to the cottage with Charles, Caroline remained in the kitchen. She turned to Rees with an expression of fierce curiosity. "Did you find out who shot Richard Bowditch and James Carleton?"

Rees glanced at Lydia. "I had to say something," she said.

"Charlotte Carleton," Rees said. Into the sudden shocked silence he added, "She was as opposed to the match between Richard and Elizabeth as Nate."

"I don't understand that," Caro said. "Nate and James were friends and business partners. I should think both of them would be overjoyed to connect the families. I mean, Charlotte has always looked down upon the rest of us as illiterate and ill-bred Colonials, but Nate knew better."

"He must have known something to Richard's disfavor," Lydia said. "No one describes Mr. Bowditch as anything less than fair."

"If anyone were to object, " Caro said, "I would expect it of

Molly. She's spoiled that boy rotten." She glanced at her brother. "You should know, Will. You and Nate were inseparable once."

"We parted many years ago," Rees replied, unwillingly recalling the treasures in Nate's trunk. "I haven't known him since we were boys."

"Maybe you don't want to," Caro suggested shrewdly. "I remember the aftermath of your final quarrel with him. Suddenly you enlisted in the Army. Suddenly you married Dolly. Maybe you should remember why." Rees stared at his sister.

"That sounds like excellent advice," Lydia agreed, turning from her position at the dishpan.

In the sudden silence, Rees inspected Caroline. The lines in her face had smoothed out and she appeared relaxed and happy. Although she wore an apron she seemed to be supervising Lydia rather than working herself. "I saw Sam," Rees said. "I met him in the Bull."

She collapsed into a nearby chair, her eyes widening with fright. "What did he say?"

"Nothing," Rees lied. Caroline was trembling with terror. "I threatened to shoot him if he set foot on the property." Recalling Sam's accusation, he couldn't resist glancing at David. Besides the red hair and the height that David shared with Rees, he and Charles both had moles under their left arms; Ree's father had an identical one. David was inspecting his aunt with dislike and unwilling pity.

"You don't know what he's like," Caroline said. "He won't give up. And he knows this farm; he'll guess we're living in the cottage."

Rees and Lydia exchanged a long look, and then Lydia went over to Caroline and touched her shoulder comfortingly. "Don't worry," she said. "We'll sort it out. He won't hurt you or your children again." But she sighed as she said it, dreading more days of Caroline's presence.

"My babies are alone in the cottage," Caroline cried, jumping to her feet. "I must go to them." She ran out of the kitchen.

"What can we do?" David asked.

"I don't know," Rees admitted. The sanctity of marriage, and a husband's control over his wife, were enshrined in law.

"Aunt Phoebe doesn't like him, and he and Aunt Caro have never visited them," David said. "Maybe Aunt Phoebe—?"

"That sounds like a good suggestion," Rees said, nodding. "If Caro agrees . . ."

He climbed the steps to the quiet second floor. Since Lydia now occupied what had been his weaving room, and dusk was fast approaching anyway, he plodded into his bedroom. Sliding off his shoes, he washed up in the basin and lay down upon his bed. Sam's cruel accusation rang in his ears even though he knew it was most certainly untrue. But what had Susannah said a few days ago about King Carleton? That he took what he wanted and pursued one woman after another. Rees knew she would never lie. Sam's accusation could be true about other women in town, maybe even about Dolly. No, that Rees couldn't believe. He yawned, his thoughts turning too slippery to hold.

He awoke with a start early the following morning, jolted awake by the sounds of Lydia and David creeping downstairs. He lay still, trying to recall the night's confused dreams. He remembered only that Nate was shouting at him about his will and even that memory was growing fuzzy.

Finally, with a sigh of frustration, he dressed and put on his shoes and followed the others down to the kitchen.

David and Lydia, involved in a discussion of the advisability of going to market on Saturday, turned to look at him in surprise. "I'm sorry," Lydia said. "Did we wake you?"

Rees shook his head, yawning, and helped himself to coffee. "Strange dreams," he said.

"That's not quite done," Lydia said, looking at his cup.

"Do you think we should go to market?" David asked his father.

Rees shook his head. "No. And not just because of the danger to Caro. Sam has already gone after you once. I want you to wait until that situation has settled out. . . ."

"I'm sorry," David said to Lydia. "But you don't know my uncle like I do."

"I'm glad of it," Lydia commented dryly.

Rees sat down at the table. She placed a bowl of mush before him with a dish of honey and a pitcher of fresh cream. He began eating, still distracted by the hints thrown up by his dreaming mind.

"I almost forgot," Lydia said, pulling a packet of paper from her pocket. "I found these yesterday as I tidied your room." Rees looked at the wad blankly. "They were on your bedside table so they must be something important."

Rees stretched out his hand and took the packet, recognizing the ribbon and spiky writing all of a sudden. "Love letters from Molly to Nate."

"From Molly?" Lydia repeated. "That's not her hand. She cultivates a dainty feminine cursive. Remember? The handwriting on the invitation? And look at the dates; the most recent is about twelve years ago. Richard is seventeen so Molly and Nate wed eighteen years ago."

"From Nate to Molly then when he was in London," Rees suggested. Of course, that could not be the case. The salutation was clearly to Nate and besides Rees knew Nate's writing and this bore no resemblance to it all. "They were in the cottage . . . ," Rees said, dropping them into his pocket. "I meant to return them but forgot."

"Good morning," Abigail caroled as she entered the kitchen.

"The sky is clouding up," David announced. "Looks like we'll have rain."

Rees jumped to his feet and crossed to the back door. Dark clouds scudded rapidly across the sky, and as he stood there peering into the heavens he heard the rumble of thunder. They all knew what that meant; the weather was changing. These dark clouds would be sweeping out this unseasonable warm weather and bringing cooler temperatures. Hailstones began pattering down upon the ground, and Rees felt a sudden cold wind swirl into the house.

David looked over his shoulder. "Let's get out and pick as much as we can," he said. Lydia and Abby had already started for the tender plants still producing in the kitchen garden.

Rees joined David and Augustus as they hurried to the fields to gather in as much as possible. Even pumpkins could be damaged by hail. He did not find the opportunity to ponder the mystery of Nate's death until several hours later when, tired and wet and very cold, he returned to the house. But his mind had continued working without his conscious direction and when he returned to the puzzle the first few steps of a solution leaped into his mind.

Rain continued all afternoon and into the night, a heavy vicious rain that ripped the changing leaves from the trees and spread them across the ground. Many of the plants in the garden had been flattened, the leaves shredded. Any grains not harvested were destroyed.

Rees joined Lydia at the back door after supper, where she stood watching the rain pelt the tattered green. "I don't like this time of the year," she said. "From now until summer, no fresh food. Well, we'll have beets. . . ." Rees nodded. Lydia and Abigail had been drying fruit and pickling vegetables for weeks and now would finish the last of it. The beets and apples that survived this weather would be picked and stored downstairs. Soon the cattle and the sheep would be brought back from the meadows and returned to the barns and the fenced paddocks.

Rees sighed. "We'll see snow before you know it. And then, I'll set up my loom in the parlor, until after we're married. Marsh told me Nate wove for many of the local housewives and I expect to pick up some of that custom. At least for the winter."

Lydia glanced at him, smiling, but with a shadow of worry darkening her eyes. "You're sure?"

"I'm sure," he said. Now that he'd made the decision and accepted it, he wished the wedding over and done with. "We'll have to speak to Father Sperling, arrange a date." Smiling, she tentatively linked her arm in his.

Rain continued through the night. Rees knew it because he heard it; he lay awake for many hours staring sightlessly into the darkness as random snippets of conversation trotted through his mind. Consciously he saw little connection between them and he kept forcing his thoughts back to the certainties he knew.

"I visited my wife in Portland," Marsh had said.

"King Carleton liked the girls young." That was Susannah.

"I left when Richard ran home," James had said. "Nate was still alive."

"Richard came back to the house," Kate said. "I saw him."

"You and Nate were such close friends." Caro's voice echoed through his head.

"Do you speak Greek?" Carleton's mocking question.

When Rees finally slid into sleep he dreamed of Nate, first of the boy, and then of the man. Nate put his arm tight around his friend's shoulders. "We'll always be together, Will," he said. "You and me." His grip tightened as he aged into adulthood and firmly commanded Rees not to marry, never to marry. Rees flung out in a temper. Why was Nate telling him what to do?

Rees woke up with his eyes moist. Rain still rattled on the roof overhead and dripped from the eaves. David and Lydia crept downstairs, but Rees remained in bed, staring at the gray early morning light. He pondered Nate and the childhood friendship that had been more vital to him than his parents and the final argument that had irretrievably broken the bond. Finally he picked up the letters and, untying the ribbon that bound them, he began to read.

Although he did not read all of them, concentrating upon the oldest and the newest, he felt he'd read enough to understand something else about Nate. Preoccupied, he finally arose and went downstairs. He replied to David's and Lydia's questions in monosyllables, so distracted, he did not notice the glance they shared. After breakfast he harnessed Amos to the buggy, which would provide more protection from the rain than the open wagon, and set off for Dugard. His coat and hat were soaked before he even left his driveway.

Although this was market day, he passed only a few wagons and other buggies. The rain had discouraged most of the farmers. Rees viewed the empty, albeit muddy, road with favor and urged Amos into the fastest gait possible.

The Potters were awake as Rees had expected, but still at breakfast. Sally regarded the dripping apparition at the back door in surprise. "Why Mr. Rees," she said.

"Who is it, Sally?" Mr. Potter asked from inside the kitchen.

"Mr. Rees," Sally called. She was too polite to say "again."

"Where's your manners, girl? Let him in out of the wet." Mrs. Potter hastened to the door and flung it wider. "Please, Will, come in."

Rees obeyed with alacrity and stood dripping upon the brick. He could see through the inside door into the kitchen, where the Potters ate en famille.

George Potter had risen from the table and, as he dropped his napkin to the table, he regarded his friend in surmise. "Why Will, what is it?" And then, "You've figured it out."

"Not all of it," Rees said, "but most." He handed his wet coat and hat to Mrs. Potter.

"Let's go upstairs to my office," Potter suggested. He cast a glance back at his wife and she nodded as though he'd spoken his wishes aloud. Rees followed Potter through the house and up the stairs to the office on the second floor. The lawyer took his usual seat behind his desk and motioned his friend into the chair in front. "All right," he said. "Tell me."

Rees smiled. "Not yet. I prefer to tell everyone at once."

"Can you at least explain why Nate Bowditch, a man I knew from childhood and someone I counted as a friend, chose a lawyer from another town to represent him."

"That's why," Rees said. "You are friend to everyone involved."

Potter frowned, unsatisfied. "He must know I would always be impartial." Rees said nothing. "Tomorrow is Sunday. So you must meet with everyone this afternoon or Monday."

"Can we do it today?"

Potter rubbed his nose thoughtfully. "I suppose. We'll have to hire a few lads to carry the message around."

Rees nodded. "I'll pay the few farthings necessary. And please, send someone to my farm to fetch Augustus. I have a few errands. . . ."

Potter looked at his friend curiously but assented with a nod.

When Rees left Dugard, he drove toward Thomas Bowditch's farm and the family graveyard where Nate was buried. Although Rees had not attended his friend's internment, he knew the location of the cemetery. He remembered joining Nate at his mother's burial. He parked on the road and walked through the sodden fields to the small plot. The stones marking the plots of Nate's parents were already weathered and dark with rain. Nothing marked Nate's grave but a muddy rectangle. Rees stood at the foot, wishing he'd brought something, flowers or a boyhood treasure, to place upon Nate's unmarked final resting place. For a moment he just stood there, staring at the mud. He'd intended to tell Nate that he'd identified the murderer, but instead he said, "I'm sorry, Nate. I'm sorry we didn't speak sooner. I'm sorry we didn't become friends again. But I know who killed you."

"It's odd, isn't it," Thomas said from behind him, "how one can be so furious with a brother and still miss him so much when he's gone?"

Rees jumped and whirled in surprise. "I didn't even know him these past few years and I . . ." He stopped, his throat closing. He turned his face away to hide the moisture in his eyes.

"I know. Come down to the house and dry off by the fire. You're soaked to the skin." Clapping Rees upon the shoulder, Thomas drew him away from the grave.

By tacit agreement, Rees and Thomas did not speak of the murder. Instead they reminisced about the boy they both knew. Thomas shared several stories about the man his brother had become, a man that, in some ways, was the same rascal Rees remembered. "So the Widow Penner kept returning the cloth," Thomas said, "and telling Nate it wasn't green enough. So, although he'd already dyed it green, he dyed it blue and then yellow. You never saw such a green. Mrs. Penner couldn't deny it was green, emerald green, but you could see from her face that she didn't like it. Nate gave her another length of cloth to make up for it, dyed a dark blue. She was grateful. I daresay she was through with green."

Rees laughed. "But he has some bright green," he said, recalling the apron hung from the ceiling of the dye room. Thomas nodded.

"Now. He found the trick of it after." Thomas paused and then added, "I suppose there won't be much demand for dyers now, with the current fashion for whites and pale grays."

"I doubt that style will last for long," Rees said. "White doesn't flatter everyone and rapidly becomes tedious."

Thomas nodded. "My brother said the same."

"He always liked bright colors," Rees said. "Remember, he used to help your mother set the pieces in her quilts."

Thomas nodded and sighed.

Finally Rees rose. "I know I'm keeping you from your work," he said. "And I have to return to town."

Thomas nodded. "I'll see you at two o'clock," he said. "I look forward to knowing the name of the villain who killed my brother."

Chapter Twenty-eight

Noon was fast approaching when Rees finally returned home. The rain had diminished to drizzle and he hoped for clearing skies by evening.

Lydia came out upon the porch when she heard the buggy wheels. "My goodness," she said, "you look half-drowned. Come inside for dinner." Rees tossed the reins over the rail and took the steps at a run. But even before he set foot in the hall, he heard Caroline shouting at Charlie. He looked at Lydia.

"Your sister does not care to eat alone in the cottage," she explained. Rees said nothing. He could hardly wait until his sister and her children found another home.

With so many hungry mouths around the table, Lydia had thought ahead and prepared a large stew. Rees recognized some of the vegetables picked from the kitchen garden the previous day. Lydia also sent around a basket of bread, the last of this week's baking. At least the children were not noisy; they still ate with a single-minded hunger that made Rees's skin crawl. Had Sam starved his children? He looked at his sister. She caught his glance but did not speak and his initial frustration at their continued presence in his home faded. He realized they were all frightened. Even Caro was too scared to stay alone in the cottage. They felt safer here, in the kitchen, with other people around them. "I'm trusting you to keep watch," he said to his son with an emphatic nod.

"Of course." David straightened his shoulders, very conscious of his responsibility. "I'll make sure nothing happens."

Rees ate little, too preoccupied to feel hungry. Lydia was nervous also; she pushed away her bowl untouched. "I think it's time to leave," he said to her. She rose instantly to her feet and went to the hooks for her cloak and winter bonnet. Rees clapped his old hat upon his head, the newer one being too wet to wear, and donned his best coat of indigo-dyed linen. They went outside to the buggy. Augustus had already put Bessie between the traces and was sitting in the backseat, waiting.

"Will my mother be there?" Augustus asked.

"I hope so. And James Carleton as well as Molly and Richard Bowditch. If he can make it."

After that no one spoke.

They were the first to arrive at Potter's office. Although they were early, he was ready for them and with a great flourish seated Lydia in a chair by the desk. As Augustus took up a position next to the wall, Potter gestured Rees to the desk. Sally brought in cake and coffee. Rees accepted a cup but then couldn't drink it. His stomach fluttered, as it always did before a presentation of this sort.

Jack and Susannah arrived next, with Rachel in tow. "She wouldn't come without us," Susannah explained to Rees. Her bright gaze fastened upon Lydia and as soon as she could Susannah hastened to Lydia's side.

"Weddings, you know," Jack said to him. Rees sighed.

Rachel clasped hands with Augustus before finding a chair somewhat removed from the others.

Dr. Wrothman was next up the stairs, quickly followed by Caldwell. The constable joined Augustus leaning against the wall. Potter, trying not to breathe, quickly flung up a window. Then James Carleton plodded up the stairs. Rees stared at him, shocked by his appearance. A sling held his bandaged shoulder still. Well, Rees had expected that. But dark circles ringed Carleton's eyes as though he hadn't slept for several days, and instead of a finely woven jacket and silk waistcoat he wore a simple linen coat, tow colored. Food spotted the shirt underneath. Potter glanced at Rees as Dr. Wrothman hurried to Carleton's side to help him sit down.

Thomas Bowditch and his wife hurried in, Thomas exchanging a knowing look with Rees. He was moved to clap the other man upon the shoulder in wordless sympathy.

Although he wasn't sure Richard could manage the journey, Rees was surprised that Molly was not attending.

After several minutes, while Sally offered cake and tea or coffee to the group, Rees cleared his throat. "Welcome," he said.

"Shouldn't we wait for Mrs. Bowditch and Richard to arrive?" Potter asked.

"Richard is badly wounded," Carleton said, stirring himself sufficiently to speak. Everyone looked at him, some with disgust, others with sympathy. In the sudden silence, the clatter at the front door floated clearly up the stairs. Rees jumped up and rushed to the top of the staircase. He peered down to the bottom. Richard, his face completely bloodless, leaned heavily upon Marsh. Behind them, Molly stood silhouetted in the light streaming in through the open door.

"Can I help?" Rees called down.

"I believe we've got it," Marsh said. Richard said nothing, but he clung to the bannister with all his strength. Step by step they climbed the stairs, Richard resting on each riser. By the time he reached the top, and almost fell into Rees's arms, Richard's gray face was dewy with cold perspiration.

"He insisted," Molly said, tears leaking from her eyes. "I tried to persuade him to stay home. I tried."

"I have to know," Richard grunted. "I have to."

Potter swung a chair forward, and together Marsh and Rees helped the boy collapse into it. Lydia sprang to her feet and fetched him a cup of coffee, liberally sugared. Richard thanked her, his expression never changing from one of hopeless despair. Rees glanced d at the boy in concern.

"Let's begin, shall we?" Richard said hoarsely. "Everyone knows I'm guilty."

"Oh? And just how did you murder your father?" Rees asked.

"I hit him with that scutching knife. Everyone knows that."

"Was he dead when you left?"

"Well no, but—"

"The blows by the scutching knife didn't kill Nate. I have two eyewitnesses to that fact. Did you set fire to the jail?"

"No, of course not. But—"

"Nate's killer went down to the cottage after you left—," Rees began.

"This is absurd," Molly said.

"So, who did kill Nate, then?" Susannah asked.

Rees ignored both women. "I have a witness who saw someone running away from the cottage after Richard left."

"Who was it?" Susannah said, leaning forward.

"Please," Rees said in frustration. "Let me begin at the beginning and go through step by step. Otherwise, we shall be here all afternoon."

Susannah nodded apologetically. "I'm sorry."

"Many past events culminated in Nate's murder," Rees said. "Some of those events took place many years ago and without describing them, none of you will fully understand why Nate was killed." He paused.

Molly, whose gaze had been circling the room, exploded. "What is she doing here?" She pointed a trembling finger at Rachel.

"She has every right to be here, and so does her son," Rees said in a chilly voice. "Especially her son. First Augustus was suspected of Nate's murder and then threatened with his own death."

"Forgive our poor manners," Lydia said, her voice tart. "Please, continue." Molly directed an angry glance at her.

"Nate was already ill," Rees said as all eyes once again turned to him expectantly. "In fact, I suspect he would have passed on in the near future anyway. His murderer simply rushed him into the grave." He looked around, his expression stern. "That night, two other men visited Nate prior to Richard's arrival." Someone gasped, but Rees did not know who. "First, James Carleton called upon Nate to press Richard's suit with his daughter. He retreated upstairs when Marsh arrived to argue with Nate about the same issue. With Richard's sudden entrance, Marsh fled through the dye room to the back. So, both Mr. Carleton and Marsh overheard the argument between Richard and his father and both swore that Nate was still alive when Richard fled the cottage."

"That's true," James agreed heavily. Marsh nodded.

"I suppose it is unfortunate neither man remained; we would already know the identity of the murderer. But they left, Marsh to visit his wi—" Recalling Marsh's secret, Rees quickly inserted the word "sister" for "wife," "—in Portland. And Mr. Carleton went home."

"Are you certain one of these men did not remain and bludgeon Mr. Bowditch to death?" Caldwell asked, his suspicious expression darting toward Marsh.

"Possible, but I doubt it," Rees said, his gaze turning toward

Richard. "When you struck your father and he fell to the floor, did you believe he had died?"

"No. He was groaning."

"You knew he was hurt?"

"He was bleeding." Richard strangled a sob.

Rees nodded. "So you went for help. Didn't you?"

"Of course," Richard said, looking at Rees in disgust. "I'm not a monster."

"You and your mother are extraordinarily close, are you not?"

"This is ridiculous," Molly said.

"Kate, the nursemaid, saw you from the window running up the slope from the weaver's cottage. I'm suggesting you went to your mother for help. And she went down to the cottage in her turn." All eyes turned to Molly.

"Now, wait a minute," she said. "I'm not strong enough to pick up that wooden blade and batter Nate with it." She looked around, and several people nodded in agreement.

"That's true," Potter muttered.

"I suspect you *are* strong enough. But that doesn't matter, since Nate wasn't bludgeoned to death. He was wounded, that's true, but the scutching knife didn't kill him." This time, when Rees paused to gather his thoughts, no one spoke. Now he would be venturing into deductions and outright guesses and needed to take great care.

"Why would I kill him?" Molly burst into speech. "And why now? We've been married almost twenty years."

"Jealousy," Caldwell said.

"Of her?" Molly flapped her hand at Rachel. "I had reason for jealousy; Augustus is Nate's son. But I did not kill Nate in a fit of jealousy."

"That's true. You did not murder your husband in a fit of jealousy," Rees agreed.

"Then who killed Nate?" Susannah asked. "Did someone else visit Nate that night?"

Rees never removed his gaze from Molly. "Molly did not murder her husband from jealousy or because he deserted her, choosing to live in the weaver's cottage rather than their home. I don't believe she went down to the cottage intending to kill him at all. But she did. She forced a cup of poisonous green dye down his throat to protect a powerful secret." He knew as soon as he saw Molly's first relieved smile change to an expression of horror that he had guessed correctly. "I saw the scratches on your arm the first day I met you. Nate struggled, didn't he? But he was weak."

"A secret?" Potter looked at Rees skeptically. "What secret could that be? I've known her all my life; she has no secrets."

"When I first saw Richard and Augustus together, I marked the resemblance between them. They are brothers. Look carefully, and you'll see a similar look to James as well. They all share a father. But their father is not Nate Bowditch, it is Henry Carleton." All eyes fastened on the three men. Once pointed out, and discounting Augustus's skin color, the brown eyes, heavy prognathic jaw, and fleshy lips shared by the three were obvious. Richard, after a glance at the other men, turned to look at his mother in disbelief.

James stared at Richard, first with interest and then in dawning revulsion. "So Nate refused to allow the marriage because he knew Richard and Elizabeth are what? Brother and sister? No. Uncle and niece?"

Rees nodded. "A very close relation, in either case. Your father never knew about Augustus, but he knew about Richard."

He threw a glance at Rachel, and she nodded. Clearing her throat and speaking very tentatively, she said, "He sold me to Nate before I began to show. I didn't want Master Henry to know. I was so afraid he would take my boy from me. But Master Nate knew."

"And of course he knew about Richard also," Rees said. "I wondered for a long time how Nate managed to begin the accumulation of great wealth. Fetching James from London might account for some of it. But I suspect King Carleton paid Nate to take Molly off his hands. After all, she was not a slave but the daughter of a well-respected craftsman."

"How can you stand there and speak these lies," Molly cried.

"That is the secret you killed Nate to hide." Rees continued as though she hadn't spoken. "He knew Richard and Elizabeth shouldn't wed."

"Charlotte must have known." James's voice trembled. "She was so determined. . . ."

Rees nodded in agreement. "Your father must have let something slip. Your wife was willing to do almost anything to prevent that marriage." He turned his attention to Molly. "You knew the truth of Richard's parentage could never be revealed; you preferred your son commit incest rather than that. And you allowed him to believe he killed the man he thought of as his father. But it was you. Did Nate threaten to tell James Carleton the truth himself if you did not?" The angry and fearful expression on Molly's countenance confirmed Rees's guess.

"But how?" Lydia asked.

"I think she's stronger than anyone believes. You told me, George, that she was able to keep up with her brothers in everything, and she was a skilled rider besides. I suspect she hasn't lost those skills. You are misled by her delicate appearance. And the jail?"

"You aren't saying she—?" Caldwell looked sick. "But she's only a woman."

Rees nodded. He knew women too well to believe them incapable of murder, or courage, or any of the other passions men kept for themselves. "Look at her. In boy's clothing, would anyone suspect a woman?" Everyone looked at her, noting her short hair, her height, and wiry build. "At first I suspected the arsonist might be Richard, although I never quite understood why he would threaten his brother. But Molly? That makes more sense. She saw him as Nate's son, Richard's competition, and he would make a handy scapegoat."

"And Nate?" Marsh asked, his face contorted with emotion. "She poisoned Nate?"

"When Molly came down from the house to study his condition, they quarreled. He swore he would tell the truth about Richard, and I think most of us know how stubborn he could be. He was already weak, bleeding from Richard's blows. So she took a cup of green dye and forced it down his throat." He turned to look at Molly. "Then you stripped off your torn and stained frock and Nate's stained apron and stuffed them in the dye pot. He was a dyer, always messing with his roots and powders, so who would notice? You wrapped yourself in Rachel's shawl and ran home. Nate died alone and in pain that night."

The image kept everyone silent.

"I hope that's not true," Dr. Wrothman said, looking at Molly. "How could you be so cruel?"

Molly glanced at him and shuddered. "Richard," she whispered, turning to her son. He refused to look at her, and Rees thought that if the boy could have risen unaided to his feet and walked away, he would have. "I did it all for you." Tears welled into her eyes. "I didn't mean to kill Nate. It was an accident."

"It was an accident that you held his nose closed and forced poisonous green dye down his throat," Rees said in disbelief.

His sneer sparked a flare of rage in Molly's eyes. "I didn't know it would kill him," she retorted. "I just wanted him to look at me—"

"Was it an accident when you burned the jail?" Caldwell asked her, the harsher from disillusionment.

Rees directed a swift glance at Richard. The boy's mouth was open in a silent scream.

"Or did you believe that if Augustus caught the blame and died, I wouldn't search any further?" Rees asked.

Molly jumped to her feet. "I will not remain here and continue to be insulted." Caldwell rapidly moved around the wall until he stood in front of the door, his arms crossed. "Move out of my way, your dirty dog," she commanded.

"Don't move a finger, Constable," James said. "I think we all deserve to hear this tale in its entirety."

Molly looked at Carleton pleadingly. "Jimmy?" But his expression went shuttered and she turned to Potter. "Georgie?"

"We want the truth here, Molly," he said.

Susannah stared at Molly. "How could you do that? Murder your husband?"

Molly looked at her in dislike. "Don't you dare judge me. Don't you dare. You don't understand what it was like living with Nate. You have a husband who loves you. Nate ignored me. For a little while after we were married, he was a good husband and we had Grace. But then he lost interest and spent all of his time down at the cottage. With her." She flung her hand at Rachel. "I didn't know he knew Richard was not his until that night in the cottage when he told me."

"So why not let it go?" Rees asked, regarding her curiously. "Did it matter so much that James Carleton would know?"

She shook her head, tears filling her eyes. "Don't you understand? Richard didn't know. And he wanted to wed Elizabeth. I had to protect my son."

Rees looked at the anguished expression on Richard's face. "No, you had to protect the secret *from* Richard," he said. "You knew how Richard would feel. So you killed the man who married you to protect your reputation and give your son a name."

"Well, she is none of mine," the boy cried. "Not now. You murdered my father, tried to murder my brother, and by your whoring, made it impossible for me to marry the woman I love."

"I was but fifteen!" Molly screamed. "King Carleton promised me I would be the mistress of his house and all his property. Then he tossed me away as though I were nothing."

"He promised everyone the same," Susannah said, sparking a sudden startled glance from her husband. "But even a fifteen-year-old should know better than to believe it."

"You were a fool to trust my father," Carleton agreed.

"I thought if you wed Elizabeth Carleton, you would succeed to all that had been promised to me and taken away."

"He will anyway," Rees said. "Nate ensured Richard's future in his will."

"But now we know Richard is not Nate's son," Caldwell said. "Doesn't that invalidate the will?"

Potter rubbed his finger thoughtfully up and down his nose. "No, I don't think so. He identifies Richard by name and specifies the properties he is to receive."

Properties Nate had won from James Carleton; that irony wasn't lost upon Rees.

"Perhaps Gracie will care for you," Richard said to his mother. "I won't. You're dead to me." He turned his face away and said, "Marsh?"

Rees joined the servant in lifting Richard to his feet. The lad winced and Rees saw a widening scarlet stain across the white bandage. But Richard refused to pause. When he was finally upright, Rees said, "And what about Kate, Richard? Are you going to allow *your* child to grow up without a father?"

Richard looked across the distance and met Rees's eyes. "No," he said, his voice colorless. "I'll do the right thing." Then he turned and began his slow and painful descent down the stairs.

"Please return, Marsh," Rees called after them.

"What are we going to do with her?" Caldwell asked, gesturing to Molly. "I no longer have a jail to put her in, and the tack room . . . Well, it just won't do."

For a moment no one spoke. Then, with a sigh, Rees said, "How long until the trial?"

"Judge Hansen is in town now, so it shouldn't be long," Caldwell replied. "Do you think she'll hang? It's an ugly business, hanging a woman."

"Oh, I doubt she'll hang," Rees said cynically. "Not with Piggy Hansen and his wife among her confidants. Although, after the ostracism and the snubs I expect will be her lot, she may wish she'd been hanged."

"Perhaps a room in the Contented Rooster?" Caldwell suggested. "Locked in and with her meals brought to her, she should be safe enough. At least until the trial. And she'll be under my eye. . . ."

Rees looked over at Susannah and Jack. They nodded somberly.

"I'll go and get a room ready," Rachel said, starting for the door.

More irony: Molly would now be the recipient of kindness at the hands of the woman she despised and had evicted from her home.

Augustus ran after his mother. Jack, looking at his wife as though he no longer fully recognized her, crooked his arm. Susannah smiled at Rees and laid her hand upon her husband's elbow.

"I'll expect to see you in the inn," Jack said.

"Of course."

"And of course we'll receive an invitation to the wedding," Susannah added, darting a sly glance at Lydia. Lydia blushed and nodded.

"I'll take my prisoner to the inn," Caldwell said, offering her a sarcastic arm. "Please, milady . . ." She turned her face away. Chuckling, the constable grasped her elbow.

Rees looked at Potter. The lawyer was straightening everything on his desk, over and over. He looked up and said, "Is that story true?"

"I'm persuaded of most of the details." Potter's expression of dismay did not change. "I did warn you about secrets."

"Yes but . . ." Words failed him.

"Molly's past behavior is not your fault," Rees said. Taking pity on his friend, he added, "And I would have looked into Nate's death without your encouragement. I owed it to him."

"Mr. Rees?" Marsh hesitated by the door. "You asked me to return. . . ."

"I have something that I believe belongs to you," Rees said, extracting the packet of letters from his pocket. Marsh approached cautiously. "I fancy these were the items you searched for," Rees added. Potter looked over, craning his neck to see the packet.

Marsh took them as though they might explode in his hands. "Thank you. Nate always loved you, you know."

"I know," Rees said, his voice thickening. "What will you do now?"

"Stay," Marsh said in surprise. "Gracie will need me, now more than ever. Besides, where would I go?"

Rees nodded. Turning to Lydia, he said, "Shall we go?" She nodded, and when he offered her his arm, she laid her hand upon it.

"I'll walk you down," Potter said. He followed Rees and Lydia downstairs, with Marsh behind him. Both Rees's buggy and the Bowditch carriage were drawn up to the curb.

Rees looked through the carriage window; Richard was slumped against the opposite wall. Rees turned and darted an anxious glance at Marsh.

"He'll be all right," Marsh said. "Eventually." He climbed in beside the boy.

Rees guided Lydia toward their buggy, and the mounting stone that would allow her to maintain her dignity when she ascended onto the high buggy step.

"Where's my wife?" Rees was suddenly driven forward by a tremendous weight that wrenched his arm away from Lydia's hand. "Where's Caroline, you interfering bastard?"

Using his powerful legs, Rees jerked himself sideways, dislodging Sam's grip. He slewed around to face the other man. "Stop!" he shouted. "Stop, I tell you." He heard Potter's running feet behind him.

Sam, whose first stop this morning had clearly been the Bull, ran at Rees again. "I want my wife and family."

Rees pushed Sam back, hard. "Stop it. You don't want to do this." He heard the carriage door open and Marsh's feet thudding to the ground.

Potter circled around and made an effort to grab Prentiss, but the bigger, stronger man pulled away and launched himself at Rees again. Out of patience, Rees pulled his arm back and let fly, smacking Sam in the nose. Scarlet blood sprayed out. Already off balance, Sam staggered and fell backwards, plummeting to the ground and hitting his head on the carriage step with a sickening crunch. Blood pooled in the hollowed granite. Both Potter and Rees rushed to Sam's side and bent over him.

"My God," Potter gasped, looking up at Rees in horror. "Look at the blood."

"He's just unconscious," Rees said, his stomach flipping over. "He can't be dead." He dropped to his knees by Sam's body and listened at the chest. He heard a faint but steady heartbeat. Sam's scarlet blood kept pumping out. Rees began ripping his shirt into strips.

"It was an accident," Potter said, staring at Rees in shock and appalled horror. "And so I shall say."

"We all saw it," Marsh agreed.

Rees looked over his shoulder. Lydia broke into a run, hurrying to his side to offer her loving support.

Don't Miss Any Titles in the Will Rees Mysteries Series

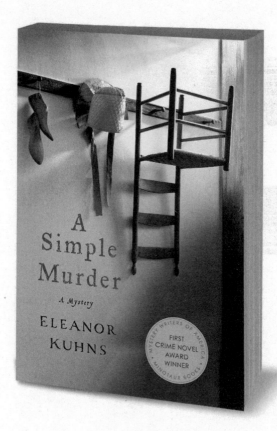

Other Will Rees Mysteries
Death of a Dyer
Cradle to Grave